Lewis Ardenley was considered society's most handsome lord, and he had never looked so overpoweringly attractive as now, as he met and held Lady Jane Derwent's gaze. His eyes were cold and glitter-bright as he said, "You want me back, don't you? Oh, yes, I know that you do, I can feel it when I'm near you."

"I'd rather die than take you back!" Jane breathed.

"You can't fool me, Jane, I know you too well," he said. Twisting her close, his grip on her wrist as viselike as steel, he forced her against him. Then his lips were over hers, bearing down with a force that almost stopped her breath.

It was bad enough that Ardenley had flaunted his mistress before her. But the power he now flaunted was even worse. The terrible truth was, the temptation he created was as mighty as his treachery. . . .

(For a list of other Signet Regency Romances by Sandra Heath, please turn page . . .)

WILLFUL BEAUTIES, DASHING LORDS

LADY JANE'S RIBBONS

SANDRA HEATH

A SIGNET BOOK

NEW AMERICAN LIBRARY

Copyright © 1987 by Sandra Heath

SIGNET TRADEMARK REG. U.S. PAT. OFF. AND FOREIGN COUNTRIES
REGISTERED TRADEMARK—MARCA REGISTRADA
HECHO EN CHICAGO, U.S.A.

SIGNET, SIGNET CLASSIC, MENTOR, ONYX, PLUME, MERIDIAN
and NAL BOOKS are published by New American Library,
1633 Broadway, New York, New York 10019

First Printing, February, 1987

1 2 3 4 5 6 7 8 9

PRINTED IN THE UNITED STATES OF AMERICA

ONE

*T*he peace of the warm June night was shattered by the commotion in the street outside. The noise of the unruly mob awoke Lady Jane Derwent with a start and she sat up in her bed, her long dark hair tumbling down from beneath her lacy night bonnet. She listened for a moment, staring at the leaping reflections from the crowd's torches, and then her heart-shaped face went a little pale as to the general din of shouting and chanting was added the unmistakable sound of breaking glass. Windows were being smashed! What on earth was going on?

For a moment she was so frightened she couldn't move. The elegant Mayfair bedroom was no longer in quiet darkness but was illuminated by a flickering light, and the gilded washstand in the blue-and-white-tiled bathroom beyond the dressing room was glittering brightly, as if on fire. The tiles themselves, usually so cool and soothing, were burnished to a dancing crimson. She gasped aloud as the ormulu clock on the marble mantelpiece began to suddenly chime. It was two o'clock in the morning, and exclusive South Audley Street was as noisy and disorderly as the market at Covent Garden! Oh, how she wished her companion, Mrs. Rogers, was with her here instead of away caring for her sick mother.

Flinging back the bedclothes and slipping into her pink muslin wrap, she hurried to the window to hold the curtain gingerly aside and peep out at the chaotic scene below. A hooting, chanting mob was gathered across the street in front of the brightly-lit residence of Sir Matthew Wood, a troublesome Member of Parliament whose sole purpose recently had been to embarrass the government and cause unrest; he would seem to have succeeded at last. But even as she thought this, she realized that the mob wasn't angry and aggressive, but cheering and happy. They were waving banners and what appeared to be little green bags on sticks. Little green bags on sticks? She stared at them, wondering what on earth they signified. The chanting became more and more strident, and gradually she realized what they were saying. *God save the queen! God save the queen!* Jane stared down in puzzlement. Why were they shouting for the queen? Caroline of Brunswick was in exile on the Continent and had been since she was Princess of Wales, long before her husband's accession as King George IV.

More glass was broken as the more unruly elements in the crowd turned their attention to a nearby house, which had remained in darkness in spite of the disturbance. Stones and missiles were hurled, shattering some of the windows, and Jane's heart leapt a little in alarm. Had Melville seen to it that some lamps were placed in their own windows? The thought was only fleeting, for almost immediately her attention was drawn to some gentlemen who were unwise enough to attempt to pass down the street. They were rudely jostled and made to doff their hats toward the jutting stone porch of Sir Matthew's house, almost as if the queen herself was standing on its balconied roof. Jane couldn't understand it, for the queen had been virtually banished from England because of her indiscretions, and since being on the Continent had persistently shocked European society with scandalous conduct which had appalled the British and had made the king more and more determined never to have anything to do with her again, even though his own conduct over the years had left a great deal to be desired. So why had the mob gathered like this? Why shout and cheer for so disreputable a heroine? Jane was a little bemused now, as well as alarmed, for evidently something had been happening during her absence at Derwent Park, the family seat in Cheshire.

At that moment a carriage turned into the street from the direction of Curzon Street, attempting with great difficulty to pass through the crowd and drive north past the window where Jane stood. The crowd immediately became more excited on recognizing the occupant as Lord Sidmouth, a high-ranking member of the government who was known to uphold the king's wishes where the queen was concerned. Jane's breath caught in horror as someone let squibs off beneath the hooves of the horses, which sprang forward almost out of control. The carriage careened away along the street, the crowd hurling stones after it. She could hear each missile striking the vehicle's gleaming black panels.

Someone tapped urgently at the bedroom door behind her, making her jump, but it was only her maid, Ellen. "My lady? I must come in and put a lamp in your window. Mr. Melville says the earl left instructions for the house to be illuminated if there was any sign of trouble."

"Yes, Ellen. Please come in." Jane was surprised to learn that her brother Henry had evidently been expecting some sort of disturbance and yet had gone out to his club, even though he knew she was coming back from Cheshire that night.

The maid hurried in with the lighted lamp, her night bonnet and voluminous night robe a startling white in the dimly lit room. Quickly, she placed the lamp on the window sill, and was rewarded by an immediate cheer from the street. With a sigh of relief, she turned to Jane, her tangled, sandy-colored hair sticking out in spikes from beneath her bonnet. "We'll be all right now, Lady Jane. Mr. Melville says they only throw things at houses that don't light up in honor of the queen."

"Did I understand you to say that the earl left instructions about this?"

"Yes, my lady. There was trouble last night as well."

"But why? What's it all about? And why wasn't I informed about it the moment we returned from Cheshire?"

"Mr. Melville says he didn't want to alarm you unnecessarily, my lady," explained the maid, gazing down at the street. "You were so very tired after the long journey from Derwent Park, and the street was quiet because the constables had managed to clear everyone away. He hoped nothing would happen tonight."

Jane nodded. She could understand the butler's reticence, but she still couldn't understand why her brother had seen fit to go out and risk exposing her to such an unpleasant situation. And anyway, what on earth was it all about in the first place? "Ellen, did Mr. Melville tell you why the crowd is here?"

"The queen has returned from Europe, my lady. She arrived yesterday and is lodging with Sir Matthew Wood. It's said she's come back to claim all her rights. The crowds accompanied her all the way from Dover and have stayed with her ever since. Mr. Melville says it's been quite dreadful, and all of Mayfair's complaining. It's worst of all when she appears on the balcony."

"I can imagine." Jane glanced out again, at the green bags in particular. "What are those funny little bags, do you know?"

The maid looked out. "No, my lady."

"Did Melville mention my letter to the earl? I confess I'm a little astounded that my brother should decide to go out when I was due back. The letter set out very clearly his error in thinking I wasn't due until two days from now."

"I, er, don't think the letter can have arrived," replied the maid tactfully, avoiding her mistress's eyes. The letter had arrived all right; the earl had simply forgotten all about it, as seemed only too usual these days.

Jane read the maid correctly. Henry Derwent, fifth Earl of Felbridge, had changed so much of late. He had become so wrapped up in his new passion for coaching that he thought of little else, his fiancée and sister included. Poor Blanche, what sort of husband was he set to be now? No doubt, he'd neglect his bride and spend most of his time at the Fleece in Thames Street, which establishment he'd gone so far as to purchase so that he could become a professional coachmaster and operate his crack Iron Duke stagecoach on the fashionable Brighton road. He bore little resemblance now to the gallant, dashing, loving, and attentive suitor he'd been when first he'd wooed and won Blanche Lyndon's tender heart.

Jane sighed inwardly. Her brother was fast slipping beyond redemption. His obsession wasn't only causing endless difficulties for his long-suffering sister, it was threatening to jeopardize his betrothal. Blanche's father, one of London's most important bankers, had wanted his daughter to turn down Henry, a mere earl, and settle instead for the loftier-titled Duke of Dursley, who had recently been paying her a great deal of attention.

Jane stared at the milling crowds. She'd gone to Cheshire for six months partly to escape from Henry's constant coaching chatter, but that had proved impossible because it followed her in the form of Blanche's sad letters, which had listed his continuing sins and which had also begun to make more and more mention of Mr. Lyndon's attempts to break the Felbridge betrothal and replace it with a Dursley alliance instead. Jane really didn't know what to do about her brother, for she knew he loved Blanche very much, but if he didn't take more care he'd lose her to the Duke of Dursley, a notorious libertine whose only reason for pursuing her was to lay his avaricious hands upon her vast inheritance. Mr. Lyndon wasn't concerned with this—he was intent only upon having one of the premier dukes of England as his son-in-law.

Jane continued to stare at the scene in the street, thinking of her other reason for hiding away in Cheshire for six long months. She'd gone there to try and forget her own desperately unhappy love affair with Lewis, Lord Ardenley, the most handsome and most unfaithful and heartless man in London. But six months hadn't made any difference. She was still hopelessly in love with him, and she knew that she always would be, in spite of all that he'd done.

Outside, the cheering became suddenly louder. *God save the queen! God save the queen!* Jane's attention returned to the present as Caroline of Brunswick, Queen of England, emerged onto the balcony of Sir Matthew's house with her smugly satisfied host and his wife at her side. The queen wasn't an inspiring figure, for at the age of fifty-two she was short and immensely fat, with a vast wig of coal-black, girlish curls and bushy eyebrows dyed the same false color. She wore a large hat adorned with enormous ostrich plumes, and a mourning gown in ostentatious respect for the late king, who had been both her uncle and her father-in-law. Her gown had a large Tudor ruff, which made her head look like a grotesque *pièce-de-la-rèsistance* on a banquet platter, but she waved as regally as Good Queen Bess herself to her adoring supporters, who cheered wildly and waved their odd green bags in the air. Jane couldn't help disapproving of her, even though the king himself was hardly a shining example, for how could a woman who kept a low-born Italian courtier as a lover be fit to be queen? Her antics, and those of the king, had left the royal family at a very disreputable ebb in this year of 1820, and if this night's events was anything to go by, things weren't set to improve just yet.

Ellen suddenly clutched at her arm, making her jump. "Oh, my lady! Isn't that the earl's phaeton returning? Surely it will overturn in such a horrid crowd!"

Jane followed the maid's gaze and her heart almost stopped with alarm as she saw that it was indeed her brother, with another gentleman at his side, driving the dangerously high, unstable phaeton toward the house. It was an eccentrically old-fashioned vehicle, once owned by their father, and it was notoriously difficult to drive, even at the best of times, which of course was why Henry chose to use it. No other vehicle could better display his considerable skill as a whip of the first order, for it was drawn by no fewer than six horses, and Henry was one of the only men in England who would risk such a large team without the assistance of at least one postilion. The horses were highly strung and very nervous indeed as they picked their way through the turmoil in the street, their heads tossing and their eyes rolling alarmingly. Ellen's fear seemed justified, for it did indeed look as if the phaeton must overturn at any moment.

Jane held her breath, relaxing only a little as Henry was recognized and cheered as the mob greeted him with approval for having his house illuminated. Beside him, his passenger's top hat was pulled down over his face, concealing his identity. She hardly gave him a second glance, believing he must be Charles Moncarm, Marquis of Bourton, her brother's closest friend and the man who had long wanted to marry her, continuing to propose even during her brief betrothal to Lewis Ardenley. She didn't love Charles; she should, for he was good and kind, but she didn't.

At last the phaeton reached the curb and two grooms hurried to attend the frightened horses. Henry and his companion vaulted lightly down to the pavement, turning to doff their hats and bow to the queen, who acknowledged them with a wave and smile. The crowd immediately cheered again, but Jane was oblivious to the noise, she could only stare in dismay at the man at her brother's side; it wasn't Charles Moncarm after all, it was Lewis!

Tall, elegant and as handsome as ever, with disheveled hair of the brightest gold, he cut a striking figure even in the flickering, uncertain light from the torches. Jane couldn't look away from him. It was as if the last six months had never been, for the pain and heartbreak of his betrayal was suddenly as fresh as if it had been discovered that very moment. She could see again the beautiful, taunting face of his mistress Alicia, the Duchess of Brantingham, when she'd come to tell his unknowing fiancée the truth. *Lewis is my lover, Jane, and he has been all along. Marry him and you'll never be anything more than second best. My dear, he's only marrying you to please his father. The old man's dying, you know, and nothing would delight him more than to see his son and heir safely married to a suitable wife. I'd have been first choice, if I hadn't already had a husband. Brantingham's being very tiresome, refusing to divorce me. Still, one can't have everything, can one? And I do have Lewis, you know. You'll never have anything more than his name. Be sensible, my dear, give him back his ring and save your pride.*

Jane blinked back the hot tears which suddenly pricked her violet-blue eyes. How could Henry bring him here, how *could* he?

Ellen looked uncertainly at her mistress, having immediately recognized Lewis. "Shall—shall you go down, my lady?"

Jane drew sharply back from the window then, for something made Lewis look directly up at the lamp. Had he seen her?

"My lady?"

"I haven't any choice. They'll know I'm awake because of the light in the window."

"I could say that you have a headache after the long journey," offered the maid tentatively.

Jane shook her head. "No, I have to face him some time, and now would seem as good a moment as any."

She sat before the muslin-draped dressing table for the maid to brush her hair, then she quickly dressed and a moment later was ready to face Lewis and her brother.

She hesitated before leaving the safety of her rooms. Six months ago, she'd vowed never to let Lewis realize how much he'd hurt her, or how much she still loved him. She'd always thought she'd have time to prepare herself for their first meeting, but that wasn't to be so, she was to be thrust into his company without warning. Please, don't let him see the truth written in my eyes; let me be able to conceal my heart from his cruel, uncaring gaze.

TWO

*J*ane reached the balustrade above the columned vestibule just in time to see the lean, elderly figure of the butler, Melville, cross the black-and-white-tiled floor below to admit the two gentlemen. The noise from the street was suddenly loud as he opened the door, then it became muffled again as he closed it and took their hats, gloves, and canes.

At first, Lewis was hidden from her view by the tall Ionic columns which stretched up from the ground floor to the gilded, domed ceiling far above, but she could see her brother quite clearly. At twenty-five, he was four years her senior, and possessed the same dark coloring and violet-blue eyes. He wore a tight black evening coat and white kerseymere trousers, and his intricately tied silk cravat was edged with fine lace. By the light of the single chandelier, she could see the diamond betrothal ring on his finger. It was a very fine ring, as one would have expected to be given by one of London's most sought-after heiresses. It was also very like the ring Lewis had put on Jane's own finger. Jane looked at it for a moment, wondering how much longer it would grace her brother's finger if he persisted with his present attitude. The Duke of Dursley might not be able to boast a fortune as spectacular as that of the Earl of Felbridge, but his family and title went back to the time of the Norman conquest, and as far as the extremely socially ambitious Mr. Lyndon was concerned, that was more important than wealth because Blanche was already fabulously wealthy.

Suddenly, Lewis moved his position and she could see him at last, his hair very golden indeed in the soft glow of the chandelier. Gazing down secretly at him, she was conscious of the familiar, bewildering rush of emotion she'd experienced the very first time she'd seen him. She'd loved him then, and she loved him still.

He was taller than Henry, with broad shoulders and slender hips, and it was not without reason that he was spoken of as the most handsome man in society. His face was romantically classic and his complexion bronzed from many hours spent in the open air. He had long-lashed gray eyes which always seemed to have a hint of devilment in them, and his smile possessed an air of sensuality which played havoc with even the most frosty female hearts. The warm, almost lazy charm of that smile promised so very much that the prospect of being alone with him had lured many a hitherto chaste young lady from the paths of innocence; it had lured Lady Jane Derwent to the depths of unhappiness.

He and Henry paused to talk for a moment at the foot of the curving marble staircase, allowing her even more time to study him without his knowing. How effortlessly elegant he was, his taste so perfect at all times. Like Henry, he wore a tight black evening coat, but its buttons were silver and its collar just high enough to touch the hair at the back of his head. His long legs were encased in close-fitting white trousers, and there was an emerald pin nestling in the folds of his unstarched silk neckcloth. His white satin waistcoat was left partly unbuttoned to reveal the fine lace trimming of the shirt beneath, and a discreet bunch of seals swung from his fob. His looks would have set him apart in any gathering, no matter how superior, but with hair of such a bright gold, he was memorable. He was thirty years old, charming, amusing, exceedingly wealthy, and confident of acceptance in any company; he was also faithless, cold-hearted, and unkind, and loving him had been a bitterly painful experience which would remain with her for the rest of her life.

Henry looked up suddenly and saw the paleness of her cream dress. "Jane? Is that you?"

She stepped reluctantly into view at the top of the staircase. "Yes."

"Are you all right? We came as quickly as we could." He

glanced a little uncertainly at Lewis and then came swiftly up the stairs toward her. "I had no idea you were returning two days early. You should have written."

"I did write." He was avoiding her eyes, which meant that he had indeed received her letter but had forgotten all about it. No doubt, he'd been too taken up with his wretched coaching to think about such a mundane matter as her return!

Outside, the mob became suddenly noisier as some unfortunate attracted its displeasure. At the sound of more breaking glass, Henry looked quickly down at Lewis, who hadn't moved from the foot of the staircase. "Come on up, we'll adjourn to the blue saloon. It's at the back of the house and is bound to be more peaceful."

Jane gave her brother a furious look, for the last thing she wanted was to sit in polite conversation with the man who had treated her so infamously, but Henry didn't notice her anger, or affected not to notice it, and drew her hand through his arm to walk to the white-and-gold doors of the main reception chamber.

Lewis hesitated, toying with the lace spilling from his cuff. He hadn't missed Jane's reaction, but they had to meet each other sooner or later. Perhaps it would be wise to get the first confrontation over and done with as soon as possible. He came slowly up the staircase.

The blue saloon lived up to its name, having walls hung with the finest Chinese silk and sofas upholstered in the richest sapphire blue velvet. It had a gilded ceiling from which were suspended no fewer than three dazzling French crystal chandeliers, and the Adam fireplace was fashioned from a blue-veined marble which seemed to reflect whatever light surrounded it. There were four tall windows overlooking the ornamental gardens at the rear of the house. Reaching from floor to ceiling, they opened onto a covered, wrought-iron balcony where in summer it had long been the family custom to take tea or liqueurs after dinner. The fringed, golden velvet curtains were drawn now and the room was very quiet indeed after the noise which seemed to permeate the rest of the house. Lit only by the two ornate girandoles on either side of the chimney breast, everything was dim and shadowy, with the glint of gold and fine porcelain shimmering in the two immense glass cabinets in the recesses beside the fireplace.

Jane was stiff and cold as Henry escorted her to the nearest sofa, and he could no longer ignore her manner. He leaned closer to whisper in her ear. "You're in a sour mood, sis. Didn't Cheshire agree with you?"

"This has nothing to do with Cheshire," she hissed back, "as well you know, Henry Derwent! Are you *really* surprised that I'm less than thrilled to be confronted with Lewis Ardenley on my first night back?"

He refrained from saying any more for the time being, handing her to her place on the sofa and then going to the console table behind it to pour some cognac. He raised the decanter inquiringly to Lewis as he came in. "A glass of restorative?"

Lewis nodded. "Thank you."

Jane looked away. How well she remembered his voice, light and yet firm. It was a voice which had haunted her dreams.

Henry handed Lewis his glass and then looked reprovingly at his sister. "Jane, I know why you're angry, but perhaps you should know that if it hadn't been for Lewis I wouldn't have known you were back."

"You wouldn't have *remembered* I was back, you mean," she replied.

"What does it matter? The fact is that I was at Brooks's and would be there still if Lewis hadn't heard about the mob at Wood's house and remembered seeing your carriage returning early this evening."

Her violet-blue rested fleetingly on Lewis and then moved away again. She didn't reply.

Henry was exasperated. "Jane . . ." he began.

Lewis shook his head warningly, not wanting him to pursue the point.

Henry glanced at him, but then returned his attention to his sister. "Jane, you're being a little unfair tonight, and I begin to wish I'd stayed with the backgammon; my luck was in. Anyway, why *did* you return two days early?"

Lewis turned away with a silent groan, for he knew full well what her answer was going to be. There were times when Henry Derwent seemed hellbent upon putting his handsome head on the block.

Jane looked coldly at her brother. "Henry," she said with ominous calm, "I haven't returned two days early. *You* were under the impression that I was coming back two days later than I actually was. I realized that when I received that hastily scribbled note which masqueraded under the title of a letter. Where did you write it? In the stables at the Fleece? Wherever it was, you had barely enough time to dash off a polite greeting."

"It was a perfectly acceptable letter, written right here, if you must know."

"Then I'm appalled at your notion of an acceptable letter, Henry Derwent. But we're digressing, aren't we? You asked me why I've returned today."

"And I'm waiting for your answer."

"Evidently, you've forgotten your promise to take me to Madame Louise's tomorrow for the final fitting of my new ballgown."

Henry stared at her, light slowly dawning on him. Lewis raised his eyes heavenward. Pray your last, *monsieur*, Madame Guillotine is about to severe you fool head from your shoulders.

Jane's smile was sweet. "And if you've forgotten the ballgown, Henry, you must have also forgotten the occasion for which it was ordered."

He drew a long, slow breath. "Oh lord," he murmured.

"Yes, well you might say that. How could I possibly be returning in two days' time when Blanche's birthday ball is tomorrow night? You'd forgotten all about it, hadn't you? I couldn't believe my eyes when that miserable note arrived at Derwent Park. After all the silly mistakes you've been making with poor Blanche, you've actually gone so far as to forget all about one of the most important social occasions of her year! I'm ashamed of you, Henry Derwent. In fact, I'd go further than that and say that I despair of you! What was it this time? Has the Iron Duke been losing to its rivals on the Brighton road? Or has Lord Sefton been involving you in the activities of the Four-in Hand? What is it, mm? Come now, don't be coy, you *know* it has something to do with your wretched coaching. You aren't capable of thinking about anything else these days."

"It was the annual race to Brighton on Midsummer Day," he admitted unwisely.

"Really? Well now, I'll warrant the Duke of Dursley hasn't been devoting his time to something as dull as a stagecoach race."

"Dursley? What on earth has he got to do with it?"

"He's pursuing your fiancée," she replied, "but then you've probably been too busy jaunting off to Brighton to notice."

"For someone who's been away for six months you seem to know a great deal," he grumbled.

"Blanche and I correspond regularly," she replied. "I know all about your many sins, Henry Derwent. Still, I suppose that if *this* is the company you've been keeping of late, your monstrous lack of consideration can easily be explained." She glanced at Lewis.

Henry was appalled. "Jane!"

Lewis merely raised his glass, smiling just a little. "It's a pleasure to see you again too, Jane," he murmured.

She was glad of the dim lighting, which concealed the swift flush which sprang to her cheeks. "Six months don't appear to have improved you, sir. You're still smooth and disagreeable."

"And you're still impetuous," he replied quietly.

Henry was glad the focus of attention had been diverted, but was still aghast at Jane's personal attack. "Jane, that's quite enough!" he protested.

She raised her chin defiantly, her violet-blue eyes very stormy indeed.

Lewis put out a hand to silence Henry further. "It's all right, Henry. I believe I've outstayed my welcome and should toddle along."

Henry hesitated, looking furiously at his unrepentant sister, then he nodded at Lewis. "I'll come down with you."

As they left the room, Jane leaned her head wearily back against the sofa's soft blue velvet. She closed her eyes to hold back the hot tears, but they welled miserably from beneath her lids. "Oh, Lewis, Lewis," she whispered to the empty room, "I love you so."

Melville was waiting patiently in the vestibule as the two men descended the staircase. Henry apologized to Lewis for Jane's behavior. "I'm sorry, I thought she'd be over all that by now."

The butler handed Lewis his hat, gloves, and cane and then withdrew, realizing that the two would talk for a while longer. Lewis looked at Henry. "Don't be hard on her. She obviously thinks she had just cause to condemn me. I shouldn't have come here tonight; it was a gross error of judgment on my part."

"But damn it all, it's been six months since—"

"Since I deceived her with the Duchess of Brantingham?"

It was the first time he'd said anything about the scandal which had terminated his betrothal to Jane, and so Henry looked quizzically at him. "Did you?"

"What do you think?"

"I've always believed what you told Jane at the time—that there was no foundation in the rumor. The fact that Alicia is your mistress now is neither here nor there."

Lewis smiled. "Then perhaps we should leave it at that, mm?"

"Is old Brantingham likely to grant her a divorce?"

Lewis hesitated. "I doubt it."

"I can't imagine why," replied Henry bluntly, "for you aren't the first lover she's taken, are you?"

"Have a care, dear boy; the lady is a friend of mine."

"Forgive me, but I just don't see her as being the right one for you."

Lewis's smile was enigmatic. "Do you think she sees me as being the right one for her?"

Henry was a little taken aback. "Eh? Well, that's obvious, isn't it?"

"Is it?"

Henry was a little exasperated. "You don't intend to discuss this, do you?"

"No."

"Then maybe you'd prefer to discuss Charles Moncarm?"

"And why, pray, should the dear, honorable Marquis of Bourton be a burning topic of conversation?"

"Because he's once more on the point of popping the question to Jane."

"*Again?* He's becoming a little tedious."

"Maybe so, but this time I think she'll accept."

Lewis studied him for a moment. "Why should she do that when she's always turned him down before?"

"I don't know. Actually, it was Blanche who said that she thought Jane would."

"And we all know that except where you're concerned, Blanche is a very perceptive lady."

"Precisely. Eh? Now look here, don't *you* start on me. It's bad enough having Jane back to torment me all the time."

"Perhaps you need tormenting."

"Rubbish. Blanche is quite content."

"Is she?"

"Yes."

"You *must* be feeling secure. I've seen Dursley's curricle outside the Lyndon residence almost every day recently."

"Blanche is too sensible to be fooled by a fortune-hunting libertine like Dursley."

"The ladies are said to find him pretty enough."

"Maybe he is, if the eye can perceive real flesh and blood behind all the powder and paint. He's a dissolute fop, too shallow by far to impress Blanche."

"Let's trust you're right."

"I am. By the way, I almost forgot, Sefton's charged me to ask you again to return to the Four-in-Hand fold. We want you back, Lewis, for although it grieves me to admit it, you're still the best whip in England."

"Coaching bores me these days, Henry, so you can tell Sefton what he can do with his Four-in-Hand, teams, axles, wheels, ribbons and all."

"Thank you very much," replied Henry, a little miffed.

"Not at all. Besides, having witnessed the feeble fist you made of it tonight with your damned phaeton, I rather think the standard of the club must have slipped far too much for me to even consider lowering myself to rejoin."

Henry was most indignant at such unfair criticism. "Feeble fist? There's a near riot going on out there and although my six might be the best blood cattle in the land, such circumstances strained even their courage!"

Lewis grinned at having so easily provoked him.

Henry looked sheepish then. "Go to hell," he muttered.

Lewis tapped him on the shoulder with the silver handle of his cane. "I've had enough of coaching, Henry, and I don't want anything more to do with it."

"Then why do you keep such an immense stable at Maywood?"

"Horses are one thing, coaches quite another. My disillusionment with coaching has been taken for an act in some quarters, but that's not the case. Coaching is a pastime which I've realized can only too easily become an obsession, and in your case, my friend, that's clearly exactly what has happened. Take a word of advice and think carefully about Jane's criticism of your recent conduct. She's right, you *don't* think about anything other than your wretched ribbons. Your reputation as the world's boldest whip is allowed to take precedence over absolutely everything else, and if you continue in this vein, you'll lose Blanche Lyndon to Dursley. It's coaching or your future wife, one or the other, but not both. You do love Blanche, don't you?"

Henry was a little put out that such a question should even be asked. "You know that I do."

"Then behave like it."

"I am, dammit!"

"Are you? How many times recently have you deigned to even call upon her?"

"I, er, don't know."

"No, because you've been wrapped up in this damned Midsummer Day race to Brighton. I take it that *all* the other coaches have withdrawn now that you and Chapman have made it a personal challenge."

Henry looked a little mutinous. "The race is important to me."

"Too important. Edward Chapman is the most formidable and most ruthless coachmaster in London, and until you and your Iron Duke came along, he regarded the Brighton road as his personal kingdom, where lesser coaches were tolerated but no more. Now you're there, springing your cattle like something demented, cutting his times, stealing his fares, and offering more luxury than his Nonpareil can ever hope to."

"Chapman's been heading for a fall for some time now. His methods aren't exactly legal, are they?"

"Which makes you all that much more of a fool to try taking him on. He hasn't made the Black Horse the most important inn in the city by abiding by all the gentlemanly rules. He's renowned for his dangerous methods, and the fact that all the other coachmasters have withdrawn from the race should warn you of what to expect."

"The Iron Duke's going to trounce his Nonpareil. I've already ordered a new coach from Henry & William Powell."

Lewis gave a wry laugh. "Bond Street? They make a fine landau, I'll grant you, but a racing stagecoach?"

"The order's been placed."

"More fool you. I hear that Sefton's agreed to marshal the race."

"Yes."

"I'll warrant his money's on the Nonpareil."

"Sefton's impartial."

"In a pig's eye! He can't cross the road without wagering on whether he'll reach the other side or not!" Lewis was more serious then. "Forget the race, Henry, it's not worth the risk."

"I can handle Chapman."

Lewis searched his face. "I trust you can, my friend, because if not, you're going to find yourself in all manner of trouble."

"I'm going to win that race, Lewis."

"I wash my hands of you. Feud with Chapman if you must, cut a dash to end all dashes by risking your very life, spring your crack coach all the way to Brighton and back as if the devil himself is on your tail, and curse with the most vulgar knights of the road, but don't come whining to me when Blanche throws you over for Dursley. Believe me, Henry, if you carry on as you are at present, she's going to give you your *congé*, and it will serve you right.''

He opened the front door then, and the noise, which had been continuing relentlessly throughout, seemed to suddenly leap in at them. Torchlight cast weird dancing shadows over the vestibule's cool cream walls as he turned in the doorway, tapping his top hat onto his golden hair. ''Have you heard Wellington's latest *bon mot*?'' he inquired, raising his voice above the din. ''It seems he was accosted in the street by some laborers, more of the queen's own regiment of yahoos, who demanded that he doff his hat in salute to her. He duly obliged, saying that he wished all their wives would be like her.''

Henry grinned, forgetting his annoyance at what had previously been pointed out to him in such unequivocal terms. ''Wellington's tongue can be as formidable as his sword; he's quite irrepressible. Which is, of course, why I named my coach after him.''

Lewis raised an eyebrow at that. ''Come now, don't tell little fiblings. You named it after the duke because your Aunt Derwent suggested it. *Her* reasons for such a suggestion remain a mystery, of course, which is probably just as well since there would be a certain lack of courtesy in inquiring.''

Henry feigned shock. ''Are you suggesting that my widowed aunt has a past, sir?''

''I'm too much of a gentleman, and far too fond of the lady concerned, to hint at any such thing, but shall we just concede that it's very likely she took full but discreet advantage of the freedom allowed by her status as widow? Good night, Henry.''

''Good night, Lewis. I'm sorry our damsel in distress turned out to be a dragon in disguise.''

''Ah, but what a splendid dragon, mm?'' Lewis stepped out into the riotous night, where the crowds continued their noise even though the queen had long since retreated from the top of Sir Matthew Wood's porch.

THREE

*H*aving committed the crime of muddling up the date of his sister's return from Derwent Park, Henry was most careful the following morning not to commit the further sin of forgetting his promise to take her to her dressmaker, whose premises were most inconveniently situated in the city. He gave her his solemn word that they would set off at ten o'clock precisely.

A little before the appointed time, Jane was ready and waiting for him in the vestibule, where the noise from the mob outside still continued unabated, as it had done all night. Her dark hair was dressed up beneath a high-crowned straw bonnet which was trimmed with lace and had sapphire-blue satin ribbons, and she wore a frilled white muslin pelisse and matching morning gown. Her blue reticule and parasol were looped over her wrist as she stood by the narrow window light beside the door, teasing on her gloves and gazing out at the turmoil in the street. It really was a disgraceful disturbance, and one she sincerely hoped would not continue for very much longer.

Banners and flags were still being waved aloft, as were the peculiar green bags on poles she'd noticed the night before. The crowd was singing now, and South Audley Street rang with the new words which had been applied to a very old song, as if the king himself was singing it.

Oh, dear, what can the matter be,
Oh, dear, what can the matter be,
Oh, dear, what can the matter be,
Caroline's come—lack-a-day!
I hoped she'd have stayed, then I'd get a new spouse, and
I mentioned my wish to my friends in the house, and
They made her an offer of fifty bright thousand
If she would keep out of the way!

Jane raised an eyebrow. Fifty bright thousand? Could that *really* be how much the king and the government had offered the queen if she would remain on the Continent and renounce her rights? They must indeed be desperate to be rid of such an unseemly consort.

Henry came down the stairs, looking very fashionable in a tight-waisted, full-skirted brown coat, baggy Cossack trousers gathered at the ankles, and a green-and-white-striped American cravat which had been starched so much that it looked positively rigid. "Good morning, sis, and how are you this fine, bright day?"

"Still not pleased with you, brother mine."

"No, I somehow didn't think you would be. I'm sorry about last night—at least, I'm sorry it went the way it did."

"Henry, I know you've always believed Lewis's version of events, so I don't think there's any point in going into it all again, do you?"

"It isn't just that I believe what he says, Jane, it's that I honestly think you were completely wrong." He put his hand momentarily to her cheek. "He wasn't being unfaithful to you, I'm sure that he wasn't."

She drew away. "He was."

"Jane . . ."

"Please, Henry, I know that I'm right in this."

"How can you *know*? It's mere intuition, and this time it's playing you false."

She took a long breath and then met his gaze. "It isn't intuition, Henry, it's the evidence of my own ears."

"I don't understand."

"I haven't told anyone this before, I haven't even mentioned it to Lewis, but Alicia came to see me. *She* told me she was Lewis's mistress."

Henry stared at her. "I can't believe it."

"It's true. So who am I to believe? Lewis with his protestations of innocence, when all the time he was seen everywhere with her? Or Alicia's confession of guilt, again substantiated by the fact that she was seen everywhere with him? Given the situation at the time, and the fact *neither* of them have since bothered to hide the truth about their liaison, can you really wonder that it's Alicia's story which has the undeniable ring of truth as far as I'm concerned?"

Henry shook his head. "No, I suppose not, but I'd like to know why Lewis proposed to you in the first place if Alicia was the apple of his eye all along."

"It was to please his dying father, who wanted to see him suitably married."

Henry raised an eyebrow. "Well, if you don't mind my saying so, I find that hard to swallow. Lewis isn't a man to marry to please someone else, and his late father wasn't a man to expect him to."

"Nevertheless, that's what happened. You're the only person I've ever told, Henry, so I don't want it getting out. I've been trying to forget all about it, especially as I found Alicia's visit deeply distressing and humiliating. The last thing I want is for it to get out all over Town."

"It won't get out through me."

"You're not even to bring the subject up with Lewis. I want it left."

"Then left it will be."

A sudden roar from the crowd made her look out again. The queen had appeared on the balcony, waving and smiling, and in the daylight her false black curls looked more dreadful than ever, especially as she wore too much rouge as well.

Henry gazed at her and sighed. "What a sight she is, almost as comical as the king himself. They deserve each other."

"I agree."

"Still, I understand she's soon removing to Portland Place, which should leave us in peace again."

"Good. Henry, just what *are* those funny green bags?"

"Ah, so there has been *some* news which has failed to filter through to Cheshire!"

"Blanche was more concerned with your sins than anything else."

"I'm a misunderstood angel. Now then, the green bags have appeared because in his efforts to rid himself of his queen, the king has produced a real green bag containing documents giving salacious details of her, er, extramarital indiscretions. Needless to say, the bag has become the target of every caricaturist and lampoonist in Town, and has made the king the object of much derision, since a similar bag of *his* scandals would need to be a positive sack!"

Jane had to smile. "He really does rather ask for it at times, doesn't he?"

"He always did, right from those early days when as Prince of Wales he fell for the charms of Mrs. Robinson, the actress. All those silly letters which were published, from Prince Florizel to Perdita!" Henry chuckled.

She glanced a little slyly at him. "Perhaps I should see to it that *my* letters are published in future."

"Eh?"

"Come on, Henry Derwent, you know perfectly well what I'm talking about. My letter from Derwent Park did reach you, didn't it?"

He shifted uncomfortably. "No."

"Henry."

"Oh, all right, yes it did."

"And you forgot all about it?"

"To be perfectly honest, I hardly glanced at it. I was just about to go out."

"To the Fleece and the Iron Duke, no doubt."

"Yes, as a matter of fact."

"You really will have to improve, you know. This isn't good enough."

"It was a simple mistake, Jane," he protested.

"One of a multitude. If you'd read my letter properly, your memory would have been jogged about the ball tonight. As it is, I'm here to remind you, but what if for some reason I'd had to stay on in Cheshire? Would you have remembered? I'll warrant you haven't any plan to see Blanche this morning or this afternoon, have you?"

He took a long breath and shook his head sheepishly. "No, I haven't. But I *would* have remembered, Jane, truly I would. I love Blanche very much indeed."

"I know you do, which is why I can't understand how empty-headed you can be where she's concerned."

"Lewis gave me a lecture last night, Jane; I don't fancy another one."

"I won't say any more if you promise, on your honor, to be good from now on. You mustn't put coaching before Blanche, and you mustn't allow that wretch the Duke of Dursley to worm his insidious way into her affections."

"Blanche wouldn't even look at him," he declared a little too airily for Jane's liking.

"Henry! Are you paying proper attention?"

"Yes."

"You'd better be, or so help me I'll wring your handsome neck for you!"

"You, Lady Jane Derwent, are a positive tyrant."

"With you around, I need to be."

"Well, we've kicked my private life around for long enough, let's turn our attention to yours."

"I'd prefer not to. Besides, there's nothing to discuss."

24

"There's Charles Moncarm, Marquis of Bourton."

She looked at him in surprise. "Charles? Why should we discuss him?"

"Because he's about to ask you to marry him again."

"I wish he wouldn't."

"Because you don't love him?"

"I'm very fond of him, but I regard him more as a brother than anything else."

"His feelings for you aren't brotherly, I can promise you that." Henry studied her for a moment. "It's still Lewis, isn't it? If it wasn't for that, your feelings for Charles would be considered strong enough for marriage."

She could feel her cheeks reddening. "No, Henry, it isn't Lewis, and no, I don't feel enough for Charles to marry him."

"I can read you like a book at times, Jane. All right, maybe I'm wrong about Charles, but I'm damned right about Lewis."

"I don't wish to discuss it."

"Six months of Cheshire don't appear to have done the proverbial trick, do they?"

"I don't require six months anywhere," she replied with more than a little bravado. "I need only think of that *demimondaine* Alicia Brantingham to be perfectly cured of any misguided affection I may have felt for that lord."

"*Demimondaine?* That's a little strong, isn't it?"

"Well, since she's married to the Duke of Brantingham, who for some reason best known to himself refuses to divorce her, and since Lewis is merely the latest in a line of her lovers, I can't think of a better way to describe her, can you?"

"I admit that she's been a little indiscreet. . . ."

"A little? What would you consider a lot, Henry?" She held his gaze challengingly. "Would you still wish to marry Blanche if you knew she was another man's mistress?"

"Eh?" He gave a quick laugh. "Don't be ridiculous, of *course* I wouldn't!"

"Why not?"

"It must be obvious to you why not."

"Then why was *I* expected to marry Lewis when all the time he was granting his favors elsewhere?"

"Ah, but that's the crux of it, isn't it? I still don't think he was doing any such thing, in spite of Alicia's claim to the contrary."

She raised an eyebrow and then pretended to suddenly see

something out of the window. "Good heavens, what was that? Why, I do believe it was a pig with wings! Yes, indeed it was."

"All right, you don't have to resort to sarcasm, you've made your point, even if you're quite wrong." He smiled, touching her cheek with his fingertips. "I'm so very sorry that it didn't work out between you and Lewis, sis."

"So am I," she whispered.

At that moment, the sound of hooves came from the street and Jane looked out to see the phaeton being brought to the door, the horses already sweating and nervous because of the continuous uproar. She looked at it in dismay. "Oh, no, not the phaeton! Do we *have* to negotiate the streets of London in that wretched thing? Why can't we go in the town carriage?"

"Because the phaeton's good practice for me."

"You don't really mean to go on with this challenge to Mr. Chapman, do you?"

"I told you last night—"

"I was hoping that in the cold light of day you'd see a little sense."

"The Iron Duke's going to run the Nonpareil off the road, and that's why I must have all the practice I can if I'm to take the ribbons myself on Midsummer Day. It's only three weeks away, you know."

"I wish you would forget all about it."

"Never."

With a sigh, she gathered her skirts and went to the door, which the ever-vigilant Melville immediately hastened to open. The noise and clamor was almost deafening as she emerged into the warm June sunshine. Henry assisted her up onto the perilously high seat and then climbed up beside her, taking the reins. The queen had retired from the balcony, so they didn't have to acknowledge her in any way, for which Jane was very grateful, since such salutes would have meant still more riotous cheering from the mob, with the consequent alarming effect upon the unfortunate horses.

The phaeton moved forward very slowly, the team inching its way reluctantly through the crush. Jane gripped the side of her seat in readiness, knowing that the moment it was possible, Henry would spring the light vehicle forward at a reckless pace. She was right; his whip cracked and the team lunged forward, setting off down the street as if the hounds of hell were behind them. Jane hung on tightly, alarmed at the wild acceleration, and wishing with all her heart that she'd *insisted* they take the town carriage!

Driving along Piccadilly shortly afterward, the team were still uneasy from the crowd, proving a handful even for Henry, so that to her relief he had to take them along at a more sensible speed. As always, the conspicuous phaeton attracted a great deal of attention, and she felt horridly on show, perched up as she was almost on a level with the outsiders on the stagecoaches.

When they reached the city, he didn't drive directly to Madame Louise's, but took a rather circuitous route by way of narrow, steep Snow Hill. She was immediately suspicious, for it was in Snow Hill that the famous Black Horse coaching inn stood. The Black Horse was owned by Henry's bitter rival, Edward Chapman, and it was from here that the crack Nonpareil stagecoach operated.

FOUR

Jane's suspicions were well founded, for as they neared the entrance of the inn, Henry maneuvered the phaeton in to the curb and took out his fob watch. "Henry? What are you up to?" she demanded.

"Just wait, and you'll see."

"I'm supposed to be going to my dressmaker!"

"And so you shall, in just a moment. It won't take long; the Nonpareil's always on time, to the very second."

She looked quickly at the inn. It was a large building, its roof adorned with an immense carved wooden statue of a black horse. The entrance giving on to the crowded, busy courtyard was guarded by similar statues, and the same black horse design could be seen on every one of Chapman's well-known scarlet coaches, thirty or more of which operated from this inn alone. He had other inns, all of them thriving, and all of them operating his famous coaches, but the Black Horse in Snow Hill was his headquarters, and had justifiably earned its reputation as one of the finest inns in London.

Glancing again at the set of her brother's chin, she became a little alarmed. "Henry, can't we please drive on?"

"There's a little matter I have to take care of first."

"What little matter? Oh, Henry, don't do anything foolish! Mr. Chapman isn't a man to tangle with!"

"I know what I'm doing, sis. Ah, here we go." The sound of a coaching horn echoed from the inn's yard, the unmistakable notes of "Cherry Ripe." Henry touched the phaeton's leaders with his whip and they moved slowly forward, held in check by a very tight rein as he inched the high, unstable vehicle slowly toward the entrance of the inn.

Jane held her breath, not knowing quite what to expect, but her heart almost stopped as she saw the splendid Nonpareil bearing down upon her, its panels gleaming and its coachman, the famous George Sewell, very natty indeed in a blue coat and white top hat, a fresh nosegay pinned to his lapel. Beside him was a young blood who had paid well over the odds for the privilege of this coveted place, no doubt hoping for a chance to take the ribbons himself on the open road. The coach started to emerge from the entrance into the steep, narrow street, the four outside passengers bowing their heads to pass beneath the archway. The guard began to give another spirited rendition of "Cherry Ripe," but the notes died on a horrified choke as Henry abruptly placed his phaeton squarely in the coach's path, making the cursing, startled coachman rein in very sharply indeed in order to avoid a collision. The outsiders cried out in alarm, thinking their end had come, and Jane closed her eyes tightly, for the Nonpareil's leaders were rearing up a little too closely for comfort.

For a moment there was uproar, the whole street turning to see what was happening. Dogs began to bark excitedly and Henry's team danced around, only just held in check by the tight reins.

The young gentleman on the Nonpareil's box recognized Henry and half rose to his feet. "I thay, Felbwidge, thith ain't the thing, you know!" he protested.

"You stay out of this!" snapped Henry, flicking his whip expertly within inches of one of the excited dogs, which had come unwisely close to the phaeton's leaders. Then he held Sewell's sly-looking eyes. "There's more where this has come from, Sewell, and if you attempt to overturn the Iron Duke again, you'll be sorry. Is that clear?"

The coachman swallowed, his lean figure motionless as he met the accusing gaze squarely enough. "I don't know what you're talking about, my lord earl. Overturn the Iron Duke?" He spread his hands with an innocent smile, and Jane distrusted him immediately.

Henry wasn't finished. "You've been warned, Sewell, and you can tell Chapman that I'll brook no more interference of any kind. Do you hear?"

"I hear. Why don't you stick to your pretty Four-in-Hand, my lord, and leave the real thing to the professionals?" The man smiled, knowing the taunt had found its target.

Henry's hands tightened on the reins, but Jane looked warningly at him. "You've issued your warning, can't we leave it at that?" she whispered urgently.

For a moment more he held the coachman's eyes, but then urged the phaeton's team forward once more, and to Jane's utmost relief, the light vehicle sprang effortlessly out of the Nonpareil's path.

She clung to the side of the seat again as the phaeton swayed out of Snow Hill, weaving its way past wagons and hackney coaches as if endowed with wings. At last she felt sufficiently recovered to be angry with him. "Have you taken leave of your senses, Henry Derwent? How *could* you do something so utterly foolish?"

"It had to be done; they tried to run me off the road last week."

"And this morning you nearly finished the job for them! What if that coachman hadn't been able to stop in time?"

"George Sewell's the best in the business. He'd stop on a halfpenny if necessary."

"I'm glad you can be so sure."

"I am. Look, sis, you're blowing this up out of all proportion."

"Henry, I don't think *I'm* the one doing that."

He slowed the phaeton almost to a trot, giving her his full attention for a moment. "I'm a coachmaster now, Jane. I'm the owner of the Fleece inn and the operator of the Iron Duke. Last week, Chapman attempted to force me into a ditch on Reigate Hill, and that can only mean I'm threatening his coach's supremacy on the road. It was meant to warn me off, but it hasn't worked. He had me off the route for two days, but that was all. I'll have him yet, and he's going to be swallowing an awful lot of the Iron Duke's dust before I'm finished with him."

"If Mr. Chapman's efforts don't succeed in turning your coach over on top of you first. Henry, you're playing with fire. It's going beyond a mere passion for coaching when you take on such an adversary."

"I'm going to better him, Jane, and I'll do it on Midsummer Day, you mark my words."

"He might yet decide to refuse your challenge," she said hopefully.

"What, and lose face? Not a chance. Besides, today's little incident will soon be relayed to him, and he'll be hopping mad about it."

There was no reasoning with him, not where coaching was concerned. Oh, how she wished he'd never gone to that dinner two years before when he'd met Lord Sefton and become embroiled in the Four-in-Hand Club. It had all stemmed from that, getting worse and worse until they'd reached this present ridiculous situation, where he lived and breathed only for his precious ribbons.

He said nothing more, touching the whip to the leaders again and urging them more swiftly through the traffic, threading deftly past a cumbersome brewer's dray and passing between a gig and a cart laden with vegetables with only inches to spare on either side. The Phaeton's fine horses didn't check or hesitate; they moved at a bold pace which drew much admiration from all who saw them. Henry grinned proudly at her. "A rare team, eh? The finest set of cattle in England."

She was still exasperated with him. "Yes," she replied tersely, "and they're driven by the most bone-headed ox."

He merely grinned all the more, flicking the whip and bringing the phaeton up to breakneck pace again. At last he halted with a flourish outside the four-story red brick building where Madame Louise, one of London's most fashionable couturieres, occupied the whole of the top floor with her flourishing business, her presence indicated only by the discreet display of millinery in the windows.

Henry vaulted from the phaeton and came around to assist his sister down. "There, madam," he said, still grinning, "you've been conveyed with supreme style right to the very door."

"I'd thank you not to look so immensely pleased with yourself, for that was the most disagreeable journey I've ever experienced." She looked past him then along the pavement, a sixth sense warning her of approaching trouble. She immediately saw the form that trouble was taking, for walking along the street toward them was none other than the proprietor of the Nonpareil, Mr. Edward Chapman.

He was a wiry little man of about forty-five, with a jutting, narrow chin, a wide forehead, and high cheekbones. He had once been a stockbroker, until three extremely fortunate marriages to rich widows had left him with sufficient wealth to purchase a coaching business and embark upon the career which had made him the most important coaching man in the whole land. His hair was a nondescript, mousy color, and he wore it with large, bushy side-whiskers. His clever eyes were like bright brown beads, and set as they were above that odious smile, it seemed a miracle to Jane that *any* woman could accept him in marriage, let alone three. His taste in clothes was gaudy, to say the least, and today he had chosen a light blue coat and yellow waistcoat, a blue-and-white-spotted neckcloth, rust-colored breeches, and gleaming black boots. His wide-brimmed top hat was pulled forward on his head, and he swung a particularly handsome ivory-handled cane in his kid-gloved hands. Jane had met him only once, and the experience had been more than enough to make her dislike him intensely. She had no intention whatsoever of risking a second meeting, and so she hastily took her leave of Henry, who promised to wait for her.

As she hurried toward the door of the building, she heard Chapman's thin, nasal voice. "Why, good morning, my lord earl, and a very fine morning it is, too."

Madame Louise's fitting room was an untidy place, cluttered with half-finished garments and strewn with bolts of fine cloth, cards of lace, and tray after tray of buttons, spangles, fringes, and many other fashionable trimmings. Gowns, pelisses, and spencers hung on hangers on the picture rail, and someone had evidently been trying to decide upon a particular shade of pink gauze, for samples of this material in every degree of that color lay on the sunny windowsill beneath the display of hats and bonnets.

The dressmaker herself was small and dark, but although she looked very French, she came from Edinburgh, and spoke with a decidedly Scottish accent. She always wore charcoal-gray taffeta, which rustled as if it were trying to attract attention, and her hair was pushed up very severely beneath a very heavily embroidered day bonnet, making her long nose look almost beaky.

While an assistant was sent to bring the ballgown from the workroom, where it was being sewn with hundreds of tiny, clear glass beads, Jane went to the window to look down at the street below. The phaeton was still drawn up at the curb, and Henry and Chapman were standing beside it, engaged in what appeared to be a rather heated conversation.

She had to put them from her mind then, for the gown was

brought and it was time to try it on. It was particularly beautiful, made of the softest and most delicate cream silk, its hem padded to make it stand out a little. The overgown was of sheer cream net, and it was this which was being stitched with the glass beads, not all of which seemed to be in place as yet. The décolletage was deliciously low and daring, and the little puffed sleeves had an edging of beads which winked and flashed in the shaft of sunlight streaming into the room.

Jane gazed delightedly at her reflection in the cheval glass. "Oh, Madame Louise," she breathed, "it's the most beautiful gown I've ever had from you."

The dressmaker nodded with some satisfaction. "I believe it's my finest creation ever, Lady Jane."

"I shall steal Miss Lyndon's thunder at the ball tonight. It *will* be ready for tonight, won't it?"

"Oh, yes. It fits quite perfectly, and there are only the beads to sew on. I'll have it delivered to South Audley Street this afternoon."

Shortly afterward, Jane was dressed in her own clothes again and with the dressmaker's repeated promise that the ballgown would be delivered in good time, she descended the many stairs to the ground floor of the building, emerging onto the pavement to halt in disbelief, for of Henry and the phaeton there was no sign at all!

She glanced swiftly up and down the busy street, but she couldn't see him anywhere. For a moment she was nonplussed, but then a flush of anger swept over her. He'd forgotten her! Something had happened because of his encounter with Chapman, and his passion for coaching had once again taken over completely. He'd simply driven off and left her to fend for herself!

She was about to go back to the dressmaker to ask her to send a man for a chaise from the post house in nearby Fleet Street, when an elegant maroon town carriage suddenly drew up at the curb beside her.

The occupant lowered the glass to address her. "Good morning, Jane, am I right in thinking you're in some difficulty?"

She looked up into Lewis Ardenley's clear gray eyes.

FIVE

*H*e smiled at her startled reaction, and flung open the carriage door to step lightly down. He wore a dark blue, high-collared coat with a sprig of forget-me-nots in the buttonhole, and his hair was very golden in the sunlight as he removed his top hat. "I was wondering if I could be of any assistance to you?"

"None at all, sir."

"Allow me a little common sense, Jane, for it's quite obvious to me that Henry has let you down. Oh, don't look so astonished. I'm not clairvoyant, it's just that I happened to drive past a short while ago and saw him in extremely animated conversation with Mr. Edward Chapman. He then departed at speed in his highflyer and as I'd already noticed that they'd been talking outside this establishment, I remembered your remarks last night and put two and two together. He's rushed off on some vital matter connected with *his* kind of ribbons, and has left you attending to yours. Am I right?"

Reluctantly, she nodded. "I think so; there doesn't seem to be any other explanation for his sudden disappearance."

"My carriage is at your disposal."

"No, Lewis, I would prefer to have Madame Louise's man procure a chaise from the post house in Fleet Street."

"Why go to all that trouble when I can so easily return by way of South Audley Street?"

"Because I don't wish to accept any assistance from you, sir, and because I certainly don't wish to travel in the close confinement of a carriage with you."

"Your high horse can be very high indeed, can't it?"

"Do you really expect anything else after what you did?"

"I didn't *do* anything."

"No?" Her eyes flickered scornfully. "Allow me a little more credit, sir."

"Credit? Why should I, when you've always shown yourself to be singularly lacking in common sense. You revealed that sad failing six months ago, and now you're doing it again. You've been stranded here and my carriage awaits, so either you get in of your own accord, or I'll bundle you in without any ceremony at all, is that quite clear? I will *not* leave you on your own." He folded his arms, holding her mutinous gaze. "I'm waiting, Jane, so pray don't provoke my patience too far."

She gave in then, angrily snatching her skirts to climb up into the carriage. She sat in the farthest corner, her eyes stubbornly averted to avoid any possibility of catching his glance and provoking conversation.

He instructed the coachman to drive to South Audley Street and then climbed in too, closing the door behind him. The carriage lurched away from the curb and drove slowly on down the busy city street.

They traveled in silence at first, but she knew that there was a mocking smile on his lips as he studied her angry profile. At last he spoke. "What an infuriating way you have with you, Jane. I wonder if you realize how very provocative it can be."

"I neither know nor care, sir."

"There was a time—"

"That was before I found out about your highborn *belle de nuit*."

"Alicia is not a *belle de nuit*."

"I suppose you'll say next that she wears a habit and resides in a nunnery."

"You would appear to have used your six months in Cheshire to perfect the art of sarcasm."

"No, sir, I used it to reflect upon how very foolish and gullible I'd been. Did you honestly expect me to believe you when you said those long hours you spent with Alicia were purely platonic? She hasn't got a platonic bone in her body, especially not with a man like you!"

"If I dig deep enough in that, I do believe I will find a compliment concerning my person."

"You will also find my irritation at your dreary insistence that you are all innocence. Tell me, did you and she enjoy a platonic time in Paris?"

"My, my, word does travel."

"It was mentioned in passing in one of Blanche Lyndon's letters."

"In passing? How unflattering! I would have thought it warranted at least a page, possibly even two."

"You haven't answered my question. I understand you didn't

encumber yourself with much of any value for the trip; you took with you only a very little baggage. Baggage indeed.''

He smiled. ''For someone who claims to be so little affected by what I say or do, you seem inordinately interested in my private life.''

She flushed at that. ''It's idle curiosity, no more.''

''Idleness is not to be recommended, so I shall not show encouragement by pandering to it.''

She looked out of the window again, wishing with all her heart that he didn't have such a devastating effect upon her. She envied Alicia every moment spent in his arms, and she longed more than anything to feel his lips over hers again and to hear that seductive softness in his voice when he whispered her name. . . . Her eyes flashed then. What a fool she was—she should despise him!

South Audley Street was still in uproar because of the queen's supporters. The coachman eased the horses through the crush, taking several minutes to reach the curb outside the Derwent residence.

Lewis didn't immediately open the carriage door, but looked at Jane again. ''Perhaps I should tell you that I'll be at the ball tonight, with Alicia.''

''It's no concern of mine, sir.''

''Is Charles Moncarm escorting you?''

''I really don't see why I should tell you.''

''I still want to know.''

''No, Charles isn't escorting me tonight, but I do expect to see him there. Will that suffice?''

''Are you going to accept him?''

She gave him a cool smile. ''No, Lewis, I think I'll become his mistress and then pretend to the world that I'm no such thing. Now then, will you please let me alight?'' Her glance rested briefly on the forget-me-nots in his lapel. ''The symbol of true love and fidelity? How singularly inappropriate!''

He caught her wrist, his gray eyes very bright. ''Pride is a perverse emotion, it can save one from humiliation or it can plunge one into the depths of needless misery. You have far too much of the wrong kind of pride, Jane Derwent, and it will please me immensely when one day you're forced to admit it!'' He released her, opening the door and stepping down to the noise and clamor of the street.

The cheering and wild chanting echoed deafeningly between the elegant Mayfair houses, but she hardly heard a thing as she alighted, ignoring his outstretched hand and hurrying into the house, blinking back the tears which had once again sprung hotly to her eyes.

For once, Melville had been caught unawares by her return, but as he hurried into the vestibule she managed to present an outward calm. "Has the earl returned?" she inquired, teasing off her gloves and dropping them onto the console table beside the vase of carnations brought that morning from the market garden in Chelsea.

"The earl? Why, no, my lady, I thought he was with you."

"So did I, but he has apparently taken himself on some other business."

"Will he be here for luncheon, my lady?"

"I really have no idea, but I somehow rather doubt it."

She was right. Henry didn't return for luncheon, and as the afternoon began to wear on with still no sign of him, she began to fear that whatever business it was which was occupying him would once again dominate him to the exclusion of all else, including the ball that night! As the clock struck four, she asked Melville to send a man to the Fleece in Thames Street, in the hope of finding her wayward brother and prompting him to return. An hour passed and the man came back to tell her that Henry had gone to Brighton, driving the Iron Duke himself.

Jane stared at him in dismay. "*Brighton?*"

"Yes, my lady."

"When is he expected back?" She hardly dared ask.

"They couldn't say, my lady. I left word, and if he does return he'll be told straightaway."

If he returned. It was a very big if, for the journey to Brighton took all of five hours, even in a crack coach like the Iron Duke, which meant ten hours on the road, *excluding* whatever time he spent there. She glanced at her little gold fob watch. She'd last seen him at about eleven that morning, and then he'd driven to Thames Street and had the Iron Duke made ready, so he couldn't possibly have set off much before midday. She sighed, for even if he drove all the way to Brighton and back at breakneck speed, with barely a halt in between, he still couldn't be back in London much before eleven tonight, at the very earliest. Then he'd have to change and drive to Lyndon house in Berkeley Square, which meant it would be nigh on midnight before there was any chance at all of seeing him at the ball! And what if he'd forgotten it anyway and intended staying overnight in Brighton?

Oh, no, surely he wouldn't. . . . But, unfortunately, it was only too possible; she knew her brother only too well.

And she had problems of her own if he wasn't there to escort her to the ball, because she didn't have her companion, Mrs. Rogers, either. Sometimes it was very tiresome being a single lady in society. Under the circumstances she'd be reduced to just Ellen, which wasn't really the thing but surely wasn't so dreadful a sin—at least she didn't think it was.

SIX

Shortly after this, she was seated at the escritoire in the blue saloon trying to write a letter to her favorite aunt, Lady Agatha Derwent, when through the open windows she distinctly heard the sound of a carriage above the noise of the crowds. Could it be Henry? Had he remembered after all and turned back? Swiftly, she got up and hurried to the balustrade overlooking the vestibule, but as she gazed down to see who was admitted, the hope faded abruptly away, for it was Charles Moncarm, Marquis of Bourton, who stepped inside and handed his hat, gloves, and cane to Melville.

"Is Lady Jane at home?" she heard him ask.

"I'm up here, Charles."

He smiled up at her. "Good afternoon, Jane."

"Good afternoon, Charles. Please come on up. Melville, will you serve some tea in the blue saloon?"

"Very well, my lady." The butler bowed and withdrew.

Charles came up the staircase toward her. He was twenty-seven years old and of medium height and build, his wavy brown hair worn in the side-whiskers which were fast becoming the rage with gentlemen of fashion. He wore a mulberry coat and gray trousers, and there was a ruby pin in the center of his discreet, uncomplicated cravat. His looks were agreeable rather than handsome, but his hazel eyes had a certain appeal which made him far from unpopular with the opposite sex. To Jane, however, he was simply Charles, the friend she'd grown up with and liked so very much, and who would never amount to anything more, no matter how much he wished it otherwise.

Reaching the top of the staircase, he drew her hand to his lips. "It's good to see you again. Six months is far too long."

"It's good to see you again too, Charles."

"I hope I haven't called at an inconvenient time."

"No, I was just about to try and write to Aunt Derwent."

"Try? I thought letter writing came disgustingly easily to you."

"It does usually, but today I've got so much on my mind. Shall we go to the blue saloon?"

He pulled her hand gently through his arm. "Can I be of any assistance with this whatever it is that's on your mind?"

"Not unless you can produce my odious brother out of thin air."

He closed the saloon's elegant double doors behind him and leaned back against them for a moment, looking curiously at her. "Produce Henry out of thin air? Have you lost him then?"

"In a manner of speaking. He's taken himself off to Brighton, would you believe, and on Blanche's big day! I could box his silly, selfish ears for him."

"From your tone, I'd hazard a guess that it's his infernal coaches that have caused this."

"Yes." She explained what had happened. "So you see, I really don't know if he's going to be there tonight or not. If he doesn't get there, he'll be positively *thrusting* Blanche into Dursley's horrid arms, and her father will be doing all he can to help her on her way. Oh, Charles, what am I going to do?"

"What are *you* going to do? I fail to see that there's anything you *can* do."

"Should I warn Blanche what's happened?"

"I rather think not. What if he arrives in time after all? You'd have upset her for nothing, wouldn't you?"

Jane sighed and nodded. "I suppose so."

"Besides, I'm sure Henry will do the right thing and present himself in good time. If he doesn't, I'll escort you." He led her to the sofa. "Now then, sit down and relax a little. You look positively fidgety."

"So would you be if Henry was your brother."

"I hardly want Henry as my brother, since that would make you my sister, and that's not how I want things to be at all."

To her relief, Melville came in at that moment with the tea, which was prompt because it had been about to be served anyway. The butler placed the elegant silver tray on the table before the sofa and then withdrew again. Jane poured the tea into the dainty pink-and-white porcelain cups and handed one to Charles. "What have you been up to while I've been away?"

"Don't change the subject."

"I wasn't aware that we were discussing any particular subject."

"I was pointing out to you that I don't regard you as my sister."

"I know you don't, Charles."

"I've thought a great deal about you since you so providently handed Ardenley his *congé*, and I've come to the conclusion that now is once again my opportunity. You know what I'm going to say, don't you?"

Slowly, she nodded. "Yes, but I wish you wouldn't."

"I can offer you a great deal, Jane."

"I know."

"I love you very much."

She met his steady gaze then. "I know, and I love you too, but it isn't the right sort of love."

"But it's still love, and I believe it would grow into that other sort of love. We could do very well together, Jane."

She shook her head. "It wouldn't work, Charles. No, hear me out. I couldn't be satisfied with what you and I would have together, for it simply wouldn't be enough. I'd need to feel very differently about you in order to marry you."

He put his cup down. "Meaning that you'd need to feel as you did about Ardenley?"

"Yes."

"And where did that get you?"

"Don't, Charles. . . ."

"No, I want to know. If that love was so wonderful and fulfilling, why did he keep the Duchess of Brantingham's charms so very close all the time? You're deluding yourself about that so-called *love*, Jane; it was a fleeting passion which was as intangible and inconsequential as a will-o'-the-wisp!"

"It was a little more than that, Charles," she said quietly.

He was silent for a moment. "Maybe it was, but the fact still remains that it came to a very unhappy conclusion." He studied her for a moment. "That is, if it *is* concluded."

"It is."

"I wonder."

"Can't we talk about something else? The weather perhaps? Or the queen's return?"

"Both are exceeding tedious subjects."

"Then shall we gaze at each other in amicable silence?"

He smiled then. "No, I'll just say my final piece and then remove myself so that you can continue your letter writing. I'm not going to give up yet, Jane. I'm determined to win you, and I rather suspect that I will after tonight."

"Tonight?"

"When you are faced once and for all with Ardenley's love for Alicia. You haven't seen them together, have you? You dashed off to Cheshire to lick your wounds, and that was that. Maybe you've thought about him being with her, but you haven't seen them for yourself. And maybe, too, in your bitterness, you've forgotten that although Alicia may have a rather scandalous reputation, she's still a very beautiful and fascinating woman, certainly beautiful and fascinating enough to keep her hold on a man like Ardenley." He got up then. "I'll ask you again, Jane, and again, until you accept, of that you may be sure. And remember, if you need me to escort you later, just ask." Leaning over, he kissed her lightly on the cheek and then left.

Later, with the letter to her aunt completed at last, Jane went up to her rooms to begin her lengthy preparations for the ball, and in the first instance that meant taking a bath. Ellen undressed her and brushed her long dark hair before pinning it up into a loose knot on the top of her head. Then the maid drew a screen around the elegant copper bath tub in the center of the little bathroom, and Jane stepped into the deliciously warm, lavender-scented water. She leaned her head back against the soft pink cloth which had been draped around the tub, and closed her eyes. The bath was meant to be relaxing, but she had far too much on her mind for that. First there was Henry and his atrociously ill-timed flight to Brighton; then there was Charles; and finally there was Lewis. . . .

Her thoughts traveled back to the first time she'd met him. It had been at Kensington Palace the previous June, when society had attended the christening celebrations of the little Princess Victoria, daughter of the Duke and Duchess of Kent. After a while, she and Lewis had slipped out into the gardens overlooking Hyde Park, and had walked between the flowerbeds which had been a riot of roses, geraniums, and honeysuckle. How sweet and warm the air had been, and how still. Above them had wheeled the rooks and jackdaws for which the palace was famous, and the sound of music had drifted out from the great assembly within. Not a word had passed between them—indeed, they'd hardly spoken at all from that first fateful moment when Henry had introduced them. As he'd taken her hand and drawn it to his lips, his gray eyes so dark and clear as they'd gazed into hers, she'd felt a shock of emotion pass through her such as she'd never known before. Then, as they walked in the gardens, their hands had brushed together again, oh, so briefly. He'd pulled her into his arms, her body crushed close to his, her lips bruised with the passion of his kiss, a passion she'd returned. She'd lost her heart and soul to him, and both would be his until the day she died; but he'd only been toying with her, he had no heart, and his soul was cold.

"My lady?" Ellen's voice roused her.

"Yes?"

"Your gown has been delivered."

"Oh, good. I don't suppose there's any word of the earl?"

"No, my lady, I'm afraid not."

Jane finished her bath and then put on her wrap. Ellen had turned back her bed for her to sleep, because the ball was bound to go on until almost dawn, but it was impossible with all the din still going on in the street. The queen had evidently appeared on the balcony again, for the noise was tumultuous.

She must have managed a little sleep in the end, for Ellen was suddenly bringing her some tea, and the crimson and gold of sunset was slanting into the room. The crowd was still chanting.

Jane sat up, looking hopefully at the maid, but Ellen shook her head. "There's still no word, my lady."

Jane's heart sank. He'd forgotten completely, she knew that he had. What was she going to say to poor Blanche? And what was she going to do about her own escort? She didn't really want to ask Charles, not so quickly after his proposal—she'd feel a little awkward being so alone with him. No, it would be better to take Ellen and trust that her predicament was understood.

"Ellen, I'd like you to come in the carriage with me tonight."

"Yes, my lady."

She only picked at the tempting cold chicken and salad Ellen brought for her. She knew she should eat before an occasion like the ball, but her appetite seemed to have deserted her.

Afterward, she sat at the dressing table for the maid to apply the face lotion she always prepared before balls and other such tiring assemblies. It was a mixture of cream, crushed grapes, and lemon, and it smoothed and refreshed, leaving the skin perfect for the subtle application of cosmetics. Opening the elegant japanned box of Chinese papers, the maid took out the ones she required. It was considered very vulgar to apply heavy rouge to the cheeks and lips, but a little shading was very necessary if one was to look well under the harsh glare of many chandeliers. The papers were applied very sparingly, leaving a soft pink on Jane's lips and cheeks, and the merest hint of pearly white on her nose, to prevent it from shining in the heat of the ballroom. The touching of a little of Yardley's excellent lavender water to her throat and wrists and behind her ears completed this part of her toilet, leaving only the pinning up of her hair and the donning of her clothes and jewels.

At last she was ready, her hair put up into an intricate knot from which fell a single long curl, while her face was framed by a froth of little curls. Around her forehead she wore a plain golden circlet graced by a large, bright amethyst surrounded by diamonds, while more amethysts and diamonds shimmered from her ears and at her throat, making her eyes seemed even larger and more violet than usual. The gown was exquisite now that the bead decorations were complete, for they caught the light so softly that they resembled the sparkle of frost. Silk stockings, satin slippers, a delicate lilac-and-cream shawl, and a spangled reticule put the final touches to her appearance, leaving only the bringing of the painted fan from the silver casket on the dressing table.

Outside, above the continuing clamor of the crowds, she heard her carriage arriving. It was time to go. She glanced at her reflection in the cheval glass. What lay ahead tonight? Would Henry do the right thing and turn up after all? She lowered her eyes. And would she be able to conduct herself as if she was completely indifferent when she saw Lewis and Alicia together? Had she enough of the actress in her for that?

Taking a deep breath, she accepted the fan from Ellen and then, accompanied by the maid, she went down to the vestibule and emerged into the noisy evening to get into the waiting carriage.

SEVEN

*M*r. James Lyndon was a very important man of finance, acting for several members of the royal family and also for a great many aristocrats and other wealthy persons, so even had it not been for his wife's enviable reputation as one of the finest hostesses in London, the annual ball celebrating their daughter Blanche's birthday would have been a dazzling highlight of every season. Mrs. Lyndon could be relied upon to make any occasion brilliant, and tonight was no exception, for both the decorations and the ambience were quite outstandingly pleasing.

Lyndon House was set in its own grounds in a corner of Berkeley Square, and was approached through two pedimented gateways set in the tall wall fronting the great courtyard. There was already a crush of fashionable carriages as Jane arrived, and as she drove beneath one of the gateways, she saw that the court-yard, usually rather plain, had been transformed with tiny fountains, each one surrounded by beautiful flower arrangements in the three colors comprising Blanche's name—white, yellow, and green, for Blanche Xanthe Lyndon. The guests exclaimed in admiration as they alighted, pausing for a moment on the herb-strewn steps to gaze around at the magical scene. Then they went up the steps to the porticoed entrance, where the columns were garlanded with still more white, yellow, and green, a mixture of laburnum, white rhododendrons, and leaves. At the doors, two little black pageboys in mock-Elizabethan clothes presented each gentleman with a white carnation for his buttonhole, and each lady with a wrist favor of tight white rosebuds.

Ellen gazed around, her eyes wide, as the carriage halted at the steps. A footman assisted Jane down to the ground, where the bruised herbs filled the warm evening air with perfume. The splashing of the fountains could be heard above the clatter of the carriages and the music and laughter emanating from the bril-liantly illuminated house. The maid remained in the carriage and would be there to chaperone her mistress home afterward. Jane hesitated, suddenly apprehensive, but then went slowly up the steps, smiling at the pageboy as he presented her with her favor. Then she was in the great vestibule, with its magnificent black marble double staircase and priceless French chandeliers, and the scene which greeted her made her halt in wonder, for she had never seen so many flowers before, all of them in the same three colors. There were blooms, boughs, leaves, and petals everywhere, garlanding columns, draped along mantelpieces, twining up the staircase, covering console tables, adorning windows and corners, and even tumbling from the ceiling, where baskets frothing with lace and ribbons overflowed with roses and irises. It was all staggeringly beautiful and must have cost a fortune, but it transformed the house into a bower where the goddess Flora herself might have appeared at any moment.

There was a great crush of people, and the noise was quite considerable, so that first she didn't hear Charles calling her as he pushed his way toward her. "Jane?"

She turned at last, smiling at him. "Good evening, Charles. What a press this is!"

"Which gives me an excellent excuse for standing rather closer to you than is quite proper," he said, bending over her hand. He looked very dashing in a tight indigo velvet evening coat and white trousers, and there was a very large diamond in the pin adorning his white silk cravat. He smiled into her eyes then. "You're more beautiful than ever tonight, Jane." He tied the favor onto her wrist. "I take it that there's no word yet from Henry?" He looked at her a little reproachfully for not asking him to escort her, but he knew why she hadn't.

"None at all."

"There's time yet."

"Maybe."

"You don't sound very hopeful."

"I'm not. Oh, Charles, what am I going to say to Blanche and her parents? How can I possibly excuse him?"

"We'll do our utmost to delay seeing them, shall we?"

"We couldn't possibly."

"Why not? Is there a rule which says we must go directly to the ballroom? No, there isn't, so we'll make an *extremely* leisurely circuit of the house first, taking in the drawing room, the music room, the library, and anywhere else we can think of, and we'll stop to talk to every living soul we meet, even those whose claim to actually being alive stands in question, since they seem to me to have been visited by a taxidermist at some point."

She had to laugh at that. "You're good for me, Charles

Moncarm, and I know I'm the end in fools not to snap you up straightaway."

"You'll come around to it, and before much longer," he murmured, drawing her hand through his arm. "Shall we proceed?"

It wasn't difficult to ensure a lengthy dawdle, for they were acquainted with almost everyone they met, and there was one burning topic of conversation which seemed to occupy everyone's interest—the rights and wrongs of the queen's return.

"My dear, if my husband had used me as hers has done, I'd think myself *entitled* to act as she has."

"Poor, dear Lord Sidmouth was going home last night with the Duke of Wellington, and he couldn't get into his house for the mobs. There were missiles hurled after his carriage, and squibs set off under his horses' very hooves! It's quite disgraceful that such vulgar elements should be permitted to rampage like that!"

"The press is paid abundantly to support the queen, all the radicals like Wood have seen to that, and the city is with her too, although I understand our wise host tonight has thrown in his lot with the king."

"*The Times* went so far today as to say that the landing of neither William the Conqueror nor William III agitated the bosoms of Londoners as much as the arrival of *brave* Queen Caroline!"

"Admiral Lord Yarmouth could stand no more of the yahoos outside his house this morning—they'd kept him awake all night and he's a crusty fellow at the best of times. Well, he rushed out at them brandishing a sword and a pistol, and they scattered in all directions, like ants. I haven't laughed so much in years, although Yarmouth was too furious to find anything amusing in the situation."

"Dursley had his carriage waylaid coming here tonight because it was seen emerging from the royal den of iniquity, Carlton House. He was forced to doff his hat to the queen, and showed astonishing presence of mind by aping Wellington and wishing her majesty all she merited. The buffoons didn't know he was being clever and actually cheered him on his way. I confess I didn't think Dursley had it in him, but then he's been positively *busy* recently, hasn't he? If Felbridge doesn't watch it, the Lyndon fortune's going to be lifted from right under his fool nose, and it'll be no more than the rash young rip deserves. Ribbons before a fortune? Ye gods, if he had any wisdom at all, he'd make sure he'd *married* the fortune before deserting it to play knight of the road. The fellow needs his head examined, and no mistake. He's changed so much recently that I hardly know him, and I'm damned sure *la belle* Blanche must be feeling the same.''

This last was uttered by a gentleman who didn't see Jane and Charles join his group in the library, and he looked very embarrassed and uncomfortable when he realized they'd heard every word. He cleared his throat. ''Er, forgive me, m'dear, I didn't mean anything. . . .''

Jane's fan wafted to and fro and she smiled in a little embarrassment too. ''Sir, no doubt all you say does indeed run the risk of coming true, but now, if you will forgive me. . . .'' She inclined her head and hastily withdrew from the room, followed by Charles.

On the crowded landing above the double staircase, she halted, turning agitatedly to him. ''I can't keep this up for much longer—I feel so guilty. Oh, I know it isn't my fault, but I still feel as if somehow it is. It really is too bad of Henry to carry on like this, and it's so embarrassing to hear him being discussed in such a way. If it's being talked of here, you can guarantee it's all over Town. I could choke him for his irresponsibility, truly I could!''

''Perhaps it would be better if I took you home.''

''Oh, no, I couldn't do that.''

''Why not? If it's upsetting you like this. . . .''

''Too many people have seen me here, I couldn't just leave; it would be most discourteous, as well as cowardly. No, I'll have to face Blanche, and her parents, there's nothing else for it.''

''If you're quite sure.''

She nodded. ''Yes.''

He drew her hand through his arm and they turned toward the staircase, but then Jane halted in dismay, for coming up in their direction was Alicia, Duchess of Brantingham.

Jane would have retreated, but the crush was too great because a large party had emerged from the card room to go down to dance. There was nothing for it but to face Lewis's odious mistress.

The Duchess of Brantingham was one of the most beautiful and most notorious women in London, having taken a number of lovers from the very outset of her marriage to the elderly but extremely wealthy duke who now refused at any price to divorce her. Her crimes, as such, hadn't been so very great, a number of important ladies had been equally guilty, but she had lacked the discretion to keep her amours secret, and that was the most heinous crime of all in the eyes of a society which thrived on such double standards. But there was something about her which turned men's heads, and there was no doubt that when she chose she could be witty and amusing, so that the *monde* had not been all that surprised that she had snapped up a man like Lewis Ardenley, stealing him from the arms of a proud but unwary rival. Now, as she slowly ascended the staircase toward that rival, a number of people realized that an extremely interesting confrontation was almost bound to take place, and so made little secret of their interest, pausing to watch, no doubt hoping for the proverbial fur to fly.

Alicia hadn't as yet noticed Jane, and engaged in a brief conversation with a gentleman. She looked particularly beautiful tonight, in a lime green silk gown the neckline of which plunged perilously low over her curving, flawless bosom. Her willowy figure would have been eye-catching even had she not been so very beautiful, for her sense of style and fashion was impeccable. Her hair was thick and tawny, and possessed of a strange air of weight which made it always seem on the point of tumbling free from its pins, but it never did; it always remained perfectly groomed and enviably shiny. She had green eyes and a creamy complexion, and her lips never seemed to need rouge, they were full, warm, and softly pink, and they curved in an inviting way which made many a man forget what it was he had been talking about a moment before. There were diamonds at her throat and sparkling from her ears, and soft white plumes springing from the tall, jeweled comb in her hair. Tonight, she was evidently at her most witty, for her tinkling laughter rang out audibly as she tapped the gentleman's arm with her closed fan and proceeded on up the staircase. Then she saw Jane, and her green eyes became almost feline. "Good evening, Jane. Charles," she said, her voice carrying plainly in the sudden hush surrounding them.

Charles inclined his head. "Alicia."

Jane merely held the other's gaze. "Good evening."

A faint, rather taunting smile played about Alicia's lovely lips. "How very pretty you look tonight, quite charming. Do tell me, how was Cheshire?"

The hush was almost deafening.

"Just to the east of Wales, as it usually is," replied Jane conversationally, steeling herself for a vitriolic exchange.

Alicia's eyes flickered with cool amusement. "My *dear*, how

47

very droll you are, to be sure. Perhaps I should phrase my question another way. Did you enjoy your stay in Cheshire?''

"I enjoyed it immensely. Did you enjoy Paris?''

"Well, to be perfectly honest, my dear, we didn't go out a great deal while we were there, so I really couldn't comment.'' Alicia's smile was positively silky.

There was a ripple of unashamed amusement from the onlookers, who were quite blatantly listening to every word.

"What a waste of Paris, to be sure,'' replied Jane smoothly. "One might as well stay in in London.''

"But, my *dear*, staying in in Paris is so much more fun!'' declared Alicia, glancing deliberately around and inviting more laughter.

But Jane wasn't about to allow her the last word. "Really? Well, I suppose I must take your word for it, since the enjoying of that particular kind of fun has been an art you've more than perfected over the years, and with so many teachers that I declare I quite forget their names.''

The barb went home. Alicia's eyes flashed with anger and her fan snapped open. Gathering her skirts she walked on past, leaving the way clear at last for Jane and Charles to proceed down the staircase. As they did so, a babble of conversation broke out behind them as the confrontation was dissected word by word, point by point.

Jane managed a smile which conveyed a high degree of triumph. "Victory to me, I fancy, Charles.''

"I had no idea you possessed such fearsome claws.''

"I needed them, since hers were unsheathed the moment she saw me. Did you see the cat in her eyes? I merely dealt claw for claw.''

"And very dextrous you were, too. I doubt if even a barber-surgeon could have wielded a sharper edge.'' Charles paused at the foot of the staircase. "If you didn't still love him, you wouldn't have bothered with her just then, would you? The mere fact that you crossed swords proved to me that beyond a doubt you still want him.''

"Want someone who treated me so very shabbily? I think not, Charles.'' But she knew she didn't sound very convincing. "Can't we forget him and just go to the ballroom so that I can attend to my guilty conscience?''

"Forget him? Oh, *I* can do that cheerfully enough, but I doubt very much if you'll ever be able to.'' He drew her hand over his sleeve and escorted her through the crowded, flowery vestibule to the equally flowery inner hall, and then on to the immense black-and-white-marble steps that led grandly down to the glittering, flower-decked ballroom, where an ocean of elegant, bejeweled people moved to the sedate music of an allemande.

The ballroom at Lyndon House was one of the most beautiful in London, a vast chamber with pink marble columns set against walls adorned with intricate gilded plasterwork. Shining Italian crystal chandeliers were suspended from an azure sky sprinkled with countless golden stars, where the gods and goddesses of ancient Greece flew in divine splendor. The orchestra played from an apse high on the wall opposite the line of tall French windows that stood open on to the lantern-lit terrace and the illuminated gardens where guests could be seen strolling among the trees. Outside, there were flowers, but there were so many more inside, festooned with almost careless abandon and yet looking so very perfect, their pale colors and sweet perfume forming the ideal foil for the harsh glare of the chandeliers and the heavy haze of cigar smoke which was already rising to dim the beauty of the ceiling.

A number of people were waiting for the master-of-ceremonies to announce their names before they could proceed down the steps to where Mr. and Mrs. Lyndon were waiting to greet each new arrival, and so Jane and Charles took their places at the end of the queue. Mrs. Lyndon had decided to look as flowery as her decorations, for her silver muslin gown was sprinkled with little artificial roses, and there were more in her salt-and-pepper hair. She wore the famous Lyndon pearls, not one of which seemed smaller than a marble, and she was flushed and smiling, evidently more than pleased with the way things had gone so far. Beside her, looking tall, dark, and a little fearsome, her banker husband glanced shrewdly around, his sharp eyes very quick and clever above his hooked nose. He was, thought Jane, for all the world like a large bird of prey, and it was just as well for Blanche's sake that she took her looks from her mother.

Jane felt almost sick with apprehension. What on earth was she going to say to them? How could she possibly smooth things over? Charles put his hand over hers, squeezing it comfortingly. "It'll be all right, Jane, don't worry so."

"I can't help it. Can you see Blanche anywhere?"

"No, but she's bound to be here somewhere. Perhaps she's dancing."

"With the Duke of Dursley, no doubt."

"If she is, Henry has only himself to blame."

Jane glanced around again, and then her gaze was drawn inexorably toward the only man who was ascending the ballroom steps when everyone else was descending; it was Lewis. Her heart seemed to skip a beat, as always it did when she saw him. He looked so distinguished, his black velvet coat cut with the excellence attributable only to Weston of Bond Street. His hair seemed more golden than ever beneath the brilliance of the chandeliers, and he was toying with the spill of lace protruding from his cuff, as if his thoughts were very far away from the ballroom. He was coming straight toward her.

She couldn't look away from him, and he seemed to suddenly sense her gaze, looking directly into her eyes. He paused, a faint smile touching his lips, and then he inclined his head before passing straight by. He didn't say a word, and his acknowledgment had been so slight as to verge on a snub. Color leapt to her cheeks and she gazed ahead again, resisting with all her power the overwhelming urge to turn and look at him again. She was trembling inside and her hands felt suddenly very cold.

Then the master-of-ceremonies staff was striking the floor and their names were announced.

EIGHT

*H*owever, even as Jane and Charles began to descend the steps, by pure chance the orchestra struck up the first waltz of the evening, and Mr. and Mrs. Lyndon decided it was time to abandon their post and begin to enjoy the ball themselves.

Jane was a little ashamed of the rush of relief which flooded through her as she watched them whirl away onto the crowded floor, but she thought it was probably just as well that the moment had been postponed yet again, for the incident with Lewis had so ruffled her that she doubted if she would have handled the meeting very well at all.

Charles smiled at her, glancing heavenward at the gods and goddesses on the ceiling. "They're smiling on you from Olympus, evidently."

"For the moment."

"Forget Lewis Ardenley, he's not worth even a moment of pain." he murmured, slipping a hand to her waist and allowing her no choice but to join the throng on the sanded floor.

Flowers, jewels, costly silks and velvets seemed to spin past as they danced, and the laughter and drone of conversation were almost lost beyond the sweetness of the music. For a few brief minutes, Jane forgot all her problems and gave herself to the pleasure of the dance, but as the final chord was struck, and she and Charles stepped off the floor once more, she at last saw Blanche.

She was seated on a small crimson velvet sofa, her ivory fan wafting prettily to and fro as she smiled attentively at her companion, the winning, rakish, slippery Duke of Dursley. He was evidently employing his every wile, holding her hand, gazing ardently into her eyes, and doing his fascinating best to impress her. At thirty-five, he was handsome enough, with dark hair, soft brown eyes, and a full, rather sensuous mouth, but there was something about him which told that the real Dursley was very different from the charming, courteous gentleman he was at present striving to appear. He looked the elegant, easy-going fop in his black satin coat and silk pantaloons, but he had a reputation which was undesirable to say the least, and his gambling debts were almost legendary. His lineage might stretch back to the Conquest, but he wasn't at all the gracious lord such ancestry should have produced, and he was certainly all that was wrong for someone as sweet-natured and trusting as Blanche.

Jane looked at her brother's fiancée. As the belle of the ball, it was most appropriate that she wear a gown which sparkled with semiprecious stones. Each tiny movement she made caused a glitter which attracted many admiring glances, for not only was the gown very beautiful indeed, but its wearer was also. She had rich chestnut hair which was dressed up beneath a diamond tiara, and her pale complexion included a sprinkling of freckles over her retroussé nose, enhancing rather than detracting from her looks. Her eyes were of the softest brown, with long lashes which made her look very shy when her glance was downcast. It wasn't downcast now, however, for she was smiling at the attentive duke and tapping his arm with her ivory fan.

Jane sighed as she watched. Oh, Henry, she thought sadly, *you* should be sitting there with her now, not that odious toad Dursley. Even as she thought this, she saw Blanche glance up at the great golden clock high on the ballroom's west wall, her expression a little perplexed; then she adjusted the feather boa resting over her arms and returned her attention to the duke. Jane knew that she'd been wondering where Henry was. The time was long overdue to tell her what had happened, but how to winkle her away from the persistent lord at her side, that was the problem. Jane was quite determined not to confess her brother's sins in front of the man who was trying so openly to take his place!

She had no chance to approach Blanche for the moment, however, for she was claimed from Charles by an extremely large and slightly merry general, who wouldn't take no for an answer where the cotillion was concerned. Since he was an old friend of her family, Jane felt obliged to accept, and so stepped back onto the floor to join one of the sets.

As the cotillion progressed, she saw Lewis and Alicia together for the first time. They were descending the steps into the ballroom, and Alicia was leaning clingingly on his arm, her lovely face turned toward him. He bent his head to say something and Alicia laughed. Jane had to look away, unable to bear watching their easy intimacy.

For the next hour she had no chance to go to Blanche, and she was forced to endure numerous glimpses of Lewis and his mistress. They danced together all the time, thus breaking one of the cardinal rules of etiquette, for it simply wasn't done for a lady to devote her attention to just one partner. Jane tried not to think about them, concentrating instead upon the problem of how to get Blanche on her own to tell her about Henry, but that seemingly simple task was proving quite impossible. The Duke of Dursley didn't leave her side to begin with, and besides, Jane was herself besieged by a succession of gentlemen anxious to dance with her. There was an elderly great-uncle who kept asking her where Henry was, and a dashing young guards officer who thought himself so much the thing that he talked of nothing else, to say nothing of the various friends and husbands of friends who whirled her onto the floor for a seemingly endless round of ländlers, contredanses, cotillions, polonaises, and waltzes. Time ticked relentlessly on, and not once was she able to draw Blanche aside to explain Henry's absence, or offer the fast-diminishing consolation that he might still arrive.

Just before supper was to be served in the adjoining room, Charles at last managed to claim Jane again, leading her onto the floor for the lancers, the new dance which had reached London from Wales only the previous summer, and which had already become all the rage. It was fashionable to try and outshine everyone else in the five separate figures, so the floor was more crowded than ever, the crush being so great that Jane wondered if the master-of-ceremonies would have to send some people off, but the dance began, and practically everyone was soon moving to the music.

As she danced, Jane noticed that for once Alicia was not dancing with Lewis but with Lord Sefton, the fifty-year-old leading light of the Four-in-Hand Club, and the gentleman who had agreed to supervise the forthcoming Midsummer Day race to Brighton. Bluff and jovial, he wasn't the most elegant of dancers. Glancing around, Jane wondered who Lewis was with, and then she saw that he'd managed to winkle Blanche away from the duke. The two seemed to be engaged in deep conversation, and soon left the floor, sitting on a sofa to continue their talk. Lewis seemed concerned, Jane thought, and even as she thought it he rose to his feet, looking around the crowded floor as if searching for someone in particular. That someone was evidently Jane herself, for his gaze became steady the moment he saw her. He seemed far from pleased about something.

The dance ended and supper was announced, but as Jane and Charles began to make their way with everyone else toward the adjoining room, Lewis paused for the briefest of moments to whisper something to Alicia before making his way through the crowd toward them.

"Jane, I must speak with you. In private."

She halted in surprise, and Charles looked less than pleased. "I say, Ardenley . . ." he began coolly, but Lewis interrupted him.

"You've every right to feel affronted, Charles, but this is very important. Jane?"

Jane nodded then, smiling apologetically at Charles. "Forgive me, Charles, I shall not be long. If there's any of that caviar, please save some for me."

He inclined his head a little stiffly and relinquished her hand to Lewis. "I don't take kindly to this, Ardenley, not in view of all that's happened."

Lewis's clear, gray eyes rested on him for a moment, but he said nothing more, drawing Jane's hand through his arm and leading her away. "Shall we adjourn to the garden?" he suggested quietly.

She halted close to the nearest French window, where the cool air breathed in from the terrace, and where there were very few people because nearly everyone had gone to sample the supper.

"Can't it be said here?" she asked, remembering his public snub of earlier and not having any intention of allowing him further opportunity to hurt her.

"No, Jane, it can't, since I've no desire at all to be overheard. And before you gain the wrong impression, let me assure you that what I have to say concerns Blanche and not our own differences." His hand was firm on her elbow as he virtually steered her out into the darkness, where the light from countless colored lanterns cast soft pastel shades over the terrace and the gardens beyond.

He led her across the cool grass to a little gazebo by a lily pond, and there he turned her to face him. "What do you know about Henry's whereabouts tonight?"

The garden lights reflected in her eyes as she looked at him in surprise. "I—I think he's in Brighton," she said after a moment's hesitation.

He gave a slightly disbelieving laugh. "So, you *do* know!"

"Why do you say it like that?"

"Because I didn't think you'd be so cruel as to leave Blanche in the dark about it, that's why!" he snapped. "I thought better of you, Jane. Isn't Blanche supposed to be your dear friend? How could you leave her expecting to see him at any moment? I haven't told her anything, it isn't my place to do so, but *you* should tell her immediately!"

She drew back a little, at once angry and hurt at his harsh tone. "Condemn me if you wish, sir, but don't presume to know my every thought. It so happens that I've made a number of attempts to speak to her alone, to explain, but all of them failed, and anyway, Henry could indeed walk in at any moment!"

He stared at her. "How can you possibly say that?"

"Because it's true . . . isn't it?" She searched his face then, realizing that he knew something she didn't. "What is it, Lewis? Why are you so sure he won't be here tonight?"

"Because he told me he was staying overnight in Brighton when I spoke to him earlier today."

Now it was her turn to stare, and to accuse. "You *saw* him? Lewis, why on earth didn't you remind him about the ball?"

"Because he gave me no opportunity. He was waiting at my house when I returned after leaving you. He brushed aside my reminder that he'd deserted you—he was interested only in a new development concerning the race. It seems that when Chapman accosted him this morning, he wagered a great deal of money that the Nonpareil would outrun the Iron Duke. It's not merely a race now, Jane, it has a fortune resting upon it. Because of this, Henry wants the best bloodstock available to pull his coach, and so he approached me about it, because my estate at Maywood lies, as you well know, directly on the Brighton road, and because there aren't any finer horses in the realm than those in my stables. I refused to help him, since I think stagecoach racing the end in foolhardy practices, and since I happen to agree with you that he's already devoting far too much time and attention to his ribbons when it's Blanche he should be thinking about. He left in rather high dudgeon, and it was as he was driving off that he said he'd be in Brighton overnight if I happened to change my mind. I called him back, but you know how he springs that damned highflyer of his; he was gone in a trice and I doubt if he heard.''

Jane turned away. ''My every instinct told me he wouldn't be here tonight, but I still kept hoping against hope that he'd prove me wrong.''

''Forgive me for speaking so harshly to you, Jane, but when I was with Blanche and it seemed so obvious that she still thought he was coming, I thought . . . Well, it doesn't really matter what I thought; I was evidently quite wrong and spoke very much out of turn.''

She was silent for a moment, the gentler note in his voice unnoticed as she wondered anew how to tell Blanche. ''What am I going to say to her, Lewis? She's going to be horridly upset and it will ruin her evening! Oh, I shall never forgive Henry for this, never!''

''Perhaps you would find it easier if I accompany you? After all, I'm the one who can say beyond a doubt that he's staying in Brighton and that you didn't know.''

She gave him a suspicious look. ''Why are you being so helpful and agreeable? It's totally out of character.''

''It isn't totally out of character, you just choose to think that it is. I'm offering because it seems the right thing to do, especially after I spoke so rudely to you earlier.''

''Ah, so it's your conscience. Tell me, sir, is that the only thing your conscience weighs so heavily about?'' She couldn't help the taunt. Would he protest his innocence again as he had before?

He met her gaze. ''Yes, Jane, it is, since I have nothing else about which to feel even remotely guilty. You've been in the wrong all along. Now then, shall I come with you?''

She wanted to take him up on it so much, but for the moment

Blanche was more important. "To be perfectly honest, I don't know if I can bring myself to tell her anything, not now that I know Henry's gone so far as to actually stay in Brighton."

"Something has to be said to her."

She nodded unhappily. "I know. But what?"

"A white lie of some sort?"

"I suppose so. Can you think of anything?"

"You said that with the firm conviction of one who believes beyond a doubt that untruths are second nature to me."

"Aren't they?"

"To go into that would be to digress quite considerably from the matter in hand."

"And would focus a most unwelcome spotlight upon the deviousness of your character," she added.

"A spotlight upon *you*, madam, would reveal a preponderance of rather ridiculous and misplaced pride, but I don't think we'll go into that either. Now then, since the object of all this is to spare Blanche's feelings, and since we can hardly disguise the fact that dear Henry has removed himself to Brighton for the night, the only thing I can suggest is that we tell Blanche that he had had every intention of being here by, er, midnight," he glanced at his fob watch, "but that since that hour has now passed and there's still no sign of him, we can only deduce that he has been unavoidably detained on some pressing matter. It's the truth, and yet not the truth, the perfect white lie."

She raised an eyebrow. "I thought you said untruths didn't spring easily to your lips, sir. This one certainly has."

"I have the odd lapse or two."

"So it seems."

"Will it do, that's the point."

She nodded. "Yes, I think so. She'll still be upset, but if she thinks he did really intend to come, it won't hurt quite as much."

"There, you see, I can be quite agreeable and lovable after all," he murmured, reaching out to rather mockingly flick the long curl falling from the knot on her head.

"When you cut me earlier you showed precious little of either quality," she retorted, moving away a little, too conscious of the effect even that small touch had upon her.

"When I declined to greet you as effusively as you no doubt think you deserve, I did so because I recalled how very irritating you were this morning," he countered.

"I was confronted by your flighty *belle de nuit* a little earlier tonight," she went on as if he hadn't spoken, "and *she* showed precious little real quality either."

Smiling a little, he folded his arms and surveyed her. "Ah, yes, the encounter on the stairs—I *have* been told."

"I'll warrant you have," she replied, looking toward the terrace where almost as if on cue, a tall, elegant figure in lime green silk had appeared. Alicia stood watching them for a moment and then went back into the ballroom, the plumes in her hair streaming angrily behind her. Jane couldn't help a secret smile; Alicia evidently felt that they'd been alone in the darkness for a little too long.

Lewis hadn't noticed his mistress, he was too intent upon ruffling Jane's feathers a little. "There's something I'm most intrigued about. . . ."

"Yes?"

"Your apparently overwhelming curiosity about my recent sojourn in Paris."

She felt her cheeks become hot. "I'm not in the least bit curious," she replied.

"No? Then why bring up the subject again with Alicia?"

"Did I?" she answered airily. "I really don't remember."

"No?" His tone was sardonic.

"No."

"I'm far from convinced, especially as I've now formed a very definite opinion on the matter."

"Indeed?"

"Yes, your insatiable interest about what happened in Paris is born of one thing and one thing only—jealousy."

She was glad of the darkness because she knew her cheeks were now aflame. "You flatter yourself, sir. Go wherever you please, with whomever you please, it's of no consequence to me since you only strike a damp in my estimation these days."

"Is that so? I must be losing my touch."

"Well, to be sure, you didn't have a great deal to lose."

"Now that, my dearest Jane, smacks of out-and-out provocation," he said softly. Before she knew what was happening, his lips were over hers and he was holding her so close that she couldn't draw away. His kiss was relentless, teasing, arousing and enticing her reluctant and unwilling senses into a response which was so urgent and demanding that she needed every last ounce of willpower to deny it.

With a laugh, he abruptly released her, and she dealt him a

57

furious blow, her fingers leaving angry marks on his cheeks. "How *dare* you!" she breathed.

But he merely grinned, rubbing his cheek. "Well, one thing's for sure, I certainly haven't lost my touch! I can raise rather more than a damp with you!"

At that moment a woman ran out of the ballroom and across the terrace, her gown glittering and her feather boa flapping wildly behind her. It was Blanche. She hurried across the grass toward them, and as she came closer they could see the tears shining wet on her cheeks.

Jane was alarmed. "Blanche? Whatever is it?"

Blanche flung herself into her arms. "Tell me it isn't true!" she begged, her voice choking on sobs. "Tell me Henry's going to be here tonight after all! He is, Jane, isn't he?"

Jane held her close, looking in dismay at Lewis.

Blanche seemed suddenly to become aware that Lewis was there too, for she drew back in embarrassment, dabbing her eyes with her handkerchief and trying to stifle her sobs. In spite of her distress, it was plain that she was a little startled to find Jane out alone in the garden with the man who had betrayed her. "I—I'm sorry to make such a fuss," she said, struggling to fight back the tears, "it's just that when Alicia told me—"

"*Alicia?*" Jane tossed Lewis a furious glance. So this was Alicia's work, was it?

"She—she said Henry was in Brighton and couldn't possibly come to the ball. It isn't true, is it, Jane?"

"Well, he *is* in Brighton," confessed Jane, feeling quite dreadful, and furious with Alicia for having so callously broken such news to poor Blanche.

Blanche was searching her face. "But he's coming back tonight, isn't he?"

Lewis stepped in then. "He had every intention of being here, Blanche, he told me so, but now it's as late as this, I can only think that something urgent has detained him."

Alarm leapt into her eyes. "You don't think he's had an accident, do you?"

"No, of course not," he said quickly. "It's most probably something to do with his coaching affairs. After all, he *is* a coachmaster now."

"Oh. I hadn't thought of that."

"He's a man of business, Blanche, and you know how seriously he takes it all."

"Yes." She sighed resignedly. "You're right, of course, and

it would have to be something very important to prevent him from being here. Oh dear, I feel a little foolish now, but when Alicia told me I was quite devastated. I think she thought I didn't believe her, so she said I'd find you out here." Again, Blanche looked a little embarrassed, as if she'd interrupted an assignation.

Jane tossed a dark look at the terrace where last she'd seen Alicia. That's what all this was really about; Alicia was getting her own back for having been defeated on the stairs, and she was making sure that the *tête-à-tête* in the garden did not continue for a moment longer. How callous and spiteful to use poor Blanche.

Blanche dabbed her eyes for a last time and then put the handkerchief away in her little reticule. "What a silly fuss I've made. What must you be thinking of me?"

"I think you were quite justified," said Jane, "especially when Alicia told you such a story."

"Oh, I'm sure she didn't mean to upset me."

Jane had to bite back the reply that blistered to her lips at this, for there was no doubt in her mind that Alicia had meant everything.

Blanche rearranged her boa. "I suppose I'd better go back. It won't be the same now I know that Henry won't be coming, but at least I know that he meant to." She gave a rueful smile. "I kept hoping that he'd come and rescue me from the Duke of Dursley, who's been a positive limpet all evening. Oh, before I forget, Jane, you are still coming to the exhibition with me tomorrow, aren't you?"

"Exhibition?"

Blanche pretended to be a little cross. "There, I *knew* you'd manage to forget, because you loathe Dutch landscapes and I adore them."

"Oh, the paintings at the Hanover Square Rooms!"

"Yes."

Jane smiled. "Of course I'm still coming."

"Good. Now I really must return to the fray, before Papa wonders where I am. He's being very difficult, Jane; he simply will not stop trying to persuade me that the Duke of Dursley would be a much finer catch than Henry. It's Henry I love, though, so that's that." With a last smile, she gathered her shimmering skirts and hurried away again.

The incident had momentarily put Lewis's previous ungentlemanly treatment out of Jane's mind. She watched Blanche hurrying away. "Henry doesn't deserve her; she's far too good for him."

"I won't argue with that."

"I didn't enjoy fibbing to her."

"It was kinder than the truth."

"Yes, which is something dear Alicia might have considered."

"I intend speaking to her about it."

"Good, because if you don't, I most certainly will!"

"I can imagine. Still, it isn't Alicia I'm concerned with at the moment, it's more important to make certain that Henry doesn't put his insensitive foot in it when he returns. We must see he's armed with a story that tallies with what we've said, so working on the principle that what drives out of the Fleece in Thames Street must sooner or later drive back there again, I shall send a man there with a note informing Henry what's been done on his undeserving behalf and warning him that unless he invents some suitably convincing excuse, he'll have me to answer to." He looked at her then, as if waiting for something. "Well? Aren't you going to thank me for my efforts?"

She remembered his considerable transgression then. "To which effort do you refer, sir?" she asked a little coldly.

He smiled. "Ah, I see that you are recalling the incredibly ineffective *damp* I raised in you a little earlier."

"I recall your monstrous indiscretion!"

"Look at me in that way, Jane, and you invite more than you realize," he replied, taking a step toward her.

With a gasp, she stepped hastily back, turning to flee across the grass. His mocking laughter followed her.

NINE

*T*he flush of humiliation remained on her cheeks as she rejoined Charles in the supper room, and it seemed that for a long time afterward she could still hear Lewis laughing at her. She'd made a fool of herself by allowing him to take such advantage; she must never let it happen again. Charles noticed the flush, but didn't say anything, though he gave Lewis a dark look when next he saw him.

News of Henry's definite absence spread like wildfire, fueling speculation about the Duke of Dursley's chances. Jane had endured enough whispering about her brother *before* the revelations about Brighton, but now it was ten times worse. She felt quite miserable, and wasn't helped at all by seeing how Lewis still devoted his ardent attention to Alicia, whose unkindness toward Blanche had apparently not put her beyond the pale as far as he was concerned. They danced together for the remainder of the ball and he didn't glance once toward his former fiancée. Alicia did though, and her green eyes were spitefully triumphant.

As dawn began to lighten the eastern sky, Jane at last managed to escape, avoiding Charles and driving back across London with a tactfully silent Ellen. South Audley Street was unexpectedly and blessedly peaceful, because the queen had earlier removed herself to Portland Place, taking her army of yahoos with her.

Jane lay awake in her silent bedroom, watching the dawn become brighter as she thought about what had happened at the ball. She wished with all her heart that she'd stayed away and thus denied Lewis the chance to hurt her all over again. Outside, the calls from the dairymaids leaving the dairy in nearby Queen Street began to ring out, but she was only dimly aware because sleep at last overtook her.

She rose very late, coming down to learn that there still hadn't been any word from her errant brother. She breakfasted alone, wondering if Lewis's message would reach him when he deigned to return, or if by some dreadful mischance he wouldn't receive it and would go straight to see Blanche without knowing what had been said on his behalf. She gazed at her cup of China tea. What point was there in worrying about it? Henry was his own master and would have to get himself out of any scrape. She leaned back in her chair, smoothing the rich folds of her cherry-and-white-checkered muslin morning dress. It was a bright, cheerful garment, making her appear much more carefree than she felt. The clock on the mantelpiece chimed, the sweet sound drifting over the quiet room. How good it was to be free at last of the constant racket from the street; it would have been very pleasant indeed had she not had so much on her mind.

Melville brought Henry's morning newspaper in and she began to browse through it. A theatrical review caught her attention. There was a new production at the Theater Royal, Drury Lane, and its first night had been a sensational success because of the appearance on stage of a well-known and very beautiful actress clad in very tight breeches. The lady concerned was the hitherto very proper Madame Vestris, and the play was entitled *Don Giovanni in London*, a burlesque on Mozart's opera. Jane made a mental note to be sure to go and see it soon.

She was about to set the newspaper aside when suddenly an advertisement caught her eye. As she read it, she became incensed.

Stimulated by the base exertions of a determined opposition, the Earl of Felbridge, proprietor of the esteemed Iron Duke stagecoach, is prepared to meet the crisis with the weight of superior force and efficiency. Passengers are assured of traveling in the utmost safety, and are promised punctuality more precise than any coach has hitherto been capable of offering. The Iron Duke is peerless, the monarch of the Brighton road, and will never again allow the intervention of jealous, inferior rivals to succeed. If further proof of this superiority is required, doubters are invited to look forward to Midsummer Day, when the Iron Duke will see off its feeble and unworthy challenger in a fitting and decisive manner, and the Earl of Felbridge will emerge triumphant and with a much fatter purse with which to toast his victory.

So, Henry Derwent had been too busy and preoccupied yesterday to be bothered to remember his fiancée's birthday ball, but he'd managed to find time not only to see Lewis about horsing his beastly Iron Duke, but also to go to the newspaper to insert this provocative clarion call aimed at goading Chapman. The phrase "fatter purse" revealed the advertisement to be yesterday's work. Her fingers drummed angrily on the table as she considered her brother's conduct. He needed teaching a lesson, and his increasingly wrathful sister was just the person to do it.

She had just finished discussing the day's meals with the cook, Mrs. Beale, when she at last heard the sound of Henry's phaeton in the street, the clatter of hooves carrying quite clearly now that the queen's supporters had gone. A moment later, he entered the breakfast room, looking travel-worn and tired, and immediately on his guard when he saw his sister's dark glance.

He was on the defensive. "Before you say anything, I know I've covered myself with mud again, and I've already been to see Blanche to make my peace."

"I trust you received Lewis's message."

"I did." He went to the sideboard, helping himself to an extremely large breakfast of bacon, eggs, kidneys, tomatoes, and sausage.

She waited until he sat down. "You received his note, so what exactly did you say to Blanche? I must know if I'm to keep up the pretense on your behalf."

"I told her a suitable tale," he replied noncommittally, grinning a little.

"You look inordinately pleased with yourself," she said suspiciously.

He applied himself to his breakfast. "Don't start fussing, Jane. Blanche accepts my excuses for not being there last night, so I think you should leave the subject alone, don't you?"

"Don't be so insufferably conceited about getting away with it, Henry Derwent. You placed me in an invidious position last night, not knowing if your lamentable memory would save the day or not. How *dare* you sit there now looking so smug with yourself for slipping out from under! Your match with Blanche is only intact this morning because Lewis and I couldn't bear to see her so upset and hurt!"

"Oh, so it's Lewis and *I*, is it?" he said, attempting to deflect the conversation. "You've changed your tune where he's concerned, have you?"

"Don't try to change the subject," she snapped, so angry that she could have tipped his plate over his impossible head. "I don't think you'd be quite so full of yourself if you'd seen the Duke of Dursley dancing constant, extremely efficient attention upon Blanche last night! The whole of London is speculating about how long it will be before he wins her."

He speared a sausage with his fork. "The damned fellow was there again this morning, grinning all over his sly, painted face and being the dandy with his lace handkerchief, flicking it in all directions as if beset by a swarm of flies. He reeks of scent, you know—it's like being in a room with a civet cat."

"Blanche doesn't appear to find him that offensive."

"He irritates her; she told me so this morning."

"More fool her. I'd have left you wondering."

"You're downright cold-hearted, sis dear. Anyway, I wasn't wondering anything, because I'd very quickly wiped the grin off his scheming face. And off old Lyndon's, for that matter." He smiled, looking more smug and self-satisfied than ever.

She looked at him with misgiving. "What do you mean?"

"Oh, I demolished them both with my wit," he replied airily.

Such airiness meant that he was loath to confess the truth, so she pressed him. "That's no answer, and you know it."

"You're like a dog with a bone sometimes, aren't you?"

"I know when you're avoiding the crux of something, Henry Derwent."

"There are times when I wish you'd stay permanently in Cheshire."

"I'm waiting, Henry."

He shrugged. "As you wish. It so happens that last night in Brighton there was a particularly bad fire. A warehouse went up like tinder and endangered a great many properties nearby. There was quite a to-do, I can tell you, with fire engines and crowds, and the flames were so high that I felt compelled to go and watch. Anyway, I didn't think anything more about it until I reached the Fleece this morning and found Lewis's note waiting. Then I had my inspiration and toddled off to Lyndon House to put paid to Dursley's hopes by telling them that I'd been kept in Brighton because I'd helped fight the fire. I described my valor so vividly that I swear by the time I finished they could smell the smoke on my clothes." He grinned. "You should have seen Dursley's fool jaw drop, I don't know if with astonishment or fury, both probably. It was a sweet moment, Jane, I promise you."

Jane was staring disbelievingly at him. He'd behaved atrociously, he'd forgotten Blanche and her ball because of his obsession with coaching, and now he'd told monstrous fibs about heroism in order to get out of it. He even had the gall to sit there now virtually patting himself on the back for his cleverness! It was too much! "Henry Derwent," she breathed disgustedly, "you are without a doubt the most selfish, odious toad it has ever been my misfortune to know, and I wish with all my heart that you soon come the cropper you so richly merit!"

"I say—" he began in protest.

"Don't say anything more in your own defense, sir, because I'm ashamed that you're my brother! How *could* you treat poor Blanche so shabbily and then have the effrontery to award yourself deceitful laurels! You're despicable, and your wretched coaches are despicable too! I hope the Nonpareil trounces you on Midsummer Day, because after this you most certainly don't deserve to win!"

Stung, he rose angrily to his feet. "And what would *you* know about coaching, madam? Coaching is men's business, and women would do better to confine themselves to embroidery and fripperies, which feeble items would seem more suited to their lesser intellects!"

She eyed him with equal anger. "I notice you choose to forget my remarks concerning your conduct toward Blanche, and reply instead *only* on your coaching! You're an insect, Henry Derwent. And as to coaching being men's business, I wonder you can say that when there exist women like Mrs. Mountain of the Saracen's Head and Mrs. Nelson of the Bull Inn. If my lesser female intellect is serving me correctly, they happen to be coach proprietors of considerable standing, their success being viewed with some envy by their male counterparts. Pour *that* unpalatable draft in your glass and drink it, sirrah!''

He was so angry that words fought for a place on his lips, but then he flung down his napkin and strode from the room, slamming the door behind him. Jane picked up his plate, in half a mind to hurl it after him, but perhaps the breakfast room door didn't warrant such punishment. She put the plate down again. Men! They were so arrogantly convinced they were superior! Oh, to bring him down a peg or two! She'd *dearly* like to teach him a lesson he'd never forget! But how, that was the problem.

She'd calmed down a little, but was still deeply angry, when that afternoon she set off in her open landau with Blanche and their maids to attend the exhibition at the Hanover Square Rooms. Wearing an unbuttoned emerald green silk spencer over a white lawn gown, her little hat adorned with emerald green aigrettes, she showed commendable restraint as she listened to Blanche extolling Henry's many nonexistent virtues. It was very difficult to bite back the truth about his jaunt to Brighton, but bite it back she did, since Blanche was so evidently still in love with him, Duke of Dursley or no Duke of Dursley.

Blanche wore blue and cream, the poke brim of her dainty bonnet casting a shadow over her face. She was light-hearted and in excellent spirits, her choice of future husband having apparently been more than vindicated by the valor he'd shown risking his very life in the searing heat of the conflagration.

Jane listened to it all without divulging a word of the real tale, but it was with an almost superhuman effort that she continued to remain silent when the landau passed a sandwich man hired by Henry to stroll around with an advertisement about the merits of the Iron Duke and the failings of the Nonpareil. Henry could so effortlessly find the time to attend to things like that, but he couldn't stir himself to remember the annual grand ball which was the highlight of his poor fiancée's social calendar!

Hanover Square was the oldest of the Mayfair squares, with its center neatly laid out in a railed garden crossed by gravel paths, and there were lamps set at intervals along the railing so that at night the garden was prettily illuminated. The surrounding houses were mostly of a uniform red brick, all of them gracious and elegant, but there was one in particular which attracted Jane's attention the moment the landau turned into the square. It occupied a prime position on the northern side, and was the town residence of Lewis, Lord Ardenley.

It was a long, three-storied building, its roof surmounted by a handsome stone balustrade, and its main entrance was in the narrow lane alongside, connecting the square with busy Oxford Street beyond. The entrance boasted a splendid columned porch, large enough for carriages to halt beneath in order to set down passengers without exposing them to vagaries of the weather, and beside this porch there was an immense bow window of such magnificent design and proportions that it was much admired by all who saw it. As Jane looked, a dark red barouche entered the lane from Oxford Street, halting beneath the porch. It was Alicia's carriage. Jane looked quickly away.

The assembly rooms stood in the southeast corner of the square, and were a fashionable venue for concerts, lectures, exhibitions, and subscription balls. As the landau halted and Jane and Blanche alighted, leaving the maids seated where they were, Jane noticed a man pinning a bill to the board by the main door. Thinking it must be an announcement concerning forthcoming events at the rooms, she went to read it. But it wasn't anything to do with the rooms, it was about the sale of a stagecoach business.

To be sold, the very superior, old-established business of J. E. Wheddle & Co., being the hostelry known as the Feathers inn, Cheapside, the Swan Ticket Office, Castle Square, Brighton, and the coaches, horses, and other appurtenances which form the Swan daily coach, famous for its security, punctuality, and reliability. The proprietor is forced to this dire length by circumstances beyond his control. All interested inquiries to the Feathers, Cheapside.

She'd heard of the Swan stagecoach, which had been running for a long time on the fashionable Brighton road, but which had never become the crack vehicle both the Iron Duke and Nonpareil could justifiably claim to be. She recalled that Henry had mentioned it recently, something about Chapman's making a determined effort to run it off the road and thus reduce the competition. Was that what the notice meant by circumstances beyond the proprietor's control?

Blanche had been looking without interest at the notice, and now she grew impatient. "Shall we go in?"

"Mm?"

"I said, shall we go in?"

"Oh, yes, of course."

"What on earth is so absorbing about a notice like that? You surely aren't thinking of becoming a coachmistress?" Blanche laughed at such a preposterous notion.

Jane laughed too, but as they entered the rooms, she paused in the entrance to look back at the board. Her expression grew thoughtful.

The exhibition was excellent, the finest gathering together of Dutch landscapes London had ever seen. The rooms were as a consequence very crowded as society came to view the delights, but as Jane wandered from painting to painting at Blanche's side, her mind wasn't on masterpieces at all, it was outside with the notice on the board. Blanche's chance remark seemed to echo in her head. *You surely aren't thinking of becoming a coachmistress?*

"Jane?" Blanche was speaking again.

There wasn't a reply.

Blanche touched her arm, a little hurt now. "Jane?"

"Oh, I'm sorry. Did you say something?"

"Yes, I was asking your opinion of this painting. Don't you think it's a remarkable performance? It's so lifelike, one could almost step into all that snow, don't you agree?"

"Yes, it's truly magnificent." Jane's tone lacked true enthusiasm.

"You haven't been concentrating at all, have you? In fact, I'd say you were totally uninterested. Is something wrong? You were all right on the way here, but ever since we arrived. . . ." Blanche looked quickly at her. "I saw Alicia's barouche arriving at Lewis's house, are you low because of that? I haven't said anything today about last night, but why *were* you alone in the garden with him? Were you making progress again? Is that why it upsets you to see her carriage at his door?"

Jane colored and glanced quickly around in case someone had overheard, for the room was a considerable crush. "Hush, Blanche, someone may hear. You're wrong anyway, it's nothing to do with Lewis. As to my reason for being with him in the garden, it wasn't what you think, I promise you."

"What was it then?"

Jane hesitated, for she could hardly tell Blanche the truth. "Oh, it was just something and nothing. If you must know, we were discussing Henry's chances in the race. After all, Lewis *was* a much-admired whip himself, if you recall."

"Yes, I suppose he was, in fact he still is. Oh dear, and there I was, hoping against hope that the two of you were getting together again."

At that moment, Jane's heart sank, for she heard the unmistakable trill of Alicia's laughter from the adjoining room. "Oh, no," she whispered, "I couldn't face that wretched woman again." She turned quickly away, anxious to escape into another room, but as on the previous evening, events conspired against her, and the crush was so great with people coming *into* the room she was in that it was quite impossible to get *out* of it. Resignedly, she turned back again, trying to look as if she was engrossed in the study of the painting she and Blanche stood before, and hoping against hope that Alicia wouldn't see her. But it was a faint hope, for Alicia's feline eyes spied them immediately, and what was worse, she wasn't alone—Lewis was with her.

He wore a charcoal gray coat and cream cord trousers, and the tassels on his gleaming Hessian boots swung to and fro as he walked. He carried his top hat under one arm, while on the other leaned his graceful, clinging mistress. Alicia looked as stylish and beautiful as ever, in a golden-brown silk pelisse and a pearl muslin gown with a Tudor ruff. Her straw bonnet was tied on with wired oyster ribbons, while under its brim was pinned a posy of golden-brown velvet flowers. There was a gauze scarf fluttering behind her, and the shoes peeping out from beneath her hem were a particularly shiny black patent leather. She looked enchanting, and was evidently at her most fascinating, whispering to Lewis and making him laugh. She halted then, drawing his attention to Jane and Blanche, and Jane's heart sank still further as they came over.

Alicia was all sweetness and charm. "Oh, what a pleasant surprise. My dear Blanche, I didn't have a chance last night to tell you how very much I admired your mother's decorations. All those flowers, it was quite wonderful."

"Thank you." Blanche was a little reserved with her, having on reflection decided that Alicia's revelations about Henry hadn't been entirely innocently or kindly meant. According Alicia only a cool nod, she reserved her smile for Lewis. "Good afternoon, Lewis. I trust you are recovered from your late night?"

"I am indeed." His gray eyes rested on Jane. "Good afternoon, Jane. Are you enjoying the exhibition?"

"I am, sir, but then some of the exhibits are more prize than others, aren't they?" Her glance flickered momentarily toward Alicia, whose eyes darkened angrily.

Blanche touched Jane's arm quickly. "We must get on, Jane, or we won't complete the exhibition before it's time to go."

With some relief, Jane seized the excuse and they withdrew, threading their way through the crush into the next room, and then on out of the rooms altogether.

Jane said nothing as they drove back toward Berkeley Square in the landau with the maids and Blanche eventually broke the silence by issuing an invitation to tea. Jane declined. "I'd love to, truly I would, but there's something I must do."

Blanche was a little perturbed. "Jane, you've been in a very strange mood for the past hour or more, and now you tell me you have something else planned? Why haven't you mentioned it before? I've half a mind to be alarmed."

"There's no need, I promise you."

"You're not going to tell me anything more, are you?"

"Not yet, but I will if anything comes of it."

"Comes of what? Oh, I do wish you'd confide in me."

"There's nothing to confide just yet."

Blanche said nothing more, much to Jane's relief, because she didn't really know how to admit what was really on her mind. Blanche would think she'd taken leave of her senses if she found out that Lady Jane Derwent, champion opponent of all things connected with coaching, was actually contemplating purchasing a stagecoach business! Jane could hardly believe it herself, but that was what had been on her mind since the moment she'd read the notice in Hanover Square, and when she had left Blanche she intended to go to the Feathers inn in Cheapside to make further inquiries about Messers J. E. Wheddle & Co. Henry was in dire need of being given a lesson in how to behave, and his sister intended to do just that, by taking him on at his own game.

TEN

Cheapside was a broad, cobbled street with a wide pavement on either side. It was a bustling thoroughfare filled with traffic and people, with a permanent line of hackney coaches waiting patiently down its center. The tall brown brick buildings, their upper stories graced by fine, symmetrically-arranged windows, their ground floors taken up by bow-fronted shops displaying an astonishing variety of goods, seemed to trap the noise of the traffic, making it echo all around. It was one of the old city's finest shopping streets and was dominated by the tall steeple of Sir Christopher Wren's church of St. Mary-le-Bow.

The Feathers inn stood close to the church and was a plain building with a low archway leading through to a large galleried courtyard. For such an establishment in a sought-after street, there was a strangely subdued air about it, as if it had withdrawn from the surrounding noise and pace. As Jane's landau approached, she felt rather apprehensive, for not only was she contemplating doing something very unconventional indeed, she was also offending etiquette by just coming here. Ladies simply did not enter such establishments alone, unless forced to do so by unavoidable circumstances; they frequented the elegant, fashionable hotels of Mayfair, and then seldom unaccompanied. And yet here she was, about to go alone into a London coaching inn, her purpose one which went against a whole legion of rules governing proper, ladylike conduct. Indeed, just about the only convention she *was* observing was that she had Ellen with her, as her obligatory chaperone. Yes, Blanche would indeed think her quite mad if she knew.

In the seconds before the landau entered the cobbled courtyard, all was quiet in the enclosed area. There were no other vehicles except a brewer's dray unloading kegs by the open cellar door, close to the kitchens. A group of grooms and ostlers were waiting for the afternoon Swan stagecoach from Brighton, and they whiled away the time by playing dice against the wall beneath the steps leading up to the gallery and bedrooms. The coach ticket office was empty, the clerk having deserted his post to join his friends in their game. The Swan was late again, but that was nothing new these days.

At the sound of hooves and wheels beneath the archway, they were all galvanized into astonished action, scattering to their various posts and looking askance at each other that the stage-coach should have failed to announce its approach with a blast of its horn. As the elegant, fashionable landau appeared in the courtyard drawn by four perfectly matched bays and driven by a liveried coachman, the men's surprise became outright amazement, especially when they saw that the landau's occupants were a very stylish lady and her maid.

Even as the landau came to a standstill, from the street outside came the anticipated note of a coaching horn, heralding the approach at last of the Swan. An ostler hurried to take the bridle of the landau's off-side leader, and another came to open the door for Jane to alight, but at the sound of the stagecoach beneath the archway, she turned in her seat to watch. Ellen turned too, her eyes wide and apprehensive, for the noise was such that it seemed the stagecoach must surely rush straight into them!

It swept into the courtyard, the burly coachman caught a little off-guard by the landau and only just managing to maneuver his sweating, ill-matched team to a standstill between it and the brewer's dray. He was a far cry from George Sewell, the elegantly attired whip of the Nonpareil, being more in the mold of the old coachmen of the past, his face round and flushed, his bulk hidden beneath the folds of a voluminous benjamin coat. The coach itself was unlike the Nonpareil as well, being rather old and in need of fresh paint. It didn't boast luxurious fittings, or shining harness, nor did it have a full complement of fares, for it carried only the coachman and guard. Jane read the words beneath the dust on its door panels: *Swan. London and Brighton. Reigate. Handcross. J. E. Wheddle & Co. License No. 3224.*

At the sound of the horn in the street, the landlord, presumably Mr. Wheddle himself, had emerged from the door leading to the kitchens. He was a tall, large-framed man with bushy sidewhiskers and a rather weary expression. He wore a crisp, starched apron, a brown coat, and gray breeches, and his neckcloth was tied as smartly as that of any gentleman. He looked up expectantly at the coachman, not seeing the landau, which was obscured from his view. "Trouble again, Johnno? You've lost ten minutes somewhere."

"What's the point of worrying about times when there aren't fares to carry?" grumbled the coachman, putting down the ribbons and searching in his coat pocket for his clay pipe, which he thrust between his teeth without lighting. "Aw, I'm sorry, Mr. Wheddle, I didn't mean to sound like that. It's just that I've had a gutful of Chapman and his tricks."

"What was it this time?"

"The usual. They boxed me in good and proper just by Maywood, and the poor old Swan just hasn't got it in her to pick up enough speed to make up. Sewell gave me the go-by on the Nonpareil, laughing fit to burst. I managed to make up some time at Handcross, but only through a fluke, and I lost it again at the Red Lion, where some darned informer had the magistrates

71

waiting to check the license. Sewell was laughing so much I hoped he'd fall off his box, but no such luck; the swine had the Nonpareil on the road again well before me, snatching all my fares, and seeing to it that the George at Crawley wouldn't have a fresh team ready and waiting.''

The guard spoke up for the first time. "That's right, Mr. Wheddle. I gave them "Cherry Ripe" more than a furlong before we got in, but they hadn't even got the cattle out of the stalls.''

The landlord nodded wearily. "So, Chapman's got the George in his pocket as well now.''

"Seems like it, Mr. Wheddle. It took us five minutes to change horses, and we should have been in and out in two. I reckon I've done well to only lose ten minutes all told. Chapman's going hard at it; he's determined to get you off the road one way or another.''

"Well, at least I won't have gone without a fight,'' replied the landlord resignedly.

The coachman pushed his hat back on his balding head. "You need a really crack whip, Mr. Wheddle. I'm not in that class, and you and I both know it.''

The landlord shook his head. "It's too late for all that now, Johnno. The Brighton road's too fashionable; a coach needs to be like a private carriage to succeed, and it needs not only a fine whip at the ribbons, but also matched teams of blood cattle, and an endless supply of funds to meet the tricks of Edward Chapman and the style of the Earl of Felbridge. It also needs a proprietor with the stomach to carry on, and I have to confess that I'm fast losing that. I've fought long enough, and now I just want to get out.''

"You don't really mean that, Mr. Wheddle.''

"No, perhaps not, but much as I love this place and want to keep the Swan on the road, I can't afford it anymore. I have to sell.''

"To Chapman?''

"No, not before I've tried hard to find another buyer elsewhere, someone who's prepared to offer what it's really worth. Anyway, take her on through, Johnno. Then you and Dick get to the kitchens; Betsy's got a handsome dinner waiting for you.''

"Right you are, Mr. Wheddle.'' Johnno picked up the reins again, clicking his tongue and easing the tired horses forward into the stableyard, which lay beyond a second archway at the rear of the courtyard.

As the coach moved out of the way, the landlord saw Jane's landau for the first time. His lips parted in astonishment, and for a moment he just stood there, but then he swiftly recovered and came hurrying over. "Begging your pardon, madam, but I didn't realize you were here. May I be of any assistance to you? Has your carriage incurred some damage, perhaps?" This was evidently the only reason he could think of for a lady to deign to enter an establishment like this.

"My carriage is quite all right, sir, but I think you could be of immense assistance. Could you spare me some of your time, Mr. Wheddle?"

"My time?" He couldn't hide his puzzlement.

"I wish to discuss the sale of this business."

"But surely such a thing is of no interest to a lady."

"Perhaps if I explained that I am Lady Jane Derwent, and the Earl of Felbridge is my brother . . . ?" She allowed her voice to trail away, no further clarification seeming necessary.

His eyes cleared and became suddenly hopeful. "The Earl of Felbridge? Is he considering purchasing the Swan, my lady?"

"Something of that nature," she replied noncommittally.

He didn't stop to wonder why a gentleman like the earl would send his sister on such an errand; he could only see the possibility of a satisfactory end to his problems. "My time is yours, Lady Jane. Perhaps you would be more comfortable if we adjourned to the coffee room?"

"By all means, sir."

He assisted her carefully down, as if he was afraid she would shatter the moment her dainty foot touched the yard's rough cobbles, and he nodded at one of the ostlers. "Tell Betsy to bring some of the best coffee, and to be quick about it."

The man dashed off toward the kitchens and Ellen remained in the landau as Jacob led his extremely grand and unlikely visitor into the quiet coffee room, which had windows looking out onto both Cheapside and the courtyard. It was a low-ceilinged room with a large, yawning fireplace at one end where gleaming copper and brass pots hung against the soot-marked stonework. The rows of white-clothed tables were enclosed by settles and partitions, and it was so quiet that the ticking of the long-case clock in the corner could be clearly heard. Afternoon sunlight streamed in through the Cheapside windows, falling warmly on the pots of scarlet geraniums blooming on the sills, and the smell of coffee hung tangibly in the still air, even though it was Jane's guess that it had been some time now since there had been any passengers to serve.

She was led to a table next to one of the windows, but before she could sit down, Jacob had to remove a slumbering tabby kitten which was curled up in the sun on the settle. Then he brushed the seat, smiling apologetically at her. "It's my daughter's kitten, my lady. Betsy dotes on it. The darned thing's always sleeping in here, even though I put it out every time I catch it. There. Please sit down."

She took her seat, gesturing toward the place opposite. "Please join me, Mr. Wheddle, for it will be most difficult to conduct a conversation if you are standing, since you are so very tall that I'm sure my neck would soon ache."

He obeyed, but rather uncomfortably, since it didn't seem right at all that he should be seated in the presence of a lady.

"Now then, Mr. Wheddle," she began, "could you explain to me exactly why you're selling?"

"Oh, the usual reasons for a man to fail in business, my lady," he replied blandly. "Expenses have become quite intolerable. I've poor horses, old coaches, and less than brilliant coachmen, which all means a loss of business when there are the likes of the Earl of Felbridge's fine Iron Duke to contend with. A new coach would set me back at least £120, and I'd need four to have the Swan running properly. I could hire, of course, but at threepence a double mile—that's one mile there and one back again—that's quite out of the question as well. Then there's the horses, an average wheeler would cost a good £30, with the leaders naturally coming out at a lot more. After all that, there's the running of this place, and the ticket office in Brighton, the wages of stablehands, horse keepers, guards, coachmen, and so on, to say nothing of government duties, licenses, road taxes, turnpike tolls. . . . It's endless, my lady, as no doubt the earl has told you."

"With all due respect, Mr. Wheddle, all the things you've just mentioned are the cross every single coach proprietor has to bear, but not every single proprietor is forced to sell for reasons beyond his control. Besides, let me be quite honest by admitting that I overheard every word which passed between you and the coachman in the courtyard, so please don't fob me off with irrelevances. You're selling because you're being driven off the road by Mr. Chapman, aren't you?"

For a moment he was silent, then he nodded. "Yes, Lady Jane. Because of his activities, I'm reduced to running only one coach a day instead of my usual four. The other three lie idle in the stableyard. I've got one coachman and one guard, my single coach cannot be relied upon to keep time, and I'm losing passengers like water through a sieve. It's costing me £50 a week, my lady, and I can't go on because I'm galloping toward bankruptcy."

"What exactly does he do to you?"

"You heard—"

"Yes, but I confess I didn't always understand. For instance, what does boxed in mean?"

He seemed surprised. "I would have thought that the Earl of Felbridge's sister would be well up with all the slang."

"I may be his sister, sir, but I assure you that I've hitherto done my utmost to avoid having anything to do with his wretched coaches."

This response surprised him all the more, for if she loathed coaching so much, why on earth had she apparently agreed to come here on such an errand for her brother? Still, who was Jacob Wheddle to wonder why the likes of the earl and his family did anything? "Well, my lady, when a coach is boxed in, it's contained on the open road by two rivals, both deliberately traveling a great deal slower and blocking any attempt to pass. They closed up on the middle coach so tightly that it hasn't a chance, and then they let a fourth coach slip by—in today's case it was the Nonpareil itself—letting it get ahead to the next stop to pick up the boxed-in coach's passengers. Chapman's running an army of coaches at the moment, most of them boxing in his competitors, while the Nonpareil waltzes along pinching all the fares."

"That sounds a rather expensive way of doing things, Mr. Wheddle, even for a man like Mr. Chapman."

"To him it's worth it, because in the end he reckons to be top dog on the Brighton road."

"I see. So this boxing in, and the buying off of inns along the road, is how he's forced you into your present predicament?"

"Well, there's a little more to it than just that."

"At that moment the door opened and a young girl came in carrying a tray of coffee. She was fair and pretty, with rosy cheeks and a rounded figure, and the tabby kitten, which had been washing itself on the stone-flagged floor, bounded over to rub around her skirts as she brought the tray to the table and set it carefully down, glancing curiously at Jane for a moment and then withdrawing to the counter on the other side of the room, where she made a pretense of polishing and dusting, but was actually trying her utmost to overhear what was being said.

75

Much to Jacob's discomfort, Jane automatically picked up the coffee pot and poured two cups, handing one to him. "Now then, sir, you were saying that there is a little more to Mr. Chapman's activities."

He awkwardly accepted the cup, for it didn't seem right at all that she should wait upon him.

She looked quizzically at him. "Have you nothing more to say, sir?"

"About Chapman? There's almost too much to say about him. He's the biggest villain in coaching, and set to be a bigger one still if he's not stopped. Anyway, yes, there's much more to what he's done to me personally than I've said so far. The Swan was never a crack coach, but it did reasonably well, especially the afternoon up coach from Brighton, which got in just in time to connect with the Holyhead mail. There are a couple of regiments stationed over in north Ireland, and their junior officers and so on liked to take their pleasure in Brighton and then get back to camp at the last minute. They used the Swan because it kept perfect time and could be relied on to meet the mail." He gazed away for a moment, smiling as he fondly remembered those halcyon days. "The Swan was always full then, and never a crazy woman like she is now."

"Crazy woman?"

"Empty coach."

"Oh."

"Anyway, I was doing so handsomely that Chapman began to cast his covetous eyes in my direction, deciding that he wanted the Swan's slice of the cake for his Nonpareil. He started off mildly enough, luring my best whips away with offers of better wages, bribing inns, and occasionally boxing in. I began to lose a minute here and there, and occasionally the Swan wouldn't get in in time for the Holyhead mail. My reputation soon suffered, passengers switched allegiance, and before long I was running at a loss. But I wouldn't give up, and that annoyed Chapman, so much so that he got a bit rougher. His coachmen would goad mine into racing along the open road, he'd squeeze, feather edge, choke up the ground—"

Jane was at a loss. "Please, Mr. Wheddle, you'll have to explain."

"Squeezing is when a rival coach forces a dangerous situation by passing too close, making the other coachman make mistakes. Feather-edging is when that's taken still further, usually by forcing a coach against a bridge parapet or a bollard. Choking up the ground, well that means putting obstacles like flocks of sheep or logs on the ground, the ground being the actual road a coach travels. The down ground is from here to Brighton, the up ground from Brighton back again.''

"Which is why we always say up to London and down to the country, no matter what?''

"Yes, Lady Jane. And to be more precise than ever about grounds, each one is divided up into stages, in the Brighton road's case into six stages, each one horsed by a local inn or landowner. I personally horse the Swan on the first stage out of London and the last one in, but for the rest I relay on others, and that's how Chapman can get at me, by bribing them to serve me badly.''

"It all sounds most irregular and dangerous, Mr. Wheddle.''

"It is.''

"To say nothing of being extremely illegal.''

He gave a short laugh. "Oh, Chapman's a sharp one when it comes to what's legal. He uses informers to see to that side of it.''

"As he did today? When the magistrates checked the license?''

"That was a mild one, designed only to delay me; he's usually more intent on having me fined.''

"But he can only do that if you break the law.''

"Ah, but there's ways and ways of breaking the law, Lady Jane. Sometimes I admit to being at fault, like when the coach panels get so dirty that the lettering can't be read, that's an infringement and carries a fine. The magistrates, naturally enough, wouldn't get to know about most of what goes on, except for the likes of Byers, Chapman's pet informer, and the most hated man after Chapman himself on the whole road. He's trapped a great many coaches by luring the coachmen into shouldering.''

"Shouldering?''

"Picking up fares along the route, carrying them a short distance, and then setting them down without entering their names on the waybill. The coachman does it to pocket the money; it's the same when he carries more passengers than the license permits. Overloading's another one the informers can get a coach on, and then there's the old one of getting a genuine passenger to sit on his luggage on top.''

She stared. "I beg your pardon?''

"It raises the coach above the legal limit of ten feet nine inches,'' he explained. "Byers waits at the next tollgate to point the fact out to the keeper, who carries out a spot check, and bingo, another appearance before the magistrates.''

She sat back thoughtfully, remaining silent for a moment before looking at him again. ''Mr. Wheddle, so far you've only told me what Mr. Chapman's sins are, but I'm not fool enough to think that he's the only coachmaster resorting to somewhat low tricks. Does my brother conduct himself in a less than honorable way on the open road?''

''May I be honest with you, my lady?''

''Please.''

''The earl's more a thorn in the side of honest proprietors than a downright poisoned arrow like Chapman. Oh, he may own the Fleece and run the Iron Duke as legitimately as I run the Swan, but for all that, he's still a gentleman amateur, in it for the prestige and little else. He's a swell whose greatest delight is to get up on the box of a crack coach and drive it like the very devil to Brighton and back. The Iron Duke's not a stagecoach, it's a spanking turnout worthy of the Four-in-Hand and Hyde Park, all trimmings, gleaming lacquerwork, polished brass, and perfectly matched teams. He doesn't carry a guard like everyone else—he has a liveried servant who hands out the best sherry and a little silver box filled with sandwiches, should the passengers feel in need of refreshment. And if, by any mischance, the Iron Duke should get in a half a minute over time, then he gives the passengers their fares back! It's a game to him, and he has more than enough money to play it as long as he likes. Losing £50 a week would be like water off a duck's back to him. But he's a gentleman, and even though he's needling Chapman at the moment, he's still playing it all strictly according to the rules, like a duel between gentlemen, only with blank shot. He's entering this Midsummer Day race in the belief that it will be conducted correctly in every way; well it won't be, because Chapman's not a gentleman and only knows how to fight in the dirtiest way possible. So no, Lady Jane, the earl doesn't conduct himself dishonorably on the open road; he's just intent upon his own pleasure and that's about it.''

''I'm glad to hear you say that, Mr. Wheddle, for it would grieve me considerably to discover that my brother had sunk to such levels.''

''Is there anything else you wish to know?''

''No, I think you've been most informative.''

''Not too informative to put the earl off purchasing my business?''

"When you've been so honest with me, sir, I think it's time that I was equally honest with you. My brother knows nothing about my visit here today. *I'm* the interested party, Mr. Wheddle, and I'm interested because I'm seeking a way of teaching him a lesson in how to go on politely. He's become a ribbon bore of the first order, and these days the only thing capable of moving him to rhapsodies is his coaching." She paused for a moment. "Did I understand from your conversation with your coachman that you don't really wish to lose this place or stop running the Swan?"

A little bemused, he nodded. "Yes, my lady."

"Good, because that means we can come to a mutually beneficial arrangement. I don't wish to become the owner of your business, Mr. Wheddle, but I am more than prepared to finance you to whatever sum you think is necessary to make the Feathers and the Swan as flourishing and important as the Black Horse and the Nonpareil, or the Fleece and the Iron Duke. I'll purchase new coaches, give you funds to attract back your best coachmen, pay for any advertising, and meet any fines you may have to pay. In return, you'll keep my involvement a secret until the very morning of Midsummer Day."

"Midsummer Day?" Light was beginning to dawn in his astonished eyes.

"Yes, Mr. Wheddle. I want the Swan to be entered in the race. I'd like to beat the Iron Duke, and the Nonpareil as well, since Mr. Chapman appears to be even less deserving of victory than my brother. It's just over two weeks to the day of the race, which I admit doesn't give us a great deal of time to prepare, but it will have to do."

He was still staring at her. "My lady, you can't possibly be serious!"

"But I am, sir. Oh, and I nearly forgot to say, I wish to travel on the Swan's box during the race. My brother must suffer the humiliation of seeing a woman come in first, and the further humiliation of that woman's being his sister. I cannot think of a more sovereign way of teaching him that long overdue lesson." She smiled at him. "Well, sir? What do you say? Do we have a deal or not?"

Had she sprouted horns and a tail he couldn't have been more taken aback, while from behind the counter his daughter could only stare.

ELEVEN

*J*acob was dazed. "You—you can't be serious," he said again, shaking his head as if he must have misheard everything.

"As I said, sir, I'm very serious indeed."

Betsy couldn't remain behind the counter, and came hesitantly toward the table. "But my lady," she said tentatively, "such things simply aren't done."

"Gentlemen do it all the time," Jane pointed out.

"Yes, but not ladies. There'd be such talk and a dreadful scandal. Your reputation would suffer."

"I don't intend to file my teeth, wear breeches, and hurl abuse at the bystanders," replied Jane, still smiling. She could understand their amazement, for what she was suggesting was indeed a little shocking. She looked from one to the other, seeing doubt written all over them. "Come now, if a gentleman came here with such a proposition, you'd both think it a splendid notion, wouldn't you?"

Jacob had to nod. "Yes, but what a man does is entirely different. Ladies just can't go around doing things like ride on stagecoaches during races."

"I fail to see why, since what's sauce for the gander is sauce for the goose as well. Don't you *want* to save your business, Mr. Wheddle?"

"Yes, but not if you're intent upon risking life, limb, *and* reputation."

She held Betsy's gaze then. "What do *you* think? I mean, what do you *really* think?"

The girl glanced uneasily at her father. "I don't know, Lady Jane, and that's the truth. I agree with you that it's not fair that what's sauce for the gander isn't sauce for the goose as well, but I agree with Dad, that for a lady to set out on something like this would be very ill-advised indeed."

"You think it would make me notorious?"

"Yes."

"Well, I don't agree. It will be a nine-day wonder, that's all, and if the Swan should win, or even come second, just think how gleeful all the women would be. I wonder how many other poor female souls there are suffering at the hands of selfish men who can only think of coaching? And I don't just mean ladies like myself; there must be countless women who have to endure ribbon talk morning, noon, and night.''

Betsy had to grin at that. ''There are indeed, Lady Jane. I've heard some of them complaining.''

''There you are then.'' Jane fixed her eye upon Jacob. ''I'm still set on this, sir, and you've yet to give me a really good reason why we shouldn't do it.''

For a moment he didn't reply; then he met her gaze. ''Very well, Lady Jane, you want reasons, I'll give you them. I haven't told you everything about Chapman's activities, not by a long chalk, and perhaps when you know *exactly* what sort of man he is, then you'll see that to go ahead with what you propose is quite out of the question.'' He glanced at his daughter for a moment. ''There's a coachman, name of Arthur Huggett. . . .''

Betsy took a deep breath and turned quickly away. Jane looked curiously at her.

Jacob continued. ''He was the finest whip on the Brighton road, and no mistake, better even than George Sewell. He used to drive for Ebeneezer Taylor, who kept the Dog Tavern down in Thames Street, close to the earl's Fleece. Ebeneezer's coaches ran the Brighton road like mine, never being exactly bang up to the mark, but fetching along handsomely enough for all that. Needless to say, Ebeneezer's business caught Chapman's eye and he began all his usual tricks, but Ebeneezer was made of stern stuff and wouldn't give in. He was also not without funds, having married a widow of some means, so he could keep going, it didn't matter to him that he was losing £50 pounds a week. That meant Chapman had to use different tactics, dirtier ones, in order to get Ebeneezer off the road. The Dog Tavern burned to the ground one night.''

Jane stared at him. ''Are—are you saying that . . . ?''

''That Chapman put it to the flame? Yes, Lady Jane, that's exactly what I'm saying. Arthur Huggett lost his wife in that fire, and he was never the same after that. He took to the bottle, couldn't keep a stagecoach going in a straight line, lost job after job, until now he's being kept by his son Will, in poor rooms above the Orange Tree Coffee House in Covent Garden. Before that he'd had his own house, he'd dressed as handsomely as Sewell does now, and he'd been the toast of the Brighton road, the acknowledged master, idolized by the likes of your brother, Lady Jane. He's a mere shadow of a man now, never sober, without any self-respect, and totally reliant upon poor Will, who daren't keep a regular job because that would mean he couldn't keep his eye on his father. Will's a fine young man, a coachman like his father, but his life's been ruined by Chapman, just as surely as his old man's has.''

Jane was appalled. ''But if Mr. Chapman did such a dreadful thing, why hasn't he been brought to book for it?''

''Knowing he's done something and being able to prove it, are two different things, Lady Jane. Anyway, the outcome of it all was that Ebeneezer threw in the towel after that, sold out to Chapman, and went to live in the country. I think he's got a place somewhere up by Oxford now. Now then, my lady, it's true that I don't want to leave the Feathers, and it's true that I want to keep the old Swan on the road, but I'm not a fool. I don't want my business to go the same way as Ebeneezer's.''

''I can't think that Mr. Chapman would risk the same thing twice,'' replied Jane. ''Surely that would be far too hazardous, even for him.''

''He's capable of anything.''

She nodded. ''He's evidently a far more black-hearted villain than I'd realized, but I'm afraid that that only makes me more determined to win. He shouldn't be allowed to get away with such dreadful things, Mr. Wheddle, and to lose the race would surely be as big a blow to his pride as to my brother's.''

With a patient sigh, Jacob got up. ''Lady Jane, I don't think you've any idea what sort of event that race is going to be. It'll be a vicious scrap, with no holds barred, and it'll be as far removed from a spin in Hyde Park as you can imagine. And apart from all that, I don't think the Swan can be got up to the necessary scratch by Midsummer Day.''

''Why not?''

''New coaches take time to build, and time's needed too to find the right sort of horses. Bloodstock is what's needed for such a race, not the poor old nags I've been running lately. Then there's the finding of a fine enough whip, to say nothing of which inns will agree to take the horses—they're all either in your brother's pocket or in Chapman's. They horse the Swan at the moment, but they certainly won't for the race; it's more than they dare risk because they'll lose custom from the other two.''

''Very well, let's consider all those points. I'm sure we can find a coach builder who will be prepared to provide the right sort of coach in such a short time.''

"Maybe.''

Betsy gave him a cross look. "Come on, Dad, you *know* a coach can be got in time. Mrs. Mountain would build one, for a start.''

"All right, but finding a coachman of the right caliber is another matter.''

Jane sat back. "What about my own man?''

He laughed a little wryly. "With all due respect, my lady, he might be a fine and fancy fellow driving a sedate landau through London, but he'd never stand a chance on the open road against the likes of Sewell or your brother. You'll need a man of different quality, a master of the Brighton road, not just a reasonable hand over any road you care to mention. It's knowing the *exact* ground to be covered that's the thing, knowing every corner, every hill and every hollow, because it's knowledge like that that gains seconds, minutes even. That's why coaches like the Iron Duke and the Nonpareil cover the distance to Brighton in five hours, reducing to as little as four and a half for a race like the one we're talking about. The Swan takes a good five and a half hours, and won't better that unless it's got a Sewell on the box. It's years of practice we're talking about, not shoving a man up out of the blue on race day.''

"But my brother hardly has years of practice,'' she pointed out.

"No, but he's a different kettle of fish. As you've said, he has a positive passion for coaching, he probably eats, sleeps, and breathes it, and that's what makes him Sewell's equal.''

She nodded then. "Yes, I suppose that does describe my brother rather accurately,'' she admitted. "So, we can acquire a coach with relative ease, but we'll find the matter of a suitable coachman much more difficult.''

"Next to impossible; they're snapped up and kept tight, of that you may be sure, since they're worth their weight in gold to a good coachmaster.''

Betsy cleared her throat. "Dad, there's Arthur Huggett.''

"Oh, be sensible, Betsy! He's a drunk; he can't see further than the next bottle. I know you love Will, but that's blinding you to the truth about his father.''

Betsy flushed a little. "That's not true, Dad. Oh, I admit that I love Will, and if he was half the coachman his father is I'd recommend him as well, but Will isn't, he's just average. I know his father, though, and I think he'd leap at the chance to get back at Chapman. He'd stay dry in order to drive the Swan in that race, I just know he would.''

Jane looked from one to the other, her gaze resting finally on Betsy. "Do you really think he would?"

"Yes. He hates Chapman, Lady Jane, because Chapman was responsible for his wife's death in that fire. He *was* the best whip on the Brighton road, and I think he still is."

Jacob groaned aloud. "For heaven's sake, Betsy, talk some sense! He'd be a positive liability on the box of any stagecoach, let alone one involved in a race like this!"

Betsy looked imploringly at Jane. "Dad's wrong, Lady Jane, I know that he is.''

Jane hesitated and then nodded. "I believe you, Betsy."

The girl tossed a triumphant glance at her father, who sighed again. "All right, let's assume that we've got a new coach and that Arthur Huggett remains sober enough to actually pick up the ribbons; that leaves us with the most difficult matter of all in my opinion—horsing the coach."

"But you already have horses."

"And I've already said that they're not anywhere near good enough, it's bang-up teams of blood and bone you'll be needing, and lots of them. London to Brighton is approximately fifty-five miles, that's six stages, and therefore six fresh teams; that's a minimum of thirty horses, not counting the spares you'd be best advised to keep on hand. Thirty of the best bloodstock horses in the realm, Lady Jane, that's what your brother and Chapman will have ready for the race; we haven't got any. The usual practice is to approach landowners along the ground, since they're usually the only ones with money enough to keep the sort of cattle we're talking about. There's only one hope I can think of, and that's Lord Ardenley at Maywood. He's a very fine amateur whip, in my opinion probably the best, and he's kept well out of coaching recently, but as far as I know he still keeps a large stable at Maywood. He might—"

"No, Mr. Wheddle, I think not. Lord Ardenley and I don't see eye to eye."

"Oh. Well, that's the best I can suggest."

She sat back, gazing at her coffee cup for a moment. "Have you told me everything I should know now, Mr. Wheddle?"

"I think so."

"I'm still set on going ahead with it, sir."

"I was afraid you'd say that," he replied resignedly. "Forgive me for asking this, Lady Jane, but what happened to make you suddenly decide upon such a startling course? The earl's passion for the ribbons has been going on for some time, it's not new.''

"No, but it's been getting worse, and last night was the last straw.''

"Last night?''

"It was his fiancée's birthday ball, but he took himself off to Brighton on some errand connected with the race. He stayed there overnight and forgot all about the ball.''

"His fiancée? That'd be Miss Lyndon?''

"Why, yes.''

He smiled a little. "Oh, I'm not well up on such things, Lady Jane; it just so happens that my cousin is a footman at Lyndon House and I know there was a grand birthday ball there last night.''

"Very grand indeed, if my brother had only been there to see. Anyway, he came back this morning and had the absolute gall to tell her fibs about his absence. He covered himself with laurels and then was odiously pleased with himself for getting away with it. It was the last straw, as far as I'm concerned.''

"So, you saw my notice and began to think?''

"Yes.''

"You'll only teach him a lesson if you bring the Swan in ahead of him.''

"I know.''

"And there's many a slip 'twixt cup and lip, for even with a fine new coach, a sober Arthur Huggett, and thirty bloodstock horses conjured out of thin air, you're still going to need more than a morsel of good luck to win on Midsummer Day. That race is far from won.''

"I realize that, sir, but I *will* win it," she replied, smiling because she knew he'd decided to agree. "Mr. Wheddle, am I to understand we have that deal?''

He gave a reluctant nod. "We do, Lady Jane, although I think I'm the end in fools for letting you persuade me.''

Betsy was overjoyed. "And will Arthur Huggett be allowed to drive the coach on the day?''

Jane nodded. "There doesn't seem to be anyone else.''

"You won't regret it, Lady Jane, I promise you! Will and I between us will keep him on the straight, but I don't think we'll have to try very hard, because he'll *want* to do it.''

Jacob sniffed and shook his head doubtfully. "I hope you're right, my girl, because a lot will be resting on this race.'' He looked at Jane. "Mrs. Mountain of the Saracen's Head was mentioned earlier about building a new coach. She's good, so unless you've any personal preference. . . ."

Jane smiled. "Mr. Wheddle, my knowledge of coach builders extends to the firm in Bond Street which provided our last landau."

"They won't do for a racing stagecoach."

"Approach whomever you wish, sir, I will leave that entirely up to you, but please do it quickly if we're to have a new Swan by Midsummer Day."

"About the cost. . . ."

"Money's no object."

"Very well."

"And please remember that I don't want anyone to know about my involvement until the day of the race."

"With all due respect, Lady Jane, if that's the case, then I strongly advise you not to come here again in a fancy open landau; it's much too conspicuous."

She smiled ruefully. "I realize that and will be much more circumspect from now on. If you need any money, please contact my lawyer, Mr. Nathaniel Payne of Curzon Street, and if you need to contact me, please do that through him as well, since it would hardly do to risk my brother's finding out because you've come to South Audley Street. Well, that only leaves the matter of the horses, and I shall have to give that a great deal of thought. They must be available somewhere."

"You'll need a magic wand, my lady."

"I'll find them, of that you may be sure. And the Swan's going to come in first on Midsummer Day."

He grinned at her. "Do you know, I'm beginning to think that's exactly what it *will* do."

She left shortly after that, arranging to call the next day to meet Arthur Huggett and his son Will, whom Betsy promised to produce at the Feathers at two o'clock in the afternoon.

As she and Ellen drove back toward Mayfair, Jane gazed at the passing streets, the full import of what she had embarked upon suddenly striking her. But she wasn't concerned with any possible scandal she might be making; she could think only of the joy of trouncing Henry and his odious Iron Duke. Yes, Henry Derwent, she thought, *then* you'll have something unpalatable to pour in your glass and drink!

TWELVE

*I*t was raining just before midday the following morning when Jane and Ellen hurried the short distance from South Audley Street to the residence of Jane's lawyer, Mr. Payne, in Curzon Street. Jane was glad of the rain, for it gave her an excuse to wear an anonymous hooded mantle over her fashionable clothes, which was just as well since after seeing Mr. Payne she had to go again to the Feathers, and in order to get there without being noticed she had decided for the first time in her life to take a hackney coach. This was a course which even Ellen thought the height of madness, and so it probably was, but what better way was there to travel incognito?

Mr. Payne was appalled to learn of her plans, but after trying unsuccessfully to talk her out of them, he at last capitulated and agreed to act for her. He also agreed, extremely reluctantly, to keep the whole business to himself and not to say a word to Henry. When she and the maid left, he was on the point of going to Long's Hotel for his favorite luncheon of deviled soles, and it was Jane's guess that after her visit this meal was almost certain to result in indigestion.

It was still pouring as she and Ellen hurried back along the wide, fashionable pavement of Curzon Street, and she pulled her hood well down over her face as they hailed a conveniently passing hackney coach. It was a disreputable vehicle drawn by a tired old horse, and its interior was very shabby indeed, with worn seats and a scattering of stale straw to soak up the wet from passengers' shoes. They sat gingerly on the edge of their seats, holding on tightly to the leather straps as the ill-sprung little carriage lurched around a corner and set off on its uncomfortable way toward Cheapside. Jane thought longingly of the elegance and comfort of her landau, and gritted her teeth as the hackney jolted over every rut and bump in the road, its window glasses shaking so much that they seemed in imminent danger of shattering.

Arthur and Will Huggett were waiting, as Betsy had promised, and as she had predicted, Arthur was more than anxious to have

87

the chance to drive the Swan in the race. He was a chubby man with a florrid complexion and a nose of that rosy hue that tells of a predilection for beverages of an alcoholic nature. His blue eyes were watery and his tongue passed frequently over his lower lip as he stood nervously in front of Jane. He wore shabby clothes that had once been of good quality, and he turned his hat anxiously in his hands throughout the interview.

His son, the Will Betsy declared she loved, was a burly young man with broad, muscular shoulders and a mop of curly brown hair. His skin was sun-tanned because he had recently had temporary work repairing roofs, and his eyes were the same blue as his father's, although clear instead of rheumy.

They both seemed eager to be part of Jane's venture, with Arthur swearing on his honor never to touch the bottle, and Will promising to see that this promise was adhered to, to the very letter. Betsy had evidently been hard at work on Jacob, who had most reluctantly agreed to let the Huggetts stay at the Feathers, but he made little secret of his disapproval, and stated quite bluntly that he doubted very much if Arthur was capable of remaining sober for one day, let alone two weeks. However, Jane was inclined to think Betsy was right about the old coachman, and she accepted his word, especially as she could see the light of revenge gleaming in his eyes at the thought of maybe beating Chapman, who had so much to answer for.

Jane and Ellen left the Feathers in the same hackney coach, and Jacob's parting words were that he would go later that afternoon to see Mrs. Mountain at the Saracen's Head about a new coach. As the hackney bounced along Cheapside on its way back toward Mayfair, Jane felt a thrill of excitement; it had really begun now, she had embarked upon teaching Henry a lesson he'd never forget, and she was enjoying herself immensely. Her only problem appeared to be the acquisition of the coach horses, and she still hadn't any inspiration about them at all.

It was still pouring with rain when they alighted from the hackney coach on the corner of Curzon Street and South Audley Street, and there were no passersby to look curiously at the rich, frilled hem of the fashionable pink lawn gown revealed briefly beneath the plain, concealing mantle as Jane stepped down to the wet pavement. She and Ellen hurried along the street, Jane glancing carefully all around before going up to the door to have it open as if by magic as the vigilant Melville attended efficiently to his duties. They stepped thankfully into the vestibule and the butler relieved Jane of her wet mantle.

She glanced at her reflection in the mirror to see that the hood hadn't flattened her hair too much, then she turned to the butler. "I would like some tea and buttered toast to be served in the blue saloon, Melville, and will you see that Ellen has some too in the kitchens?"

"Certainly, Lady Jane, but maybe you would prefer to join the earl?"

"The earl?"

"He's already taking tea in the library."

"Oh. Very well, the library then."

"Yes, my lady." He bowed and withdrew in the direction of the kitchens, spiriting the damp mantle away with him. Ellen discreetly followed him, hoping that he would be mindful of Jane's instructions to see that she had some tea and toast too.

Gathering her skirts, Jane hurried up to the library, pausing in the doorway to compose herself. She mustn't appear different in any way, and she was sure that at this precise moment she was positively aglow with scheming excitement. She drew a long, steadying breath, and then calmly went in.

Henry was slumped dejectedly in a chair by the window overlooking the gardens at the rear of the house. Unlike the blue saloon's windows, there was no roofed balcony outside, so the rain washed dismally down the glass, distorting the gray scene outside. He seemed sunk in gloom as he watched it. His neck-cloth was untied and hanging loose, his shirt was partly unbuttoned, and his favorite maroon coat lay crumpled on the sofa where he had tossed it. He looked anything but happy, and since he hadn't returned from Watier's until six in the morning, and then more than a little tipsy, she could only imagine he'd lost heavily and was suffering from the effects of both that and a monumental hangover.

She sat in the chair next to his, seeing at a glance that he hadn't touched the tray of tea which Melville had set on the little octagonal table beside him. "Henry? What's the matter? Did you lose last night?"

"As a matter of fact, I won. Handsomely."

She was a little surprised. "You seem very low for someone who won handsomely. Is something wrong?"

"Everything."

"Are you going to tell me?"

"And risk an 'I told you so' lecture? Thank you, but no."

She sat back. "Is it to do with the race?"

"No."

"Then what?"

He scowled at the rain-washed window. "As a matter of fact, it's to do with Dursley."

Her eyes widened. "Blanche hasn't . . ."

"Ended it with me and accepted him? No, but she probably soon will."

"Henry, I think you'd better explain."

"He was at Watier's last night, and he told me that he had grave doubts about the veracity of my story about the fire in Brighton, such grave doubts that he's going to send a man down there tomorrow to check. He'll lose no time at all in telling Blanche, and it'll finish me with her. Goddamn him, I should have called him out there and then for questioning my word!"

"It's just as well you didn't, since although he may be a dissolute rake, he's one of the most accurate shots I've heard of."

Henry sighed heavily. "Yes, well it isn't with lead that he's going to pick me off now, is it?" He met her gaze. "Don't you dare say I told you so."

"I don't need to."

"What am I going to do, sis?"

"Well, I don't really see why I should try to help you at all, since you know what I think of you and your despicable lies. But at the same time, I don't see why the Duke of Dursley should be assisted in his blatant attempts to poach Blanche, so it seems to me that the solution to your problem is very simple indeed."

"It is? Pray elucidate then, for I'm damned if *I* can see any solution at all, let alone a simple one."

"Well, the duke's man is going to find out that the fire was a very bad one indeed, with crowds of people, isn't he?"

"Yes." He looked puzzled. "That's obvious, even to me."

"So he's going to have to go to your inn to try and find out what you were or were not doing that particular night. All you have to do is send someone there ahead of him to prime them with what to say to any suspicious questions. If they value their positions, they'll come up trumps for you."

He was staring at her, then he leapt to his feet, dragging her bodily from her chair and kissing her roundly on the cheek. "Sis, you old darling! What *would* I do without you? I'll write a letter straightaway and have it sent down on the evening Iron Duke. I'll spike Dursley's rotten guns for him!"

"Henry, about Blanche . . ." But he'd rushed from the room, almost colliding with Melville bringing her tea and toast.

When the butler had gone, she sat down in resigned silence sipping the tea. Henry should have been left to stew in his own selfish juice, but she could hardly have done that and thereby indirectly assisted the duke in his deceitful and dishonorable suit. She sighed, picking up a slice of toast. It was becoming more and more obvious that the only way to make an impact on her self-indulgent, careless brother was by taking him on in the race. He *had* to change, or he'd lose Blanche. She nibbled the toast, gazing at nothing in particular. Where on earth was she going to get the horses for the race? She couldn't use Derwent stock because Henry would find out straightaway, and for the same reason she couldn't approach any of their friends. So what *could* she do? Where could she go to find thirty such horses? Perhaps it was going to prove too much of a stumbling block, just as Jacob Wheddle appeared to think.

She was still giving the matter her consideration shortly afterward when someone tapped discreetly at the library door. "Excuse me, my lady?" It was Ellen.

"Yes, Ellen?"

"Begging your pardon, my lady, but there's something I think you might like to know."

"Yes?" Jane looked up with interest.

"Lady Partridge's maid has just called on me, and she mentioned that her mistress was going to the Grafton House haberdashery this afternoon because they've had a new delivery of French lace, direct from Paris. I know how much you like French lace, so I came up straightaway to tell you."

Jane's eyes brightened. "French lace? Oh, yes, I certainly do like it, and since it's so wretchedly hard to come by, I suppose I should take myself there as quickly as possible, otherwise everyone else will have bought it. Will you tell Melville to have the landau—no, it's raining too much, have him see that the town carriage is brought around immediately."

"Yes, my lady."

"And Ellen, you shall pick a piece of lace for yourself for being so vigilant on my behalf."

The maid's face lit up with delight. "Oh, my *lady!*" She hurried out, her skirts rustling.

Jane finished her toast and licked her fingers. She only hoped the lady gannets of Mayfair hadn't picked everything clean before they got there! She glanced approvingly at the rain. It was always a good deterrent, she thought, so with luck Grafton

House wouldn't be as full as might otherwise have been the case. She crossed her fingers and then hurried up to her room.

Shortly afterward, with Melville holding a large umbrella over their heads, she and Ellen emerged from the house to enter the waiting carriage. Within seconds of that, they were on their way to Grafton House, the fashionable drapers in New Bond Street.

Rain or not, news of the lace had traveled and ladies had converged upon the shop from seemingly every corner of London. The place was dreadfully full, and very noisy indeed as ladies vyed with one another to attract the attention of the harassed young gentlemen assistants, who were doing their utmost to please everyone but were succeeding in satisfying only a very few. The polished oak counter was littered with drawers and trays, and cards of lace lay everywhere, their precious loads sometimes spilling over to trail perilously close to the damp floor and being trampled by the elegant shoes of the ladies pressing closest.

It was half an hour before Jane and Ellen managed to reach the counter and secure the services of one of the assistants. He brought them several trays filled with cards of lace, and they began to search eagerly through them for the ones they liked best. They were quite absorbed in this pleasant task, when quite suddenly, a gentleman leaned between them from behind. Such conduct wasn't to be tolerated and Jane was on the point of turning indignantly toward him to request him to step back, when she found herself staring at a bunch of gaily colored ribbons which was being dangled before her eyes.

"I understand that these aren't the only kind of ribbons to interest you, Jane," the gentleman murmured, dropping the ribbons onto the tray of lace in front of her.

She recognized the voice only too well. With a gasp, she turned to stare into Lewis's mocking gray eyes.

THIRTEEN

*I*t seemed to amuse him to see how startled she was, but it was a disapproving sort of amusement. "My, my, it seems that what I've been told is unfortunately only too correct."

She recovered her composure a little, adopting a cool, dismissive manner. "I don't know what you're talking about, sir." Deliberately she returned her attention to the lace.

"Come now, Jane," he said softly, "don't let's play games. You know perfectly well what I'm referring to."

"I'm afraid I don't. Please leave me alone."

"I'm prepared to discuss it in rather loud detail, if that's what you wish," he replied, glancing around at the crowded shop, where a number of ladies would have overheard had he raised his voice even slightly.

Turning back toward him, she couldn't hide the anger and dismay she felt that her secret had so swiftly been discovered. "I would prefer not to discuss anything with you, Lewis, especially as it's none of your business."

"I'm making it my business."

"By what right?"

"By right of being someone who will not stand idly by and watch you make a spectacle of yourself. Now then, shall we go outside? It's a little crowded in here for serious conversation."

She wanted to defy him, but she knew there was little to be gained from that. Snatching up her reticule from the counter where she had placed it, she bade Ellen wait where she was and then made her way out into the rainy afternoon.

A sea of umbrellas swayed to and fro along the wet pavement, and the metallic clinking of pattens filled the air, as two elderly ladies, unable or unwilling to adopt the new fashion for overshoes, hurried by on their outmoded little platforms, their shoes and hems raised safely above the rain-soaked ground. Jane would have stopped in the shelter of the doorway, but Lewis took her elbow and steered her through the rain to where her carriage waited. Opening the door he almost thrust her inside, climbing in after her and sitting opposite, flinging his top hat and cane on to the seat and then holding her unwilling gaze. "Now then, are you going to stop being difficult and tell me what all this is about?"

"I fail to see why I should tell you anything, Lewis."

"If you don't, I'm quite prepared to spread the rumor far and wide."

"Yes, I do believe you'd stoop to that."

"It could be that I regard such ungentlemanly conduct rather necessary if you're to be protected from yourself."

"I find it quite insufferable that you, of *all* men, should preach about my protection."

"Don't try to change the subject. Is it true that you've involved yourself in a stagecoach company, with a view to entering this damned race on Midsummer Day?"

"Will you answer me one thing? How did you find out?"

"Perhaps if I mentioned that I dined on deviled soles at Long's today the answer would become quite clear."

"Mr. Payne! He had no right!"

"He's worried about your safety, and justifiably so. And please don't think he rushed to tell me straightaway. He hesitated quite considerably before eventually mentioning it."

"I'll warrant he did," she replied drily. "He pondered the matter at great length, all the way from the first course to the last. I wonder who else he told? The entire dining room?"

"Hardly. I'm the only one who knows. After I left him, I went to South Audley Street and Melville told me you'd come here."

"Should I be flattered to think you've chased across Mayfair after me?"

"I'm not in the mood for any nonsense, Jane. Now then, although you haven't come right out and admitted everything, it's quite obvious that all I've been told *is* true, which surprises me since when I look at you, you appear quite sane, but then looks are evidently misleading. You must have taken leave of your senses to embark upon something as wildly improbable, not to say dangerous, as this. It's dangerous not only because of the natural jostling for position that occurs during a race, but because Chapman's eager to relieve your brother of a small fortune and the presence of a third coach might jeopardize that little plan. Chapman's probably confident of beating the Iron Duke, but he can't be certain of beating an unknown quantity in the form of another challenger. He'll do his utmost to prevent that third challenger from even starting, so forget this imprudence, Jane, it's too hazardous.''

''Imprudence is Alicia's stock in trade, not mine. I suppose she knows all about this? By the time you get back, the story will be all over Town.''

''Alicia knows nothing about it.''

''Ah, so the business at the ball taught you a little wisdom after all.''

''Your tongue is so sharp it will surely cut itself one day,'' he replied drily, his eyes veiled so that she couldn't tell if her barb had found a target. ''Now then, about this horror you think to perpetrate upon society.''

''Upon Henry,'' she corrected.

''The *monde* is going to witness it, Jane, not just Henry. Have you any idea how many elegant souls intend to follow the race all the way to Brighton? The start on Tower Hill is going to be a mill to end all mills, it's even being suggested that the queen herself intends to be there, so assuming that Chapman allows the Swan to get as far as the start, your grand gesture is going to be witnessed by *everyone*.''

''A large proportion of the ladies will be cheering me on. Ribbon bores are the worst bores of all, and London seems to have more than its fair share.''

''You're quite set on this, aren't you? Nothing I say will deter you.''

''Nothing. Which I suppose means you'll spread it far and wide in order to try and stop me.''

''It so happens that I was about to tell you my price for silence.''

She stared. ''Lewis Ardenley, if I didn't know you better I'd think—''

''That I was on the point of propositioning you?'' He gave a faint smile. ''Well, tempting as that notion might be, I have to confess that it isn't what's on my mind.''

''Which is as well, sir, since I'd rather tell the world myself than submit to you.''

He was still drily amused. ''Really? It seems that I can recall a time when you didn't feel at all like that about me.''

''I'm older and wiser now.''

''Are you?'' His voice was suddenly soft, like the touch of silk, and there was a dark, practiced warmth in the lazy way his gray eyes moved over her.

She managed somehow to meet his gaze without wavering.

"Yes, Lewis, I am." Her voice was commendably level, even though he'd so easily managed to once again play havoc with her unwilling heart. He wouldn't slip past her guard this time, not this time.

He laughed lightly. "Very well, my *wise* Lady Jane, we'll leave that highly debatable point for the time being and return to the matter in hand. Have you ever traveled to Brighton on a stagecoach?"

The question took her by surprise. "No, of course I haven't."

"Precisely, so you really haven't any idea what it's like, have you? To you, traveling to Brighton means the comfort of a private carriage, with very little inconvenience or danger."

"I think I know what stagecoach travel is like, sir. I've been very thorough in my inquiries."

"Have you indeed? Well let me point out that there's a world of difference between *hearing* about something and actually experiencing it. Which brings me to my price for silence. I want you to travel to Brighton on a stagecoach—with me to escort and protect you, of course."

She stared at him. "I'm not the one to have taken leave of my senses, Lewis, you are."

"Take it or leave it, Jane. Either you do as I ask, or I blow the proverbial gaff on your madcap plan."

"But why do you want me to go to Brighton? What on earth purpose will it serve?"

"It will show you that traveling on the king's highway in a public coach is a vastly different experience from your private carriage! And what you see from the stagecoach, whatever it might be, will only be a shadow of what you're likely to encounter if you're stubborn and foolish enough to insist upon being on a coach in a race Chapman's determined to win for the money."

She raised her chin defiantly. "And if at the end of this forced excursion I still remain firm in my intentions?"

"If you do—and to my mind it's a rather big if—then I'll say no more on the matter."

"You won't tell Henry?"

"I won't tell anyone."

She considered for a moment. "Very well, I agree."

"I trust that you're not saying that because you have every intention of continuing with your idiocy even if you're alarmed by what happens on the way?"

"You'll have to trust me, sir, since there's no way you can know the answer."

"Don't be overconfident, Jane. Those fifty or so miles to Brighton might prove the undoing of you yet."

"You say that as if you know something is going to happen."

"I've a shrewd notion that it will, especially since we'll be traveling on the Nonpareil. Chapman has made himself many enemies, and he's introduced a considerable spice to the race proceedings by laying that hefty wager with your brother. The Brighton road has become exceeding boisterous, with all manner of skulduggery afoot, and between now and Midsummer Day you may count upon it that the dirty deeds will flow thick and fast. The road on race day will *not* be a place for a lady, Jane, and that's what I'm hoping to prove to you."

"We'll see then, won't we?"

"Yes, we will, the day after tomorrow."

She gave an incredulous laugh. "So soon?"

"Midsummer Day isn't that far away. I'd insist upon tomorrow itself were it not for the fact that it happens to be Sunday, and you'll no doubt need a day to pack a portmanteau and concoct a believable excuse to fob Henry off."

"Pack a portmanteau?" she repeated warily. "Are you suggesting that we stay overnight in Brighton?"

"I am."

"I fail to see why."

"I have no intention of traveling to Brighton and back in one day. We'll travel down on the afternoon Nonpareil and return the next morning in my private carriage." He smiled a little. "Public transport need not be suffered in both directions—I'm too fond of my creature comforts for that."

She was cool. "I trust you don't harbor hopes that *I* will become one of those creature comforts."

"Hardly, since you're not even a comfortable creature most of the time."

She ignored the remark. "And I trust that you've considered the implications of what you're suggesting, for if this little jaunt is discovered, my reputation will be damaged beyond redemption."

"I doubt very much if we'll be found out. We're hardly likely to be recognized traveling as insiders on a public coach, and even if I am, you won't be if you're sensible enough to wear a veil of some sort." He paused. "I've already taken the liberty of sending my coach to Brighton."

Color leapt to her cheeks. "You *were* sure of my answer, weren't you?" she said a little angrily.

"Yes."

She looked away.

"As I was saying, I've already sent my coach ahead, to the White Lion in Bedford Lane, where rooms will be booked for us in the names of Mr. and Miss Havers, brother and sister. Accommodation will also be reserved for your maid, to be sure that propriety isn't offended."

"Propriety may not be offended, sir, but I most certainly am." She glanced at him. "Why Havers?" she demanded.

"It's my mother's maiden name."

"False names can look extremely suspicious, especially if we're seen at this White Lion."

"It isn't an establishment exactly haunted by fashionable society."

"Really? I trust it isn't a den of iniquity."

"It's merely a comfortable hostelry which provides tidy accommodation and a reasonable table."

"One wonders how you know about it. Did dear Alicia acquaint you with its existence? Yes, to be sure that must be it, for I'll warrant she knows a great many establishments which are, shall we say, off the beaten track?" She gave him another sweet smile.

"My, my, I had no idea you had so much of the *chienne* in you, Jane," he reproved, shaking his head and tutting disappointedly.

"One learns from the dogs of this life, sir."

"Aye, and some of us appear to be more adept at learning than others." He picked up his hat and cane. "I shall have to tear myself away from your fascinating company now. I shall expect to see you in the coffee room of the Black Horse, Snow Hill, at just before four in the afternoon the day after tomorrow."

"Perhaps I should remind you that Mr. Chapman is acquainted with me and might quite easily recognize me."

"Wear a veil, as I suggested. And don't tog yourself out in the highest tippy of fashion, for that would most certainly draw attention on a stagecoach."

"Lewis, I only possess the highest tippy of fashion," she replied acidly.

"How very inconvenient for you. Still, I'm sure you'll come up with something, especially since you're so very eager to protect your reputation."

"I loathe you, Lewis Ardenley."

"Then I'm afraid you're going to find the visit to Brighton extremely tedious, since you'll be closeted with me for such a long time." He gave her a lazy half-smile. "But no doubt a creature of such indomitable spirit will not permit such petty adversities to weigh her down for long." He flung open the carriage door and stepped down into the pouring rain, turning to help her out. "Until the day after tomorrow then."

She snatched her hand away. "I do *not* look forward to it," she said, gathering her skirts and hurrying across the wet pavement to go quickly back into Grafton House, where the ladies still fought over the best of the lace.

Lewis remained where he was for a moment, then he tapped his top hat onto his golden hair, closed the carriage door, and strolled on down the street, apparently quite oblivious to the torrential downpour, which soon soaked the costly fabric of his excellent coat.

As she and Ellen returned to South Audley Street with their purchases, she regaled the astonished maid with the story of her plans and Lewis's arrogant, interfering ultimatum. Reaching the house she found Charles Moncarm's carriage waiting at the door. He and Henry were in the billiard room at the rear of the ground floor, the French windows open onto the gardens. The noise of the rain filled the room, and the air was a little cool, but the two men didn't seem to notice, they were too engrossed in their play. The ivory balls chinked against one another on the green baize table, and the smoke from Charles's cigar curled up thinly from the dish where he had placed it while he played his shot.

Jane entered quietly, going to stand by the open windows to look out at the gardens, still thinking angrily about Lewis's unwarranted intervention in her private affairs. She took a deep breath, reaching out to touch the moisture-laden blooms of the climbing rose growing against the wall by the window. She didn't want to submit to his will in this way, but there was a secret part of her which thrilled very treacherously to the thought of being alone with him.

"Jane? A penny for your thoughts." Charles was leaning on his cue, smiling at her as Henry prepared to play.

"They aren't worth a penny," she replied, turning. "I trust you're winning and that Henry is soon to be trounced."

He nodded at the marking board on the wall. "I'm afraid not."

"Charles, you'll simply have to do better," she said lightly, forcing away thoughts of Lewis Ardenley and Brighton, and concentrating upon the state of the game.

"I know, and it's most disagreeable, since I came here to see you and instead end up being demolished on the green baize by your brother's superior play. I think I should have remained in bed today; the idleness would have been much more comforting."

"You came to see me? What about?"

"I thought it was time we toddled along with the rest of the *monde* to see Madame Vestris's legs in *Don Giovanni in London*. I gather her pins are well worth a viewing."

She smiled. "So I understand. The newspapers say the rest of the production is superior as well."

"But of course. What do you say then, are you ready for such a *succès de scandale*?"

"Yes, and I think I shall manage without recourse to the sal volatile."

"Excellent. I'm afraid I'm dining with friends tonight, and tomorrow I have to visit my mother, but Monday is quite free."

"Oh. I—I'm afraid I can't manage that day."

Henry looked up from his game. "Can't manage it? Why not? You don't have any engagements do you?"

Telltale color was creeping into her cheeks. "I shall be away that night," she said lamely.

He was surprised. "Away? Why haven't you said anything before? Where are you going?"

Her mind was racing. "Aunt Derwent," she said, plucking inspiration from nowhere.

"You're going to Beaconsfield? When was this arrangement made?"

Oh, this was dreadful. Henry had such penetrating eyes at times. She managed a light laugh. "Henry, is this an interrogation? It so happens that I received a letter from her this morning telling me that she felt it was too long since she'd seen me and hinting that I should put in an appearance there. The thought appealed to me and I dashed off a note straightaway telling her I'd be there sometime the day after tomorrow to stay overnight and then return the next day." She hoped she sounded light and airy.

He was still looking at her. "Why didn't you mention it to me earlier?"

"You were somewhat preoccupied with other matters, as I recall."

"Yes, I suppose I was. Still, it seems a little odd to me that you're going to scramble all the way to Beaconsfield only to stay for one night. Why not stay longer?"

"I believe she's going away herself," she answered, the whole fabrication becoming more and more elaborate as one fib led to another.

"Ah, that explains it, I suppose."

To her relief, he seemed satisfied at last, returning his attention to the green baize.

Charles was preparing to play, but he looked up at her. "Tuesday it is then?"

"I look forward to it."

He glanced at Henry. "Perhaps you and Blanche would come too, we could go on to dinner afterward."

Henry nodded. "That's a capital notion."

As Charles bent over the table again, Jane decided to withdraw. "Well, I think I'll go up and change. I stepped down into a puddle earlier and got my hem quite wet."

"Yes, you toddle off, sis," murmured Henry, his attention apparently firmly on the play.

She made her escape.

Behind her Henry leaned thoughtfully on his cue. "Charles, my old son, she's up to something."

"Eh?" Charles was distracted and played a poor shot, looking up a little crossly. "Up to something? Whyever do you say that?"

"Well, to begin with, Lewis Ardenley was here looking for her earlier. Melville told him she was at Grafton House and he took off after her. I'll warrant he found her, too, but she hasn't mentioned it, has she?"

"Perhaps he didn't find her."

"Ardenley? He did."

"Then perhaps it wasn't worth mentioning. Oh come on, Henry, let's get this wretched game finished."

Henry straightened. "I still say she's up to something. It's written all over her. I think I shall keep an eye on her from now on."

"An eye on the next shot might be more appropriate," said Charles a little drily.

"All right, dear boy, don't get in a pet. It mightn't have anything to do with Lewis."

Charles didn't reply, but he lowered his gaze.

Up in her room, Jane had changed into a dry dress and was by the window watching the rain. Opposite, the roof of Alderman

Wood's porch was quite empty, and the street itself was deserted; it had always been like this, except for a few days' interruption, but somehow it seemed as if those disturbances had gone on and on.

She turned away, pulling her shawl more closely around her shoulders and sitting down at her dressing table, where Ellen had placed the writing implements she'd requested. The maid withdrew then, carefully closing the dressing room door, so that should Henry enter the bedroom itself, he wouldn't catch sight of his sister hurriedly composing a rather complicated explanatory letter to Aunt Derwent.

Having used her aunt's name, Jane now had to make sure that Henry didn't somehow stumble upon the deception and feel obliged to make embarrassing inquiries about what exactly his sister *had* been doing on the night in question. Lady Agatha Derwent was a lady whose inclination in the past to speak her mind in no uncertain terms had earned her the reputation of being eccentric and unpredictible. Widowed after only two years of an arranged match, her beauty had soon won her much attention, and very quickly there had been whispers of a liaison with the Duke of Wellington himself. These whispers had been given substance as far as Jane was concerned when her aunt had virtually insisted that Henry name his newly-acquired stagecoach the Iron Duke. Yes, it was certain that Aunt Derwent had a past, but she'd always been discreet, so no one knew the facts for absolute certain. One thing Jane did know about her, however, and that was that she had a sense of fun and adventure, and that she disapproved of Henry's recent selfish conduct where his coaching was concerned. She must be drafted in on her niece's side, and in order to achieve this, nothing less than a complete explanation would suffice. This meant not fibbing about the visit to Brighton, or the identity of the gentleman concerned, and it also meant taking the risk that her aunt would be so appalled by such indiscretion that she'd rush to tell Henry straightaway. Jane picked up her pen, wondering how to begin. Then she dipped it in the ink and started to write.

It took her an hour to compose the letter satisfactorily, and when it was finished she sat there thoughtfully. She had worked everything out. The day after tomorrow she and Ellen would set off in the traveling carriage, which would be driven by Thomas, the coachman, who happened to be very sweet on Ellen and who could therefore be relied upon to hold his tongue about what really went on. Instead of driving his two passengers out to

Beaconsfield, Thomas would take them to Snow Hill, and then he'd drive out alone to Aunt Derwent's residence, give her the letter, and—hopefully—be allowed to remain there until the day after, when he'd return at an appointed hour to Snow Hill to wait for his mistress and Ellen to return. They'd then drive back to South Audley Street, for all the world as if they'd been to Beaconsfield all along.

She got up and went to the window again. Fair weather was spreading from the west now, and a rainbow arced magnificently against the leaden skies to the east. She thought again about what was to happen the day after tomorrow, and the mixture of feelings of earlier passed through her once more, a blend of apprehension, anger, and secret anticipation. It was against the last that she must be on her guard. She stared at the rainbow. She could only be on her guard if she had the will, and after the kiss in the gardens at Lyndon House, she knew that Lewis Ardenley still had the power to seduce her every sense.

FOURTEEN

*T*he rain had long gone when the time at last arrived on Monday afternoon for Jane and Ellen to set off, ostensibly for Beaconsfield. The weather was bright and clear when at three o'clock the two women emerged from the house to climb into the waiting carriage. From the box, Ellen's young man managed to give her a sly wink, which made her blush very much.

Jane had deliberated for a long time about what to wear, and in the end had chosen a plain, dove-gray pelisse over a white lawn gown, the pelisse being the least conspicuous garment in her wardrobe. There was a blue gauze veil attached to her straw bonnet, although for the moment it was tossed back, since she seldom covered her face and to suddenly do so might rearouse Henry's curiosity about the visit. He hadn't said anything more, but she knew that he was suspicious about something, although he hadn't as yet managed to put his finger on what exactly it was. Her outfit was completed by a blue reticule and gray gloves, and in her reticule she carried the explanatory letter to her aunt.

As the carriage drew away, there was nothing in her manner to suggest that she was setting out on anything other than the stated visit. She smiled and waved to Henry, who stood at an upstairs window; then the carriage turned a corner and she couldn't see him any more. A minute or so later, instead of driving west along the Oxford road toward Beaconsfield, the carriage moved smartly eastward into the city, bound for Snow Hill and the Black Horse. Jane pulled the veil forward over her face, and as she did so it seemed that she drew on the strange blend of apprehension and anticipation which had descended intermittently over her ever since Lewis had first insisted upon this expedition to Brighton, except that now, with the final moment virtually upon her, the feeling was stronger than ever; and more confusingly mixed than before.

The city, always a crowded, congested place, was today worse than ever, its road choked with slow-moving traffic, its pavements thronged with people. Moving at little more than a snail's pace, the carriage entered Snow Hill and passed the entrance of the Saracen's Head, the inn owned by that same Mrs. Mountain who was to be approached to build the new Swan stagecoach for the race. Jane wondered if Jacob had called upon her yet. She also wondered again about the matter of horsing the coach. How on earth was she going to manage it?

As the Black Horse loomed ahead, she put the race temporarily from her mind to concentrate instead upon the business in hand, crossing her fingers that all would go off without incident and that she would return to Town the next day with her reputation and character intact. Thomas maneuvered the carriage into the curb a short distance from the entrance to the inn, and then climbed down to assist the two women out and take their portmanteaux. He would have escorted them right into the inn, but Jane stopped him—a liveried coachman would almost certainly draw everyone's attention, it would be much wiser to carry the little cases in themselves. She gave him the letter for her aunt and repeated her instructions that he was to be waiting in Snow Hill from noon onward the following day. Then she and Ellen took a portmanteau each and made their way along the busy pavement to the inn. Jane's resolve almost deserted her then, and she hesitated before going in. What if she really was discovered going to Brighton with Lewis? But then she thought about the race and the need to defeat Henry at his own game, and with a deep breath she pushed open the door and went inside.

The contrast with the Feathers couldn't have been greater, for all was noise and bustle. The inn was a thriving establishment, filled with travelers, waiters, and serving girls, with no one standing idle. There was only one table free in the coffee room, and Jane and Ellen made their way quickly toward it, for two gentlemen evidently had the same notion and were bearing purposefully down on it. The two women reached it first, sitting down firmly and placing their portmanteaux on the empty chairs to discourage any notion the men may have had of joining them. Taking the hint, the gentlemen moved away again, muttering beneath their breath.

Jane glanced around the busy room, half-expecting to see Lewis at another table, but they were early as yet and there was no sign of him. A waiter came to inquire if they wished to take some coffee and Jane nodded, but as it was placed before her and she automatically made to fling back her veil, she realized that the coffee, delicious as its aroma suggested it was, would have to be foregone. Ellen wasn't subject to any such restriction, however, and sipped hers appreciatively, much to her mistress's secret chagrin.

The drone of conversation and the clinking of cups made a pleasant background noise as Jane gazed out of the window next to the table. It looked out over the courtyard, where two stagecoaches, the Birmingham Thunderbolt and the Lincoln Flyer, were preparing to leave. Got up in Chapman's famous scarlet livery, the black horse emblems prancing proudly on the dazzling panels, they made a handsome sight, their well-groomed teams tossing their heads and stamping restively. Jane found herself watching the door on the opposite side of the courtyard, for she'd noticed earlier that it led to the room provided for the coachmen, who were the elite of the inn's many employees. It was the Nonpareil's whip Sewell she'd noticed, lounging with a number of other men at a large, circular table, his white top hat tipped rakishly back on his head, his lapel again adorned by a fresh nosegay. He was laughing and joking with his friends, but there was something about him which suggested, even from that silent distance, that he considered himself to be their superior.

As the final outsider settled onto his precarious place on the Birmingham Thunderbolt, two of the men in the coachmen's room rose to their feet, simultaneously adjusting their hats and repinning their nosegays before draining their glasses of sherry and emerging into the yard, where an expectant hush had now fallen. An eager young gentleman approached the driver of the Lincoln Flyer, who gave him a condescending nod, at which the young blood hurried keenly to the coach, clambering up to the coveted seat on the box. As the coachman climbed up as well, Jane saw a half guinea change hands. The team waited in readiness. It was a quarter to four precisely, and both coachmen nodded at the stableboys holding the bridles of the leaders. The boys released the horses and at a barely perceptible instruction from the ribbons, the teams strained forward, hooves striking sparks from the cobbles. The guards put their bugles to their lips again, one playing "Cherry Ripe," the other "D'ye ken John Peel," then the outside passengers bent their heads, holding onto their hats as the coaches swept out beneath the low archway into Snow Hill. The bugles could still be heard long after the coaches had gone, leaving behind an oddly quiet yard, where everyone snatched a brief moment of rest before the departure of the Nonpareil itself, the jewel in Edward Chapman's considerable crown.

In the coachmen's room opposite, Sewell was alone now, enjoying a final glass of sherry before setting off. As Jane watched, he was joined by Chapman himself, his gaudily clad figure a startling contrast to the coachman's natty attire. The two spoke quietly together, their heads close, their manner secretive; Jane didn't need to be told what they were talking about, her every instinct told her it was the race.

"A fine pair of honest, upright fellows, eh, Jane?"

Lewis spoke behind her and she turned quickly to see him standing by the table. He wore a brown coat and beige trousers, and his cravat, naked of jeweled pin, was full and unstarched. A cane swung lightly in his hand and he carried his top hat under his arm. His golden hair was a little tousled, giving him an air of nonchalance which on many men would have been careless, but which on him somehow managed to be graceful. He seemed unconcerned about being recognized, which wasn't really surprising since his reputation would not suffer from discovery.

Behind her veil, she remained poised. "Good afternoon, Lewis."

He smiled, evidently faintly amused by the deliberate coolness in her voice. "Good afternoon, Jane. I note that you're in full disguise—are you hiding from the enemy without, or the enemy within?"

The veil concealed the blush which leapt to her cheeks, but

she had the uncomfortable feeling that he could see it anyway. "You talk in riddles, sir, but then that's nothing new, is it?"

"The sharp edge of your tongue would seem to be accompanying us all the way to Brighton. How very tedious." He glanced toward the room opposite again. "How much would you wager upon the topic of that little conversation?" he murmured.

"Betting on certainties is hardly exciting," she replied.

"Maybe not, but if it's excitement you want, you're about to have it in plenty." Again the faint smile. "Don't look so alarmed. I'm only referring to the journey not my personal intentions."

At that moment, the Nonpareil itself was brought through from the yard at the rear of the inn. It was a splendid sight, its panels somehow more gleaming and scarlet than those of the other coaches, its team not a hotchpotch of colors but splendidly matched skewbalds, their harness polished until it glittered in the afternoon sunlight. The black and gold lettering on its doors stood out almost challengingly: *Nonpareil. London and Brighton. Reigate. Handcross. E. Chapman & Co. License No. 3561.*

As it halted by the ticket office and the passengers' luggage was immediately carried out, Lewis beckoned to a waiter and told him to take the two portmanteaux out, his own being already in the yard. The guard climbed up to his place at the back of the coach, his bugle at the ready, and as the final two portmanteaux were placed in the boot and the lid closed, he raised the instrument to his lips and gave the usual warning note to summon the passengers.

Jane rose slowly to her feet, her nerve faltering again. She was quite mad to be yielding to this. . . .

Lewis saw her hesitation and interpreted it correctly. He took her gloved hand and drew it firmly through his arm. "It's too late now," he murmured, putting on his top hat. "Besides, just think of the mirth if your activities so far should get out."

"I find you quite odious," she replied, removing her hand and gathering her skirts to stalk out ahead of him into the yard, where the outside passengers had now taken their places and only the insiders had to climb on board. The hands of the clock on the wall of the inn pointed to almost four o'clock.

Lewis assisted Jane and Ellen into the coach, and they took their places, Ellen sitting next to the only other inside passenger, a large, extremely portly squire whose girth took up not only his own seat but some of the maid's as well.

Jane hardly noticed the other passenger as she sat nervously on the crimson-and-beige striped seat, looking at the coffee room window where a minute before she had been sitting. There was someone else at the table now.

The hands of the clock moved to four. The guard put his bugle to his lips again, waiting just long enough for Sewell to take his place on the box. Then the coach moved forward, the team straining as they pushed into their collars. Jane was holding her breath. For a brief, dreadful moment she found herself staring out directly at Chapman, who stood hands in pockets in the yard, watching his pride and joy departing. He seemed to be looking directly at her, and she felt as if he could see right through her veil, but he gave no sign of recognition, and then the coach was sweeping out into Snow Hill, the bugle trilling proudly to the notes of "Cherry Ripe."

Jane managed to make herself sit back on the seat, conquering the overwhelming desire to sit bolt upright. She glanced at the squire, who was settling himself comfortably, ignoring the fact that he was doing so at the expense of poor Ellen, who was pressing into her corner as much as possible to keep away from him.

Jane's nose wrinkled disapprovingly, for he reeked of the curry and wine he'd consumed in the inn's dining room, and he showed every sign of going to sleep, which would inevitably mean they would be subjected to his snoring. She glanced at the carved ivory timetable on the wall above his head. Four o'clock, Black Horse, Snow Hill. Nine o'clock, Black Horse Ticket office, Castle Square, Brighton. Five hours to go. The squire's head was nodding already. A first snore rattled jarringly out. She gritted her teeth, praying that he wasn't going all the way to Brighton.

Sewell was a master of the ribbons, moving the coach swiftly along without having to greatly check its speed in order to negotiate corners. The dazzling coach, bugle blaring with "Cherry Ripe," sped through the city toward London Bridge, threading its way through the maze of traffic as if possessed of some magic which kept the horses at a smart trot, while everything else on the road was in difficulties.

They crossed the Thames, where the sun flashed on the water of the pool of London, and a forest of masts swayed on the swelling afternoon tide. The towers of Southwark cathedral rose splendidly to the right as the coach gained the southern shore, entering a high street which before the improvements to the bridge and its approaches had been a place of gabled medieval houses and galleried, half-timbered inns, but which was now a broad, modern thoroughfare.

Jane glanced at the timetable again. It was fifty-five miles to Brighton, twelve to the end of the first stage at the Cock Inn, Sutton. After that there were stops at Reigate, Crawley, Handcross, and Bolney, before the final run into Brighton itself. She sighed as the squire's snores intensified, shuddering through the coach like the roars of a disgruntled lion. Public transport wasn't at all agreeable, she'd found *that* out already.

They passed Marshalsea prison and then the brown brick facade of St. George's church, overlooking the junction of five busy roads, where London traffic seemed to flow endlessly to and fro. They passed through the St. George tollgate and then drove on to an even busier crossroads at the Elephant & Castle, where they stopped briefly to take on another outsider. After that, they began to leave the older part of the capital behind. The road was now lined with houses built only five years before, after the battle of Waterloo, and behind them there were market gardens and the suggestion of open fields.

The city began to fade away to the rear as they drove on south, passing over the wide openness of Kennington Common and again halting briefly, this time at the turnpike in Kennington village. Then the Nonpareil drove on, coming up to a fine pace as it traversed Streatham Hill and then branched to the right for Mitcham. There were fields of crops and flowers on either side of the road now, and they had nearly covered the first half of the first stage. Men paused in their work in the fields to wave their hats as the famous coach passed. The guard gave them "Cherry Ripe," telling them that the finest coach on the Brighton road was on its way, and on time to the very second.

The roadside was laced with cow parsley and blue flax, and the fields looked almost drowsy beneath the warm summer sun. It was all so peaceful that Jane couldn't help glancing at Lewis. "Where's your excitement, sir?"

He didn't have time to reply, for at that moment the Nonpareil suddenly leapt forward as Sewell got a rival coach in his sights and prepared to overtake it with as much dash as possible. Jane's breath caught on a gasp as she saw the other coach, its startled passengers staring as the Nonpareil swept by dangerously closely. She was vaguely aware of Jacob's patient explanation of coaching slang. *Squeezing is when a rival coach forces a dangerous situation by passing too close, making the other coachman make mistakes. Feather-edging is when that's taken still further, usually by forcing a coach against a bridge parapet or a bollard.* There was a bridge ahead now, and the road suddenly became much narrower! She stared as the other coachman overreacted, just as the laughing Sewell intended he should, grabbing at his ribbons and bringing his already unsettled team's heads up far too sharply. Jane heard the outsiders on both coaches crying out in alarm as disaster stared them in the faces. The two coaches were racing neck-and-neck for the bridge, and it was a battle of nerves then, to see which coachman would give in and halt his coach, except that the other men seemed frozen with fright and incapable of making any sort of sensible decision.

Jane's heart was suddenly cold as she stared, but then, at what seemed like the eleventh hour, the other coachman reined in with all his might. His coach slipped away behind and out of sight as the Nonpareil swept triumphantly over the bridge and on toward Sutton.

Ellen sat rigidly in her seat, her eyes round and frightened. Jane twisted around to look back at the other coach, which had now come to a standstill on the far side of the bridge, its wheels perilously close to a deep ditch, its team capering and tossing as the miserable coachman still fought for absolute control.

Jane sat back then, her heart thundering in her breast. Opposite, the squire slept on, oblivious to everything.

Lewis glanced at Jane's pale profile and smiled. "What was that you were saying about excitement?" he murmured.

FIFTEEN

*J*ane had scarcely recovered her composure after this when a second incident occurred, this time at the expense of the Nonpareil.

The lavender and herb market gardens of Mitcham were two miles behind them when the road entered a dell where lilies-of-the-valley bloomed sweetly in the shade. Sewell was taking the stagecoach along at a spanking pace, mindful of having lost a minute at Mitcham because a small flock of sheep had blocked the way. There were high, leafy banks on either side of the road, completely concealing a muddy track joining it from the right. Without any warning whatsoever, a cumbersome ox-wagon emerged from this lane, pulling directly into the stagecoach's path and coming to an abrupt halt right across the highway. The outsiders gasped with renewed alarm as Sewell immediately checked the team, gathering them to a miraculously sharp halt within inches of the wagon.

Inside, all was confusion for a moment, with Ellen squealing as she was jerked roughly back in her seat. Jane was flung forward, and had it not been for the firmness of Lewis's grip as he held her, she would have fallen to the floor. The squire was shaken a little, but although he awoke long enough to glance around, he soon closed his eyes again and went back to sleep as if nothing had happened.

The moment the ox-wagon had halted in front of the stage-coach, the carter had leapt down from it, running swiftly away through the trees, which soon folded over him completely, as if he had never been. Sewell shouted furiously after him, and the outsiders, severely shaken, climbed down for a moment to recover. The guard went to lead the ox-wagon off the road, and within a minute or two the Nonpareil was on its way again, the team being urged up to a very smart pace indeed to clip back yet more lost time.

Still trembling, Jane stared out at the passing trees, thinking about the carter's flight. The wagon's sudden appearance hadn't been an accident, it had been planned; and the incident was a sharp reminder to her that Chapman too had his rivals, the chief among them being her own brother. . . . Oh, please, no, don't let Henry be behind such a low, despicable, and dangerous act.

Lewis glanced at her. "Are you all right now?"

"Yes. Lewis, that wagon. . . ."

"It wasn't an accident."

"No."

"And you're wondering if Henry had a hand in it?"

She looked at him. "Could he?"

He shrugged. "It's possible."

"But do you think he'd stoop to something like that?"

"If I'm honest with you, Jane, I have to say that I really don't know. I wouldn't have thought him idiotic enough to be goaded into the madness of this race, but he has been."

She said nothing more, looking out as the coach emerged from the trees into open countryside again.

Shortly afterward, they reached the Cock Inn, Sutton, the end of the first stage. As the team was changed, a serving girl brought out a tray of sherry for the passengers, and the glasses were taken gladly, for everyone was still a little unsettled. It was with some satisfaction that Jane watched the squire slumbering on, missing the sherry.

Her hand was shaking a little as she held her veil aside to sip her glass, and Lewis couldn't help noticing. "I trust that what's happened so far is enough to change your mind about the race."

"My mind is still made up."

"We've only covered one stage," he warned.

"When we reach Brighton my answer will still be the same. It would serve both my brother and Mr. Chapman right if they were beaten by a mile in that race, for neither of them deserves to win."

"You'll find it hard to even stay with them without the right cattle," he reminded her.

She met his gaze boldly. "Maywood has such horses." It was a spur of the moment remark, one she'd had no intention of uttering.

"Yes, and they're staying there. I'm here to dissuade you entirely from this lunacy, not to aid and abet you."

She wished she'd never said anything.

With the horses changed, the guard gave his customary blast on his key bugle and the Nonpareil set off once more, heading toward the rolling chalk beauty of the North Downs, which now lay directly ahead. The squire's snores rattled on, checking only for a brief moment when he sprawled a little too much on his seat and his legs encountered those of Lewis, who kicked them sharply aside. With a start, the squire awoke, looking angrily at his assailant, but refraining from a forthright complaint when he saw the cold, angry glint in Lewis's gray eyes. Muttering under his breath, but saying nothing aloud, the squire drew himself in to his proper part of the coach and closed his eyes.

Within moments, his snores were jarring upon them all again. Lewis leaned across to prod him, but Jane restrained him. "Perhaps his snores are preferable to his conversation."

Lewis gave a wry smile at that. "Perhaps you're right," he murmured, sitting back again, "but if his disagreeable conduct continues, I shall put him in his place."

The Nonpareil climbed up onto Banstead Downs, where skylarks tumbled in the clear blue sky. Grazing sheep scattered in alarm as the guard gave the empty countryside another rendering of "Cherry Ripe," and the hens pecking in the dust outside the remote Tangier Inn fluttered wildly in all directions as the stagecoach swept magnificently past.

From the village of Banstead, where the cottage gardens were sweet with purple thyme, Jane gazed across to the right and the high point of Tumble Beacon, where a warning had been lit centuries earlier to tell London that the Spanish Armada was in the Channel. Recalling Lewis's obvious assumption that the upsets suffered on the journey to Brighton would be more than sufficient to extinguish her frail female spirit, she amused herself for a while imagining a modern-day beacon being lit there, this time to warn Henry, Earl of Felbridge, and Mr. Edward Chapman that their supremacy on the famous road was about to be impudently challenged—by a feeble woman!

They reached the top of Reigate Hill, with its magnificent views over the clay weald that formed the middle portion of the journey. Leaving the North Downs behind, the coach made the steep descent to the small town of Reigate itself, where the team was to be changed again. The town was a place of timber-framed houses and had a picturesque town hall with arches and a splendid clock which indicated that it was six o'clock precisely as the Nonpareil drew up at the White Hart. They were exactly on time.

Leaving Reigate behind, a fresh team harnessed, they set off on the third stage a few minutes later. The weald countryside was very different from that of the chalk downs, with daisies and buttercups scattered in the grass, pale pink dog-roses arching out of the hedgerows, and a lacy fringe of cow parsley fluttering in the verges as the stagecoach passed. Jane gazed out at the fields. White daisies and yellow buttercups shining amid a sea of fresh green grass. White, yellow, and green—Blanche Xanthe Lyndon. She couldn't help thinking of the ball, when Henry's conduct had finally reached the point when something would have to be done. And so here she was, doing something, and getting herself into all manner of embarrassment and difficulty because of it!

They completed the third stage without event, arriving on time at the George Inn, Crawley. They were to halt here for a little longer than at previous stops, to allow the passengers time for some refreshment. The squire, who seemed woefully likely to be with them all the way to Brighton, stirred as if by magic as the guard called out the George's name. Flicking open his fob watch with thick, stubby fingers, he sniffed, stretched, and then alighted, taking himself into the inn to partake of a hearty helping of bread, cheese, and pickle, washed down by several mugs of strong ale. He didn't speak to any of the other passengers, and his ill-mannered attitude toward all and sundry was such that had Lewis been present, Jane had no doubt the squire would have been brought up very sharply indeed. But Lewis was outside in the yard, leaning against the gallery steps smoking a leisurely cigar.

Jane and Ellen sat at a window seat drinking the inn's indifferent tea. Lewis was in plain view and Jane tried not to keep glancing toward him, but she couldn't help herself. Why did she have to love him so? Fate was most unkind, making her so wretchedly susceptible to a man who'd betrayed her and who'd consistently lied about his infidelities. She gazed at him, taking in the gold of his hair, the clear gray of his eyes, and the grace of his elegant, manly figure. Would she ever be able to pull free of the spell he could so effortlessly cast over her?

Shortly afterward, they set off in the fourth stage, and soon the squire was snoring again. Jane glared at him and sighed, which made Lewis grin. "Look upon it as part of the rich pageant of public transport," he said.

"I prefer to look upon it as something disagreeable which has been forced on me because of your interference in my affairs," she retorted coldly, still angry with herself for her thoughts at the George. Damn him for having such an effect upon her!

"So, the sharp edge of your tongue had decided to rejoin us, has it?"

"I'm merely pointing out that I wouldn't have had to endure this wretchedness at all were it not for your arrogant intrusion. What I do has nothing to do with you any more, and I resent your meddling."

"Come now," he answered in an infuriatingly reasonable tone, "it isn't because of *me* that we're here, it's because *you* are a stubborn, strong-willed minx who refuses to be sensible when it comes to things like stagecoach races."

"I'm at liberty to be as stubborn and strong-willed as I please, sir." She met his gaze. "You made your decision six months ago, and I'd be grateful now if you remembered that."

"I didn't make the choice six months ago, Jane, you did," he reminded her.

She looked deliberately away, terminating the short conversation.

The Nonpareil drove on for some time and the land ahead began to rise, covered with the green cloak of Peasepottage Forest. Jane suddenly began to feel unaccountably nervous. The nervousness grew stronger as the coach passed through the forest and emerged into open countryside again. She glanced at Lewis and saw that he too seemed disturbed about something. He caught her eye and knew how she was feeling. "It's the pace

Sewell's taking," he said. "We're on good, straight, open road, but he's moving at barely above a walk, indeed he's been going just a little too slow since we entered the forest."

Opposite them the squire was still asleep, and even Ellen's head was beginning to loll against the seat. Jane's hands twisted uneasily in her lap. Something was about to happen, she could feel it. She craned her neck to see ahead as the road began to sweep around a long curve. There were two stagecoaches in front of the Nonpareil, the nearest one in a green livery she didn't recognize, the leading one in Chapman's distinctive scarlet. She touched Lewis's arm. "Look in front," she murmured.

He lowered the glass and leaned out, then he sat back again. "The green one is the Venturer, and it's been doing rather well recently, no doubt incurring friend Chapman's wrath," he explained in a lowered tone so as not to disturb Ellen, who was now soundly asleep. "The leader is Chapman's, but a lesser coach, probably the Century or the Lion. Sewell's waiting for a third coach, another of Chapman's, that's why he's biding his time."

"A third coach? Why?"

"I think they're going to box the Venturer in. We're only a couple of miles from Handcross, where I'll warrant the Venturer usually picks up some regular fares. Chapman's going to start boxing him in so that the Nonpareil can slip past and pick up the fares instead." He glanced out of the other window, for the road was curving in the other direction now. There was a crossroads ahead, and through a copse of trees he saw the glint of sunlight on harness. He nodded toward it. "There, behind those trees. The third coach. It's going to slip out behind the Venturer, boxing it tightly in behind the leading coach. Then you watch Sewell go. Hold on now." He put a firm hand on hers, his fingers warm and safe.

She held her breath as they drove closer and closer to the crossroads. She saw the waiting stagecoach spring into action, sweeping quickly up to the junction and onto the Brighton road immediately behind the Venturer, just as Lewis had predicted it would. She heard the angry shouts of the Venturer's trapped coachman, but then the Nonpareil seemed to leap forward as Sewell urged the team from a walk to a swift canter. Ellen's eyes flew open as the coach began to sway and jolt, and Jane instinctively gripped Lewis's hand, her heart thundering as the Nonpareil dashed past the other three. She saw the two grinning faces of Chapman's coachmen, and the furious, gesticulating figure of the helpless man on the Venturer's box. Soon all three were left behind, moving at a snail's pace toward Handcross, while the Nonpareil flew on its way, sure of reaching the Red Lion and the Venturer's passengers well ahead.

It was just as Lewis had said, for as the Nonpareil swept into the Red Lion's yard, Jane heard George Sewell shouting to the landlord that the Venturer had met with a slight mishap and would be greatly delayed. He offered two outside places to the two gentlemen who came out anxiously on hearing the news, and they gladly accepted. The coach swayed as they climbed up on top. Jane lowered her eyes. This was what was happening to her Swan. Edward Chapman was getting away with so very much, but if she had her way and luck smiled upon her regarding the horses as well as everything else, he wouldn't be winning that race on Midsummer Day!

Lewis touched her arm, pointing up toward one of the inn's bedroom windows. A man with a sallow face was looking down into the yard, holding the curtain aside so that he couldn't be seen very well. "I think that's Byers, the informer. He probably put the Venturer's fares Chapman's way."

She stared up at the window, but the informer had already drawn back out of sight. She wished she'd seen him, for his appeared to be one of the most infamous names on the Brighton road.

With another fresh team harnessed, the Nonpareil set off once more. It was seven o'clock and in two more hours they would be in Brighton. The road was new now, having been built only ten years earlier to replace the old route which led through Cuckfield and then over the long, wearying, dangerous climb of Clayton Hill. The new route had once been a much lesser highway, threading through hamlets and past farms, and making a circuitous detour around the perimeter of Lewis's estate at Maywood because one of his ancestors had approached King Charles II for permission to build a great house in this lovely part of the countryside.

Jane leaned her head back against the coach's soft upholstery watching for the first glimpse of Maywood. At last she saw the stone phoenixes on the gateposts, and then the armorial wrought-iron gates themselves, and beside them the elegant little north lodge. Hanging over the lodge, its bronzed leaves bright in the afternoon sun, was an immense copper beech tree. There were horses in the paddocks, horses which would do so well for the Swan; but they'd be staying where they were and she'd have to think of something else for the race. Dappled leafy shadows moved on entrance to the driveway, which swept on beyond the gates, leading up a long incline to the magnificent house. It was a Jacobean masterpiece with no fewer than sixty-three windows gazing out over its beautiful park and mirror-like lakes. There was a prospect tower on a nearby hill, from which on a clear day six counties could be seen, and in which, one cold, snowy afternoon the previous winter, Lewis had asked her to marry him. It had been a frozen November day, the air crisp and sharp, and the snow had seemed to stretch away into icy oblivion on all sides. Her cheeks had been pink with the cold, and she'd worn a fur-trimmed pelisse, her hands plunged warmly into a large muff. She gazed at the tower as the Nonpareil swept past the lodge. In little more than a month the betrothal had been over.

If Lewis was remembering that day in the tower, he gave no sign of it. He remained silent as the coach swept past the estate, taking more than ten minutes to reach the great copper beech marking the place by the south lodge where the drive emerged onto the highway again. Maywood's drive had been the original highway, before the petition to the king which had forced the public road to make a circuitous detour around the estate. The rise of fashionable Brighton and the need for a better route for the swift new stagecoaches had brought the old road to prominence again, but still it had to sweep around Maywood, which barred its way as surely as a great rock bars the smooth flow of a river.

Bolney, where the team was changed for the final time, was on the southern slope of a ridge close to a windy common, and it was renowned in the spring for its cherry orchards. Then it was a sea of pink and white blossom, but now the trees were in full foliage, waiting for the fruitfulness of autumn. With fresh horses harnessed, Sewell took the Nonpareil on its way once more, carefully negotiating a very sharp bend by an ancient stone barn, and then bringing the coach up to a good pace for the climb over the chalky South Downs, which alone now lay between the travelers and their destination.

Unlike the North Downs, those in the south were treeless, bare and hump-backed, a place of tufty grass and scattered gorse. Silver-blue butterflies fluttered in the thyme-scented air, where the tang of the sea was already perceptible. Cloud shadows flitted over the open slopes, and the white wings of gulls flashed brilliantly against the clear evening sky.

At last the final hill was behind them and they could see Brighton stretching elegantly along the shore of the azure sea. Jane gazed ahead at the clean, white villas spreading out from the edge of the town. She glanced quickly at Lewis from beneath lowered lashes. What was going to happen during the coming hours? Would she surrender to the emotions which only this man could arouse within her?

SIXTEEN

*I*t was as much the thing to be seen on the fashionable pavements of Brighton as it was to be noticed driving in Hyde Park, and as the Nonpareil drove through the elegant streets on its way to the terminus in Castle Square, Jane noticed a number of ladies and gentlemen strolling along, seeing and being seen. Among them were several faces she recognized, and she nervously adjusted her veil, praying that it was as concealing as she hoped.

Castle Square was very noisy and crowded, for it was here that most of the stagecoaches arrived and departed each day, indeed it was such a busy and colorful place that many people came there just to watch the spectacle. There were at least five stagecoaches drawn up outside their individual ticket offices as with a final flourish of "Cherry Ripe" the Nonpareil was brought to a dashing standstill outside the Black Horse office. Two gentlemen standing there took out their fob watches to check the time—it was nine o'clock precisely and the most famous crack coach on the Brighton road had accomplished its fifty-five mile journey from the capital without losing a single minute on its timetable. No one seeing it now could possibly guess the truth about that eventful journey.

As Lewis turned his attention to the business of tipping and then recovering their luggage from the boot of the Nonpareil, Jane glanced around the square at the various ticket offices. There were so many, from the Spread Eagle office, Capp's and Snow's, to the Red and Blue offices and the Fleece, which belonged to her brother and outside which stood the splendid bright green Iron Duke, on the point of departure on its evening up run. It was a handsome vehicle, its panels shining like mirrors and its team of bays so perfectly matched and groomed that they were worthy of royalty. The liveried servant Jacob Wheddle had told her of was standing by the coach, a bottle of sherry and a silver box of sandwiches on an elegantly held little tray. The coachman, as sprucely attired as Sewell, was looking across at the Nonpareil with undisguised loathing, reminding her quite sharply of the race and her reason for being there. That steady gaze reminded her as well of the incident just before Sutton when the ox-wagon had so nearly caused a terrible accident. Had that been Henry's work? She looked away from the Iron Duke, hoping with all her heart that her brother hadn't had anything to do with it.

Lewis had recovered the luggage and was beckoning to his private carriage, which by previous arrangement was waiting to convey them across the town to the White Lion inn.

She looked around the square again, searching for one ticket office in particular, that associated with the Feathers and the Swan stagecoach. She saw it at last, its doors and shutters closed because the only up coach of the day had long since departed and there wouldn't be any more business until the down coach the following morning. How sad and neglected it looked when compared with the others, and with the Nonpareil's and the Iron Duke's in particular. Her veil lifted in the light breeze as she looked at the other two again. What she'd witnessed on the road today had been proof enough to her that Henry wasn't alone in needing to be taught a lesson, Chapman had more than joined him. She was going to do her utmost to deal them both a salutary blow on Midsummer Day, and nothing Lewis Ardenley said in the meantime was going to change her mind.

Sitting in his private carriage a few minutes later driving toward the White Lion inn, she reflected that her only experience of public conveyances had been exceedingly unpleasant and she was relieved to think that tomorrow's return journey would be in this luxurious vehicle and not the Nonpareil.

They entered the Steyne, the wide, fashionable thoroughfare where the king's famous pavilion was built and where the race would finish outside the Castle inn. On such a quiet summer evening the Steyne was peaceful, with only a few elegant couples strolling, but on Midsummer Day it would be crowded with people, all anxious to see which stagecoach crossed the finishing line first.

She looked across at the king's magnificent pavilion, which was almost complete now, having been altered from its original Italianate style to one which was oriental, being Indian on the outside and Chinese on the inside. With its shining domes and cupolas, it was rather like a set of ornate pepper pots, but she didn't find it as ridiculous or eccentric as some. On the contrary, she found it exciting and alluring and was in complete agreement with the king, who adored it.

Leaving the more fashionable streets behind, the carriage drove toward narrow Bedford Lane, passing on the way the burned-down warehouse of which Henry had spoken, and for the fighting of which terrible conflagration he had claimed such false credit.

The White Lion was a low building, built some hundred years before when Brighton had still been a fishing village. White-washed, with windows which peeped out almost sleepily from beneath overhanging eaves, it seemed to hug its position as if afraid that at any moment the more fashionable part of the town might come to brush it aside. The carriage halted at the door and Jane looked approvingly at the flowers in the windows and the new paintwork of the inn, deciding that although the White Lion wasn't the most fashionable inn she'd seen since arriving in Brighton, it was certainly the most welcoming. She turned her head as a soft sighing sound carried to her ears. It was the sea, the waves of the incoming tide lapping gently against the unseen beach nearby.

As the coachman took the carriage around to the stables at the rear of the inn, Lewis ushered the two women inside, and the landlord came hurrying immediately to attend them. He was a small, bustling man, his apron as crisp and clean as Jacob Wheddle's, his manner all that was pleasing and agreeable. Jane felt uncomfortable when Lewis gave their names as Mr. and Miss Havers, and she was glad she could hide behind her veil, for she was sure her embarrassment was written large upon her face.

The hall was as neat and well-kept as the outside of the building, with red tiles on the floor and chintz on the furniture and at the windows. The clock on the wall above the fireplace pointed to just gone half past nine, and the inn, in spite of being in an unfashionable part of the town, was doing a brisk trade. The tap room was very crowded, but it was evident that most of the custom came from local people, for the dining room opposite was almost deserted, indicating that very few guests were actually staying. Even though she knew it was highly unlikely that she'd know anyone at such an establishment, she was nevertheless highly relieved when a swift inspection of the faces presented to her revealed no one with whom she was even remotely acquainted.

Assuring them that dinner would be served the moment they came down to the dining room, the landlord called to a boy to carry their luggage up to the rooms which had been reserved for them on the first floor. Ellen went with the landlord to her own room, which was near that already occupied by Lewis's coachman, somewhere close to the kitchens and other similar offices. Jane and Lewis followed the boy up the staircase.

Lewis drew her hand through his arm. "It may not be Grillion's or the Clarendon," he murmured, "but it will suit our purposes, I fancy."

"Since the purposes are entirely yours, sir, you must be the sole judge of whether it suits or not."

"That's very true," he agreed, halting outside her door while the boy placed her portmanteau inside and then hurried away, "so perhaps you should be a little on your guard, Lady Jane, for I might have any number of dastardly plans in store for you tonight."

"Plan away, sir," she replied with forced lightness, "for it will avail you nothing." Then she went into the room and gladly closed the door behind her, leaning back against it for a moment, her eyes closed. It was madness to be here like this; utter madness. . . .

She looked around the room then. It was plainly but comfortably furnished, and was dominated by an immense carved-oak four-poster bed in the center. Hung with dark green velvet and piled with several thick mattresses, it was so high that in order to climb into it one had to use a small flight of wooden steps, and once inside, with those heavy curtains drawn, it would be like being in a huge cocoon. The rest of the room was less impressive, with a small dressing table and chair, and a wardrobe in the alcove next to the chimney breast. The grate had been freshly blackened and even though it was summer, there was a plentiful supply of good coal in the bucket next to the highly polished fire irons. On the dressing table there was a fine porcelain jug and bowl, together with some hand towels and a face cloth, and there was even a cake of Windsor soap. The scent of crushed lavender hung in the air from the little bags in the drawers and wardrobe, and a posy of newly picked herbs swung to and fro in the light breeze coming in through the open window. She went to the window, looking out over the stables at the rear of inn toward the sea, which was only about a hundred yards away. She could see the beach, with its rows of huts on wheels for bathing, and the shelf of shingle leading down to the smooth expanse of sand, which was being covered more and more with each incoming wave as the tide crept slowly in. The sun had almost gone now, staining the western sky with a glory of crimson and red which shimmered on the water like liquid jewels, and the calls of seagulls echoed around the surrounding rooftops.

Ellen came up to assist her in dressing for dinner. Jane had deliberated for a long time about what to wear, for she could hardly sit down to dine in the same gown she'd worn all day, but at the same time she couldn't appear at the White Lion in something too Mayfair and fashionable. It was a problem she'd solved in the end by opting for a lilac muslin gown which she usually wore with her amethyst necklace but which was itself plain and unadorned, and which she knew traveled well, even after being crushed into a fairly small portmanteau. Ellen piled her hair up into a knot at the back of her head, leaving a single curl to fall to the nape of her neck, and added the only item of jewelry Jane had allowed herself, a little crystal-studded comb which sparkled very prettily in the glow of the sunset pouring in through the window. Draping her shawl over her arms and picking up her reticule, Jane was ready to go down. Trepidation seized her again then and she looked anxiously at the maid. "How do I look?"

"Very well indeed, my lady."

"I don't know if I can trust myself, Ellen. He still sets me at sixes and sevens." But she took a deep breath and went out, closing the door quietly behind her.

Ellen lowered her eyes sadly. Lady Jane Derwent was one of the loveliest women in society, but she was also one of the most unhappy, and all because of her hopeless love for Lord Ardenley.

The long, low dining room was completely deserted as Jane went in. She waited, listening to the muffled sounds from the tap room opposite, sounds which suddenly became loud as the dining room door was opened and then closed once more. It was Lewis. He came toward her, and raised her hand to his lips. "Good evening again, Jane."

"Good evening." Oh, how she wished her hand wasn't trembling so, for surely he must feel it.

He didn't seem to notice anything. "I've taken the liberty of already ordering, and trust that you approve of my choice. It was either mutton, which I'm told is the finest in England because the flocks hereabout graze on pasture impregnated with salt from the sea, or lobster, caught fresh this very afternoon. I chose the lobster, since I seem to recall that it's a favorite of yours.''

"It is indeed.''

"Excellent, then at least we shall not fall out over the menu. Shall we sit down?'' He indicated a table where a waiter stood patiently with a bottle of wine.

As Lewis drew out her chair for her, he glanced at the bottle. "I trust that that is the Portuguese?''

"Yes sir, the very last bottle.'' The man quickly poured a little into a glass.

Lewis took his seat and sampled the wine, nodding appreciatively. "The last bottle, you say? What a pity, it's quite excellent.''

The lobster proved to be excellent as well, and was served with new potatoes and a crisp, fresh salad. They'd finished the course before Lewis mentioned the reason for their being there. He sat back for a moment, his wine glass swirling in his hand as if it was a brandy glass. "How very agreeable this is, Jane. I'm almost tempted to be pleased you've been hatching such wildly improbable schemes of late.''

"Yes, the *food's* agreeable,'' she replied.

"A deliberate qualification? The food's good but the company isn't? That's hardly polite, Jane.''

"Should I be polite, Lewis? I fail to see why, when you've forced all this upon me.''

"Since when did lobster have to be forced on you?''

"That's not what I mean, and you know it.''

"Perhaps I do.'' He swirled the glass again and then put it down. "On the way here today you told me that you wouldn't change your mind about the race. Is that still so?''

"Yes.''

"In spite of everything you saw today?''

"I told you, what I saw today has only made me more determined than ever.''

"And this determination still includes the ultimate idiocy of sitting beside Huggett on the day?''

"Yes.''

"You'll be putting your life at risk.''

"I think not.''

"Be sensible, Jane, the fellow's forgotten what it's like to look at the world without a protective haze of alcohol.''

"He hasn't touched the bottle since the thing was put to him."

"He promised you, I suppose." There was more than a hint of irony in his tone.

Her violet eyes flashed. "Yes, he did."

"I can't believe that you actually accept his word, Jane. Since when has a drunkard's promise been his bond?"

"He's promised because he wants the opportunity to be avenged on Chapman for the death of his wife. That's a very strong reason, Lewis, strong enough for me to believe in him."

He looked at her for a moment. "Well, all I can say is that you've placed far more faith in him than I ever would."

"No one's asking you to."

A faint smile touched his lips. "That's very true," he murmured.

She held his gaze for a moment and then sipped her wine.

Lewis watched her. "I understand Mrs. Mountain of the Saracen's Head is to build a new Swan for you."

She put down her glass. "I suppose you're about to tell me she's incapable of building a brewer's dray, let alone a race coach."

"On the contrary, I was about to remark that you couldn't have chosen better."

"You mean, I've actually managed to do something right?"

"Right? I suppose so, if anything can be right in this whole silly business."

"Ah, that's more like you, Lewis—build me up with a compliment and then dash me down with a sly backhander."

"I had no idea you saw me in such a brutish light."

"I see you in a great many disagreeable lights, sir."

"All of them quite wrong."

"So you keep insisting."

"Can't you put away your imagined grievances for once, Jane?"

"No, because they aren't imagined."

"I'm flattered that it still matters so much to you."

"You delude yourself, sir, if you imagine that I care two figs about you anymore. You can bed Alicia morning, noon, and night, every day of the week for all that it matters to me."

He feigned amazement. "Good God, what do you take me for? Morning, noon, *and* night seven days a week? Virile I may be, but not *that* virile!"

She flushed. "I haven't given your virility much of a thought recently, Lewis," she replied, attempting to end the conversation with a crushing retort.

There was a lazy mockery in his gray eyes. "No?" he inquired softly.

"No."

"Well, that being the case, you will no doubt feel perfectly safe when we take a romantic stroll along the beach after dining."

"I don't wish to stroll anywhere with you."

"Come now, admit that you'd *adore* a little toddle along the sand."

"Maybe I would, but you don't figure very prominently on my list of suitable partners."

"Who would then? Charles Moncarm?"

"He's much more agreeable than you are."

"Does this herald a change of heart? Are you reconsidering his proposal?"

"If I am, it's none of your business."

"No, it isn't," he agreed, "but the truth is that I was merely sympathizing."

"With me?"

"Good heavens, no. With Charles."

"If I don't ask why, you'll no doubt tell me anyway."

"Naturally. I was thinking that he'll be in a very sorry position—he'll have a wife he adores, but every time he kisses her she'll be thinking of someone else."

There was silence. She looked at him. "Meaning, I suppose," she said in a voice which quivered with anger, "that *you'd* be that someone else?"

"Yes."

"What effrontery," she breathed furiously, tossing her napkin onto the table and rising to her feet. "How *dare* you presume to speak to me like this!"

"Effrontery? My dear Jane, I rather thought it was honesty."

"I've eaten enough, sir. You may finish alone." She gathered her skirts and hurried out. She heard his chair scrape as he followed her. He caught up with her at the foot of the staircase, turning her sharply back to face him. "Aren't you forgetting our stroll on the beach?" he asked coolly.

"I'd as soon walk with the devil himself!"

Her slightly raised voice attracted the attention of two gentlemen waiting to be attended to by the landlord. Lewis glanced at them and then back at Jane. "I'm quite prepared to make a scene, if that's the way you wish it, but it would be much more agreeable if you simply gave in like a good girl and came along with me."

"I would prefer not to," she replied stiffly.

"But I'm insisting," he said, taking her cold hand and drawing it through his arm. "There, that wasn't too difficult, was it?"

She said nothing more, but unwillingly allowed him to usher her out into the dark warmth of the summer night, where stars glittered like diamonds against the deep indigo of the sky.

SEVENTEEN

A man selling Sussex gingerbread had a stall by some steps leading down to the beach. He would usually have gone home by this time, but the night was so fine that a number of people were still out, and it was therefore worth his while to stay just a little longer.

Not a word had passed between Lewis and Jane since they'd left the White Lion, indeed her manner was so stiff and angry that it didn't encourage conversation of any kind. It wasn't only her anger with him which made her so quiet, it was her unease at being out without the protection of a veil. There were so many people about, and at any moment they might come face to face with someone they knew.

She was so intent upon inspecting each approaching figure, that she hardly glanced at the gingerbread stall, but Lewis halted very deliberately by it, looking closely at the array of sticky shapes displayed so carefully on a clean white cloth. Gingerbread was a local delicacy and was made in a variety of traditional patterns, from cats, grandfather clocks, and birds, to the royal arms and figures on horseback, the Duke of Wellington being a particular favorite.

Lewis picked up one of the latter, glancing at Jane with feigned hesitation. "The Iron Duke, eh?" he murmured. "Well, perhaps under the circumstances that's not entirely appropriate. Maybe this is more fitting." He replaced the gingerbread and picked up another piece, this time a bird, a swan. He gave the man a coin and then presented the gingerbread to Jane. "You rushed off from your dinner without a dessert, my lady, so please accept this instead."

Giving him a dark look, she reluctantly accepted the offered piece.

He raised an eyebrow. "Do you always do things with such bad grace?"

"Only when they're forced upon me," she replied, glancing toward a small boy who had been watching everything with longing eyes. She smiled at him and held out the gingerbread. "Here, I'm sure you'll enjoy it far more than I would."

The boy came hesitantly forward, his eyes warily on Lewis. Then he almost snatched the gingerbread and ran away down the steps and across the beach, scattering the shingle with his bare feet.

Wiping her sticky fingers on her handkerchief, Jane then proceeded down the steps as well, lifting her muslin skirts above her ankles as she picked her way between the row of bathing huts, which stood to silent attention gazing out to sea. Further along the beach there were fishing boats, drawn safely above high water level, their rigging absolutely still in the quiet air. The smell of salt was very strong and fresh even though the lack of breeze meant that the waves only whispered against the shore, lapping almost timidly as if anxious not to disturb the peace of Brighton. The town glittered with lights, and from time to time Jane caught drifts of music from the Castle inn on the Steyne, but apart from that the night was quiet.

Still anxious to avoid encountering someone she knew, she walked away from the lights, making her way toward a deserted part of the beach. She was very aware of Lewis as he caught her up at last and firmly took her hand, drawing it through his arm. They were on sand now, hard, smooth sand only recently deserted by the tide.

He halted at last. "I think we've walked far enough, don't you?"

"I didn't want to walk in the first place," she reminded him.

"Can't we set aside our personal differences for a moment? I want to talk about your venture into coaching."

"What is there to talk about? You hoped that by making me travel on the Nonpareil you'd change my mind. It hasn't worked."

"Please reconsider."

She looked at him in surprise. "Was that actually a polite request?"

"It was an earnest one. What you intend to do is dangerous and ill-advised, and will cause a great deal of unwelcome and unnecessary talk."

"I endured unwelcome talk before, Lewis, when you chose to make a fool of me with Alicia. I survived that; no doubt I'll survive this as well."

This exasperated him. "Don't be so damned tedious, Jane. This is far too important. Can't you see that the only way to achieve anything worthwhile is to actually win the race? And to be perfectly honest with you, I don't think the Swan stands a cat in hell's chance."

She met his gaze. "I'm going to win," she said quietly.

"You haven't even got suitable cattle," he replied.

"I'll find them."

"Thirty bang-up horses in so short a time?"

"Yes." But this was said with more bravado than real conviction. The horses were the real problem, and she was no nearer solving it now than she had been at the outset. Her mind was a blank, for if she approached any of her aristocratic friends, then the story would soon filter back to Henry.

"So, you'll find them and you'll win the race." He gave a satirical laugh. "Well, I admire your spirit, Jane, but *spirit* isn't going to slip that race into your pocket. Didn't the journey today teach you anything?"

"Yes, it taught me that men who resort to such foul and odious methods should not be allowed to get away scot free. They think they've got it all sewn up, don't they? Between them, they've frightened all the other coaches out of the race, so that it's just a battle of giants. Well, they *haven't* got it all to themselves, as I'm going to prove. What I witnessed today was absolutely appalling, and although I know that Chapman was behind most of it, I cannot be absolutely certain that Henry didn't arrange that incident with the ox-wagon. If he did, I shall never forgive him for stooping to such despicable depths; if he didn't, I shall be very glad, but I still will not forgive him for behaving as he has done toward Blanche. He's been very shabby, Lewis, and he has to realize what's he's become. I must turn the tables on him somehow; it's the only way to make any impression. He'll lose her if he doesn't change, and without Blanche, he'll be desperately unhappy. He's taking her for granted, and he can't afford to do that, not with the Duke of Dursley paying her such clever attention. She's unhappy and vulnerable. I love my brother, and I don't want to see him heartbroken. His coaches aren't worth it. He has to grow up." She paused to draw a deep breath, surprised at herself for such a long outburst.

He looked at her for a long moment. "So, your plan goes ahead?"

"Yes. Are you going to split on me?"

"I should do, for your own sake."

"Yes, but will you?"

For a long moment he didn't reply; then he ran his fingers through his hair, giving a slightly incredulous laugh. "No, I won't split on you."

It was the answer she wanted, but it still took her slightly aback. "You—you won't?"

He shook his head. "No, Jane, your secret's safe with me," he said softly. "In fact, I'll even go so far as to offer you my assistance."

She stared at him. "Assistance? What do you mean?"

"You'll be astonished to learn that your eloquent little speech has made an ally of me, Jane. I'll help you all I can to win the race. Your motives are admirable and I ask you to forgive me for ever having treated them lightly."

She was still staring. "I must indeed have been eloquent."

"You always were, when something really mattered to you. Very well, I shall grant you your wish, I'll horse the coach for you. I'll provide the bang-up cattle—something slap, as the coaching parlance goes."

She was absolutely nonplussed, taken completely off-guard by his dramatic turnabout; indeed, her astonishment was so great that she couldn't believe he meant it. "Lewis, if this is your notion of a jest. . . ."

"No jest, Jane. I mean it. Maywood's stables are at the Swan's disposal. Mind you, this is not to say that I approve of your intention to be on the coach on the day, for I most certainly do not and I'll do all I can to dissuade you between now and Midsummer Day. Sitting on that box in front of the whole of society will do your reputation no good at all, as even you must eventually see. Surely it's enough that Henry should know you're behind it? Does he really have to *see* you as well?"

"Yes."

"You're a stubborn woman, Jane Derwent."

She searched his face in the darkness. "You—you *do* mean it about the horses, don't you?"

"Don't you trust my word?"

She lowered her eyes then. "Since you are a gentleman, sir, then I must accept that your word is your bond."

"It is indeed, as it was six months ago when I told you that I was innocent of deceiving you with another."

She drew back slightly. "Please don't say any more, Lewis."

"But I must. If you can accept my word where the horses are concerned, why can't you accept it about what happened six months ago?"

"I'd rather not discuss it," she said stiffly.

"Well, I'm afraid that I intend to discuss it, since there will not be many occasions when I have you alone. I didn't do anything wrong six months ago, Jane. I neither betrayed you nor cast a roving eye in anyone else's direction."

The bitter anger and resentment welled up uncontrollably inside her then, and she could no longer stay silent. "Stop it, Lewis! Don't say anything more, because I cannot bear your lies!"

He caught her wrist, his fingers like a vice and his gray eyes like flint in the darkness. "I'm not lying," he breathed.

"Yes you are!" she cried, trying to wrench herself free. "Alicia herself came to tell me all about your unfaithfulness!"

He was very still, not releasing her as he looked intently into her angry eyes. "She came to see you? When?"

"The day before I gave you back your ring."

Slowly, he released her. "And what did she say?"

"That all the rumors were true and she *was* your mistress, and that you only proposed to me in order to please your father on his death bed."

He continued to look at her for a moment, then gave a brief, cold laugh. "And you *actually* believed her?"

"Yes."

"Didn't it occur to you that she had a vested interest in lying about it? Dammit, she *wanted* to be my mistress!"

"If she was lying, sir, why have you both since gone out of your way to prove the very opposite? She *is* your mistress now, isn't she?"

"What she is now and what she was then are two entirely different things."

"I'm afraid that I find that impossible to believe."

"Why?"

"Lewis . . ." she began.

"No, dammit, I want an answer. Why is it impossible to believe?" She didn't reply.

He put his fingers to her chin, forcing her to look at him. "What a fool you are, Jane Derwent—a prideful creature without the wit to see beyond the end of your pretty little nose. You've been gulled, and not by me. As for Alicia gracing my bed, well to be perfectly honest with you, I failed to see why your childish outburst should force the life of a monk on me!''

''How dare you!'' She was so angry that she raised her hand to strike him, but he caught her wrist.

''I'm not in the mood to tolerate more of your ridiculous pride, Jane, so don't even attempt to demonstrate your endless capacity for throwing tantrums!''

''*Tantrums?*'' she cried furiously, trying to wrench her hand away. ''If that's what you call my refusal to believe your lies . . . !''

''I haven't lied to you—you've been lying to yourself. Your pride is the villain in all this, and if you want things to ever be again what they once were, then you're going to have to set that pride aside once and for all!'' His eyes were cold and glitterbright as he looked down at her. ''You want me back, don't you? Oh yes, I know that you do. I can feel it whenever I'm near you.''

''I'd rather die than take you back!'' she breathed, still trying to pull free.

''You can't fool me, Jane, I know you too well!''

''Not that well, sirrah!''

He gave a cool smile. ''Oh yes I do,'' he said softly, ''well enough to be certain that I can read your every thought. Admit you've been wrong all along, Jane, admit it on your knees if necessary, and I might, just might, forgive you.''

''You arrogant, insufferable . . . !''

''Is the prize worth winning?'' he interrupted. ''Don't you remember how good things were between us? Well *I* remember, but I'm damned if I'm going to make it easy for you to put yourself in the right again. It's going to be uphill from now on, Jane, and I'll make you struggle every inch of the way. And in case you should still be vain enough to pretend that you don't want me, perhaps this will go some way toward convincing you.''

Twisting her close, his grip on her wrist as vicelike as steel, he forced her against him. A small cry of pain escaped her before his lips were over hers, bearing down with such a force that it almost stopped her breath. She could feel the hardness of his body through the soft muslin of her gown. His heart was beating close to hers. The kiss offered her no quarter; it was brutal and demanding, sending a dizzying, bewildering weakness flooding through her veins. She wanted to surrender, to succumb to him right there on the dark, secluded beach, but a harsh sanity called to her from beyond the bonds of passion and desire which coiled so irresistibly around her. Reaching into the depths of her being for the strength to withstand the almost overwhelming temptation, she at last managed to wrench herself free.

"No!" she cried, her heart thundering in her breast and a bright flush staining her hot cheeks.

He gave a thin smile, not attempting to touch her again. "You'll come to me, Jane," he said softly, "and you'll do so on *my* terms."

"Never!"

"You've got too much passion in your soul, Jane Derwent, and it's a passion which only I've aroused. Charles Moncarm could never stir your blood as I do, and you know it. I can reach into that soul at any time and rouse that passion, but I'm not going to any more. I'm not even going to try to meet you halfway. You're going to be treated with all the cool distance you've been claiming you want, and I don't think you're going to find it at all to your liking."

"It will be very much to my liking, sir!" she replied coldly, but inside her pulse was still racing with treacherous excitement. She was confused and upset, and striving with all her might to hide the fact from him. He spoke of allowing her back on his terms, but he hadn't once mentioned loving her. Did he really think his skill as a lover would convince her to accept his lies? But, oh, how she wanted to accept them, how she wanted to reach out to him. . . . Her heart was close to betraying her, and she turned abruptly away toward the sea, where the waves broke gently against the sandy shore.

"Behave as you wish from now on, madam, for as I've said, I don't intend to offer any assistance to your monstrously misguided pride." He spoke in an almost detached way, toying with his cuff and glancing back toward the town, where the lights shimmered against the looming shadow of the downs beyond. "However, in one way I shall indeed still offer my assistance, and that is in connection with horsing the Swan. As I said earlier, I respect your reasons for going ahead with the race and I stand by what I said. Maywood's horses are at the Swan's disposal."

"Thank you." She said the words so quietly that they were barely audible.

"Saying that evidently pinched your pride to the quick."

She turned back to face him then. "I said thank you, and I meant it."

"Good. Then we both know where we stand, don't we?" he replied, his voice still cool and detached. "Now then, I'm going back to the inn, so unless you wish to remain here on your own, I suggest you accompany me." Without waiting for her to reply, he turned and walked away.

She stared after him. A breath of night wind stole in from the sea, touching her hot skin and making her shiver. Drawing her shawl a little closer, she followed him across the beach.

As they had left the inn earlier, so they returned, without a word passing between them. His manner was distant and chill; he was like a stranger. At the inn's entrance, he seemed to change his mind about going in. "Good night, madam, I trust you sleep well." With a slight bow he left her, walking away toward the town. She saw the flare of a lucifer and the curl of smoke from a cigar; then he turned a corner and was gone.

She stood where she was for a long moment. Quite suddenly, the thought of the return to London in his private carriage was too much to contemplate. How could she sit there with him for all those hours now that this had happened?

Taking a deep breath, she went into the inn, ringing for the landlord, who came hurrying into the hall straightaway. "Yes, Miss Havers?"

"I will require a post chaise first thing in the morning, to convey me back to London."

"But I was under the impression that you and Mr. Havers were returning together."

"There has been a change of plan. I'm now returning early."

"Very well, Miss Havers. At what time did you wish to leave?"

"Six o'clock."

"I will see that a chaise is ready at that time. I'll send a man around to the posting house straightaway."

Jane informed Ellen of the change of plan, but didn't explain her reasons—she couldn't bring herself to discuss what had been said on the beach, not yet anyway. She climbed the little flight of steps into the vast bed and the maid drew the heavy curtains around her. Ellen withdrew then, extinguishing all the candles and closing the door softly behind her.

Jane lay in the velvet darkness. She couldn't forgive Lewis for the past, she just couldn't. She still believed he'd been unfaithful. Tears stung her eyes and she hid her face in the pillow, her shoulders shaking as she wept.

EIGHTEEN

*I*t was very late indeed when Lewis returned to the inn. Jane lay awake in her bed, her eyes dry at last. She heard his steps on the stairs and sat up, holding the curtain aside to watch the wavering candlelight beneath her door. He walked past and into his room; then there was silence again.

He was still asleep the next morning when she and Ellen left in the post chaise, which arrived promptly at six. It was a handsome enough vehicle which had until recently been a private carriage, and it was well sprung and comfortably upholstered. Its team of mixed bays and chestnuts moved along at a smart pace, urged on by the yellow-jacketed postboy riding one of the leaders. Jane gazed at the passing scenery. She felt unsure of herself. Half of her wanted to turn back, to rush to Lewis and tell him how much she really loved him; the other half, that proud side of her, bade her drive on. She lowered her eyes. It was to that second half that she must pay heed, because it was that half which gave her the strength and which reminded her of his betrayal; but it was so very hard when the memory of the kiss burned on her lips with a fire which warmed her still, as if a flame flickered deep within. She gave no order to turn back and the chaise drove on toward London, but she found herself confiding the whole story to the sympathetic maid.

Maywood looked very lovely in the early morning sunlight. The lakes lay like sheets of glass among the trees, and the sun flashed on the windows of the house, as if trying to attract her attention. She gazed at it as the chaise drove around the great loop in the road, and then her glance was drawn to the meadows to the east of the house, where several horses had just been released and were galloping with pure joy. She thought about Lewis's insistence that he'd still horse the Swan. Would he really, especially after she'd fled from Brighton like this? It was a matter of conjecture now.

The return journey was uneventful. At Handcross, she remembered the informer Byers and wondered if any of Chapman's other rivals would suffer today as the Venturer had yesterday. Two miles further on, she saw the spot where the Venturer had been so dangerously boxed in, and then the chaise was descending through Peasepottage Forest to Crawley. After Reigate, the road climbed steeply up to the North Downs, where the song of the larks tumbled sweetly through the warm air, and then they were in Sutton, where the day before the passengers of the Nonpareil had been so glad for a glass of sherry after the horror of the ox-wagon's sudden appearance. As the chaise drove through the dell shortly afterward, Jane wondered again if her brother had had anything to do with it. She would have to find out somehow; she couldn't rest until she knew.

Soon London stretched before them, its church spires rising toward a sharply blue June sky. It was a beautiful day, the sort of day when spirits should be light, but Jane only felt low, and so very tired that the last thing she felt like was a visit to the theater, which was what she'd agreed to that night.

On London Bridge, she saw the Swan. She didn't know what made her look out of the opposite window at that very moment, but something did, and she saw it pass, the only down Swan of the day, with Arthur Huggett at the ribbons. She lowered the glass then, leaning out to watch it. Will sat at his father's side on the box, and she distinctly heard Arthur's rather throaty laugh as he expertly tooled the old coach past a lumbering dray. The guard put his bugle to his lips and the notes of "D'ye ken John Peel?" rang out over the river and the rooftops of Southwark. A strange thrill passed through her and she sat back again. On Midsummer Day her Swan was going to come into Brighton first; she was absolutely resolved that it would!

At the Black Horse, they had rather a long wait before Thomas was due to arrive with the traveling carriage. As she and Ellen sat in the coffee room, Jane wondered what her aunt's reaction had been on reading her letter. Maybe it was all up already and a shocked Henry had been informed of his sister's underhanded and unladylike activities. Even as this awful possibility crossed her mind, it was pushed aside by a more immediate disquiet, for Chapman came into the crowded coffee room, pausing close to their table and looking around, evidently searching for someone. Suddenly he was looking directly at her. Her heart almost stopped. Could he see through the veil? He continued to look at her for a moment, but then, he left again, and a surge of relief rushed through her. If he'd recognized her, he'd have done his utmost to embarrass Henry with the story, seeing to it that the world knew that the Earl of Felbridge's sister had been seen traveling incognito at the Black Horse! A titillating scandal could have been made of just that, but how much more of a stir could be provoked if he'd found out any more? The chaise she'd traveled in was still in the yard, and the postboy could identify her as the Miss Havers who'd been staying the night at the White Lion in Brighton with her "brother"! Jane closed her eyes, feeling almost faint at the thought of the ripples which would pass through society if such a story got out.

To her relief, Thomas was very prompt and they didn't have to wait much more. He handed her a letter from her aunt, and then they were driving away, back toward Mayfair. Jane hurriedly broke the seal on the letter, her trepidation soon vanishing as she read of her aunt's thorough approval. She smiled. Henry wouldn't find anything out from Aunt Derwent, that much was certain, for that lady indicated that she thought he deserved to be taken to task for his odious conduct. Indeed, the general tenor of the letter was that Lady Agatha Derwent thought her niece's actions so spirited and splendid that her only regret was being so far away from the area of excitement and intrigue. Jane folded the letter, silently agreeing with her aunt's sentiments, for it would have been very good indeed to have had such a kindred spirit close at hand.

On arriving at South Audley Street, she wasn't displeased to find that Henry was out at luncheon with Lord Sefton. She needed time to rest after so much traveling and so little sleep, to say nothing of the strain of her latest dealings with Lewis. She had to relax if she was to manage any sparkle at all at the theater. She sighed, for she wasn't in the mood for *Don Giovanni in London*, or for Madame Vestris's famous legs.

Before taking a long bath, she dashed off a quick note to Jacob, telling him about Lewis's promise to horse the Swan, but not holding out too much hope that the promise would be honored. After the bath, she lay on her bed. What was Lewis doing now? What had he thought when he'd risen and found her gone? A wry smile touched her lips, for no doubt he'd put it down to yet more childishness on her part.

She sighed, remembering all that had passed between them on the beach the night before. He'd been so right about her, and he *did* know her too well to be fooled by what she said. She thought about the way he'd kissed her, and the memory stirred through her again. He was indeed the only man ever to have aroused her passion like that. She closed her eyes, for it was a passion she must learn to quench and she'd be a fool indeed to give herself into his hands again. But she'd find it easier to cope from now on, for if he carried out his threat to be distant with her, then surely she'd learn how to deal with her treacherous heart? She wished that he'd never chosen her as the bride required to please his dying father. The best thing would have been for him to have persuaded the Duke of Brantingham to grant his unfaithful wife her freedom so that she could marry her lover.

She was composed and refreshed when Henry returned, and was taking tea in the garden, seated on a cane chair close to the roses which were in such magnificent bloom this summer.

He sat down on the grass close to her, plucking a blade to place between his teeth before lounging back to survey her. "I trust Aunt Derwent was in fine fettle?"

"As ever."

"And your visit went off well?"

Did he know something? She met his gaze. "Yes."

"I'm relieved to hear it, since such a short stay hardly merited the effort involved."

She relaxed, for she sensed that he didn't know what she'd really been doing. She hesitated then, for she wanted to broach the matter of the ox-wagon and the Nonpareil. "How—how is the Iron Duke going along?" she inquired lightly.

He looked slightly incredulous. "Good God, I do believe you're actually showing an interest!"

"It merely occurred to me that the race is less than two weeks away now."

"I'm staggered that such an unusual thought should cross your mind. It so happens that the Duke's going on very well indeed, clocking up a very handsome time on today's trial run."

"Trial run?"

"With the new coach."

"Oh."

"I'm on to Chapman's tricks. He's been waiting for me on all my scheduled runs, so I confound the fellow by toddling off any old time in the new coach. He can't be watching all the time and have his cronies waiting on every corner."

"Nor can you."

"No, but then there's nothing I need to watch yet, since he hasn't got his new coach. Besides, I know Sewell's driving like the back of my hand; I know every command he gives on every corner."

"You sound a little too confident, Henry."

"Overconfident?"

"Yes."

He grinned. "Sewell's a master, but predictible. If I'm confident, it's because he's made me so."

"I wonder if you dare be so sure."

"Sis, the day Sewell does something different, I will personally climb up the dome of St. Paul's and fling myself off."

"Yes, well they do say that pride comes before a fall," she remarked a little drily.

He picked another blade of grass, twirling it between his fingers. "I know what I'm talking about where Sewell's concerned."

"But if Mr. Chapman is so very devious—"

"He's a damned corkscrew, incapable of doing anything honest."

"What of you, Henry? How much of a corkscrew have you become?"

"Oh, I'm a positive angel," he replied, grinning again and flicking the grass onto her skirt.

"I find that hard to believe," she answered, sipping her tea and watching him closely.

"Well, perhaps I do resort to the odd trick" he admitted then.

"Oh?"

He looked curiously at her then. "Why are you so interested all of a sudden? The last I knew, you couldn't stand my coaching at any price. Now you're all agreeability and questions."

"I thought you wanted me to be interested."

He shrugged at the perverseness of women. "Yes, I suppose that's true."

"So, what odd tricks do you get up to?" she asked lightly.

"As a matter of fact, I've started using informers."

"Like Mr. Byers?" she said without thinking.

He gave another incredulous laugh. "How on earth do *you* know about Byers?"

"You must have mentioned him," she replied quickly, sitting forward to pour herself another cup of tea. "Would you like some?"

"Tea? No, thank you. I'm in the mood for something stronger."

"In the middle of the afternoon? That's hardly the thing."

"I know, dammit."

"You were telling me about your informers. What do they do?"

"The usual things, sneaking on license breaking, fixing passengers, and so on. Nothing horrendous, I promise you. I don't use foul tactics on the king's highway—unlike Chapman, whose latest efforts have paid off handsomely."

"In what way?"

"He's rid himself of another rival, the Venturer."

She was very still then. "What happened?"

"Two of his coaches boxed it in near Handcross yesterday, and caused an overturn. It was the last straw for Davey Williams, the Venturer's proprietor. He's caved in without any more resistance—just thrown in the towel and let Chapman win."

"Would you do something like that?"

"Like what? Throw in the towel?"

"No, box a rival in, or maybe put an obstacle in the road to slow it down."

He stared at her with more than a little hurt indignation. "What do you take me for? I wouldn't resort to such tactics, and I'm put out that you should even think it."

She could barely hide her relief, for his injured expression was obviously quite genuine. He hadn't had anything to do with the ox-wagon the previous day, and she was suddenly ashamed of ever wondering if he had.

"Well, you might look contrite," he said then, "for whatever else you might have thought of me recently, I'm mortified to think you believe I'd sink so low."

"I'm sorry."

"So you should be." He lay back on the grass, his hands behind his head as he gazed up at the cloudless sky. "To go back to Davey Williams's capitulation," he said thoughtfully, "I must admit that it took me by surprise. I thought he had more in him than that. Even Jacob Wheddle's put up more of a fight."

"Jacob Wheddle?" She was all innocence as she sipped her tea.

"The proprietor of the Swan. I'm sure I've mentioned him to you before. Maybe I haven't."

"I think you did."

"I didn't think he'd still be on the road after all this time—he must be losing money hand over fist. And then this morning I saw the down Swan, with none other than Arthur Huggett at the ribbons. A very strange thing."

"Strange?" She hoped she sounded only mildly interested.

"Huggett's a drunkard, and has been since his wife died, but there he was, with his son up beside him, tooling the Swan along just like his old self." Henry took a deep breath, shaking his head admiringly. "The man's a genius, a delight to watch, and seeing him again like that made me realize what a loss he was. He'd leave Sewell standing any day."

"Really?"

"Without a doubt."

"Would he leave you standing as well?"

He grinned. "That's another matter. He certainly wouldn't if he only had that crate of a Swan to drive, that's for sure." A frown creased his forehead then. "That's what's so very strange. Why the Swan? If he's dry again, he could have the choice of any coach, but he picks the Swan, which is on its last legs in more ways than one. It's very curious, and I confess I'm more than a little intrigued."

"Perhaps he's just friendly with Mr. Wheddle," she said, not wanting him to find the thing too intriguing.

"Maybe. Maybe not. I've got a feeling there's more to it than that. I think I'll send someone along to the Feathers to have a little nose around. There's something going on there, I know there is."

It was more than time to change the subject. "How's Blanche?" she asked.

"Eh? Oh, well enough, I suppose."

"You only suppose? Don't you know?"

"I haven't seen her since the day before yesterday."

"Henry, are you neglecting her again?" she demanded.

"No, it's just that something came up, that's all."

"Something coaching, no doubt," she said drily.

"It so happens that it was, but I'm *not* neglecting her. She's joining us at the theater tonight, remember?" He studied her for a long moment. "You should accept Charles, you know."

"We've been through all that."

"So we have. What was it now? Ah yes, Lewis Ardenley and grand passion."

She flushed a little. "I won't marry Charles because I don't love him, that's all." She got up. "I must go in. I have to see Ellen about what I shall wear tonight."

"The conversation is making you uncomfortable, is it?" he called after her as she hurried away across the grass.

NINETEEN

Charles had already arrived and the carriage was waiting at the door when Jane went down. She wore an ice-blue silk gown with petal sleeves and seed-pearl trimming. Her earrings and necklace flashed with diamonds, and her hair had been dressed up into her favorite knot, the long curls tumbling from it twined with narrow blue velvet ribbons and scattered with tiny artificial flowers. Her long fringed shawl dragged on the floor behind her, and a painted fan dangled from her white-gloved wrist; she looked very well, and knew it.

Charles, splended in black velvet, smiled admiringly at her as he drew her hand to his lips. "I shall not be able to tear my gaze from you to look at the stage tonight," he murmured.

She returned the smile. "For Madame Vestris's legs, you'll somehow make the supreme effort."

Henry swirled the glass of cognac he was enjoying before setting off. "For Vestris's legs, the entire male audience will strain to watch the stage."

Jane eyed him. "You, sir, would be better advised paying attention to Blanche, and only Blanche."

He groaned. "You've already made your point, Jane. You don't have to start on me again."

"But that's just it, Henry. It seems to me that the point has to be made over and over again, *ad yawnum*."

Charles nodded in agreement, allying himself with Jane. "It does indeed, and it becomes exceeding tiresome."

Henry finished the cognac and put the glass down, giving them both a disgruntled look. "A pox on the pair of you, and before you have notions of continuing with this unfair attack, I think it's time we left." He ushered them out before him.

They went first to Berkeley Square for Blanche, and then on to Drury Lane, the carriage making a very elegant sight amid the crush of traffic still thronging the London streets. A chance remark by Charles about the merits of a racehorse he fancied soon had the two men engrossed in conversation, and it was left to Jane to quickly perceive that all was not well with Blanche, who looked particularly lovely in a dusty pink satin gown trimmed with blond bobbin lace. Her hair was concealed beneath a turban adorned with feathers, and she had a feather boa which trembled constantly as the carriage drove along. She was trying very hard to appear lighthearted, but Jane could tell that it was a facade. There wasn't an opportunity to ask her what was wrong until they'd actually reached the theater.

The Theater Royal was a new building, its predecessor having met with the fate of so many London theaters by burning to the ground. The replacement was considered by most to be a dull and uninspiring place from the outside, but the general concensus of opinion was that the interior was magnificent. From the vestibule, where many people had gathered prior to taking their places, a splendid double staircase ascended to the domed Corinthian rotunda above, and it was on this staircase that Jane at last managed to draw Blanche aside for a moment.

"Blanche, is something wrong?"

"Wrong? No, of course not."

Jane touched the other's arm. "You're fibbing. Please tell me. Perhaps I can help."

Blanche hesitated then. "It's my father. He's been subjecting me to an almost continuous barrage of criticisms where Henry's concerned. He keeps on and on about how I'm being neglected and insisting that I'd be so much happier and more cherished if I accepted the Duke of Dursley. It's dreadful, Jane, especially when Henry is so guilty and the duke is indeed all gallantry and charm."

"Are you beginning to succumb to that gallantry and charm?" Jane asked gently.

Blanche began to shake her head but then looked sadly at Jane. "No, it's just that I wish with all my heart that it was *Henry* who was wooing me like that. I've missed him these past few days, and I was so looking forward to tonight, but what happens? He and Charles have talked incessantly about a wretched racehorse, and Henry's said barely a word to me. I *do* feel neglected, Jane, and I'm beginning to wonder if I've made a mistake by accepting him. I love him very much, but he makes me very unhappy." Gathering her pink skirts, she hurried on up to the rotunda, her boa fluttering behind her.

Jane slowly followed. Then, seeing that Charles had been delayed talking to some acquaintances and wouldn't be going directly to the box, she hurried on, anxious to speak to Henry and warn him how things were with Blanche. She caught up with him just before he followed Blanche into the box. "Henry," she whispered urgently, catching his arm and halting him, "if you don't stop talking about horses and start paying proper attention to Blanche, you're going to regret it very much indeed."

He looked a little crossly at her. "Oh, lord, Jane, don't start *that* all over again!"

"I'm not starting anything, you idiot! Look at her, can't you *see* how miserable she is? For heaven's sake, stop being so thoughtless and look after her properly." Her hand remained on his arm and her violet eyes implored him. "You're losing her, Henry, and I don't think you've any notion how precarious your position is becoming. You've been neglecting her too much, and unless you do something about it, it's going to end unhappily for you."

He stared at her and then looked into the box, where Blanche sat alone, her eyes downcast and her fan resting quietly on her lap. He said nothing more to Jane but went quickly in, sitting next to Blanche and taking her hand to kiss its little palm. He smiled into her eyes, exerting his considerable charm, but although she returned the smile, Jane could almost feel her hesitation. It would take more than a few smiles and kisses to repair the damage he'd had so foolishly allowed to be done.

Anxious to allow them as much time on their own as possible, Jane waited outside for Charles. A few minutes later, with still no sign of him, she wished with all her heart that she'd gone into the box after all, for she saw Lewis and Alicia coming toward her on their way to his box nearby.

Lewis looked superb in formal black velvet, his lace-trimmed shirt adding a dash of fashionable elegance to an otherwise almost austere appearance. With his golden hair and handsome looks, there was that air of grace and refinement about him, and that hint of sensuality which always turned female heads. Jane had never been more aware of the confusion of her emotions than in those brief moments as the two approached her.

Alicia was breathtakingly beautiful in white watered silk, her gown's neckline plunging shockingly low over her creamy bosom. Her tawny hair was twisted up beneath a golden velvet beret from which sprang tall white plumes, and there were diamonds at her throat and in her ears. A suggestion of rouge colored her cheeks and lips, and her eyes had a sparkle which made her more lovely than ever. She perceived Jane immediately, and glanced quickly at Lewis, whose manner hadn't altered in the slightest on seeing his former fiancée. Alicia hesitated and then snapped open her fan, saying nothing at all to Jane as they walked past.

Lewis didn't speak either, although he gave a brief, polite inclination of his head. They passed by, entering his box a little further along the passageway, and as the door closed behind them, Jane was sure she heard Alicia's tinkling laughter. Embarrassed color had already rushed to her cheeks at being so publicly snubbed, for a number of people had witnessed the incident. She felt suddenly as if the story of the trip to Brighton was common knowledge, that Alicia had been regaled with it and hadn't wasted any time spreading it over Town. It was a horrid feeling, making her feel dreadfully conspicuous, and she was glad beyond belief to at last see Charles hurrying toward her.

She returned his smile and tried to appear composed and at ease, but as they entered the box, she was very affected indeed by the chill in Lewis's manner. As she took her seat, she could suddenly hear his voice again. *I can reach into that soul at any time and arouse that passion, but I'm not going to any more, I'm not even going to try to meet you halfway. You're going to be treated with all the cool distance you've been claiming you want, and I don't think you're going to find it at all to your liking.*

The auditorium of the Theater Royal was said to be the finest in London, having been modeled on the celebrated Grand Theater of Bordeaux. Illuminated by chandeliers, its horseshoe shape was richly decorated and boasted a particularly impressive array of tiered private boxes, most of them occupied tonight as society came out to enjoy a production which was set to remain the rage for the rest of the season. Voices murmured and jewels flashed, while down in the pit the fops and dandies displayed themselves, lounging on their seats and making a great thing of opening their snuffboxes or rattling their canes to draw attention to themselves and thus to the splendor, or ridiculousness, of their attire.

In the last few minutes before the performance began, Jane tried hard to resist the temptation to look toward Lewis's box, but in the end she gave in, glancing around in a manner as surreptitious as possible. They were seated together, Alicia's white-gloved hand resting on his arm, her head tilted toward him as she whispered something. There was a lazy humor in his gray eyes as he smiled and for a second his hand touched hers. Jane looked sharply away, opening her fan and wafting it busily to and fro before her suddenly hot face. It was something to do, something to occupy her and fend off the tears which that shared intimacy brought so close to the surface.

Don Giovanni in London commenced at last, and in spite of her secret distress, Jane soon saw why it had taken the capital by storm, for it played havoc with Mozart's opera. Don Giovanni himself, or rather herself, was such a wicked libertine that he was too much even for hell and so was dispatched to that most dissolute of cities, London, where the love of a good woman at last saved him. Madame Vestris was splendid, displaying her celebrated legs in her equally celebrated tight breeches, and singing the songs very sweetly indeed in her mellow contralto voice. She was only twenty-three years old and very beautiful, and had previously captured London by playing only very suitable, proper roles; Don Giovanni was decidedly *un*suitable and *im*proper, and taking such a part had been a considerable risk, but it had paid off very handsomely indeed and her success was sealed. The performance, to say nothing of the shapely legs, drew rapturous applause, especially from the pit, where there was much stamping of approval and shouting for encores.

With the intermission a babble of conversation broke out, and under the guise of dropping her reticule and bending to retrieve it, Jane managed to steal another glance at Lewis's box. To her utter horror, she found herself staring directly into Alicia's triumphant eyes. Lewis didn't turn at all; it was as if he was unaware of her presence. Jane looked quickly away again, her cheeks flaming with embarrassment and anger at having been caught so obviously looking. Taking a deep breath to steady herself, she did her best to join in the others' conversation about the performance. Determined to ignore the other box, she entered into the discussion as attentively as possible, and she soon forgot Alicia's gloating glance as she noticed that Blanche's mood was still rather withdrawn and quiet.

Henry was paying her every attention now, striving to put right the wrong he had allowed to happen, but he too realized that all was far from well. A little perplexed at how to go about regaining all his lost ground, he was doing his utmost to charm and amuse her, but then something happened which was to shatter his good intentions and bring about the very thing he had at last come to fear—the ending of his betrothal.

It began when the intermission was almost over. There was a tapping at the door and a head of dark brown hyacinthine curls peered around it. It was the Duke of Dursley, his soft brown eyes at once apologetic and crafty. Advancing into the box, looking very dandy in a black satin coat and tight pantaloons, he flicked open his jeweled snuffbox and took a pinch before sweeping them a very elaborate bow. "Greetings, *schöne leute*, I trust I'm not interrupting anything too private."

Henry's face had darkened the moment the head had appeared around the door, and now he gave a grunt of annoyance, scowling at the newcomer in a way which was anything but polite or encouraging.

Jane looked quickly at Blanche, whose cheeks had gone a little pink and whose eyes were swiftly lowered.

While Henry remained deliberately seated, Charles had no option but to rise courteously to his feet. "Good evening, Dursley. I trust you've been enjoying the performance?"

The snuffbox closed with a sharp click and the duke smiled. "Couldn't find a seat, dear boy, all taken." He glanced deliberately at the empty place on Blanche's far side.

Charles cleared his throat uncomfortably, but there really wasn't any way he could avoid issuing the required invitation, since the box was his and as the host it was incumbent upon him to do the polite thing. "Do join us then," he murmured, studiously avoiding Henry's furious face.

The duke's smile became positively sleek, and his hand described another elaborate pattern in the air as he bowed again. "Bourton, dear fellow, you're a trump, an absolute trump." Without looking at Henry, he took the seat, immediately leaning closer to Blanche and taking her hand, drawing it to his lips, at the last moment turning it palm uppermost.

Jane watched him. There was something very suspicious about his sudden arrival, something which smacked of conspiracy. Intuition told her that this was Mr. Lyndon's doing, that he'd told the duke where Blanche would be and had advised him that she was almost ripe for the plucking.

On Blanche's other side, Henry was so furious he seemed in imminent danger of exploding, but somehow he managed to contain himself. His eyes were very bright and angry and his fist was clenched as if he'd dearly like to punch the smile from his rival's sly face.

Charles sat down again, looking askance at Jane, who smiled sympathetically. There really hadn't been anything else he could do; it was too bad of the duke to place him in such a difficult and embarrassing position.

The performance continued, but now their box was subjected to the duke's constant whispering as he paid blatant court to

Blanche right in front of Henry. It was quite inexcusable, and unfortunately Blanche had to take a share of the blame, for she didn't do all she might have to discourage him.

Henry grew steadily more and more incensed, until at last he couldn't stand it any more. "I say, Dursley, can't you pipe down a little? Your damned whispering's driving me up the proverbial wall!"

The duke made a show of being affronted. "There's no need to be offensive, dear boy."

"*I'm* not the one who's being offensive!" snapped Henry.

Blanche bridled at that, knowing that she was guilty too. "You *are* being offensive, Henry."

It was too much. "Well, I like that!" cried Henry, his voice raised so that those in the surrounding boxes couldn't help but hear. "The damned fellow hasn't stopped whispering in your ear since he arrived, and you've been encouraging him! So don't tell me *I'm* being offensive!"

Jane looked at them both in rising dismay, but as she sat forward quickly to intervene, Charles put his hand warningly over hers, shaking his head. Leave it, his glance said; there's nothing you can do.

Blanche got quiveringly to her feet. "Henry, it evidently hasn't occurred to you that I might have good reason to encourage such gallant attention!"

"And what good reason might that be?" he demanded, ignoring the interested glances the altercation was attracting from all sides.

"It's very refreshing to have a gentleman actually appreciate me! It's so much more flattering than being ignored in favor of a stagecoach!" There were titters of laughter at this, for the Marquis of Bourton's box was now causing such a stir that the audience was ignoring the stage. Madame Vestris, unused to losing attention, hesitated a little, almost missing her cue.

A stir of whispering and more laughter rippled through the auditorium as Henry jumped to his feet as well, so furious that he didn't care what he said or who heard him say it. "Gallant appreciation! The toad's after your fortune, and you appear to be the only one in Town who doesn't know it!"

The duke leapt up then. "I say, Felbridge, I demand you take that back!"

"I never take back the truth," replied Henry coldly.

There were gasps now and Jane looked urgently at Charles, afraid that her hotheaded brother was about to provoke a challenge.

Charles got up quickly, putting a warning hand on his friend's arm. "Henry, steady now, don't be so hasty."

"I'll not brook any more that—that—that. . . ." Words failed Henry and he could only gesture derisively in the duke's direction.

Jane felt utterly wretched. By reacting as he had, Henry had played straight into his rival's hands, and Blanche's mood was such that she was allowing herself to be manipulated away from the man she really loved.

Blanche was alarmed at the situation she'd unthinkingly allowed to arise, but Henry's reaction made her too angry to care. "You're a beast, Henry Derwent," she cried, her voice breaking a little, "and I don't know why I ever thought I was in love with you. Here, take your horrid ring and put it through one of your wretched coachhorse's noses instead!" She thrust the ring into his hand and then snatched up her boa and reticule, turning to the duke, her face flushed and her eyes bright with unshed tears. "Sir, will you do me the honor of escorting me home?"

He smiled, tossing Henry a final triumphant glance. "By all means," he murmured, offering her his arm. She flicked her skirts as if afraid they would be spoiled if they brushed against Henry, and then they left the box, to the continuing murmurs of astonishment from the audience.

Jane was so shocked by the suddenness of Blanche's action, that she could only sit there, gazing in dismay at her brother's stunned face. He was very pale, staring at the ring as if turned momentarily to stone. But even as she watched, his hurt disbelief turned to rage again and his fingers closed convulsively over the ring.

The disturbance apparently over, the audience returned its attention to the stage, where Madame Vestris was valiantly continuing with her performance, and in a moment the Marquis of Bourton's box ceased to be of interest.

Jane looked anxiously at her brother, who still stood where he was. "Henry?"

He turned to her, his face still very pale, but his eyes bright with anger. "She showed me her true colors tonight, didn't she? How blind I've been, thinking her so perfect when all the time she is the most two-faced flirt who ever walked, beckoning to her precious dukeling and making an utter fool of me at the same time!"

"Oh, Henry, you mustn't say that. It just isn't true."

"Isn't it? Did she discourage him? Did she withdraw her hand when he kissed her palm? No, she didn't; she enjoyed every moment of my humiliation. I wish her well of him, for he'll undoubtedly make her as wretched and unhappy as she deserves to be." He turned on his heel then and strode out, slamming the box door behind him with such a force that the noise resounded around the auditorium like a thunderclap, causing yet another stir.

Jane would have hurried after him, but Charles stopped her. "Leave him," he said quietly. "He's too angry to be reasonable at the moment."

"But—"

"No buts." He sat down again, taking her hand and squeezing her fingers. "It had to happen some time; he'd allowed things to go too far."

"Charles, Blanche doesn't love the duke, she loves Henry. She didn't mean to give him back his ring, it was an impulse, a spur-of-the-moment thing!"

"Then let them sort themselves out. Be sensible now, Jane. All you'll achieve if you rush off after him is more heartache for yourself, and if you think otherwise, you don't know your brother very well. He'll take himself off to Brooks's now and I should imagine they'll have to bring him home in the early hours."

"Then you must be with him, to see that he's all right."

He groaned. "Henry won't thank me, Jane, of that you may be sure."

"Please, Charles," she begged. "Do it for me."

He met her earnest gaze then and reluctantly nodded. "Oh, all right. I'll take you home and then go and find him, although he doesn't deserve it you know. He behaved very foolishly tonight."

She lowered her eyes again. "I know."

He drew her hand to his lips. "But for you I'll see that he gets home safely, although as to his sobriety, that I cannot answer for."

He got up then, putting her shawl about her shoulders. As she rose from her seat, she couldn't help glancing for a last time toward Lewis's box. It was empty.

TWENTY

*H*enry was very much the worse for wear when Charles at last managed to bring him home at dawn. Jane had been lying in her bed, plagued by a guilty conscience about her secret plotting with Wheddle, for she imagined him to be devastated and heart-broken and at the very least plunged into the depths of despair; but the truth was very different, as she discovered when she went to see how he was. He was still very disagreeable and unreasonable where Blanche was concerned, roundly condemning her as being solely to blame for what had happened, and declaring himself over and over to be well rid of her. He considered himself to be the injured party, not deserving in any way to be treated as shabbily as Blanche had treated him, and it wasn't long before Jane's sympathy and conscience flew out of the window and she was as determined as ever to teach him the lesson he apparently still had to learn.

He rose very late the next day, coming gingerly down in the early afternoon to the blue saloon, where she was writing another letter to Aunt Derwent, informing her of the latest developments. He eased himself into his chair, leaning his aching head back and announcing that he'd never touch a drop of maraschino again, ever.

She put the finishing touches to the letter and quickly sealed it, placing it in the dish for Melville to see that it was posted. Then she surveyed her brother, who looked very sorry for himself, his dark hair disheveled and his face somewhat pale and fragile. She wondered if he was feeling any more remorseful now that he'd had a little time to think. "Have you taken any honey and lemon?" she asked.

"I loathe honey and lemon."

"It's a sovereign remedy for the aftereffects of being disgustingly in drink."

"I wasn't in drink."

She gave a laugh of disbelief. "How can you possibly say that when you had to be positively dragged home?"

"I remember everything and know that I wasn't in drink."

She decided to drop the subject. "Are you going to see Blanche today?" she asked tentatively.

"No."

Her heart sank. He evidently hadn't changed his mind. "Don't you think you should?"

"No."

"But—"

"I've no desire to ever see her again," he interrupted flatly, reaching over to pick up a journal and flick through the pages in a way which was meant to terminate the conversation.

She wasn't so easily deterred. "I can't believe you're persisting with this silly pretense."

"Pretense?"

"About Blanche. You know you still love her."

"It isn't a pretense and I most certainly do *not* still love her. In fact, I can't imagine that I ever deceived myself I loved her in the first place." He looked deliberately at the journal again, as if engrossed.

"That, sir, was a whopper."

"As you wish." He shrugged.

She sighed. "This is quite ridiculous."

"You can save your breath, sis, for nothing you say will make any difference. My betrothal to Miss Blanche Lyndon is at an end, and I'm glad that it is. I certainly don't intend to go crawling to her, not now that I've seen her for what she really is."

"Which is what?"

"A spoiled, selfish, fickle strumpet who richly deserves a wretch like Dursley."

Jane was appalled. "Henry, you don't mean that!"

"Oh, yes I do."

"How could you possibly say such a dreadful thing?"

"With great ease, since it happens to be the truth."

"Please stop this, Henry. Go to her this afternoon."

"I've better things to do than waste my time and energy upon someone like her."

"Things connected with coaching, no doubt," she said drily.

"Why not? You surely don't think last night's little episode is going to make me change, do you?" He would have given a derisive laugh had he not been so mindful of his aching head. "Damn it all, Jane, she gave me back my ring and then waltzed off with Dursley."

"It wasn't quite like that, and you know it. You could quite easily go to her now if you wished. You're just being beastly and stubborn."

"I've already planned what I'm going to do today," he replied airly. "As I think I mentioned yesterday, when you were being so uncommon interested in my coaching, I'm very curious about Arthur Huggett's reappearance and so I'm going to send someone around to the Feathers to take a sly peek at what's going on there."

She gave no outward reaction. "Henry, what on earth difference does it make what's going on there? All that really matters is that you do your utmost to win Blanche back!"

"I don't want her back."

"Go to her. Please."

"No."

"Henry—"

"I said no and I meant no. Don't be boring, Jane. I'm tired of talking about Blanche and would much prefer to read this journal."

"Then I suggest you stand on your head."

"Eh?"

"It's upside down."

He scowled and turned it the other way. "Leave me in peace, can't you? All I want is to sit here and have a quiet read."

Exasperated, she got up. "You're behaving very badly, Henry, and I only hope you still think your precious coaching is worth it when you've not only lost Blanche but probably that wretched race as well."

His smile was infuriatingly smug. "Lose the race? Not a chance, dear thing, not a chance."

She could have boxed his ears. "Well, maybe *you* don't care about Blanche, but I certainly do, and I'm going to see her right now."

"Toddle off to her if you wish, it's immat rial to me. But don't think you can do anything to make me change my mind, because you can't."

It was the last straw, and she couldn't bear to be with him any longer. Flinging from the room, she slammed the door behind her as loudly as she possibly could, taking a savage delight in knowing that the noise would throb horridly through his aching head.

She instructed Melville to see that the town carriage was brought around immediately instead of the landau, for it was extremely windy and threatened to rain, and she was careful to ask that Ellen's Thomas was the coachman, because after visiting Blanche she intended to go to the Feathers to warn Jacob about Henry's plan to send someone to snoop.

Shortly afterward, wearing a brown-and-white-checkered morning dress and matching pelisse, a lace veil draped in readiness over her straw bonnet so that she could conceal her face when on the way to the Feathers, she emerged from the house with Ellen. The wind was very strong indeed, whipping her skirts around her ankles and almost tugging the bonnet from her head as she climbed quickly into the waiting carriage.

Blanche received her gladly, relieved that the previous evening's events hadn't jeopardized their friendship. In a rustle of pale green lawn, she hurried to hug Jane the moment she was shown into the library at Lyndon House. "Jane!" she cried. "Oh, I'm so glad to see you. I was afraid you might fall out with me after last night!"

"I don't blame you for last night—well, not entirely anyway."

Blanche bit her lip and lowered her eyes guiltily. "I was a bit naughty, wasn't I?"

"Just a little."

"I was just so angry with Henry, even though he started out by doing all he could to make things up to me. He was just so horrid when the duke arrived. . . ."

"I know."

Blanche sat down, nervously toying with the finger which had so recently been adorned with Henry's ring. "How—how is he?"

Jane joined her on the sofa. "I'd be a fibber if I said he was displaying any overwhelming heartbreak. In fact, he's doing all he can to show that he couldn't care a fig."

"Oh." Tears filled Blanche's eyes.

"It's an act, Blanche," went on Jane more gently. "He's quite devastated, I'm sure of it, but he's determined not to show it."

"I love him so much, Jane. I only wanted to teach him a lesson. I didn't mean to let it all get out of hand like that."

Jane smiled wryly. "I think we *all* want to teach him a lesson, and no one more than me."

Blanche looked curiously at her. "You sounded very strange when you said that."

Jane hesitated, but then on impulse decided to tell her everything. "I've been up to no good of late, Blanche. In fact, I've been scheming, because I've had enough of my brother's selfish antics."

Blanche's eyes widened. "Jane, whatever is it?"

"I've been financing a stagecoach so that it can enter the race on Midsummer Day."

Blanche stared at her.

"And what's more," Jane went on, "I'm going to be on that coach when it comes in first."

Blanche couldn't speak for a moment, she was so taken aback, but at last she found her tongue. "You can't possibly be serious."

"I'm afraid I am." Jane then described in detail all that had happened since the afternoon she'd first seen the notice outside the Hanover Square Rooms.

Blanche remained in stunned silence throughout, and when the visit to Brighton was related in full, then her eyes grew rounder than ever. "You actually went to Brighton with Lewis and stayed overnight in the same inn?"

"Yes, but I assure you, we slept in separate beds."

"I believe you, but think what sport the scandalmongers would have if it got out."

"I'd rather *not* think about it, thank you," replied Jane with feeling.

Blanche took a long breath. "I can't believe you've been doing all this and I didn't guess a thing." She looked at Jane. "Is Lewis still going to horse the coach for you?"

"I doubt it. He cut me at the theater last night." Jane lowered her eyes.

"When did he do that?"

"While I was waiting outside the box for Charles." She paused, her voice catching in her throat. "I love him, Blanche."

"We all know that."

"It was awful when he wouldn't speak to me."

Blanche put a sympathetic hand on hers. "I know the feeling, since I appear to be in the same boat now. What a pair we are, both of us hopelessly in love, and both of us guilty of perverse behavior which has alienated us from the objects of that love."

"Maybe we're at fault, but they haven't exactly behaved well, have they? Henry's been a beast to end all beasts, and Lewis— well, Lewis has just been two-faced."

"Has he? He was right when he told you in Brighton that Alicia had a vested interest in lying to you."

"I don't think she was lying."

Blanche got up, gazing out at the windswept garden where the summer leaves were occasionally torn from the branches to dance wildly through the air. She turned suddenly back to Jane. "I want to be with you on the coach."

"But—"

"I want to be there when Henry sees the Swan's dust in front of him."

"Blanche, he won't like it when he sees *me* on the coach. He'll like it even less if he sees you as well. Besides, I'm told that even my presence is more than is wise, since every extra ounce will count, especially if we can't find the right horses," she added.

"Very well, then I shall follow the race in my own carriage. I'm going to be there, Jane, I'm set on it."

"The road will be a mill," warned Jane. "The world and his wife will be following that race, maybe even the queen herself."

"I like mills." Blanche smiled. "I think this whole thing is a splendid idea and I wish I'd thought of it myself. Oh, it will be so *good* to see Henry trounced!"

"To trounce anyone we'll have to hope Lewis still provides the horses."

"I'm sure he will."

"I wish I could feel that confident," replied Jane. "Oh, well, I really must go. I want to tell Jacob and Betsy about Henry and his snooper. I thought about writing another note, but really I'd prefer to go there in person."

"How are you getting there? You're surely not driving openly in your carriage."

"I shall have Thomas wait somewhere while Ellen and I take a hackney."

Blanche was aghast. "You're actually going to hire a *hackney?*"

"I've done it already and it was most disagreeable, but at least no one gives such vehicles a second glance." Jane smiled, tying on her bonnet. "Besides, this veil makes me exceeding anonymous, don't you think? Oh, no! I've almost pulled one of the ribbons off!"

"Shall I have a maid sew it back on for you?"

"No, there isn't time. It'll be all right."

The wind tugged alarmingly at the bonnet as she left the house to rejoin the patient Ellen in the carriage, and for a moment it seemed the ribbon would give, but it didn't, and soon they were being conveyed to the corner of Arlington Street in Piccadilly. Jane chose this spot because it was close to a long rank of waiting hackneys, and because there was so much noise and traffic that she wasn't very likely to be particularly observed.

Arlington Street was where Lord Sefton resided, and as she and Ellen alighted, Jane glanced along the street, holding onto her tugging bonnet as she did so, while at the same time keeping the veil pulled down, otherwise the wind would have billowed it up in a cloud about her head. Looking at his lordship's town house, she pondered the shock waves which would spread through society when the Swan's late entry in the race was announced.

The hackney coach they took on this occasion proved to be even more rickety than its predecessor, but it carried them safely across London and they alighted in the Feathers' yard without having attracted any undue attention. Jane was once again forced to hold on tightly to her bonnet and veil, for the wind was almost savagely determined to whisk both from her head.

The veil lifted and fluttered as she glanced around the yard, which had a very different air about it now. A down Swan was preparing to leave, the first afternoon one for some time, and Will was to take the ribbons. Betsy was standing proudly at his side, for he looked very smart indeed in a white top hat as splendid as that worn by the Nonpareil's Sewell. As Jane watched, the innkeeper's daughter pinned a fresh nosegay to his lapel and then stretched up to kiss him on the cheek before hurrying away toward the kitchen entrance. A moment later, two passengers emerged from the coffee room to take their places inside the coach. Then the guard put his bugle to his lips and Will climbed up onto the box. The Swan drew out, the sound of its departure echoing loudly beneath the archway as it pulled out into the crush of Cheapside.

Ellen went to join Betsy in the kitchens, the two having gotten to know and like each other, and Jane found Jacob in the coffee room, humming cheerfully to himself as he checked the waybills of the past two days. He looked up as she entered, and a grin spread across his face as he rose to his feet. "Lady Jane, how pleased I am to see you again."

She teased off her gloves and sat down. "Did I actually espy two passengers a moment ago?"

"You did indeed, and they're going all the way to Brighton."

"On the *afternoon* coach?"

His grin broadened. "Well, I thought it was a shame to leave young Will twiddling his thumbs when there was a coach to get running again." He paused. "Arthur's return has caused quite a stir, you know."

"It certainly has with my brother, so much so that he's going to send someone here to spy."

"He won't be the first. We've had three snoopers here already, two of Chapman's and one from the Swan with Two Necks. We recognized them all, and they were turfed out."

"What if there's been someone you *haven't* recognized?"

"If so, there's been nothing yet to find out. Everyone here's been put on their guard to say nothing to anyone, especially not about the race or about you."

Betsy's kitten came to jump up on Jane's lap, and Jacob immediately made to remove it, but she stopped him, "Please leave her, I love cats."

"If you're quite sure . . ." he began doubtfully.

"Quite sure."

At that moment there was the sound of hooves and wheels in the yard and they both turned to see a smart scarlet cabriolet arriving, drawn by a very handsome gray horse. It was driven by Lewis, Lord Ardenley.

TWENTY-ONE

*F*or a moment, she was motionless with surprise. Why had he come? Was he going to honor his word about the horses after all? She didn't know what to think, and she didn't know how he was going to be when he came face to face with her again. Would he snub her as he had at the theater? Slowly, she put the kitten down and then hurried toward the window, peeping out carefully so that he wouldn't notice her.

He had maneuvered the light cabriolet to a standstill close to the archway into the stableyard, and a boy hurried out immediately to take the horse's bridle and lead it through out of her sight.

Lewis paused for a moment, tilting his top hat back on his head. The wind ruffled his hair and raised the tails of his light blue coat. He wore beige trousers and gleaming Hessian boots, the tassels of which swung as he turned, glancing along the gallery as if looking for someone.

A maid was emerging from the kitchen door and she almost dropped her pail of potato peelings as he spoke to her. With wide eyes, she pointed toward the coffee room, and Jane drew hastily back from the window as he began to walk toward her.

Jacob had come to stand by her. "That's Lord Ardenley, isn't it?"

"Yes."

"Do you think he's going to horse the Swan after all?"

"I don't know. I didn't think he would, but I can't imagine why else he'd come here." The kitten was rubbing around her ankles, anxious to be picked up and cuddled, and automatically she did as it wanted, scooping it into her arms and returning to her seat with it. It purred and kneaded her sleeve with its little claws, looking the picture of feline bliss.

The door opened then and Lewis stepped in, bowing his head beneath the low lintel. He didn't immediately see her, but noticed only Jacob, still standing by the window. "Mr. Wheddle?" he inquired.

"Yes, my lord." Jacob smoothed his apron a little nervously, his glance moving involuntarily toward Jane.

Lewis saw her then and paused, evidently a little surprised. He removed his hat then, bowing politely enough, but his face revealed nothing of his thoughts. "Lady Jane?"

"Sir." She met his eyes briefly and then continued stroking the kitten.

"I didn't expect to find you here," he said.

"I could say the same of you."

A light passed through his eyes. "I gave my word," he reminded her.

"You're still going to horse the Swan?"

"If you still require horses." He looked at Jacob then. "I take it that you do?"

Jacob nodded immediately. "Oh, yes, my lord, we need them very much indeed."

"Then perhaps we should discuss the details, mm?"

"Certainly, my lord. Would—would you care to take some coffee?"

Lewis nodded. "Yes. Thank you." He put his top hat down on the table as Jacob hurried out calling for Betsy. The coffee room was horridly quiet then, with Lewis teasing off his gloves finger by finger and then putting them into the upturned hat.

Jane was shaking a little, and tried to hide the fact by continuing to stroke the delighted kitten. She was relieved when Jacob hurried back almost immediately, asserting that the very finest coffee in the city would be served to them in a moment.

Lewis sat down and bade Jacob join them. As the landlord complied, he couldn't help glancing at the rather stiff faces of his two aristocratic companions. The atmosphere between them could have been cut with a knife. Jacob cleared his throat and shifted a little uncomfortably.

Betsy brought the coffee and as she withdrew again, the kitten followed her, rubbing around her ankles as she turned to close the door behind her.

Jacob poured the coffee and gave Jane the first cup. Then he handed one to Lewis. "Do you know how many horses we'll need, my lord?"

"Thirty minimum, thirty-four to be on the safe side. There's no problem—I've that many at Maywood. Tell me about the new coach you've ordered. Does it have brakes?"

Jacob shook his head, a little taken aback. "No, my lord, no coach master worth his salt would think of such a thing. Brakes place too great a strain on the wheels."

"Brakes also give a greater advantage on hills."

"It's preferable to rely on drags and on the strength of the wheelers." Thinking that he might have spoken a little too forcefully, Jacob cleared his throat again. "Begging your pardon, my lord," he added tactfully.

A thin smile touched Lewis's lips. "You're entitled to your opinion, sir, just as I'm entitled to mine. I happen to think that brakes are an excellent invention which should be much more universally fitted than at present. I certainly think that they should be fitted on a coach which is to take part in a race, since wheels can surely take such a strain for one day."

Jacob pursed his lips. "Men like Arthur Huggett prefer to stick to the old tried and trusted ways."

"And men like Edward Chapman are just as likely to latch on to the benefits of new ways," replied Lewis.

Jacob looked quickly at him. "Do you know something about Chapman's plans, my lord?"

"No, I'm just guessing. Word has it among the fraternity that the new Nonpareil is under very close wraps at the Black Horse, so close that my suspicions are more than a little aroused. There's a small fortune resting on this race, and Chapman's determined to win it, so I believe he's struck out of the usual mold and that the coach which sets off in his colors on Midsummer Day will give the Iron Duke and the Swan a great deal to think about at such an eleventh hour."

Jacob sat back thoughtfully. "Too much to think about, is that what you're saying?"

"I'm not *saying* anything—I'm surmising. Chapman knows the new Iron Duke is conventional. There's been no secret about it."

"We'll need to find out then, to be sure."

Lewis raised an eyebrow. "Penetrate Chapman's inner sanctum? That won't be easy, not when he's clamped down so very much to keep his rivals out."

Jacob looked at Jane then. "Has the earl said anything to you, my lady?"

"No, but I'm sure he doesn't think it's going to be anything out of the ordinary."

Lewis drew a long, doubtful breath and then shook his head. "Well, I'm probably wrong. Let's hope I am, because if the Nonpareil has brakes, it's going to give you much more than a run for your money on hills and tight bends. Still, enough of the coach. I need to know exactly where each stage is set to begin and end." He looked at Jacob. "Are you using your usual bases?"

"We had planned to, my lord."

"And they are . . . ?"

"Sutton, Reigate, Crawley, Hardcross, and Bolney."

"Inns where Chapman's influence is rather too great for comfort, if you don't mind my saying so."

"What other choice do we have, my lord?"

"Dispense with inns altogether. I could have my grooms waiting with the fresh horses at predetermined places along the ground, directly outside each town or village where the stages usually end, for instance. That way we'd be sure of steering clear of friend Chapman, and of any nonsense the proprietor of the Iron Duke might feel inclined to perpetrate on an occasion by which he sets such great personal store."

Jacob was gaping at him. "Dispense with the inns? But that's unheard of."

"It isn't against the race rules—I've made certain of that. There's nothing to say we must stick to the inns."

"But what about the men that'd be needed for such changes? We'd need a small army."

"I don't keep vast stables at Maywood without having the men to look after them."

Jacob cleared his throat a little uncomfortably. "No, my lord, I don't suppose you do."

Lewis smiled a little. "It's settled then?"

The landlord nodded. "Yes, my lord."

"Good, then I'll have my men find the most suitable places and I'll let you know." Lewis finished his coffee and got up, pulling on his gloves. "I'll keep in close touch between now and Midsummer Day."

Jacob rose as well. "Thank you, my lord. With your bloodstock, I think we'll have a more than even chance of holding the others down."

"Not if Chapman uses brakes you won't," replied Lewis, tapping his top hat on his head. He left after according Jane no more than a civil nod.

She remained seated as Jacob escorted Lewis out. Then she went to the window again, watching as the two men paused by the inner archway, talking for a moment more before Lewis took his leave, vanishing from her sight as he went through to the stableyard where his cabriolet was waiting.

Until that moment, she hadn't really believed he'd just go without saying anything more to her, but it was plain that he was doing just that. He'd said that he was going to treat her this way, and it was becoming more and more obvious that he'd meant every word. The realization came as a bitter shock, even though at the theater the night before he'd made his intentions perfectly clear by cutting her as he had. She stared at the archway. Earlier, when they'd been seated around the table discussing the race, she'd been painfully aware that she might as well have not been there for all the notice he'd taken of her; he'd predicted that she wouldn't like such treatment, and he'd been so right—she'd didn't like it in the slightest. Damn him for knowing her as he did.

Suddenly the situation was too much. She *had* to talk to him. Gathering her skirts, she hurried out, the wind fluttering her veil behind her and snatching at her bonnet as if it had been waiting for another chance to seize it.

The scarlet cabriolet had been drawn up by the open door of an empty stable, and Lewis was just tossing a coin to the stableboy who had been looking after it for him.

She hesitated some distance away from him. "Lewis?" The wind was too strong and he didn't hear. "Lewis?"

He turned. "Yes?"

She went closer and the stableboy hurried tactfully away. Through the stable's open door she could see the fresh straw piled inside, and the kitten Tabitha playing in it, chasing imaginary mice. Jane halted a few feet away from the cabriolet, conscious of the coolness in Lewis's gray eyes as he looked at her. The wind made her skirts flap, and she had to steady her bonnet, which was tugging at its ribbons as if it was alive. "Lewis, I must talk to you."

"Indeed? I can't imagine what about." He was detached and could have been addressing anyone.

She moved into the lee of the open stable door, where the wind wasn't quite so fierce. "Is it really necessary to treat me quite like this?" she asked, her voice suddenly much more audible.

"I was under the impression it was what you wanted," he replied.

"I don't *want* to be cut at the theater, nor do I *want* to be ignored during conversation."

"What happened at the theater was hardly a cut, for as I recall I acknowledged you."

"Barely."

"I still acknowledged you. As to ignoring you during conversation, well there didn't seem to be anything to say, did there? To be perfectly honest, my lady, I find your present complaint a little rich, since I seem to remember your departure from Brighton being anything but courteous."

"Courtesy was hardly high on anyone's agenda on that occasion," she replied.

At that moment a strong gust of wind sucked through the stableyard, swinging the stable door so sharply that it almost wrenched from its ancient hinges. Jane's skirts flapped more wildly than ever, and the ribbons of her bonnet at last gave up their struggle. The bonnet was whisked from her head, sailing high into the air with its veil fluttering prettily like a large butterfly. Jane stared at it in dismay, and then her dismay deepened still more, for her hair tumbled down from its pins, whipping across her face as raggedly as a gypsy's.

"I don't think there's anything more to be said," Lewis murmured, inclining his head and turning back toward the cabriolet.

She stared at him, disheartenment flooding miserably through her, but then something made her look toward the archway to the outer courtyard. A man was coming beneath it, a small, nondescript fellow in shabby gray, with bow legs and highlows, and strings dangling from his knees. Normally, she wouldn't have paid any attention, his sort abounded at inns and stables, but there was something unusual about him which struck a chord. It was the way he chewed upon a straw, flicking it to and fro like a viper's tongue. She's seen him at the Fleece when she'd gone there with Henry. She'd been perched up on the phaeton and this very man held the team while Henry had gone to see someone. If he looked in her direction now he was bound to recognize her, even with her hair loose. Oh, no, he mustn't see her—he'd go straight to Henry and it would be all up!

Lewis sensed that something was wrong, for he turned back to her. "What is it?"

"That man, he's from the Fleece! He knows me."

"Get in there," he said quickly, taking her arm and thrusting her bodily into the empty stable.

The man didn't see her, but a moment later he noticed the cabriolet and recognized Lewis. He paused thoughtfully and the straw stopped flicking.

Lewis could read his thoughts. He was wondering why a man like Lord Ardenley was paying a visit to a lesser inn like the Feathers.

Jane whispered almost inaudibly from the stable. "Has he gone? Is it safe to come out?"

"Stay there. Goddammit, he's coming over!" In a moment, Lewis had come into the stable as well, and before she knew what was happening, he'd caught her wrist and flung her backward on to the pile of straw. In a blur, she saw Tabitha erupt toward the door, spitting angrily, her little ears back, but then the kitten was forgotten, for Lewis was on top of her, pinning her back against the straw, his lips only inches from her. "Be still, my lady, or you'll give the game away. His suspicions are aroused and so I have to give him something he'll believe." He smiled coldly at her then, tightening his hold and she began to struggle. "He'll believe this," he murmured, bending his head to kiss her roughly on the lips.

She had to submit, she hadn't the strength to stop him. It was a bruising, hurtful kiss and simmering behind it she could taste the anger which had been burning within him since the day she'd returned his ring. She writhed beneath him, but her struggles were futile. He could have taken her, used the ultimate force, and there wouldn't have been anything she could have done to resist.

She was only dimly aware of a shadow at the stable door as the man's curiosity got the better of him and he had to look in to see what was going on. She didn't see the sly, knowing grin which spread over his thin little face. So that was it, the smile said; his lordship was here to tumble a serving wench in the hay, taking all the liberties a fine lady wouldn't permit! The man's eyes lingered appreciatively on her legs, noticing only the smooth, pale skin and not the rather costly silk stockings and fine shoes which were hardly the apparel of a serving girl.

Suddenly someone shouted behind him and he turned sharply to see Jacob striding toward him, demanding to know who he was and the nature of his business.

"Me, sir?"

Jane saw the shadow move away.

"Yes, you," replied Jacob, standing before him with his hands on his hips.

"I'm Jack Smith, sir. I'm looking for work."

"Oh, yes? Out of here, my laddo, and don't come snooping around again or you'll get hotter treatment, is that clear?"

"Yes, sir." The man moved hastily away, almost running toward the archway.

Jacob glanced toward the open stable door, hesitating for a moment and then withdrawing. Best leave well alone.

As silence fell again, Lewis at last relaxed his grip on Jane, raising his head to look down at her. A mocking smile twisted his lips, then he rolled from her and got up, brushing the straw from his clothes.

She lay there trembling, and didn't say anything.

He stood over her, his gaze cold again as he looked at her, taking in her tousled hair and disarranged skirts. "Madam," he said softly, "you lack all modesty."

She found her tongue then. "And you, sir, lack all gallantry."

"Ah, so you begin to recover your lost composure, do you?" He held his hand out to her then. "Don't lie there like that, my lady, I might take it as an invitation."

She accepted the hand, but he paused in the act of pulling her to her feet. "Forgive me, madam, I've just remembered that you said I lacked all gallantry, so I suppose I should act the part completely." Abruptly, he released her so that she tumbled back into the straw.

He turned on his heel then and strode out, climbing into the cabriolet and driving off without giving her another glance.

TWENTY-TWO

A week was to pass before she saw him again, because he left Town for Maywood, taking Alicia with him. For the Swan the week was very eventful indeed, and not pleasantly so.

The reappearance of Arthur Huggett and the excellent times he immediately began to make, brought renewed determination from Chapman to be rid of this unwanted rival on the Brighton road. The boxing-ins and feather-edgings continued, and the use of informers was stepped up. It was due to the activities of the latter that four days before the race Jacob was hauled before the magistrates to explain no less than three separate infringements of the law.

The first incident had taken place at the Kennington tollgate, when, unseen by either Arthur or the guard, a rosy-faced, honest-looking outsider had perched himself on top of his luggage and broken the coach-height regulations, a fact which was pointed out to the tollkeeper by none other than the hated Byers himself, who was waiting by the gate. An on-the-spot inspection had resulted in the matter being reported, and Arthur had been left cursing the momentary lapse of concentration which had allowed the thing to happen.

The second and third incidents lay at the unfortunate Will's door, and they happened not because he had been careless but because he had been too soft-hearted. On Banstead Downs during a thunderstorm, he had been persuaded to stop the Swan and "shoulder" a young mother and child to Reigate without entering their names on the waybill. At Reigate, naturally enough, one of Byers's men was in waiting, since the mother and child weren't innocent travelers but were there to deliberately trap Will into some foolishness. The third incident, and the one which finally brought poor Jacob to court, had taken place in the yard of the Red Lion at Handcross, when Will had unwisely accept as genuine an anxious parson who had implored him to carry a large hamper, said to contain medicines, herbs, and fortified wine for an extremely ill relative in Brighton. Even after the business with the mother and child, Will proved foolish enough to agree, because the parson seemed so distressed. But the moment the hamper was loaded, the Swan's luggage allowance was exceeded and the vigilant Byers was there to record the fact.

Three violations of the law in as many days had proved too much for the magistrates, who were no longer prepared to deal only in fines. A summons had arrived at the Feathers and Jacob had been hauled off to court to answer for his coach's misdemeanors. He had gone very reluctantly indeed, because not only was his license in jeopardy but the magistrates, if they felt so inclined, might imprison him.

Jane waited at the Feathers for his return, having gone there straightaway with Ellen when she'd heard the news. They sat in the kitchen with Betsy, Will, Arthur, and the two guards. Betsy was in tears, holding Will's hand and dabbing her red-rimmed eyes from time to time with her handkerchief. Jane glanced around the low-beamed room with its spotless whitewashed walls and immense dressers. The smell of baking hung in the air because Betsy had earlier felt she must do something while she waited for news of her father. Mutton was roasting on the jack before the open fire, which was always lighted for this purpose instead of using the range, and a kettle sang softly as it simmered. Baskets of fresh vegetables stood on the red-tiled floor ready for the day's meals, but no one felt hungry. They all sat despondently around the scrubbed table, the four men sunk with gloom and guilt about what they had variously permitted to happen, but it was Jane who felt worst of all, for if it hadn't been for her wild schemes, Jacob wouldn't be in his present predicament.

She felt wretched, and in spite of the humiliation she'd suffered at her last encounter with Lewis, she wished he was at the Feathers now instead of at Maywood with his odious mistress. She lowered her eyes. She'd been on the point of going to him to admit that she wanted him still and to beg him to forget all that had gone wrong between them, but then Charles had told her that Alicia had gone to Maywood as well. Her confession of love had remained unsaid, and so matters remained the same between them, but, oh, how she wished he was here now, his mere presence would have comforted her. She smiled wryly to herself then, for if he had been there no doubt he would have reminded her that all this was her fault, because she'd refused his advice to leave the whole business alone. He'd have been right, too, it *was* her fault, and if Jacob went to prison she'd never forgive herself.

It seemed that they'd been sitting there for hours, but it wasn't that long, and Jane was just about to suggest that Will go along to the court to see what was happening when they heard the familiar and welcome sound of Jacob's steps approaching the door.

With a glad cry, Betsy jumped to her feet, running into her father's arms as he came into the room. "Dad! Oh, Dad, they let you go!"

He held her tightly for a moment. "Yes, love, they let me go, but only just." He fixed his gaze on the four men around the table. "And we still have our license."

They all sat back in relief, but Jane didn't share their smiles. She got up. "Mr. Wheddle, this has all been my fault and I feel very much to blame. I'm persuaded that my whole notion of winning the race was the height of foolishness—"

"You've changed your mind?" He looked at her in concern.

"I think it best that I do. If they'd sentenced you to prison—"

"It wouldn't have been your fault, Lady Jane, it would have been the fault of these four fools here." He approached the table looking darkly at the men, and at Will in particular, since he had been the greatest offender. "All three of those infringements were avoidable, gentlemen, and yet you still proceeded to commit them, even though you knew how Chapman's after us for still being on the road. You broke the law, and when you were caught you still went on and did it again! I've had to pay a hefty fine this morning to get the Swan off the hook, and I've been warned that if there's another infringement, no matter how small, I'll forfeit the license *and* go inside. Things didn't go how friend Chapman wanted them to this morning, and he won't be pleased that we're still operating. Be more on your guard from now on; don't let anything else happen in the next four days, or so help me I'll come down on you like a ton of bricks and there won't be one of you with your heads above the surface ever again. Is that quite clear?"

He'd said it all in a slow, reasonable tone, but there was a steeliness in his voice and manner which told them that he meant every word he said. The four men shifted uncomfortably and nodded, while poor Will looked so miserable that Betsy had to go to put a reassuring hand on his shoulder. Jacob turned to Jane then. "Begging your pardon if I've spoken roughly in front of you, my lady, but it all had to be said. It also has to be said that no one's twisted my arm to make me agree to your plan, and I can honestly say that the last thing I want to do is give up, not now that Chapman's leaned on me like this. I'm damned if I want him to get away with it. Begging your pardon again," he added quickly for having sworn in front of her.

"But if something else should happen. . . ."

"It won't," he replied, eyeing the men again. "All right," he said to them, "hop it now, and don't cross my path again. My temper isn't the best."

As one, they rose to their feet and went out, followed by a rather cross Betsy, who wasn't too pleased with her father for singling Will out so particularly. Ellen hesitated for a moment, but then decided to follow the others and leave her mistress to speak privately with the innkeeper.

The door closed behind them all and Jacob looked a little ruefully at Jane. "Now Betsy's displeased with me, and *that's* down to Will Huggett as well!"

"Will's a good man, Mr. Wheddle."

"I know, I just wish he could be a little more hard-headed. He's too soft by far, open to every hard-luck story he's told, and if he's going to marry my daughter and one day have this place. . . ." He shook his head.

"To have the Feathers he'll have to marry Betsy, and I don't think *she'll* listen too much to hard-luck stories."

He grinned at that. "No, she's got a sensible head on her shoulders, except where that great softy's concerned," he added.

Jane sat down again. "So, we're still on the road and still going to be in the race. You do think Mrs. Mountain will deliver the new coach in time, don't you?"

"She will, you can count upon it. I've been thinking though. . . ."

"Yes?"

"About what Lord Ardenley said. Maybe he's right about the new Nonpareil."

"Having brakes, you mean?"

"That, and more. I've found out that it was delivered at the Black Horse in the dead of night, covered in a tarpaulin and conveyed on a wagon. The man who saw it reckoned it was far too low to be an ordinary stagecoach. It could be one of those new-fangled safety coaches."

"And if it is? Surely they aren't any faster than the more conventional coach?"

"Maybe not faster, but some of them are much more steady on corners and bad cambers. If the new Nonpareil has brakes and safety design, then we might indeed be taking on more than we bargained for. I'd give my eye teeth to get a glimpse at it, but he's got it well under lock and key, and guarded all the time. I'm tempted to follow Lord Ardenley's advice and have brakes fitted."

"Perhaps we'll be able to find out before the race."

"How?"

"I don't know," she admitted.

"And four days isn't very long, is it? If only I could feel confident that brakes wouldn't strain the wheels in just one day. . . ." He sighed. "Still, there's not much to be done just yet, and I doubt if there's anything which *can* be done, for if there was, your brother the earl would have done it. I happen to know that he's had men crawling all over the Black Horse trying to get to the new coach, but Chapman's picked each one out and sent him packing."

"Henry is as alarmed as we are, Mr. Wheddle, because he has chosen to place his faith in a conventional coach too."

Jacob grinned. "Aye, a fancy drag with silver harness and lamps, shining bright green panels and green *velvet* upholstery! From Powell of Bond Street! No doubt he has teams of perfectly matched bloodstock lined up at the ready—grays, I'll warrant."

She had to smile. "Strawberry roans, actually."

"He means to cut a dash or two on the day, doesn't he?"

"He means to and he will."

"Aye, and what sort of spectacle are we going to cut?"

"What do you mean?"

"The new Swan might have fancy bloodstock, but it isn't going to be a fancy coach; it's built for a purpose, to very basic requirements."

"We don't need silver harnesses and pretty lacquer panels, sir, we simply need to come in first, and with Lord Ardenley's horses, Arthur's skill, and Mrs. Mountain's coach, we're going to do just that."

Jane and Ellen returned to South Audley Street in their usual secret manner, taking a hackney to the corner of Arlington Street and then slipping into the waiting carriage, with Thomas at the ribbons. Jane gladly flicked her veil back the moment she was inside. She had quickly become used to the secrecy, even finding it exciting, especially when things happened like the moment on their last expedition when she'd stepped down from the hackney almost onto the toes of none other than Lord Sefton himself! He hadn't recognized her and had walked on, muttering that it wasn't safe for a fellow to walk abroad without some strange female treading all over him. She'd wondered what the marshal of the race would have said had he known who the strange female really was.

She arrived at South Audley Street to find a pleasant surprise awaiting her; Aunt Derwent had come to stay and was waiting for her in the blue saloon.

Lady Agatha Derwent was a soft, rosy person, her rounded figure laced tightly beneath her blue sprigged muslin gown. Her light brown hair was sprinkled with gray now, but still shone and curled beautifully beneath her large, lace-trimmed day bonnet. She had rather short-sighted hazel eyes and wore spectacles on the end of her nose, giving her a quaintly prim appearance which somehow did not take away at all from her general attractiveness. In that brief moment, Jane wondered again about the whispers concerning the Duke of Wellington, but knew that she would probably never know the answer, because those hazel eyes, which were usually so warm and soft, could freeze in a moment at an unwise or unwelcome question, and could freeze the unfortunate questioner as well.

Not knowing her niece was there, Aunt Derwent continued with her work for a moment. She was seated at her tambour frame embroidering a shawl, and her hook was flashing busily in and out. Then she sensed Jane's presence and looked up with a glad smile. "My dear! How good it is to see you again! Come and give me a hug!"

Jane hurried to comply. "Oh, Aunt Derwent, why didn't you let me know you were coming, I'd have been here to greet you."

"Well, arriving unannounced, or at least pretending one is about to do so, appears to be a recent penchant of Derwent women," replied the older woman, smiling and raising an eyebrow to remind her niece of the fake visit to Beaconsfield.

Jane bit her lip. "I'm truly sorry about that."

"Please don't be. I don't mind being dragged into it—in fact, I'm enjoying the whole business. That's why I'm here. I couldn't bear to stay out in the sticks any more. I *had* to be here, where everything's happening. Tell me, how did your Mr. Wheddle get on today?"

Jane stared at her. "How on earth do you know about that?"

"I've been pumping Melville."

Jane stared even more. "Melville? But how does *he* know?"

"My dear girl, don't be so innocent. Servants know *everything*. That butler rules below stairs with a rod of iron and it's more than your maid's life is worth to hold her tongue about what's happening up here. I knew that if I wanted to know how things were going on, all I had to do was fix him with an even steelier eye than he fixes upon his minions, and I'd learn the lot.''

Jane had to smile. "You're quite incorrigible, do you know that?''

"Yes. Now then, about Mr. Wheddle's court appearance.''

"Well, we still have our license and Mr. Wheddle isn't languishing in jail but is safely back at the Feathers.''

"Excellent. And have you found out about the new Nonpareil yet?''

Jane sat down, laughing a little in astonishment. "Well, I'm sure that Melville didn't tell you about *that!*''

"No, Henry did—indeed, he talked of little else throughout luncheon, it was most disagreeable. I'm at a loss to understand the change in him. Tell me, is coaching now his sole topic of conversation?''

"Yes.''

"Then he does indeed warrant teaching a lesson he won't forget. Otherwise he'll sink beyond all hope of retrieval. Do you know, he didn't mention poor Blanche once, not once. Anyway, where were we? Ah yes, the new Nonpareil.''

"We don't know anything, just that it seems to be very low, which suggests that it might be one of those new safety coaches.''

"Is it very important that we find out before the race?''

"Yes, because if it's fitted with brakes it will have an advantage.''

"Brakes? Is this Chapman fellow likely to be that new-fangled?''

"Lewis—Lord Ardenley thinks he is.''

"And Lewis's judgment in such things is always so very sound, isn't it?''

"So I'm told.''

"Don't be huffy, dear, it isn't becoming.'' The tambour hook began to move again. "So, Nonpareil permitting, we're well on our way still?''

"*Our* way?''

"You don't think I've come here to sit and do nothing, do you? *Au contraire, ma petite*, I've come to do my bit. I have to earn my place in the Swan with you on the day.''

Jane was startled. "But you can't possibly!''

"Why not?''

"Because not even Blanche will travel on the Swan with me.''

Now it was Aunt Derwent's turn to be surprised. "Blanche? Is *she* in on it too? How splendid! *That* will teach young Henry to be so silly. You say she isn't traveling with you on the day? Why not?"

"Because the Swan has to be as light as possible. Blanche's following in her carriage, and I'm sure she'd be only too pleased to have you join her."

"That would be most agreeable. Very well, I'll forgo the Swan, just as long as I'm there on the day, that's all that really matters." She continued her work a moment longer. "Actually, I've come up with rather a capital plan myself," she murmured.

"You have? In what connection?"

Her aunt's smile was positively sleek. "That would be telling."

"But. . . ."

"Wild horses wouldn't drag it out of me—it's going to be my little secret. Oh, by the way, I forgot to mention, I shall be staying here tonight, but tomorrow I'm going to visit Lady Lindleigh and I shall stay there for a day or so. I intend to be back here in time for the race."

"Lady Lindleigh? Isn't she in Paris at the moment?"

"Paris? Oh no, of course not, for if she was, how could I be staying with her?" Aunt Derwent drew a deep, satisfied breath. "Do you know, I haven't enjoyed myself so much since I pretended to elope to Gretna Green with that odious Percy Byrde.'

Jane stared. "Since you what?" she asked faintly.

"It's not something I care to talk about now, but at the time it was such a scream, Jenny Lindleigh and I laughed until our sides split."

"What happened?"

"It was a bet. Jenny said that no one could persuade a stuffy miser like Percy to do something as rash as that, so naturally I took her up on it. I got him as far as Doncaster, which was pretty good going, if I say so myself, but the fellow was such an unmitigated bore that I couldn't carry on any more and so came home with no one any the wiser, excepting Jenny—and Percy himself, of course. He hasn't spoken to me since."

"I'm not surprised. Well, I've heard a whisper or two about you, but never in connection with Percy Byrde."

Her aunt chuckled. "No, well he was hardly likely to spread abroad how much we'd fooled him, and Jenny and I were always mindful that discretion meant we could be a little naughty in the future, if we felt so disposed. It was all harmless, of course. We never did anything too wicked." She became more serious then. "No, you won't have heard about Percy, but I can well imagine who you *have* heard about. You may ask me about it if you wish; it's only fair considering I'm in possession of facts concerning *your* secret amours.''

"My secret what?''

"Amours, dear, amours. I was referring to the jaunt to Brighton with Lewis.''

"It wasn't a jaunt, and it certainly wasn't an amour.''

"I used the latter word as meaning affection, not liaison,'' pointed out her aunt. "Don't be so huffy each time Lewis's name is mentioned, it's really rather tiresome and it doesn't fool me in the slightest. But to change the subject, before coming here today I called on several friends in order to become *au courant* with all the gossip. I understand that Lewis is at Maywood with that Cyprian Alicia Brantingham.''

"Yes.''

"They're far too much together for comfort, my dear.''

"Are they? I really wouldn't know, and I certainly don't care.''

"Stuff and nonsense, you care to your very marrow. I know all about the little scene on the beach at Brighton.''

"Melville, I suppose.''

"Melville.''

"I wonder if the milkmaid knows, and the butcher?''

"I doubt it, Melville's tongue-wagging stops with me. So, Lewis told you it was on your knees or nothing, did he?''

"That would appear to be his requirement. Then he *might*, just *might* consider me again.'' She mimicked his voice. "He's insufferable.''

"And quite, quite irresistible. Just like the dear Duke of Wellington. Yes, my dear, those whispers are all true, and I freely admit it to you. He was *such* a man, and such a lover. I threw caution to the winds with him, and have never regretted it. In fact, my toes curl with pleasure even now when I think of some of the . . . Well, perhaps some things are better kept secret.'' She looked over her spectacles at her niece. "You should go to him, my dear.''

"I nearly did.''

"What happened?''

"I learned that he'd taken Alicia to Maywood with him.''

"I see. Well, if you don't mind my saying so, that shouldn't make any difference.''

"It makes all the difference.''

"I'm afraid I don't agree with you. If you want Lewis Ardenley, you're going to have to fight for him, not shelter behind your bruised pride. He's far too good to let slip through your fingers, my dear, and that's what's going to happen if you're not very careful." She said this last rather mysteriously.

"Why do you say it like that?"

"All in good time, and *now* isn't the time." The tambour hook began to dart in and out again. "Jane, if you're not prepared to get up and *do* something to get Lewis back, I'm afraid that I'm going to have to do it for you, so I hereby give due warning that I've a trick or two up my sleeve to do just that."

TWENTY-THREE

*T*he following afternoon, Aunt Derwent declared that she wished to drive in Hyde Park, and accordingly at four o'clock she and Jane set off in the open landau, the wind having gone now and the weather being fine and warm. Jane wore a pink velvet spencer over a cream muslin gown, and she carried a cream pagoda parasol, which she twirled a little from time to time. The pink ribbons of her straw bonnet were very firmly attached, and there was no chance today of a repeat of events in the Feathers's windy stableyard.

Opposite her, in a russet silk pelisse and matching gown, her aunt was in high spirits, smiling and nodding at friends and acquaintances as the landau drove past. She hadn't elaborated on what her mysterious plan was, and Jane felt vaguely uneasy about it, knowing now that her aunt was capable of attempting anything if she felt so disposed.

Hyde Park was a crush, much more so than usual, and soon after the landau had driven through the elegant gates, the traffic became so congested that it barely proceeded at all. It wasn't long before Jane realized why, for in the distance she heard familiar chanting and shouting—the queen was making another of her progresses. Luckily, they had happened upon the end of her procession, which was emerging from the far side of the park as Jane's landau entered, but they were still inconvenienced by the delays as fashionable carriages were forced to wait for the way to clear completely.

There were, as always, a number of horsemen in the park, and one of them detached himself from his group of companions to ride over to the landau. It was Charles Moncarm. He reined in, doffing his hat and smiling as he controlled his capering mount. "Good afternoon, Jane, Lady Agatha."

Aunt Derwent was delighted. "Charles! What a pleasure it is to see you! You appear to be in fine fettle."

He glanced at Jane. "I could be even finer."

Aunt Derwent pursed her lips and nodded. "Dame Fortune isn't always kind."

"So I've discovered. Well, Lady Agatha, you've deserted darkest Beaconsfield for the pleasures of the wicked city. I trust I will be welcome if I call upon you?"

"My laddo, if you don't call, I shall make a monstrous fuss and cause you no end of embarrassment over Town."

He grinned. "Then I shall be careful to avoid any such dread possibility by calling on you in the very near future."

"I shall be at home this evening, but then I'm visiting Lady Lindleigh for a day, possibly two, I can't really be sure."

"Lady Lindleigh? Hasn't she gone to Rome?"

"Why does everyone keep insisting she's abroad? Jane thinks she's in Paris, you think she's in Rome, when all the time she's languishing at home in Kensington."

The traffic was beginning to move again and he gathered his reins to take his leave. "I shall call then, Lady Agatha."

"I look forward to that."

"Good-bye."

"Good-bye."

He looked at Jane. "Good-bye, Jane."

"Good-bye, Charles."

They watched him ride away, a dashing figure in a dark green coat on a fine mettlesome bay. Aunt Derwent's eyes slid thoughtfully toward her niece. "He'd make a splendid husband, Jane, although I concede that as a lover he most probably lacks Lewis Ardenley's flair."

"If I loved Charles I'd marry him, whether he had flair in that direction or not."

The landau drove on, completing the circuit of the park and emerging again into the busy thoroughfare of Park Lane, but having to wait for some time for a chance to join the constant flow of vehicles. As they waited, Jane looked out and saw

Lewis's traveling carriage driving smartly southward toward the narrow, congested corner of Piccadilly with both Lewis and Alicia inside. Alicia wore white, from the soft plumes springing from her velvet hat to the snowy lines of her modish pelisse. Her eyes were downcast and she wasn't smiling—indeed, there was something strange about her demeanor, although Jane couldn't have said exactly what it was. Opposite her, Lewis wore a wine-red coat and, as was his habit, he had tilted his top hat back on his golden head. His expression was thoughtful, and he gazed out of the carriage window without seeming to be looking at anything in particular.

The carriage passed out of sight among the rest of the traffic, and at last the landau could pull out as well, turning south toward the corner of Curzon Street and then into South Audley Street. Aunt Derwent hadn't said anything about seeing Lewis and Alicia, but as the carriage drew to a standstill at the door of the house, she remained in her seat looking at her niece. "They didn't appear to be in the seventh heaven of delight, did they?"

"Not really."

"Now he's back in Town, are you going to do anything about things?"

"Things?"

"Winning his affections again."

"There's nothing I can do."

"Rubbish."

"This is old ground, Aunt Derwent."

"Yes, well now I think it's time to tell you what I've heard. When I called upon my various friends yesterday, I heard a snippet of information which I doubt very much you've been told, since it's very new. It's about my dear old friend the Duke of Brantingham."

"The *duke*?"

"He has a new love, Jane, and he adores her so much that he intends at last to divorce Alicia."

Jane stared at her. The duke had always refused to countenance such a course in the past, even though Alicia had given him more than sufficient grounds. It was said that he still loved her. "Who—who is this new love?"

"Lady Mary someone or other—I really didn't recognize the name. Anyway, that's hardly the point. All that matters is that he's so besotted that he's all eagerness to rid himself of Alicia, and the moment he does so, she will be free to marry Lewis." Aunt Derwent held Jane's gaze. "It's time to make a move, my dear, because if you don't, Alicia Brantingham is going to emerge the final victor, and you are going to be miserable for the rest of your life. Oh yes, I mean exactly that, and I speak as one who knows only too well the result of apathy and pride. I could have married the Duke of Wellington, Jane, but I was foolish enough to take a stance, just as you are doing now. Kitty Pakenham won him instead, but she hasn't the spirit to stand up to him and so he walks all over her. He wouldn't have walked all over me, I'd have taken him on and oh, how those sparks would have flown. I'd have loved every minute of it, and so would he, but I allowed my vanity to cloud my vision, and I've regretted it ever since. I still love him with all my heart, Jane, just as you will always love Lewis Ardenley. I said last night that I had a trick or two up my sleeve, and so I have, and I shall use them on your behalf, you mark my words. The rest is up to you. Either you want him back or you don't, there's no in-between anymore."

Jane felt cold all over, in spite of the warmth of the June sunshine. Until this moment, she hadn't realized how much she'd come to rely inwardly upon the elderly duke's obstinate refusal to consider divorce, but now that small comfort was being removed.

Her aunt was looking at her. "Well? Does what I've just told you make any difference?"

Slowly, Jane nodded. "Yes," she whispered.

"I trust that that means you're going to fight for him?"

"Yes."

"Good."

Jane and her aunt dined alone that evening, prior to her aunt's departure for Lady Lindleigh's house in Kensington. Henry wasn't at home, having sent word that he was having problems with his new coach and didn't know how long it would take to put right. Jane wondered if he'd managed to find anything out about the new Nonpareil, and thinking about this inevitably led to thoughts about the new Swan. Would it be ready in time for the race? With only three days left, time was beginning to run very short indeed.

Aunt Derwent was a stickler for dressing correctly at all times, and that meant dressing formally for dinner even when there were only two of them. She had chosen a lilac-and-gray-striped taffeta gown trimmed with matching ribbons, and a lilac turban looped with a number of strings of pearls. A black lace shawl was draped lightly over her shoulders, and there were matching fingerless mittens on her hands. At her throat was a black velvet ribbon bearing a golden locket, the contents of which had always been a closely guarded secret, but Jane guessed now that it contained a likeness of her aunt's great love, the Duke of Wellington.

As Jane sat down in the chair Melville drew out for her, she reflected that if she didn't somehow manage to win Lewis back soon, then she too would probably one day wear such a locket. . . . She'd chosen to wear primrose muslin that night, a gown of very simple lines but heightened by Marie sleeves of great intricacy. With it she wore topazes, including a jeweled comb decorating the knot of hair Ellen had pinned up so expertly on her head, and as she made herself comfortable, arranging the folds of her skirts, she knew that she looked well enough to take her place at any fashionable dinner party.

Her aunt looked approvingly at her. "You'll do, my girl, you'll do."

"Thank you."

"I can't abide sloppiness at the dinner table. It's quite unnecessary and shows ill breeding. Not that I'm suggesting you are ever anything less than well groomed, you understand, it's just that I happen to think that dinner is a meal to be enjoyed to the full, and for me that means dressing up as much as possible."

"I trust it also means enjoying your favorite dishes."

"Naturally." Her aunt paused. "Am I to understand that you've chosen my favorites for tonight?"

"You are. It was too late yesterday, I'd already arranged the meals with Mrs. Beale, but today I've taken great care to consider your particular taste."

"What are we to have?"

"Tomato soup, made to Mrs. Beale's special recipe, the one you've always lamented she will not divulge to your own cook. Then boiled gammon garnished with spinach and dressed with carrots and beans, followed by strawberries and cream, and if you still have room there is cheese, with nectarines, walnuts, and that peach liqueur you once swore you'd sell your very soul for."

Her aunt was beaming. "My *dear*, I shall have to walk all the way to Kensington to pay penance for such overindulgence!"

After the meal, they took the fruit, nuts, and liqueur on the blue saloon balcony. The evening was very fine indeed, the sunset just beginning to tinge the houses and trees with a warm blush. Time was marching on and Jane was beginning to wonder exactly when her aunt intended to set off for Lady Lindleigh's, but the minutes passed and still she sat there, surveying the gardens and appreciating the scent of roses and honeysuckle filling the air.

In the saloon behind them the long-case clock chimed half-past nine and Jane looked at her aunt. "Please don't think I wish to be rid of you, but shouldn't you be thinking of leaving?"

"There's time yet."

Melville entered the saloon then, clearing his throat discreetly as he approached the windows standing open onto the balcony. "Begging your pardon, madam, but Lord Ardenley has called."

Jane sat up quickly, but it was her completely unruffled aunt the butler was addressing.

Aunt Derwent nodded. "Very well, Melville, please show him up."

"Yes, my lady."

The butler withdrew and Jane looked accusingly at her aunt. "You've been expecting this, haven't you?"

"Yes, my dear, I have. I sent a note to Lewis when we returned from the park this afternoon."

"You might have warned me!"

"That wouldn't have done at all. You'd have worked yourself up to a fine old pitch if I had. As it is, it's been sprung upon you and there's little you can do."

"Why has he come? What have you told him?"

"If you think I've told him about your change of heart, you may rest easy, because I haven't. As a matter of fact, I've invited him to discuss purchasing a particular Canaletto of mine that I happen to know he's long wished to add to his own collection. It's all perfectly innocent, my dear. I haven't hatched anything improper behind your back. Hush now, I can hear him coming."

Jane's heart was thundering as she heard Melville approaching, Lewis's steps close behind. The butler stopped at the open door. "Lord Ardenley," he announced.

Lewis paused in the doorway for a moment, toying with the lace spilling from the cuff of his dark blue single-breasted evening coat. There was more lace on his shirt front, and his cravat was tied in a soft, loose style. His tight trousers were of white kerseymere and he wore white gloves. The silver buttons on his coat gleamed a little in the fading evening sunlight as he crossed the room toward them.

He bowed first over Jane's hand, his gloved fingers warm and firm about hers before he released her.

"Good evening, Lewis," said Aunt Derwent, looking approvingly at him. "You're looking as splendidly attractive as ever."

"The same can more than be said of you, Lady Agatha," he said, raising her hand to his lips.

She smiled. "Ah, still the silken tongue. Do sit down, sir, and take a liqueur with us."

He flicked his coat tails and sat on the chair she indicated. Opposite him, Jane was very conscious indeed of the warm blush which had stolen into her cheeks. She felt very vulnerable now that she'd decided she must fight to win him back. Her hands were trembling and she clasped them in her lap.

Aunt Derwent poured him a glass of the liqueur and then sat back. "Now then, Lewis, I didn't explain fully in my note earlier, I just mentioned that a painting you'd long desired just might be available. I was referring to the Canaletto, the view of St. Paul's from Southwark. Are you still interested?"

"Naturally."

"I thought you might be, since you once droned on at considerable length about how perfect it would be for the head of the staircase at Maywood."

"For the library at Maywood," he said, correcting her. "I fear that even such a splendid Canaletto would be rather lost at the head of Maywood's staircase."

"Ah yes, I remember now," she replied, nodding, "Maywood *is* rather vast, isn't it. The library it is, then. I confess that I shall be sorry to part with it, but something has to go because I've purchased several very fine portraits by Reynolds."

He smiled. "A little old-fashioned, surely?"

"I happen to like them very much indeed."

"Which is, of course, the best reason for acquiring them."

"Naturally. Oh, I think Jane is in agreement with you about Reynolds, especially as she likes Canaletto so very much. Is that not so, Jane?"

Jane smiled a little weakly, still flustered by the suddenness of his arrival. "Yes, indeed it is."

He looked a little quizzically at her. "I had no idea you found Canaletto so much to your liking, Jane. You never mentioned the fact when you were inspecting my collection at Maywood."

"Didn't I? Well, there is so much that is beautiful at Maywood that I suppose I couldn't possibly mention absolutely everything." She met his gaze for a moment. "Indeed, I suppose that that's always been a failing of mine, not showing my full appreciation.''

He continued to look at her for a moment, as if undecided how to take her last statement. Then he smiled a little. ''Perhaps that is a wiser course than showing too much,'' he said.

''Have—have you been to the Feathers today?'' she asked, not knowing what else to say.

''Yes, I went when I arrived back from Maywood.''

''Is there any news?''

''Of the new coach? No.'' He glanced at Aunt Derwent. ''I take it from Jane's openness that you are fully *au fait* with the situation.''

''I am, sir. Indeed, that's why I'm here in Town—I couldn't bear to stay away. It's very exciting, isn't it?''

He looked at Jane again. ''A little too exciting when a certain lady insists upon traveling on the coach in the race.''

''My dear Lewis,'' said Aunt Derwent, ''how very stuffy and male you sound. I might tell you that if it wasn't that we'd be putting the Swan at a disadvantage, Blanche and I would be on the coach as well.''

''Blanche is in on it all too? Poor Henry, he doesn't stand much of a chance, does he?''

''Does he deserve to?''

He smiled. ''Probably not.''

''Of course he doesn't. He's being very shabby and silly, and by turning his back on the woman he quite obviously adores, he's being the end in fools as well.''

There was a silence. Jane felt the color deepening on her cheeks and felt she had to say something to turn the conversation from the rather embarrassing course it suddenly seemed set to take. ''Some more liqueur, Lewis?'' she asked, taking up the beautiful cut-glass decanter and smiling.

''Thank you but no, I must not stay any longer. I—''

He said no more for at that moment the doors of the saloon were opened and a rather harrassed Melville just had time to announce Alicia before that lady swept regally in in a rustle of exquisite deep purple silk.

Jane froze, the color draining from her cheeks, and Aunt Derwent stared at the newcomer in such surprise that she almost dropped her glass.

Lewis rose to his feet in some embarrassment, giving his mistress a dark look which showed that he was far from amused by her sudden appearance.

Alicia affected not to notice, indeed she was all smiles and effusive charm as she approached Aunt Derwent. "Lady Agatha," she said, the diamonds in her hair sparkling brilliantly, "I simply *had* to come up and pay my respects. Lewis said to wait in the carriage, that he wouldn't be long, but I knew that once he sat talking, he'd be a positive age and we'd be late at Grillion's. How are you? You're looking very well." Her green eyes slid coolly toward Jane's still face. "Good evening, Jane."

Jane couldn't bring herself to reply. She was devastated by the realization that Lewis had come to her house bringing his mistress with him. True, he'd left her outside in the carriage, but that didn't excuse him in the slightest. With a superhuman effort, she managed to put the decanter down without revealing how much she was trembling with anger. What a fool she'd made of herself, being all agreeable and signaling that she'd suffered a change of heart; how amused he must be.

Aunt Derwent managed to recover a little, giving Alicia a rather tight smile. "Good evening, Alicia, I had no idea you were here."

"Lewis and I had already arranged to dine at Grillion's tonight when your letter arrived, so we decided to call here on our way." Alicia smiled again.

Lewis still seemed angry, although he didn't give vent to it in front of Jane and her aunt. Glancing at his fob watch, he went determinedly to his mistress, taking her arm and then giving the others a stiff smile which could either have signified his irritation with Alicia or his supreme embarrassment at being caught out bringing her to South Audley Street. He inclined his head at Aunt Derwent. "Thank you for offering me the Canaletto, Lady Agatha. I'm sure we can agree upon a price to our mutual satisfaction. Good night, Jane."

But Jane couldn't bring herself to look at him, let alone manage a reply. How dared he bring that woman to her door, how *dared* he!

They withdrew then, and as the door closed behind them, Aunt Derwent turned sadly and apologetically to her niece. "Oh, my dear, I'm so very sorry."

"It wasn't your fault."

"But it was. I deliberately invited him here tonight, thinking that . . . Well, it's obvious what I hoped would come about. Instead, that—that *creature* came up to spoil it all."

"That creature wouldn't have been here at all if he hadn't brought her. News of her husband's changed mind has most

182

probably made the world of difference, and I'll warrant she put those few days at Maywood to excellent use. I made an utter fool of myself, Aunt Derwent, and I shall not do it again, of that you may be certain.''

"But my dear, he didn't look very pleased when she came up.''

"Don't make excuses for him, Aunt Derwent. He still brought her to the door, and I cannot excuse him for that!''

"Jane . . .''

"Please Aunt Derwent, I don't want to talk about it any more.''

Her aunt got sadly to her feet. "I have to leave now. I only wish I didn't, but plans are plans. I wish you'd think very carefully, Jane.'' She touched the locket at her throat. "I don't think Lewis wished Alicia to come up, in fact I'm certain of it, and if they had indeed planned to dine at Grillion's tonight, well it would have been insulting of him to leave her to make her own way there, wouldn't it? Whichever way he did it, he was bound to hurt someone. By leaving her outside, he did at least attempt to spare your feelings, and he wasn't to know that the wretched creature would take it into her head to actually come up here. Look at me, Jane. He's still worth fighting for, and if you let this incident deter you, then you stand only too much of a chance of ending up as I have, reduced to carrying around a portrait of the man you love because you can't have the man himself. Think very carefully about it.''

She left the balcony then, and Jane closed her eyes, fighting back the tears which stung so very much.

TWENTY-FOUR

*H*enry returned to the house before breakfast the next morning, causing something of a stir below stairs by immediately demanding a hot bath. Jane was awoken by the to-ing and fro-ing of footmen past her door as they carried the water. She sat up in bed, pushing her dark hair back from her face. Henry seemed to be in a good mood, she could hear him whistling as he changed, but she felt very low indeed, unable to forget what had happened the previous evening.

She said very little as Ellen pinned up her hair, and then she put on a pretty pink muslin gown scattered with white dots. It was a cheerful gown, putting color into her cheeks and distracting attention from the lack of sparkle in her violet eyes.

Sitting at the breakfast table waiting for Henry to join her, she ignored the array of silver-domed dishes on the sideboard, choosing instead to take only toast and coffee. Outside, it was another glorious day, the sun shining warmly down from a clear blue sky. Light streaming in through the windows lay brightly on the folds of her skirts as she sat toying with the corner of her napkin, her toast and coffee untouched.

Henry came in at last, his face very clean and pink after the bath. He wore his paisley dressing gown over his shirt and trousers, and she could smell the cologne with which he'd splashed himself rather liberally. His manner was breezy, to say the least, as he went to the sideboard and selected himself a large plateful of scrambled eggs and bacon and then sat down to tackle it. He didn't say a word to her.

"Good morning, Henry," she prompted at last.

"Mm?"

"I said good morning."

He lowered his knife and fork and pretended to see her for the first time. "Good heavens, there's someone else here! You were so still and silent as I came in that I didn't notice you."

"What would you have me do when I'm on my own, dance on the table?"

"That *would* be different." He surveyed her for a moment. "I gather Alicia Brantingham was here last night."

"Yes."

"And that's the reason for your reserve this morning?"

"If I'm reserved, you seem the very opposite," she said, attempting to change the subject. "A bath before breakfast? A cheerful whistle or two while you change? It's quite unheard of."

"It isn't *that* unheard of," he replied, a little miffed, "because unlike several gentlemen of my acquaintance, I happen to appreciate the benefits of bathing."

"That's very true, but before breakfast? I've never known you to do that before. What's happened to put you in such high spirits?"

"Everything's ready with the Iron Duke, absolutely everything."

"Have you found out about the new Nonpareil?" she asked lightly.

"Eh?" He was applying himself to his breakfast again.

"The new Nonpareil."

"No, Chapman's keep it too close to his conniving chest. Still, I don't care anymore, I think all this secrecy's just a ploy, a trick to worry me."

"Did you find out about the Swan?"

He paused then, his blue eyes resting speculatively on her for a moment. "No, but there is something a little strange."

"Strange?"

"Lewis Ardenley apparently frequents the Feathers."

"He—he does?" She hoped she was registering astonishment. "Whatever for?"

He hesitated. "That I couldn't say," he said at last, thinking better of telling her what his spy had reported seeing in the stable—Lewis Ardenley taking exceedingly improper liberties with a tavern wench! He ate a little more breakfast. "Where's Aunt Derwent? She's usually up before this."

"She's gone to stay with Lady Lindleigh for a day or so."

"Lady Lindleigh? Isn't she in Vienna?"

Jane had to smile. "Apparently not. It's strange you should say that though. I thought she was in Paris and Charles was convinced it was Rome. We're all wrong, for she is at home in Kensington."

"I could have sworn old Lindleigh told me . . . Well, no matter, I evidently misheard." He finished his breakfast and pushed his cup toward her. "You're neglecting your duties, sis. I've been gasping for coffee and you're hogging the pot."

"Gasping for coffee?" She obligingly poured some for him. "You've been so busy gobbling you haven't given yourself time to drink as well."

"I felt ravenous."

"You must indeed be pleased with your preparations for the race."

"I am. Two days to go and I'll have Chapman by the scruff of his scrawny little neck."

"If you're in such a good mood, might it not be the very time to make your peace with Blanche?" she asked tentatively.

His smile faded. "No, it might not."

"But you know you still love her, Henry."

"I don't know any such thing. Jane, I wish you'd stop all this.

185

Blanche encouraged Dursley and gave me back my ring, and so I regard her as being completely at fault."

"You're the one who is mostly at fault, Henry," she replied quietly. "You continually put Blanche in second place."

He misunderstood. "Are you suggesting that *I* was the one who was being unfaithful?"

"That isn't what I mean, but since you put it that way, then yes, you were. With a stagecoach."

With an exasperated sigh, he flung his napkin down and got up. "I'm not going to listen to any more of this. I came back here today feeling on top of the world, but you've soon put a stop to that. Leave my love life alone, Jane, and concentrate upon your own, which appears to be in a far worse state that mine ever was or ever will be. And in case you should think you still have a chance to work upon me where Blanche is concerned, let me tell you that for the next two days at least you'll have to twiddle your interfering thumbs, because I'm going to stay at the Fleece until after the race." He left the room then, closing the door firmly behind him.

Shortly afterward, his phaeton was brought to the door and he lingered in the vestibule discussing a few minor matters with Melville prior to departing. Jane had just finished going through the day's meals with the cook, Mrs. Beale, when she happened to glance out of the window to see a groom from the Feathers approaching the door, a note in his hand. She rose to her feet in dismay. Whatever could have happened for Jacob to risk sending someone directly to her instead of through Mr. Payne? She hurried out into the vestibule, where Henry was just taking his hat and gloves from Melville. The groom knocked at the door and the butler went to open it, taking the note from the man, who immediately hurried away again.

Henry glanced after the groom, raising an eyebrow. "Can't say I recognize the fellow," he murmured, holding out his hand for the note.

Jane's breath caught. "No?" she cried. "No, the note's for me, Henry."

He paused. "For you? Jane, the fellow's quite obviously a groom—I could smell the stables even from here—so why on earth should you think the message is for you?"

"He—he's Madame Louise's groom," she said quickly.

Melville had been looking intently at her, and now came to her rescue. "Her ladyship is correct, my lord. The messenger said the note was for her."

Henry still seemed uncertain. "Did he? I'm damned if I heard him open his mouth." Then he shrugged, thrusting the note into her hand. "Oh, very well, if it's for you it's for you."

Jane gladly took the note and pushed it into her sleeve, relieved that he hadn't decided to read it anyway, just to be sure. Melville was still holding the door open, waiting for Henry to go out to the waiting phaeton, so they all heard the carriage drawing up outside. It was Blanche, wearing a green sprigged muslin walking dress and a matching bonnet, the ribbons of which lifted prettily in the light summer breeze.

Jane was a little taken aback to see her calling, since she must have realized Henry was at home because his phaeton was at the door. The two hadn't seen each other since the night at the theater, and until now Blanche had been very careful to avoid all chance of encountering him. Why then had she changed her mind this morning?

Henry had stiffened the moment he recognized the carriage, and his face was now very stony indeed. He accorded her only the very briefest of nods as she entered the vestibule, but she didn't even allow him that small civility, ignoring him completely as she went straight to Jane, a warm smile on her lips. "Good morning, Jane. I was passing and thought I'd call upon you to take a cup of your excellent coffee and enjoy your more than agreeable conversation."

Just happened to be passing? Jane was more surprised than ever. She glanced at her brother's icy expression and then back at Blanche. "A cup of coffee it is, but as to the more than agreeable conversation. . . ."

Henry's smile was very cool. "Don't concern yourself about *that*, Jane, for whatever conversation there is will be taking place without me!"

Blanche's eyes flickered disdainfully. "Then it will indeed be agreeable, sir."

Angrily tugging on his top hat, he strode out to the waiting phaeton, and Melville closed the door, turning to Jane. "Shall I serve coffee in the blue saloon, my lady?"

"Yes, please."

"Very well, my lady."

"And Melville, thank you for coming to my rescue with the note."

He bowed and withdrew.

Blanche looked curiously at her. "Your butler rescues you with a note? How very intriguing."

"It was nearly all up with me, Blanche. Jacob sent a note and Henry almost read it."

"Oh, no. Whatever did the note say?"

"I don't know, I haven't had a chance to read it yet." She took the paper from her sleeve and unfolded it. Her eyes brightened immediately. "The new Swan's been delivered! It's being taken out for the first time right now and he suggests I go to the Feathers at about eight this evening to see how everything's gone! Oh, Blanche, I was beginning to think we'd have to enter the old coach!"

"How exciting! Will you go this evening?"

"Of course."

"May I come too?"

Jane smiled. "Of course to that too. Oh, and by the way, if you still intend to follow the race in your carriage, you will have a passenger."

"I will?"

"Aunt Derwent would like to join you."

"I'd be delighted. Actually, it was partly to see her that I called this morning, or at least, she was my excuse."

"She's not here. Why did you call when you saw Henry's phaeton?" she asked curiously.

Blanche lowered her eyes. "I just wanted to see him."

"You gave a masterly display of the very opposite, if you don't mind my saying so."

"I wasn't going to let him know the truth, especially not when he still puts his coaches before everything else. And now, having seen how he reacted the moment he saw me alighting from my carriage, I'm more glad than ever that you're doing what you are, and nothing, *nothing* will keep me away on race day!" She looked at Jane then, noticing for the first time how pale she was. "Is something wrong? You look—well, I don't know exactly what, but you don't look right."

"Lewis came here last night."

"And?"

"And he brought Alicia with him."

Blanche stared incredulously at her. "He did what?"

"She actually came up to the blue saloon. It was awful, and I was so humiliated because I'd decided . . . Well, it doesn't really matter anymore."

"But—"

"I don't want to talk about it, Blanche. The subject is closed."

Blanche nodded sympathetically. "I'm so sorry, Jane. Right

then, we'll talk about something else. I came here hoping to see your aunt, but you say she isn't here?''

"She's gone to stay with Lady Lindleigh for a day or so."

"Lady Lindleigh? But I thought she was on the Continent."

Jane gave a slightly incredulous laugh. "Not you too! *Everyone* says she's out of the country, but she isn't."

"I'm sure she is. She and Lord Lindleigh invited my parents to dinner last week, prior to leaving for Dover. They've definitely gone, Jane, I know they have."

Jane was very still then. "But if that's so, how can my aunt possibly be staying there?" She looked at Blanche in growing alarm. "Something's wrong, I know it is!"

"I expect it's just that Lady Agatha has muddled the dates up," replied Blanche reassuringly. "She'll arrive at Kensington, realize her mistake, and be back again before you know it."

"But she left last night. She's had more than enough time to go there and come back. I must send someone there straightaway!" Jane rang for Melville.

TWENTY-FIVE

A footman was dispatched to Kensington but soon returned to report that the Lindleigh residence was shut up for the summer, its owners having definitely gone to spend several months on the Continent. The news made Jane more uneasy than ever, but she was persuaded by Blanche that Lady Agatha Derwent wasn't accountable to anyone for her movements and that to make an unwarranted fuss would probably mean incurring that lady's considerable wrath.

By seven o'clock in the evening, there had still not been any word from her, and Jane was very anxious indeed, but Blanche, who had stayed with her all day, insisted that her aunt had quite obviously known what she was doing and that therefore they must leave well enough alone. It was time to leave for the Feathers to inspect the new Swan, but Jane didn't want to go. Blanche virtually bullied her into ordering the town carriage so that at half-past seven exactly they set off with their maids for the usual corner of Arlington Street and the line of waiting hackney coaches. It was Blanche's first experience of such vehicles, but it wasn't long before the initial excitement wore off and she declared it to be an extremely disagreeable business.

They arrived at the Feathers at almost exactly eight o'clock. The new Swan was being kept out of sight of the street in the stableyard, and Betsy hurried from the group of people clustered around it to greet the new arrivals as they alighted from the hackney, the maids withdrawing to a quiet corner. "Lady Jane, I'm so glad you've come." She hesitated then, dropping a hasty curtsy to Blanche, whom she didn't know.

Jane introduced them. "Blanche, this is Betsy Wheddle. Betsy, this is Miss Blanche Lyndon."

Betsy smiled. "Good evening, Miss Lyndon."

"Good evening, Betsy."

At that moment, they heard another vehicle entering the yard from the street and turned to see a smart scarlet cabriolet. It was Lewis. Jane stiffened, while Blanche shifted a little uncomfortably, wondering how many sparks would fly from the inevitable confrontation.

Betsy, who knew how things were between Lord Ardenley and Lady Jane Derwent, wisely withdrew to the inner yard again, not wanting to intrude upon any argument.

Lewis handed the reins to the small boy who had appeared from nowhere to attend to the cabriolet, and then he alighted, pausing for a moment to remove his top hat and run his fingers through his golden hair. He looked very Bond Street in his perfectly cut dark brown coat and tightly-fitting beige breeches, and the diamond pin in his russet silk neckcloth caught the sunlight as he turned toward the two ladies.

Jane walked away immediately, cutting him as surely as he had cut her at the theater, but she didn't do so from any calculated intention, she did so because she couldn't bring herself to face him, the pain, hurt, and anger of the previous evening were still too fresh.

He watched her hurry away toward the stableyard and then turned to Blanche, who remained where she was. "Good evening, Blanche."

"Sir."

The coolness of the greeting couldn't be mistaken. "I'm in your bad books as well, it seems."

"You are, sir."

"May I inquire why?"

"I think you know the answer to that, sir."

He pursed his lips, a wry expression in his gray eyes. "If I must guess, then I suppose it must be Alicia's appearance at South Audley Street last night."

"Correct."

"Blanche, you surely don't think I did it intentionally, do you?"

"Are you telling me that Alicia's presence in your carriage was a complete accident?"

"Hardly."

"Then there's nothing else to be said, is there? You took Alicia to Jane's house, and that was monstrous. I begin to think, sir, that when Alicia obtains her freedom and marries you, there will be some sort of poetic justice about the match, for you certainly deserve each other."

He smiled a little. "I will allow that it's your prerogative to believe what you wish, Blanche, even if you are wrong about the whole thing. Now then, if I offer you my arm to proceed into the stableyard, will you accept?"

She looked at him for a moment, but accepted the arm. "You're a beast, Lewis Ardenley."

"Ah, but I'm a very charming one."

"I suppose even a toad has charm, sir, at least as far as other toads are concerned."

They walked beneath the arch and saw everyone gathered around the new coach, which was a very eye-catching vehicle, its lacquerwork the brightest of blues and its wheels a particularly splendid yellow. It was handsome, but it lacked the fine silver harness and elegant lamps Henry's new Iron Duke sported, and inside it had only very basic upholstery, looking nothing like the Nonpareil with its ivory timetables and velvet seats. The gold lettering on its side was bold and almost defiant, and the whole effect was very challenging, as if the coach couldn't wait to come out of hiding to take on its unknowing rivals.

Jacob turned, having been primed by Betsy about Blanche's presence. "Good evening, Lord Ardenley. Miss Lyndon."

Blanche nodded. "Good evening, sir."

Lewis glanced at the coach. "I hope she flies, Jacob."

"She does indeed, my lord. Arthur reckons that with your cattle she'll take to the air itself."

"I've managed to get a sly look over the new Iron Duke, and I think we'll be able to hold our own against it. That just leaves the Nonpareil."

Jacob was still looking at the coach. "I'd give an arm and a leg to know what Chapman's got hidden under that tarpaulin at the Black Horse, but I'm more and more afraid that you've been right all along, my lord—it's a safety coach with brakes, and it'll have the edge on every incline and corner between here and Brighton. Still, whatever miracle he's got, it's too late for us to do anything to the Swan, except perhaps put on some brakes."

Lewis suddenly looked toward Jane, as if something of considerable urgency and importance had occurred to him. "Jacob, has Lady Jane said anything to you about trying to somehow find out about the Nonpareil?"

The landlord was a little taken aback. "Lady Jane? Well, she's just mentioned that perhaps we'll be able to find out before race day. . . ."

"Yes, and I think I know what she meant!" The reply had darkened Lewis's eyes and now he strode toward Jane and caught her arm, jerking her angrily around to face him. "A word with you, madam!"

She stared at him in astonishment, too startled to react with equal anger, and Blanche hurried over to her rescue, looking furiously at him. "How *dare* you use her in such a fashion!" she cried.

"I dare, Blanche, when I begin to suspect her of conduct leaving a great deal to be desired!" He held Jane's gaze. "Where is your aunt?" he demanded.

"My—my aunt?"

"That is what I said. Well? Where is she?"

"She said that she was going to stay with Lady Lindleigh, but— "

"Lord and Lady Lindleigh are on the Continent."

"I realize that now, but I didn't when she first told me! Lewis, what's all this about? Have you seen her?"

"Oh, stop this ridiculous play-acting, Jane, it doesn't fool me in the slightest!"

"Play-acting? Lewis, I don't know what you're talking about."

Blanche was still looking furiously at him, and now the whole stableyard had fallen silent, with all eyes on them. Blanche put a protective hand on Jane's trembling arm. "Lewis, you'd better have a sovereign reason for this," she breathed, "for if you do not, then so help me. . . ."

"I do have a most sovereign reason, Blanche." He held Jane's gaze. "I didn't think you'd carry things to this length, Jane. Indeed, I didn't think you'd sink so low. Endanger your own life in the pursuance of victory at Brighton if you must, but don't endanger the lives of others as well, especially not someone like Lady Agatha!''

Her eyes widened and the color drained from her face. "What do you mean?" she whispered.

"Must you persist with this charade of innocence? You decided that finding out about the new Nonpareil was of paramount importance, and you've involved your unfortunate aunt in order to do so."

She still looked helplessly at him. "I don't know what you're talking about, truly I don't."

"Oh, what a consummate actress you are—you really do look puzzled and innocent. You could almost convince me you don't know that at this very moment your aunt is at the Black Horse trying to inveigle Chapman into telling her his closely guarded secrets. When my footman mentioned to me that at noon today, while he was meeting his brother from the Birmingham Flyer, he'd seen a lady looking uncommon like Lady Agatha Derwent dining *à deux* with an exceeding attentive Chapman, I didn't give it a great deal of thought, but then when Jacob mentioned a moment ago about how important it was that we find out about the new Nonpareil, so that we're as prepared as possible, it all suddenly fell into place. Your aunt has been persuaded to go there anonymously, probably posing as a rich widow—Chapman has a penchant for rich widows, he's married three of them—and she's bent upon finding out about the new coach so that if necessary we can have brakes fitted to the Swan in time for the race. Am I right, Jane?''

A surge of guilt swept through her, even though she was blameless. She remembered her aunt's words the first evening she'd arrived from Beaconsfield. *Is it very important to find out before the race? I've come up with a rather capital plan myself. That would be telling. Wild horses wouldn't drag it out of me, it's going to be my little secret. I'm going to Lady Lindleigh's for a while, I'm not sure how long, but I promise to be back in time for the race.* Jane closed her eyes, for she could even see her aunt's rather conspiratorial smile. It was all so obvious now, with hindsight. But at the time. . . .

Lewis saw the guilt on her face. "You can't deny it, can you? You *did* work upon your aunt to do this, and you knew that it was wrong, so you've invented this tale about Lady Lindleigh."

"No! You're wrong." She looked desperately at Blanche, but

Blanche was too shaken at that moment to offer the required support.

Lewis was still looking at Jane. "I'm disappointed in you, for I never for one moment believed you'd behave so callously. I tell you here and now that if it was not for the fact that so many other people are involved in this madness with the Swan, I'd withdraw my assistance immediately and have nothing more to do with either you or your schemes. But my word has been given and I will stand by it. Right now, however, I intend going to the Black Horse to remove your aunt, and then I shall take her directly to South Audley Street. I suggest, madam, that you go there now and wait, so that you can belatedly show a little concern for her safety and welfare."

She met his accusing gaze then, from somewhere finding the composure to reply calmly, even though she was devastated by his cold contempt and by the realization of the danger her aunt had placed herself in. "I will be at South Audley Street, sir," she replied.

He turned on his heel and strode away. A moment later they heard the cabriolet leaving at speed.

Blanche looked anxiously at Jane, who was so very still. "Are—are you all right?"

"Yes." The single word was uttered so quietly that it was barely above a whisper.

Putting a gentle, apologetic hand on her arm, Blanche lowered her eyes a little guiltily. "I should have spoken up, Jane, but I was so shocked by what he said that I could only stand there. I'll tell him the truth, Jane, I promise that I will."

"Don't bother. Let him think what he wishes, I really couldn't care less."

Blanche said nothing more, for everything in Jane's voice and demeanor said that the very opposite was true—she still cared very much indeed about Lewis Ardenley and what he thought of her.

Tears filled Jane's eyes, but she blinked them furiously back. "I—I must go to South Audley Street," she said, her voice breaking a little. Then she gathered her skirts and ran through the archway to where the hackney coach still waited.

Blanche turned to look at the silent group by the new coach and then she too gathered her skirts, hurrying in Jane's wake.

TWENTY-SIX

*J*ane needed time to compose herself when she and Ellen arrived home after leaving Blanche and her maid, but that was not to be, for as she entered the house Melville informed her that Charles had called and was waiting in the blue saloon. Dismay spread through her, for the last thing she felt like was polite conversation, but there was nothing for it but to go to him. She went up still in her pelisse and bonnet, pausing at the door to take a long, tremulous breath to steady herself. Then she went in, forcing a rather too bright smile to her lips. "Charles, I do hope you haven't been waiting too long."

He was standing by the fireplace, a foot resting on the polished fender as he glanced through her copy of Lord Byron's *The Corsair*, and he immediately put the volume down, coming to take her hand and raise it to his lips. "Hello, Jane. No, of course I haven't, and if I had it would have been my own fault for insisting on waiting even when told that everyone was out." He looked into her eyes then and saw immediately that all was not well. "What's wrong?" he asked, cupping her hand in both his.

"Nothing," she replied lightly, trying to draw her hand away.

He refused to let her go. "Don't fib to me, Jane. You've been crying, haven't you?"

"No."

"Jane," he said, "I won't be fobbed off, so you may as well tell me." He reached up to unfasten her bonnet and toss it on the table, then he tilted her pale face toward his, looking concernedly into her eyes. "Now then, what is it?"

"If—if I tell you, you'll be very shocked."

He smiled. "I can't imagine that you've done anything shocking."

"But I have." The tears filled her eyes again then, rolling hotly down her cheeks. "I've been s-so foolish, Charles, and now Aunt Derwent's in danger because of me. I wish I'd n-never started it all, t-truly I do."

"Started what? Jane, I think you'd better explain properly."

Gently taking her arm, he led her to a sofa, sitting her down and then joining her. He smiled a little. "What's all this about, mm? How on earth can your aunt be in danger because of you?"

She drew a deep breath. "She's become involved in all my plotting behind Henry's back." her voice was steadier now.

"Plotting?"

"I was so angry with him after his absence from Blanche's ball that I decided to teach him a lesson." She met his gaze. "I've been financing the Swan stagecoach, Charles, and it was my intention to enter it in the Midsummer Day race. Now I'm not so sure. . . ."

He was staring at her. "You've been financing a *stagecoach?*"

"Yes." She lowered her eyes. "I told you you'd be shocked."

"*Amazed* would be a more appropriate word. So, you decided to teach Henry a lesson, I can understand that, but I still don't see how this involves your aunt in any danger."

"It was all my fault for embroiling her in the first place, but I had to think of someone when Henry kept questioning me."

He looked more closely at her then. "You're talking about that day in the billiard room, aren't you?"

"Yes. I wasn't going to be away because of Aunt Derwent, but I couldn't tell Henry the truth, he simply wouldn't have understood, and anyway, I didn't want him to find out about the Swan."

"Where were you going if not to Beaconsfield?"

She hesitated. "I—I would rather not say."

He searched her face for a moment. "Very well, I won't press you."

"Well, having said I was going to my aunt's, I thought it best if I wrote to her and explained, in case Henry should become suspicious and make inquiries."

"He *was* suspicious. He thought you were meeting Lewis Ardenley."

Hot color rushed into her cheeks at that. "It—it doesn't really matter where I was, it only matters that I dragged Aunt Derwent into it. I told her all about my plans to trounce Henry in the Midsummer Day race and she thought it was all splendidly exciting." She gave a wry, ironic laugh. "Exciting? Well, I suppose it was in the beginning, but now it's all gone sour and I wish I'd never embarked upon it."

"Don't digress, Jane, you were telling me how you'd involved your aunt."

"It was because of my plotting that she came to London. She

196

said she couldn't bear to be left in the sticks in Beaconsfield. She wanted to be on the coach with me on the day, but I said—"

"Let me get this straight, you're actually going to be *on* the Swan during the race?"

"That was my intention, yes."

"I trust you've changed your mind, because if not, I think you'll be doing something very imprudent and hazardous indeed."

She looked at him. "The way I feel at the moment, Charles, I don't think the Swan will be entering the race at all, let alone with me on the box. Where was I?"

"Your aunt wished to join you on the coach."

"Oh, yes, well as it now is, she's going to be following with Blanche."

"*Blanche* is in on all this nonsense?"

"Yes."

"Have I been walking around with my eyes and ears closed these past few weeks?" he asked a little helplessly, sitting back on the sofa with an air of such bewilderment that she could almost have smiled, except that she was too miserable and upset to see humor in anything at the moment.

"We've been very careful to keep it all secret, Charles, because we were determined to spring it all on Henry on the day of the race. But I won't be going on with it now that my aunt has got herself into such an alarming fix." She rose agitatedly to her feet, glancing at the clock on the mantelpiece. "Oh, where are they? I do hope she's all right."

"Where is she?"

"At the Black Horse."

He stared at her. "*The* Black Horse?"

"Yes."

"Why?"

"To find out about the new Nonpareil. Oh, I didn't know that was where she was going. She told me she was staying at Lady Lindleigh's."

"I know, she said so that afternoon in Hyde Park."

"So she did. Well, I believed her, and by the time I realized it was a fib, it was too late. Anyway, one of Lewis's footmen saw her with Mr. Chapman at the Black Horse and—"

"Lewis?" His face became still. "He's in on this too, is he?"

"Yes."

"I suppose you went to him about it."

"No, he found out and came to me."

He got up then, returning to his place by the fireplace and

picking up the book, flicking rather angrily through the pages. "The fellow has a way of staying in your life, doesn't he? After all he did to you, I would have thought you would have grown a little wiser by now."

"It isn't what you think, Charles, truly it isn't. He's been trying to dissuade me from riding on the coach during the race."

"But apart from that he's been assisting you, I suppose." He looked rather accusingly at her.

"He—he's horsing the race. At least, he would have been if the race was still on as far as the Swan's concerned."

He gave a slightly incredulous laugh. "Is he, by God!"

"Yes."

"And you'd still have me believe there's nothing between you?"

"It's true, Charles. Oh, I admit that I still love him, but I didn't seek his help, he forced himself into it all. He's not doing it because he loves me, he's doing it because he agrees with me about Henry."

He studied her face for a moment. "Henry was right, wasn't he? You *were* with Lewis Ardenley when you claimed you were with your aunt?"

She knew that her cheeks were flaming and had to turn away, looking again at the clock. "Oh, *where* are they? They should be here by now."

"Were you with Lewis?" he demanded again.

"Yes, but not in the way you think."

"Don't treat me like a fool, Jane," he replied abruptly, closing the book with a snap and replacing it on the mantelpiece.

"Please don't be like this, Charles," she begged, her voice on the verge of breaking again, "for I have enough to contend with at the moment. Lewis is absolutely furious with me because my aunt is at the Black Horse. He won't believe that I didn't know anything about it and he said some very cruel things." She drew another steadying breath, forcing away the bitter memory of what had happened in the stableyard at the Feathers. "He's gone to bring her back now, before Mr. Chapman finds out who she really is. Oh, I do hope she hasn't come to any harm. Why did she have to take such a risk? It wasn't important enough for that. Nothing's that important."

The misery in her voice made his anger dissolve and he went to her, pulling her into his arms and holding her close. "Forgive me," he whispered, "but I can't help my jealousy, even though I know that you'll never love me enough to marry me. Please don't worry any more. I'm sure Lady Agatha will be quite all right and that Lewis will bring her safely back. I'm sure too that she'll put him right about you, for she knows that she tricked you."

At that moment the saloon doors were suddenly opened and Lewis and her aunt came in. Jane turned in Charles's arms, looking involuntarily into Lewis's eyes. His glance flickered coldly over Charles and then away.

She drew sharply away then, almost running to hug her aunt and hold her tightly. "You're safe! Oh, I'm so glad! I've been desperately afraid for you! You *are* all right, aren't you?"

"Perfectly. In fact, I really can't understand what all the fuss is about. Mr. Chapman was quite the gentleman, wining and dining me as elegantly as any fine lord." She sat down on the sofa, looking up at her niece's anxious face. "I'm sorry, my dear, but if I'd told you the truth, you'd never have agreed to my going, would you?"

"No." Jane didn't glance at Lewis, who had placed himself behind the sofa, one hand resting lightly on its velvet smoothness.

"I just couldn't resist the temptation," her aunt went on. "I knew how much you all needed to know about the new Nonpareil, so that you could have brakes fitted to the Swan if necessary, so I concocted the tale about Lady Lindleigh and went to the Black Horse. I knew about Mr. Chapman's liking for wealthy widows, you see, Henry had told me all about him at luncheon the day I arrived, so I thought that I could pose as just such a lady and win his confidence. He latched on to me immediately, of that you may be sure. The fellow's quite incorrigible, you know. He quite obviously saw me as a possible fourth Mrs. Chapman! Anyway, it all went very well and I didn't have any trouble at all persuading him to show me his new coach." She looked around at them all, evidently very pleased with herself. "Even if I say so myself, my thespian talents are quite considerable, and were it not for my wealth and situation, I'm sure I could have been the queen of Drury Lane. Anyway, where was I? Oh, yes, the new Nonpareil. I must say that it is an extremely ugly vehicle, quite unlike any stagecoach I've ever seen before."

A spark of interest lingered in Jane. "Is it a safety coach?"

"From what Lewis tells me, yes it is. It's lower and much wider, and isn't designed to carry anyone on top. All the outsiders are supposed to sit in an open compartment behind the driver's box, with their luggage in a boot underneath them. It's a very novel idea, I suppose, and much safer than perching on the top and hanging on for grim death, but it looks most peculiar. Its wheels are small, to lower the center of gravity, or so Mr. Chapman says, and this will also give it more stability and speed when cornering. And it has brakes, which he tells me are worth the resultant strain on the wheels, because it is only for one day." She looked urgently at Lewis. "You were right, sir, and I sincerely hope that we will be able to match his brakes with some of our own. Do we have time to fit them to the Swan before the race?"

He nodded. "I believe so. After all, there's all tonight, tomorrow, and tomorrow night, and—"

Jane interrupted. "There's no point in discussing it further," she said, "because I've decided to forget the whole thing. The Swan isn't going to enter the race anymore. Everything has got out of hand, and I want nothing more to do with it."

Aunt Derwent was appalled. "Jane, you can't possibly mean it!"

"I'm afraid that I do."

"But I won't let you. My dear, after all we've done, you can't simply bow out. Think of all the others, of Mr. Wheddle and his daughter, of Mr. Huggett and his son. Oh, Jane, you mustn't let my naughty and irresponsible escapade sway you like this."

"It isn't just that," she replied, finding the will at last to meet Lewis's steady gaze. "It's just that I realize how very foolish the whole business is and I wish to withdraw from it before it's too late."

Aunt Derwent looked a little crossly at Lewis. "Sir, this is all your fault, for you were most definitely out of line in speaking to Jane as you told me you did at the Feathers. It was very wrong of you and I think that you owe her an apology."

He drew a deep breath and turned toward Jane. "Jane, I—"

"Don't bother to say anything, sir, for it would make no difference. Besides, when you spoke earlier, you left me in no doubt at all what you really think, so I rather think that any apology would be worthless."

"Nevertheless, I do apologize. I had no right to speak to you as I did. It was unforgivably hasty and harsh."

"Yes, sir, it was." She looked at Charles and her aunt. "If—if you will excuse me. . . ."

Aunt Derwent put out a restraining hand. "Please, my dear, don't stop the Swan from entering the race, not when there are others to think about."

Jane hesitated, torn between a desire to forget everything

she'd started and an acceptance that her aunt was right and she shouldn't cast aside the feelings and efforts of everyone else. At last she nodded. "Very well, let it all proceed, if that's what you really want."

"It is." There was an understanding gentleness in Aunt Derwent's eyes as she watched her niece withdraw, for she understood only too well the anguish which was besetting her now.

Lewis hesitated only a moment and then went out after her, much to Charles's anger. Aunt Derwent glanced at him. "There's nothing you can do about it, Charles. There will always be something between them, whether it's the passion of love or of anger."

Lewis caught up with Jane at the foot of the staircase. "Jane, I must speak with you for a moment."

"I don't think there's any point, sir."

"You have every right to be angry with me. I behaved abominably and I wish with all my heart that I hadn't said those things to you."

"But you did say them, Lewis, and I could tell that you meant every word. Your opinion of my integrity is evidently very low indeed, which I had not realized until today. But still, they do say that it's better late than never."

A cold light passed through his eyes then. "Oh, you're so right, madam, for after tonight I've seen you in your true colors as well."

"And what do you mean by that?"

"I was referring to the touching little scene your aunt and I interrupted on our return. You and Charles were clasped so intimately in each other's arms that I can only imagine that I've been wrong all along about your feelings for him. You evidently want him as much as he wants you."

"Shouldn't you be leaving, sir? No doubt Alicia is becoming quite impatient."

"Yes, no doubt she is. Very well, Jane, I will leave, since that is quite obviously what you wish. However, in spite of everything, I will still honor my word concerning the race. I will go now and inform Lord Sefton that the Swan is a late entrant. There seems little point in delaying the matter any further, especially as we now have the new coach."

"Then by all means do that," she replied with an icy mien which concealed completely the hot misery she felt deep within.

His eyes were very dark and angry. "You may rest assured

that your involvement will remain secret. Good night, madam. I trust that you will be very happy in the future as the Marchioness of Bourton.'' He strode across the vestibule to snatch up his hat and gloves from the table, leaving the house and slamming the door behind him before Melville had time to come to his assistance.

Jane remained motionless for a long moment, and then she went slowly on up the stairs.

TWENTY-SEVEN

News of the Swan's last-minute appearance on the race scene spread over Town like wildfire that very night, with Lewis's association adding a new dimension which electrified the coaching fraternity and caused a considerable stir throughout fashionable society. Before the night was out, there was brisk betting at Brooks's and White's, with the Swan being given a very good chance of holding the other two to a close finish because it had Arthur Huggett on the box and Lewis Ardenley's bloodstock in harness. At the Black Horse, Chapman was already in a disgruntled mood because of the mysterious disappearance of his fascinating widow; he was more disgruntled and displeased than ever when told about the Swan. A great deal of money rested on the race, money he intended to win, so something would have to be done to keep any unwelcome latecomers well and truly out of it. The Nonpareil must be free to deal only with the Iron Duke if the Earl of Felbridge was to be relieved of his cash. Chapman was disquieted on another score too, for Lord Ardenley's involvement with the Swan was disturbing; he was too good, better than the earl, and his presence made the Swan more of a threat than ever. The Swan would have to go as quickly as it had come.

By breakfasttime the next day, there was hardly a household in London where the race wasn't being discussed, and by midmorning it was evident that the start of Tower Hill was going to be more of a crush than ever, with the Brighton road a mill to end all mills as society sallied forth *en masse* to watch.

Henry was at the Fleece when he heard about the Swan, and the news brought him back *post haste* to South Audley Street in order to change to call on Lord Sefton and find out all he could. He bounded up the staircase two at a time, almost colliding with Jane as she was coming down from sitting with poor Ellen, who was feeling most unwell with hay fever.

"Jane! Have you heard?" he demanded.

"Heard what?" she inquired innocently.

"Your damned Lewis has had the gall to back Wheddle and enter the Swan in the race!"

"He isn't *my* Lewis."

He hardly heard her. "No *wonder* he refused to horse the Iron Duke—he had designs on the race himself all along! By God, I should have known when I was told about him being at the Feathers, he wasn't there just because he had an eye for a. . . ." He cleared his throat, once again deciding not to mention Lewis's activities with the serving girl in the stable. He looked at his sister then, noticing that in spite of her pretty apricot muslin morning gown she was rather pale. "Are you all right, sis? You look washy."

"Thank you, I'm quite all right."

"You don't look it," he answered, untying his cravat and drawing it thoughtfully off, forgetting her again. "I had a feeling about Wheddle from the moment he somehow managed to keep going when other coachmasters would have caved in under such pressure from Chapman. Of *course*, he could keep going, he had Ardenley's money behind him! Still, I've seen the new Swan, and to be quite frank, it doesn't stand an earthly."

"Why do you say that?"

"Because it hasn't got brakes."

"Nor does the Iron Duke."

"That's what you think," he said, tapping a conspiratorial finger against the side of his nose.

"You mean you've had them fitted?"

"Yes. Chapman's not going to steal my money as easily as *that!*"

"But I don't understand, I thought you disapproved of brakes."

"I do, but the new Nonpareil has them."

She stared then. "How do you know that?"

"One of my men managed to get into the Black Horse while Chapman was wining and dining a new lady friend. It's funny, actually, I'm told she looked a lot like Aunt Derwent. Anyway, the new Nonpareil he's got hidden away under wraps is a new-fangled safety coach, very flashy and revolutionary. No doubt he fondly imagines it's going to give him the edge to lift my £50,000, but he's sadly mistaken, tried and trusted is still best.''

"Did you say £50,000?" she asked faintly.

He shifted a little uncomfortably, for he hadn't intended to let that slip. "Yes.''

"Oh, Henry!''

"It's safe as houses, sis. The Iron Duke's going to win and it's Chapman who's going to have to cough the money up.'' He grinned then. "Safety coaches indeed! They're nothing more than wide carts. He might think it's going to be faster on corners and so on, but I don't. He's going to be eating the Iron Duke's dust all the way to Brighton, and so is Lewis Ardenley's Swan.''

The irony of the situation was enough to make her want to laugh out loud. After all the anxiety of the previous day because of her aunt's dangerous visit to the Black Horse, the information they'd wanted had fallen into their laps anyway, courtesy of Henry.

Henry smiled at her. "Cheer up, sis, it might never happen. Well, I must toddle on up to change. I have to collar Sefton and find out all I can about the Swan.''

"I thought you'd dismissed the Swan as a nonentity.''

"I have, but it never does to be complacent, especially when someone like Lewis Ardenley is involved. Besides, chit-chatting with Sefton will while away a pleasant hour or two, and whiling away the time's all I have to do now until tomorrow morning.''

"You could while it away making it up with Blanche.''

His smile faded. "The onus is on her, Jane, not me.''

"Rubbish. You're the one in need of manners, not Blanche.''

"She was in the wrong at the theater and has been ever since.''

'You're being very stubborn.''

"Then it must be a family trait, because you've given a splendid display of Derwent obstinacy where Lewis is concerned. Mind you, after what he's done now, I can't say I really blame you—the fellow's a blackguard.''

"Because he's involved with the Swan?''

"Yes.''

"You're being very childish. But I don't want to talk about Lewis. I'm more concerned about you and Blanche.''

"Then don't bother yourself, the whole matter is closed.''

"Why won't you admit that you still love her? You *know* that she loves you.''

"Then let her come to me and tell me so.''

"Why don't *you* go to *her* and tell her so?" she countered.

"Because she's in the wrong. Damn it, Jane, don't start on your dog-with-a-bone act again, I'm not in the mood."

"Do you still love her?" she asked again, determined to corner him.

He hesitated. "She made her choice at the theater."

"Answer me, Henry."

"Oh, very well, yes, of *course* I do, but I'm not crawling to her while Dursley's still sniffing around."

"Isn't she worth fighting for?" Oh dear, how very familiar *that* was.

"I'll go to her after the race."

"*After?* Henry, on your own admission you have nothing to do today but while away the time—put that time to good use."

"I said after the race, and I meant it."

"You're still being very shabby."

"She was in the wrong and so she can wait until *I'm* ready to let her have a chance to beg my forgiveness."

He went on up the stairs then, leaving his incredulous sister to stare after him. Of all the pompous, conceited, arrogant, mutton-headed beasts, Henry, Earl of Felbridge, took the biscuit!

The rest of the day dragged by on leaden feet. Jane wanted it all over and done with now, but each hour seemed to tick by so slowly it was like a day in itself. She sat in the garden with her aunt, attempting to read *The Corsair* while her aunt continued with her tambour work. It was warm and sunny, promising well for the following day, and the sounds of London were muted by the more immediate drone of bees in the flowers, and by the full-throated song of the blackbird in the branches of the walnut tree.

She gazed at the page before her without really seeing it, for her thoughts were elsewhere, with Lewis Ardenley. He would be at the Feathers now, seeing that the brakes were fitted correctly to the new coach, because he wanted to be certain there was no risk to his costly horses. When that was done he was going to Maywood, to wait there during the race in case he should be needed at all, Maywood being placed so handily along the ground. She knew this from a hasty note he had dashed off to her aunt. The words of *The Corsair* swam before her. She couldn't help remembering what he'd said the night before about her intentions toward Charles. Let him think it, because that at least would make it easier for her to face him when his forthcoming betrothal to Alicia was announced. Easier? It would never be *easy*.

"Will you read aloud for me, my dear?" There was no reply and the tambour hook stopped. "Jane?"

"Mm?"

"I asked you if you would read aloud for me."

Jane smiled apologetically. "I'm so sorry, Aunt Derwent, I didn't hear what you said."

Her aunt smiled too. "You were many miles from this garden, weren't you?"

"Forgive me."

"There's nothing to forgive, my dear, for I'm sure I more than understand."

Jane smiled. "Yes, I suppose you do."

"Well, perhaps now isn't the time to talk about it. I was wondering if you would read to me for a while. I have a notion to hear a little of Lord Byron."

"Of course." Jane turned back to the beginning of the poem. *"O'er the glad waters of the dark blue sea, Our thoughts are as boundless, and our souls as free, Far as the breeze can bear, the billows foam, Survey our empire, and behold our home!"* Her reading was colorless and she knew it. She looked regretfully at her aunt. "I'm afraid I cannot do his lordship justice this afternoon."

"No, I think you are right. The wretched fellow may be wicked beyond belief in his private life, but his genius with the written word deserves a little more than you seem capable of giving today." Aunt Derwent put down her tambour hook. "I'm sorry that my foolishness brought things to such a sorry pass between you and Lewis."

"It wasn't your fault."

"If I hadn't rushed off to the Black Horse, yesterday's, er, contretemps would not have occurred, you cannot deny that."

"It would have occurred at some point or other, Aunt Derwent, whether you'd gone there or not. Lewis and I are incapable of simple polite courtesy toward each other."

Her aunt studied her for a moment. "Once you seemed almost one, one heart, one thought, one will, just as I was with the Duke of Wellington, and would be still if I'd had any sense of my own."

"I don't think it's the same."

"No? Well, no matter, there's time enough for such deep discussions. My dear, why don't you stay at the Feathers tonight?"

"*Stay* there?"

"Yes. Then you'll be right on the spot and ready to take your place beside Mr. Huggett on the box in the morning."

Jane stared at her. "But I couldn't possibly."

"Why not? Henry isn't going to know, he's staying at the Fleece until after the race, and besides, if he does return for some reason, I can tell him you're indisposed with a headache. Ellen's ill, I know, but it won't hurt just this once if you toddle off on your own, and once there I daresay Miss Wheddle will be delighted to attend you and thus placate convention. Look, my dear, you don't know what to do with yourself right now, do you? And you're certainly not sparkling company, I can vouch for that. You need something to divert you, and there will be plenty going on at the Feathers, tonight of all night. You could leave in less than an hour."

"Lewis might still be there."

"And if he is?"

"I don't want to see him."

"Then go this evening. I'm sure it would be the best thing for you."

"But what about you? I can't simply rush off and leave you."

"As the senior member of the family here present, I'm advising you to go, and I shall be perfectly happy because I shall invite Blanche to dine with me. The matter's settled, my dear. The decision's been taken out of your hands—you're going to the Feathers. I suggest you have Melville inform Thomas and then send someone ahead to warn them to expect you—I'm sure Miss Wheddle will want to prepare their best chamber."

"You seem almost anxious to be rid of me."

"You remind me a little too much of myself, when I was so very foolish about the Duke of Wellington. Now then, off you toddle to make your arrangements before we take tea. I will see you in the morning, when Blanche and I come to the Feathers ready to follow the Swan to the start." She thought for a moment. "Jane, have you considered what you're going to wear tomorrow?"

"Wear? No, not really."

"Excellent, then after tea we'll go up and inspect your considerable wardrobe. I'm sure an agreeable hour or so can be passed deciding *exactly* what togs will be best for the occasion." She got up, putting a firm hand on her niece's arm. "I'll hear no more argument, my dear. The rest of your afternoon and the early evening has now been taken care of, and after that you are going to the Feathers."

Jane got up as well then, setting her book down on the seat and then turning anxiously to her aunt. "You don't think I'm being too shocking by being on the box during the race, do you?"

"No, my dear, I don't, but then you share my rather unusual spirit, don't you? Besides, isn't there a point to be made in all this? Was it not originally your intention to prove to Henry not only that his behavior is odious, but also that a woman is just as capable as a man of seeing a coach to victory in a race?"

"Yes, but—"

"Why but? You must ride on the coach, my dear, and I'll warrant that every woman in the realm will be cheering you on, even if mostly in secret. Blanche and I will not be secret, though, you may count upon it. We'll be following you every inch of the way and showing them all that we support you. Men are tiresome creatures, Jane. They need shaking up now and then to show them that they're the inferior sex. This is one of those times." Aunt Derwent sighed then. "Aye, tiresome they may be, but what *would* we do without them? Come along now, we'll see that the carriage is ordered and then take tea, and after that your wardrobe will receive a visitation."

TWENTY-EIGHT

The evening shadows were so long and dark as the town carriage conveyed Jane to the corner of Arlington Street that she knew it would not be long before the light had gone. Her portmanteau was on the seat beside her, containing what she would need overnight, and the clothes she and her aunt had chosen for her appearance on the Swan the next morning. It was strange to be without Ellen, but the poor maid really was indisposed, sneezing constantly. She suffered with hay fever each year and had only a day or so before been saying that it was a miracle how she'd escaped so far this summer; providence had evidently felt too tempted. Still, being alone at this particular time was perhaps the best thing, for it gave Jane time to think.

She had left her aunt and Blanche taking a cozy dinner *à deux*, the latter being worked on by the former to patch things up with Henry, but proving as stubborn as he was when it came to making that first all-important move.

Thomas drew the carriage to a standstill and Jane prepared to alight, to procure a hackney coach for the last time. Piccadilly was still crowded and along Arlington Street she could see Lord Sefton's house, with a positive gaggle of sporting vehicles outside it, from cabriolets, curricles and gigs, to a phaeton almost as outlandish as Henry's. Evidently, the marshal of the race was entertaining his fellow coaching enthusiasts to a congenial dinner on the eve of the great event, so that they could all talk about their pet subject to their hearts' content. She wondered what they would have said had they known that a mere woman and not Lord Ardenley was the mastermind behind the Swan.

Thomas wished her well as she took her portmanteau and beckoned to one of the hackneys waiting nearby, but as she smiled and turned away from Ellen's young man, she froze, for another carriage was approaching the corner, apparently making for Lord Sefton's house; it carried a number of young sporting gentlemen, among them her brother. She could hear great hilarity—evidently they'd imbibed a little too much at a club—but Henry sat in almost morose silence by the window nearest to her. His expression was withdrawn and she knew instinctively that he was thinking about Blanche. She couldn't have said why this conviction was so strong, but she was certain. He was gazing out without seeing, and although he stared directly at her carriage as he passed, he didn't seem to see it at all.

She breathed out with relief as the noisy carriageload turned the corner and drove away toward Lord Sefton's residence, where a moment later they all poured out and went rather rowdily to hammer on the elegant door. They were admitted and the street became peaceful again.

Her hackney carriage drew alongside then, and with a final smile at Thomas, she climbed into it and sat on the worn seat with her portmanteau. The little coach lurched away, its window glasses rattling alarmingly.

The streets were almost completely dark, the lamps shining above the pavements, as she drove across the city toward Cheapside. She felt better now that she'd taken her aunt's advice, for if she'd stayed at South Audley Street she knew she'd have been dismal company. She was still a little uncertain about how she'd be if Lewis was still at the Feathers, but on reflection it seemed hardly likely that he was—he must have left now in order to be at Maywood for the race.

The little coach entered Cheapside, and quite suddenly she became aware of shouting somewhere ahead. At first she thought it must be yet another of the queen's excursions, but then realized that the shouting was tinged with alarm. People were hurrying along the pavement in the same direction the hackney was traveling, and she lowered the glass to lean out and see what was happening. The air was acrid, and a little way ahead, just where the Feathers was, a pall of thick smoke cloaked the street. The Feathers was on fire!

Unable to proceed because of the crush of people, the hackneyman drew his vehicle to a standstill, unwilling to press through the smoke. Jane flung open the door and alighted, snatching up her portmanteau before putting the fare into the man's outstretched hand. He looked concernedly down at her. "Don't go that way, miss, it's too dangerous!"

"I must!" she cried, gathering her skirts and hurrying away along the smoky pavement, where people were reduced to mere shapes and shadows by the thick, choking fumes. The smoke caught in her throat and stung her eyes, but in a moment the air was relatively clear because of the way the light breeze was blowing, and she could see the entrance of the inn. People were gathered there, staring through the archway and courtyard at the fire in the stables beyond. The leaping light from the flames dancing horridly on their faces and on the cobbles where they stood.

Jane was about to push through them to go inside when the sound of hooves and wheels echoed beneath the archway. One of the stableboys led a cabriolet out to safety, the frightened horse capering and tossing its head. It was Lewis's cabriolet. He was still here! But was he safe? Alarm span wildly through her then and she pushed through the small crowd and hurried into the yard, where the breeze carried the smoke high over the inn and down into the street beyond. She could see the flames leaping beyond the inner archway, and the noise and roar of the conflagration was loud and fearsome, an eager, greedy crackling which told of how strong a hold the fire had upon the tinder-dry buildings.

There was pandemonium beyond as men dashed to and fro with buckets, trying to contain the flames while they waited for the insurance company's fire engine to arrive. She searched each shadowy shape, but couldn't make Lewis out among them. And what about the others? Were they all right?

Behind her came the sound of a jangling bell as the fire engine reached the inn, its team striking sparks from the gleaming cobbles as they clattered to a standstill in the yard. The firemen followed on foot, two teams of fourteen to take turns manning the engine's long handles. They unharnessed the horses and then dragged the engine past Jane into the stableyard, where within moments it was at work, spraying water into the searing flames and adding another sound to the already deafening din, a hissing, bubbling roar as the fire resisted with all its might.

Jane moved slowly toward the inner archway, her heart thundering as she went through into the mayhem beyond. The flames leapt into the blackness of the sky above, sending a shower of sparks into the shimmering air. The heat was intense, beating against her face and making her throat more dry and painful than ever. Sparks were carried toward the adjacent properties to the west, and the firemen worked hard at their pumps to try and stop the fire spreading.

Jane searched the scene, hoping that each dimly seen figure would be someone she knew, but they were all strangers. She cast around desperately for a familiar face, and then heard Betsy calling tearfully for her kitten as she searched a row of empty stables nearby, the horses having long since been removed to safety. "Tabitha? Oh, Tabitha, where are you?"

"Betsy?" Jane hurried gladly toward her. "Is everyone safe?"

The girl whirled about with a gasp. "Lady Jane! You shouldn't be here—it's dangerous!"

"Is everyone safe?" Jane asked again.

"Yes, my lady."

"Lord Ardenley?"

"Yes, he's helping Dad and the others put out what they can by the coachhouse. The new coach is in danger."

"How did the fire start?"

"Will saw one of Chapman's men hurrying away."

Jane stared. "You don't mean . . . ?"

"It's no accident, Lady Jane."

Dismayed, Jane glanced around at the dreadful scene again. It was all her fault—her foolishness had put them all in danger! And it might mean the end of the Feathers!

Betsy touched her arm. "Have you seen Tabitha, my lady?"

"No."

"I can't find her anywhere. She's terrified of fire."

"I'll help you look. Have you searched those stables over

there?'' She pointed through the smoke and heat to the other side of the yard.

''No, my lady. I've only just realized she's not safe in the kitchens.''

''I'll go that way then,'' said Jane, putting down her portmanteau and hurrying across the slippery cobbles where water from the engines had begun to spill.

The jet forced out by the pumping men made a boiling roar all the time, and the flames recoiled a little, their brilliance shining in the collecting puddles and reflecting in lurid shapes on the walls of the surrounding buildings. The firemen were chanting, working rhythmically at the pumps. She reached the other stables and began to look in each one, and she didn't see the sparks settle on the roof above, taking hold and springing into small flames which began to lick stealthily along the eaves before slipping inside the building, to burn unseen for an almost fatal minute or two more.

She paused in one of the doorways for at last she saw Lewis. He was working with a group of men by the coachhouse, his face glowing in the firelight, his excellent shirt torn and smoke-stained. He and the men with him stopped work for a moment, watching to see if the fire engine was tipping the scales in their favor. Most of the stables along the north side of the yard had been gutted now, and one of the coachhouses was going up like touch paper. She saw him glance toward the inn itself, where the windows glowed as if the fire was inside, although actually it was only shining on the glass.

The firemen's chants were compelling, making those who watched join in. ''One, two; one, two; one, two . . .'' Up and down they moved, first one side and then the other, their faces gleaming with perspiration, their muscles bulging with the effort. It was thirsty work. The men were called Beer-Ohs, and such parching labor earned them their name. If they saved the inn, they would be well rewarded with its finest beer, as much as they could swallow.

Jane watched them, almost mesmerized by their pumping rhythm. Then, quite suddenly, she became aware of another sound, a tiny mewing coming from the stable behind her. Tabitha! She'd forgotten Betsy's kitten! Whirling about, she went into the shadowy stall and immediately the noise and searing heat of the new fire was all around her. She stared up at the roof, where the flames roared and licked in the darkness. Involuntarily she screamed, the shock rooting her to the spot.

She was terrified, it was as if the flames had been lying in wait, ready to reach down to her the moment she stepped too near. But beyond her dread she could still hear the kitten's pathetic mewing. It was coming from the straw in the corner. Distracted at last from the fire above, she turned, hurrying to the straw and searching wildly through it for the terrified kitten. Finally, her fingers touched trembling fur and with a glad cry she scooped the little creature up into her arms, but as she did so there was a splintering, groaning noise and a sudden scorching heat as a beam fell from the blazing roof.

Sparks showered over her, catching in her hair and skirts. She screamed again. Then someone had hold of her, lifting her bodily into his arms and carrying her out into the safety of the yard. It was Lewis—she could feel the gold of the pin in his cravat pressing against her cheek, and beyond the acrid tang of smoke she could smell the richness of costmary on his clothes. He held her tightly, and she clung to him, sobs catching in her stinging throat. Her eyes smarted with tears and she could barely hold on to the struggling, ungrateful kitten, which was soon whisked safely from her by Betsy.

As Lewis set Jane gently on her feet again, Betsy was very anxious. "Are you all right, my lady?"

Coughing and almost overcome by the smoke, Jane could only nod. The firemen were turning their attention to the blazing stable now, and Lewis nodded at Betsy. "Take her somewhere safe, Betsy. The kitchens are out of danger now."

"Yes, my lord." Betsy took Jane's hand to lead her away.

Jane looked back at Lewis. He smiled at her, the flames reflecting in his gray eyes; then he turned away to continue helping fight the fire.

She hesitated, wanting to go after him. She could feel the strength of his arms around her again, bearing her so surely to safety. She loved him and she had to tell him so, but Betsy was drawing her away. "Come, my lady, there's nothing more you can do."

"I must speak to him. . . ."

"Later, Lady Jane, there'll be time enough. You're in no state now. You must come to the kitchens and rest a while." Betsy would brook no further resistance, firmly ushering her aristocratic charge through the arch to the outer courtyard and into the kitchens. In a blur, Jane glanced at the entrance from Cheapside, a sea of faces gazed in, kept back only by the determined efforts of two constables who wouldn't allow anyone in.

It was quiet in the kitchens and somehow the smoke hadn't penetrated, leaving the air soothingly fresh. The moment the door closed behind them, Tabitha made a final bid for freedom, leaping from Betsy's protective hold and dashing off into the laundry. Betsy let her go, for there was no escape that way and the kitten was safe. Leading Jane to a settle close to the range, she then hurried to fill a kettle from the hand pump above the stone sink, placing it on top of the range to make a restoring cup of tea. As the kettle began to sing, she brought a bowl of clean water, some soap, and a cloth to wipe the smoke stains from Jane's face. Jane could only sit there, suddenly feeling drained of all strength. It was delayed reaction, she knew that because she was trembling, and she was only now beginning to realize how very close to death she had come in those few brief moments in the blazing stable. If it hadn't been for Lewis. . . .

Betsy put the bowl on the table and looked concernedly at her. "How are you feeling now?"

"All right. I think." Jane managed a weak smile.

"I think his lordship got you out just in time. Another few seconds and . . . Well, best not think about that, eh?"

The kettle was boiling now and soon the sweet aroma of the tea filtered through the still air. The blue-and-white cups and saucers clinked and a moment later Jane was accepting the universal cure-all which without fail seemed to produce a beneficial effect upon those in need. It tasted good, better than any tea she had ever had before, and this in spite of the lingering acridity of smoke in her mouth and throat.

Betsy sat by the table, her eyes downcast for a moment. "None of us really thought Chapman would try this again, not even Dad."

"Will's really sure it was Chapman's man he saw?"

"Yes. We don't know how he got in, but he must have seen that we've got brakes on the new coach now. Dad reckons we'll have to stay on our guard even if the fire's stopped, because Chapman will know now that the Swan's got a better chance than he thought."

"Surely he won't try again, not after this."

"You don't know him, my lady. He's staked a lot of money on winning the race, and Dad doesn't think he can afford to lose. A third coach might get in his way and allow the Iron Duke through in first place, so he'll do all he can to stop the Swan getting to the start tomorrow."

They didn't speak again. Jane finished the tea and then sat

wearily back. She felt weak, and the horror of coming so close to death was a chilling, unnerving experience which made her just want to sit there. She stared at the kettle on the range, and the faint curl of steam issuing from its graceful spout. Like smoke. She closed her eyes then. She was so tired.

An hour or more passed and Jane had fallen asleep. Betsy stood by the window watching through the archway to see the smoke drifting across the stableyard. The fire engine was still at work, but there were no leaping flames now, only the wink and flash of sparks among the blackened embers of the stables. The new Swan was safe, its coachhouse hadn't caught fire, and Lord Ardenley's fine horses had been taken to a safe place nearby, so the Swan would still be able to take part in the race tomorrow.

Jane was still asleep when the fire was finally put out and Jacob had a keg brought up from the cellar to quench the firemen's thirst. They all laughed and talked together in the yard outside the kitchen door, but their noise didn't disturb her slumber. Lewis's cabriolet was brought back, the horse stamping impatiently as it shook its head in an effort to loosen the hold of the boy in charge of it, but he was more than mindful of his duty, and mindful too that his lordship was a handsome tipper.

Betsy left Jane in the kitchens and went out to help her father dispense mugs of beer. She saw Lewis go to the kitchen window and look in. He hesitated for a moment and then turned away again, climbing into his cabriolet and telling Jacob that he was on his way to Maywood now, and would be there should he be needed during the race. Then he flipped a coin into the boy's eager hands and turned the cabriolet, driving off at a smart pace out into Cheapside, where a curious crowd still lingered in the hope of something else happening.

Will came to stand next to Betsy. "A penny for your thoughts then," he said, slipping a muscular arm about her plump waist.

"Lord Ardenley should have gone in to speak to Lady Jane."

"Perhaps he didn't want to wake her."

"The speaking should have been more important than the sleeping, Will." She sighed, looking up into his warm, dark eyes. "You won't ever leave me sleeping when there are things to be said between us, will you? I couldn't bear to think we'd ever reach that pass."

He bent his head to kiss her on the lips. "Betsy," he said softly, "it could be that Lord Ardenley doesn't have anything to say to her."

"He has, I'm sure of it. Just as she has things to say to him."

"When they speak together, they don't speak kindly," he reminded her.

"I think they still love each other."

"He has the Duchess of Brantingham, Betsy."

She lowered her eyes. "Then why does he bother so with Lady Jane? Why doesn't he let her go? He could so easily if he wanted to, but he doesn't, and that's because he still loves her as much as she loves him, but they're both too proud and obstinate to admit the truth." She looked at him again. "I know I'm right about them, Will. You do promise me that you'll never let it happen to us, don't you?"

He smiled then. "I promise," he whispered, squeezing her.

She was silent for a moment, watching her father gradually emptying the keg for the firemen's seemingly endless thirst. Then she looked through to the stableyard, where smoked drifted quietly now and where the light from a lantern illuminated the silent fire engine. "Do you think Chapman will try again between now and tomorrow morning, Will?"

He drew a long breath. "Your dad reckons so. Chapman's not a man to sit back and take failure, and tonight he failed in what he tried to do. We'll have to be on the look-out all night, Betsy. He'll try every trick in his dirty book to keep the Swan away from the start in the morning. I'm going to sit guard over the horses where they're hidden, and I'll have quite a few of the lads with me, so don't go worrying about me." He kissed her again. "We've a score to settle with Chapman, Betsy, and we'll settle it tomorrow by getting into Brighton ahead of his fancy Nonpareil."

TWENTY-NINE

It was quiet when Betsy at last roused Jane to take her up to the gallery bedroom which had been prepared earlier. It was a large chamber, the inn's principal bedroom, and it was handsomely furnished, although everything smelled of smoke because the window had unfortunately been left slightly open during the fire. The night breeze had shifted now, however, and the fresh air breathing coolly in was gradually making the smell of smoke less pervasive and unpleasant.

Jane lay in the bed, her hair spreading in a dark tangle on the pillow as she gazed up at the unfamiliar shadows on the ceiling. Betsy had whisked away the clothes she'd been wearing on arrival to launder them as best she could and rid them of the taint of the fire. The portmanteau containing her clothes for the race had been retrieved from the stableyard and its contents carefully hung in the capacious wardrobe. They'd somehow escaped the smoke, but Betsy nevertheless placed several bunches of lavender in the wardrobe with them, just in case a night at the inn might spoil them.

Jane's throat was sore from the smoke, and her eyes still stung. She felt tired, but sleep was once again proving elusive, as if that hour or so snatched in the kitchen had been sufficient. Lanterns had been lit in the courtyard below, and whenever anyone passed them, the slanting shadows moved grotesquely over her ceiling. It was all so peaceful now; the fire engine had gone, together with its slightly tipsy band of Beer-Ohs, and Will and his companions had taken themselves off to stand guard over the horses. The task of clearing away the mess left by the fire had begun, the men working in silence. No one felt like talking. Shovels scraped as the litter and wet, black ash was cleared up, and occasionally there was a splintering noise as an unsafe, half-burned timber was dragged down and stacked away at the side of what was left of the yard. Jacob looked on, his heart very heavy. He was wondering how he could carry on his business after such a catastrophe.

Alone of the men, Arthur was sent to his room, Jacob not countenancing any notion of his staying up; the Swan's coachman had to be as alert and fresh as possible for the race. Still awake in her room, Jane heard the coachman come up the wooden gallery steps and walk past her door to his room opposite. His door closed and after a moment a dim light percolated her room as he lit a lamp.

She gazed at the ceiling, thinking about what had happened. How she wished she hadn't fallen asleep earlier, for then she would have had a chance to speak to Lewis again before he left, and this time she would at last have been able to confess the truth about her feelings for him. She couldn't pretend any more, nor could she act the very opposite of the truth—she'd gone beyond that. That look she'd exchanged with him before Betsy had pulled her away to the safety of the kitchens had seen the final crumbling away of her pride and resistance. But maybe it was too late now, for the Duke of Brantingham's change of heart had released Alicia. Jane closed her eyes to shut out the image which seemed to hover in the room before her. But she couldn't shut it out, she could see Alicia lying in his arms. . . .

Time crept slowly by and she lost count of the chimes of St. Mary-le-Bow. Finally, she got out of the bed and went to the window. The men were still working in the stableyard and Jacob was with them, helping with a heavy wheelbarrow filled with rubble and ash. A movement on the gallery steps caught her eye. A man she didn't know was coming up them. As she watched, he went to Arthur's door and knocked. There was something a little odd about him, for he kept glancing almost surreptitiously toward the stableyard as if he didn't want to be seen. Then Arthur opened his door and the lamplight from within flooded out, leaving the man in stark silhouette. He was small and wiry, with a round-crowned hat pulled well down over his face. Whoever he was, Arthur knew and liked him, for a grin of delight broke out over the old coachman's face and he immediately invited the caller inside. The door closed, cutting off the sharp light, and a moment later Arthur drew the curtains. After that, it was barely possible to see that there was a light on inside at all.

Jane remained by the window for a moment longer and then returned to her bed. She lay back once more, determinedly closing her eyes. She must have some more sleep. . . .

Sleep must have overtaken her at last, for when she opened her eyes again the first pale fingers of dawn were lightening the eastern sky, and the church clock was sounding four o'clock. She flung the bedclothes back and went to the window again. There was no movement in the stableyard now; everyone had gone to his bed for a well-earned sleep. The doors at the main entrance into Cheapside had been closed and locked as a precaution against Chapman's men returning to cause more trouble, and Jacob had left a man on guard in the courtyard. But he was now so tired that he too had fallen sleep, sitting on the bottom steps of the gallery stairs, his head lolling against the wall.

Jane looked across at Arthur's room, thinking about the man who'd called so late the night before, but as she looked, she grew puzzled. Surely the light was still on inside. Yes, she was sure the light was on. Had Arthur been awake all night? Was the man still there? She picked up her wrap and put it on, going out onto the gallery where the dawn air was sharp and cool and touched very slightly with the lingering smell of the fire. Her bare feet made little sound as she went around the gallery to the coachman's room. There was a tiny crack in the curtains and she could just see in. The lamp inside was still burning, although it was guttering now because the oil had run very low. Arthur was stretched out on his bed, still fully clothed, and even though she was outside, she could hear his shuddering snores. They were the snores of a man in a drunken stupor, and the reason for that stupor lay on the floor beside his bed, in the form of an empty gin bottle. Jane stared in utter dismay, then she gathered her skirts and ran toward the gallery steps, calling loudly for Jacob and Betsy.

Her cries echoed around the silent inn, and almost immediately Jacob emerged into the yard below, looking very strange indeed in a voluminous night shirt, a blue-and-white cap tugged down over his wiry hair. At the foot of the steps, the guard didn't move, and as Jane hurried down and reached out to shake him, another cry escaped her lips, for there was a stain of blood on his forehead where someone had struck him. For a moment she thought he was dead and her heart almost stopped, but then Jacob was there, examining him quickly and reassuring her that he was only unconscious.

By now the disturbance had aroused the whole inn, and several stablehands carried the man away to the kitchens for Betsy to attend him, while another went for a doctor. Jane hurriedly explained about Arthur, and she and Jacob went quickly up to the coachman's room. Jacob cursed beneath his breath as he tried to rouse him, but to no avail—Arthur's snores rattled on undisturbed. Jacob picked up the empty bottle, controlling the urge to smash it furiously against the wall, and with considerable restraint placing it intact on the table instead. He looked at Jane then. "Reckon you can kiss farewell to the Swan's chances in the race, Lady Jane, for he's in no condition to get on the box. Seems I was right all along about him, only I wish I wasn't."

"A man called on him last night."

The landlord's eyes sharpened. "Who was it?"

"I don't know. He seemed to be a friend of Arthur's. He was small and thin, and he wore a round-crowned hat."

"That describes just about any groom in any stable." He drew a long breath. "Whoever he was, he put old Arthur in a jovial mood, that's for sure. He'll have been Chapman's man, no matter how much of a friend to Arthur he might have been in the past."

"Why do you say that?"

"It stands out a mile, my lady. Chapman failed with the fire, so he turned his attention to our coachman instead. Arthur's weakness is too well-known and too easy to play on, as you can see for yourself." He gestured toward the bed.

Jane nodded sadly. "What can we do now? If we give him some black coffee—"

"He'll sober up a little, but not enough. He's too far gone, Lady Jane, and the hangover he's going to have will stop him thinking quickly enough for the race."

"But we can't just give up."

"We have to, unless we can find another coachman in time."

"What about Will? He's been doing the Brighton run, hasn't he?"

"He's adequate, Lady Jane, but that's all. He's better than Johno, but he lacks his father's genius."

"But if Johno's not good enough, Will's all we have."

"Aye, he's all we have. Lord Ardenley's the right man, but he's out at Maywood and we'd never get word to him in time, even supposing he'd agree to do it if he was asked."

Outside, the messenger returned with the doctor and so they hurried down again to see how the injured guard was. The man had regained consciousness now and confirmed that in the second before he'd been struck he'd recognized the intruder as a man from the Black Horse, once a close friend of Arthur's. The guard was taken to his own room and given a draft of laudanum to ease the pain and help him to sleep. Then Jane, Betsy, and Jacob sat forlornly around the kitchen table, drinking tea and wondering how Will was going to take the news that not only had his father let them down but *he* was going to have to drive the Swan in the race.

At six o'clock, Cheapside echoed with the noise of the mail coaches on their way to Lombard Street, and the first street calls began to be heard. Through the open window Jane could see the ravages of the fire in the stables and she looked at Jacob. "You mustn't worry about payment for the damage, I regard that as my responsibility."

"Oh, no, Lady Jane, I couldn't possibly agree to that."

"I insist, Jacob," she said, putting the matter on a very personal basis by using his first name. She smiled a little. "Please don't refuse, for it is the very least I can do after visiting all this upon you."

"I shall not deny that I'm relieved, Lady Jane," he admitted then, the gladness plain in his eyes, "for I couldn't see how I was going to keep the old Feathers going."

"Have whatever repairs and rebuilding done that you require, and send the bills to Mr. Payne."

"Thank you, my lady, and I say that from the bottom of my heart."

"And from the bottom of my heart I say how sorry I am to have caused all this. I really had no idea what I was stirring up that day I came to you with my crack-brained notions of teaching my brother a lesson." She smiled wryly. "Well, it seems that Mr. Chapman is going to have his way after all, for as you say, without Arthur I doubt if the Swan has much of a chance."

Outside, the sun was quite high in the sky and a small crowd had gathered as Lewis's horses were brought back by Will and his small band of helpers.

Betsy immediately hurried out to tell him what had happened, and through the window Jane saw how his face drained of color. He came slowly into the kitchen, turning his hat nervously in his hands as he looked at Jane and Jacob. "I—I can't do it," he blurted out. "I'm just not good enough, not for a race like this."

Jacob held his gaze. "If you don't do it, Will, the Swan won't even get to the starting line."

"Can't someone be sent to fetch Lord Ardenley? He's the finest whip I know!" pleaded Will.

Jacob shook his head. "There's no time, or guarantee that his lordship would agree."

Betsy squeezed Will's hand. "Please, my love, do it for me."

"But Betsy. . . ."

"Please."

He looked down into her adoring eyes and then gave a reluctant nod. "All right, Betsy, for you I'll try."

Jacob got up then, grinning and clapping the younger man on the back. "That's my laddo, you have a go! If you'd kept on saying no, I'd have known you weren't man enough to take my Betsy on as a wife. Now then, let's get on up and see if we can sober up that old fool of a father of yours; he may not be fit to drive today, but there's still a lot of advice he can give you about how to take those other two on."

It was possible to rouse Arthur now, and as Jacob had predicted, he had the grandfather of all hangovers. His face was ashen and his eyes hollow, and he felt so guilty about letting them down that he was almost in tears. He was utterly wretched and could only say that he'd been so pleased to see his old friend Fred Green that he hadn't thought it at all suspicious to have him turn up out of the blue like that. He'd only intended to have one glass, for old time's sake, never meaning that glass to lead to another and another. He shook his head in bewilderment, unable to believe that that one glass had had such an immediate effect.

Betsy picked up the empty bottle and as she sniffed it she realized straightaway that it had contained more than just gin—there had been something added to the liquor. Arthur felt a little better after hearing this, but he still blamed himself for letting them all down.

Preparations for the race continued, but there was a lack of heart in everyone now because it was believed that Chapman had succeeded in nobbling the Swan, as the latest slang went for such a situation. Men polished the coach's brasswork and panels, and grooms attended to the horses until their coats gleamed, while in the kitchens, becoming more and more sober as the minutes passed, Arthur did his best to instruct the unhappy Will about every inch of the ground from Tower Hill to the Steyne. Cup after cup of Betsy's strongest coffee cleared his head a great deal, but nowhere near enough to contemplate risking his taking the Swan's ribbons.

News of the fire was all over Town, and word of the goings-on of the night somehow leaked out as well, so that a large crowd was now waiting outside the inn, including a number of elegant carriages as those members of society who hadn't been able to find a place in the crush on Tower Hill decided to view the Swan's departure instead.

Blanche and Aunt Derwent still hadn't arrived when Betsy at last finished helping Jane dress for the race. The freshness of lavender filled the room from the bunches placed in the wardrobe the night before, and the summery perfume seemed to envelop Jane as she looked at her reflection in the plain mirror on the dressing table. She and her aunt had decided she should wear a sunny yellow for the race, an eye-catching shade which brought out to perfection her clear complexion and glossy dark hair. The frilled muslin pelisse and matching gown were the work of Madame Louise, as was the Leghorn bonnet, beneath the brim of which had been pinned lots of little very pale blue flowers. She carried a blue reticule and pagoda parasol, and her blue gloves had been intricately embroidered by her aunt with the very finest tambourwork.

Betsy stepped back to admire her. "You look lovely, Lady Jane."

"I wish I felt as brave now as I did when I first embarked on all this."

"We're going to win, my lady. Will's a good coachman; he'll bring the Swan in first." But the words were spoken with less than full conviction, for the girl, no matter how loyally she praised her lover, knew in her heart that he didn't have his father's talent and didn't really stand much of a chance, even with Lewis's prime bloodstock and a fine new coach. She went to the window, peeping down into the courtyard where the horses were being harnessed now and Arthur was instructing Will about the new brakes. "I wish I was going to be following the race," she said wistfully. "I'd love to be there to cheer my Will on."

"Put on your best mantle then. I'm sure you'd be welcome to travel with Lady Agatha and Miss Lyndon."

Betsy's eyes shone. "Could I really?"

"Be quick now, for they might arrive at any moment."

The girl was gone in a flash, and from the window Jane watched her hurry down the gallery steps and vanish in the direction of her own room.

In the courtyard, the Swan was looking splendid now, its polished panels reflecting like mirrors, the letters on them so proud and defiant that they seemed ready to taunt the two other coaches: *Swan. London and Brighton. Reigate. Handcross. J. E. Wheddle & Co. License No. 3224*. Lewis's horses had had their manes plaited and ribboned as fashionably as any carriage team, and were stamping and snorting now, impatient to be off as they became infected with the growing excitement from the crowd in the street.

More hooves sounded suddenly and a little curricle drove into the yard. For a breathless moment she thought it might be Lewis, but then realized that it was Charles. Why had he come? Had something happened to Aunt Derwent or Blanche? Anxiously, she hurried out onto the gallery to call down to him as he alighted from the little vehicle and handed the reins to a waiting boy. "Charles? Is something wrong?"

He looked quickly up and smiled. "No, nothing's wrong, I've just come to wish you *bon chance*." He came up the steps toward her, the spurs on his boots jingling lightly. He wore a pale green coat and dark gray trousers, and the sunlight caught his light brown, wavy hair as he removed his top hat to bow over her hand. "Forgive me, Jane, I didn't think I'd alarm you."

"I'm the one who should be asking forgiveness, but I'm so edgy at the moment that I think the worst at every turn."

His hazel eyes were very clear as he looked down into her pale face. "I didn't just come to wish you *bon chance*, I came because I heard about the fire and wanted to be certain you were all right.''

"As you can see, I'm quite all right." It was better not to tell him how close to death she'd come.

"You look very lovely."

"Thank you."

"I still wish you wouldn't go on the Swan in the race."

"Charles . . ."

"It's all right, I'm not going to be difficult." He smiled. "Not very long ago I asked you to marry me and you turned me down, but I said that I wouldn't give up. So, here I am, asking you for your hand again."

She looked at him in puzzlement, for now was rather an odd time to choose. "Charles, are you sure nothing's wrong?"

"Must there be something wrong for a man to propose to the woman he loves?"

"No, of course not, it's just that . . . Well, nothing really."

"What is your answer, Jane?"

She lowered her eyes then. "I can't marry you, Charles, because I don't love you enough."

He turned away a little, gazing down at the coach in the yard below. "Is that your last word?"

"It has to be. You deserve so much more than I could give you, Charles, and I know that in time you'll find the right woman for you."

"You are that woman, Jane."

"No," she said quietly, "I'm not, and if you're honest with yourself, and with me, you'll admit that you know it too."

He was silent for a moment, his cane tapping thoughtfully against his boot, then he faced her again. "Maybe I do know it, but that doesn't stop me from loving you with all my heart. Nor does it stop me from telling you something which will dash my chances forever but which will no doubt gladden your foolish heart more than anything else in the world."

"What are you talking about?"

"Alicia has returned to her husband."

Jane was stunned. "I—I beg your pardon?"

"The Duke and Duchess of Brantingham are reconciled."

"But I thought the duke wanted a divorce."

"He did, and the thought apparently galvanized Alicia into action."

"Are you sure about this?"

"I had it from someone who spoke with Alicia herself this

224

morning." He smiled a little. "She isn't generally out and about at such an unearthly hour, but it seems that she and the duke are going to follow the race to London. I encountered them as they were on their way to the Monument, where I understand they intend to join the mill when it passes."

Jane was staring at him. "When did she return to her husband?"

"Several days ago, I believe. It seems that at dinner at Grillion's Lewis persuaded her of her true feelings."

Jane looked away then. At Grillion's? That must have been after Alicia had so brazenly entered the house in South Audley Street. But why hadn't Lewis mentioned anything about it?

"Jane, I confess to being taken aback by your reaction. I expected you to be over the moon because your way to Lewis is now surely clear."

"Is it? I don't think the way will ever be entirely clear, Charles. He must have known that Alicia had gone back to the duke, but he hasn't said anything to me."

"I see. Well, I've done the honorable thing, and now I can only hope that one day you'll forget Ardenley and see me for the fine upright fellow I am." He smiled, putting a gloved hand to her cheek. "Good luck, Jane. I wish you every happiness, and if that happiness means winning Lewis Ardenley, then so be it."

She stretched up to kiss him on the cheek. "You're far too good for me, Charles."

"I know," he replied lightly. "By the way, I trust Henry is feeling buoyant this morning."

"Why?"

"Because not only is Blanche going to be following the race, but I understand from one of Dursley's less loyal cronies that the infernal duke is too. No doubt he's hoping to see Henry come unstuck so that he can rush gleefully back to tell Blanche—except that if he did but know it, she's going to be following as well. Anyway, I've sent a note to Henry warning him about Dursley's presence. Forwarned is forearmed, and it wouldn't do for the shock of Dursley's foxy face to overturn the Iron Duke at the first ditch!"

"I wish *Dursley* would overturn at the first ditch," she replied with feeling.

"Tut, tut, that's not the Christian thing, my dear."

"I know."

Down in the courtyard, Will appeared ready for the off. He wore the fine new clothes Arthur had ordered for the race, but he looked utterly miserable as he listened to his father's last-minute instructions. He wore a white top hat like Sewell's, and there was a nosegay of fresh flowers in the lapel of his brown coat. He carried a fine new whip and had somehow squeezed his rather large feet into his father's new boots, but they pinched his toes and made him shift uncomfortably from time to time as he listened to what Arthur was saying about the brakes.

Charles waited a moment more and then tapped on his top hat. "Well, I'll toddle along now. I hope to find someone at Brooks's to give me a game of billiards."

"Aren't you following the race?"

"No, I think not. I don't think I could bear to see you perched up on that wretched box in all sorts of danger. Besides, if I follow you to Brighton, I'll only be tempted to propose to you again, and that wouldn't do at all, would it." He leaned over to kiss her lightly on the cheek. "Good-bye, Jane, and good luck."

"Good-bye, Charles."

He descended the steps, pausing to wish Will good luck as well before climbing into the curricle and leaving again. Will gazed after him, not knowing who he was beyond the fact that he was obviously a fine gentleman, one of Lord Ardenley's friends, no doubt. Then the coachman returned his attention to the Swan. His expression was almost sickly, for he was wishing with all his heart that he was asleep and only dreaming all this.

Betsy came into the courtyard to join him. She wore a white-ribboned straw bonnet and a new cream linen mantle, and she took his hand, stretching up to whisper that she'd be following the race.

Blanche's landau arrived at last, its hoods up because of the dust which would undoubtedly be churned up on the road. Blanche alighted, looking very lovely indeed in a pink pelisse over a white lawn gown, a matching pink hat resting on her chestnut hair. Aunt Derwent stepped down next, looking particularly splendid in white-dotted turquoise, her hair almost entirely concealed beneath a dignified turban from which sprang tiny white aigrettes.

Jane went down to greet them and saw immediately that they'd heard about Alicia. "Jane," said Blanche urgently, drawing her aside, "have you heard . . . ?"

"That Alicia has gone back to the duke? Yes, Charles told me."

"Are you glad about it?"

"I don't know what to think. No, if I'm honest I'm not glad, because it hasn't made any difference. Lewis knew about it but he didn't tell me, which can only mean that he's indifferent to me."

"That's one thing he'll never be," declared her aunt, coming to join them.

"What else am I to think?"

"That he probably thinks you're going to marry Charles," replied her aunt candidly. "Think about it, my dear—we *did* come in and find you entwined in each other's arms the other night."

"It wasn't what it seemed."

"No doubt, but how is Lewis to know that?"

Jane looked away, for she knew that Lewis *did* think there was something between her and Charles, and she knew that she hadn't said anything to disillusion him.

Aunt Derwent was still eyeing her. "Jane, I suggest that the first moment you have, you tell Lewis what's what."

Jane didn't answer.

Blanche had been looking curiously at Will and Arthur. "Jane, correct me if I'm wrong, but isn't that *Will* dressed in race finery?"

"Yes. Arthur's, er, indisposed."

Then Blanche noticed the fire damage. "Oh, no! What on earth has been happening here?"

"It's a long story, Blanche, and Betsy will be able to tell you all about it on the way to Brighton."

"Betsy?"

"She wants to be there to cheer Will on. You won't mind taking her with you, will you?"

"Of course not."

Betsy heard and smiled gratefully. "Thank you, Miss Lyndon."

It was time to go, for Will climbed up onto the box and took up the reins. Jane's nerve almost failed her then. "Oh, Aunt Derwent, I feel positively ill!"

Her aunt put a concerned hand to her cheek. "Now then, my girl, if you're likely to have the vapors, it will be better if you travel with us instead of going on the Swan."

"I'm determined to be on the Swan," declared Jane.

"Then take a grip on yourself. You can't let womankind down by being seen in a flap."

Jane couldn't help smiling. "Womankind?"

"You carry a great responsibility, Jane. You are the only woman in a positive army of men, and you have to flick your petticoats scornfully at them all. So, take a deep breath and tell yourself that you're as cool as the proverbial cucumber. Do as you're told, Jane."

Jane obeyed, still smiling. "I'm as cool as the proverbial cucumber," she said.

Her aunt hugged her then. "Good luck, my dear, we'll be willing you on."

Blanche hugged her too. "Be lucky, Jane. Show Henry what you're made of."

"At that moment it would undoubtedly be jelly."

She went to the coach then and Jacob assisted her up onto the box beside Will. She felt almost light-headed, gazing down at the four splendid horses stretching away from the coach before her. Then, she took another deep breath—she was as cool as a cucumber! She put up her parasol and twirled it gaily above her head.

Arthur was hovering anxiously beside the coach, calling up to his apprehensive son. "Confidence now, Will; you can do it if you set your mind to it. You've got excellent eyes, strong arms, light hands, and an even temper, and with cattle like these to do your bidding, you have it all going for you. Don't pull or haul like you might need to with lesser animals; let every horse get on with its work, and always handle their mouths gently, like they were made of silk. They'll fly for you if you treat them right."

Will nodded, the beads of perspiration clearly visible on his forehead. He waited until the three ladies had entered Blanche's landau, then he gently touched the team into action. Jane's heart began to thunder so wildly that she was sure everyone must be able to hear it. The coach rolled slowly toward the archway, and as the leaders appeared in the sunlight beyond, a great cheer rose from the waiting crowd.

The chestnuts made a splendid sight, stepping high and proud as they drew the gleaming blue carriage out into the street. Approval was shouted from all sides, but there was astonishment mixed with it, for all eyes were drawn to Jane's yellow-clad figure, seated so prominently beside the coachman.

Most of those who saw her didn't know who she was, nor did they know who the ladies were in the following landau, but there were a number of ladies and gentlemen in the watching carriages who recognized them all straightaway.

A dandy in green satin stood up in his curricle, his quizzing glass raised incredulously to his astonished eyes. " 'Pon me soul," he murmured to himself. " 'Pon me soul."

THIRTY

*T*he whole of London, both fashionable and unfashionable, seemed to have gathered on the hill where William the Conqueror built his great fortress. Overlooking the city and the river, the immense square tower presided over an impressive assemblage of castellated buildings, and the whole was surrounded by an impregnable wall and a large moat. It was one of the most formidable strongholds in the world, and today it seemed to be under siege from the huge crowds that had come together to watch the start of the race.

On the green slopes outside the medieval defenses, the grass was almost completely concealed by thousands of people, their numbers swollen by the arrival of the queen and her multitude of supporters. The queen was in her element, acknowledging the huge gathering as if it was there to see her and not the race.

Every sporting gentleman worth his salt had turned out for the event, and the air was full of their knowing slang and loud laughter. The younger bucks swaggered among the crowds, conducting themselves as if they were every one the equal of professional coachmen like Sewell. Many of them were the friends of Lord Sefton, and intended to accompany him all the way to Brighton in their curricles and cabriolets. These light vehicles were to be seen everywhere, as were the more elegant and comfortable carriages which choked the roads leading to the hill, and all intended to pursue the three competitors the fifty-five miles to Brighton.

At their posts in the Tower, the Beefeaters tried to maintain an air of indifference to the excitement all around. Their scarlet and gold Tudor uniforms made vivid splashes of color against the brooding Norman stonework, and for a long time those specks of color didn't move from their posts, but in the end it was too much, and they came to the battlements to gaze down at the seething crowds below. The famous ravens wheeled and dipped excitedly in the clear sky, their raucous cries echoing all around.

229

Deep within the tower, their roars muffled by the thick walls but still audible, the lions and tigers in the royal menagerie paced restlessly up and down, agitated by the sheer numbers of people they sensed to be close by.

The Swan's two rivals had already arrived, the amazing new Nonpareil having caused a tremendous stir when it appeared, drawn by a team of extremely eye-catching skewbalds. The coach's scarlet livery was familiar enough, as were the black horse emblems on its shining panels, but the novelty of the revolutionary design made it the object of a great deal of astonished attention. It was exactly as Aunt Derwent had described it—low and wide, with an open compartment behind the box for outside passengers, only today, of course, Sewell was to be the only person on board.

He looked as smart as ever, in a coat to match the color of the coach and trousers as fashionable and white as any gentleman's. He sat elegantly on the box, the ribbons held almost nonchalantly in his kid-gloved hand as he leaned down to talk confidentially to Chapman. The coachmaster himself was dressed in peacock blue with a yellow cravat, and the satisfied smile on his lips told of his confidence that the Swan had been eliminated and the Iron Duke was easy prey.

Nearby, Henry's gleaming green coach stood at the ready, its team of mettlesome strawberry roans stamping and tossing their splendid heads. The Iron Duke exuded an air of excellence and style, everything about it proclaiming it to be the product of Powell of Bond Street. Its lacquerwork was glossy, its metalwork the finest silver, and its rich appointments were worthy of a royal carriage; it was a very elegant and stylish vehicle, as aristocratic as its owner.

A group of gentlemen stood in its shadow, discussing the burning topic of brakes. Among them were Henry himself and the marshal of the race, Lord Sefton. The marshal was a large, bluff man, much given to wearing his favorite sporting pink, and possessed of such a commanding manner that he was the natural leader of the sporting fraternity and therefore the obvious choice to see that all was as it should be on an occasion like this. A stickler for the rules, he intended to pursue the contestants in his yellow curricle, and that splendid vehicle waited behind the Iron Duke, a smart groom attending to the spirited pair of bays, Lord Sefton being famous for his predilection for horses of that color.

Behind the curricle there was another dashing sporting vehicle, this one a purple cabriolet drawn by a single gray. It was the property of the Duke of Dursley, who wore purple to match and who was lounging on the seat with a secret, knowing smile on his lips, for alone among the huge gathering he knew that Blanche was going to follow the race. He had happened upon the information because he'd overheard her maid discussing the matter with her footman beau, and he intended to use it to the best advantage. With luck, Henry wouldn't show up well against the Nonpareil, and that would surely lower his stock in Blanche's eyes—if indeed his stock could fall much more anyway. The duke's lips curved into a smile more sleek than ever. The Lyndon fortune was falling neatly into his hands after all. It had been a tiresome business, especially as the lady wasn't exactly to his taste anyway, lacking the full-bosomed figure of the actresses he much preferred, but her fortune was sufficient to make it all worthwhile, and once she was safely married, he could ignore her. His eyes glittered as he pondered the delights of spending his way through such wealth. Ah, sweet delight, he'd be able to indulge his many vices, and pursue a certain young creature who'd caught his eye at the opera house the other night. What a divinity, absolute perfection; but disagreeably expensive. That would change when he had old Lyndon's pennies in his ducal pocket.

Next to the Iron Duke, Henry was attempting to concentrate on his friends' conversation. He wore a double-breasted beige coat with a high collar and large brass buttons, and his cream cord trousers were tucked into particularly elegant Hessian boots. His brown silk neckcloth was adorned with a fine diamond pin, and his top hat was tall and shining. He was in the very tippy of fashion, looking very handsome and dashing, but although he smiled and laughed with apparent unconcern, he was wishing with all his heart that he'd gone to make his peace with Blanche as Jane had wanted the previous day. It would be so good to have Blanche with him now, cheering him on as he tooled the Iron Duke down the hill toward Eastcheap and London Bridge. Goddammit, how he missed her. His cane tapped impatiently. How much longer did they have to wait for Ardenley's wretched Swan to put in an appearance? And how much more of Dursley's smirking stares did he have to endure? Charles' note had been appreciated, for at least he'd had advance warning.

Lord Sefton took out his fob watch and flicked it open. Was the Swan's late arrival due to a sense of the theatrical, or had the events of the previous evening proved too much, even for Ardenley? Mulling over the latter thought for a moment, his lordship swiftly rejected it, for Lewis Ardenley wasn't a man to be put off by the scurrilous activities of someone like Chapman. Lord Sefton glanced at the Nonpareil's proprietor for a moment. Chapman had been sailing close to the wind for too long now, but everything he'd done had been impossible to prove. The day of reckoning was surely at hand, and if he tried anything during this race, anything at all, then he'd have the might of Sefton to contend with and he'd pay dearly for his many past sins.

Distant cheers from Eastcheap heralded the approach at last of the third and final competitor, and everyone strained to look down the hill. Chapman's smile faded for a moment. So, they'd decided to start even without Huggett, had they? Who had they found to take his place? What if they'd managed to get Lord Ardenley back from Maywood in time? Fleeting alarm seized him then and he scrambled quickly up on the box beside Sewell.

It was the women among the crowds in Eastcheap who first alerted those on the hill that there was something of more than mild interest about the Swan, for their mixed cries of delight and disbelief were clearly audible. The fashionable ladies at the start stood up in their open carriages the better to see what was causing such female fuss, and soon their gasps of astonishment were to be heard as well.

The Swan drew nearer, its blue panels very bright and its fine chestnuts stepping high as they effortlessly pulled the coach up the hill. The dainty figure beside the coachman was the cause of all the attention, as the ladies soon whispered to their male companions.

A great stir began to pass through the crowd as Jane acknowledged the cheers, her parasol twirling and her bonnet ribbons fluttering in the light breeze. Chapman stared, knowing her immediately. Felbridge's sister! So that was the real reason for Ardenley's interest in the Swan! But the coachmaster wasn't really interested in Jane; he was relieved to see Will with the ribbons. Ardenley was evidently still tucked safely away at Maywood, and long may he remain there! Chapman's sharp eyes were thoughtful, though. Maywood was too handily placed and Ardenley might get on the box yet. He leaned closer to Sewell. "You've got a passenger, George; I think it might be wise if I'm on the spot, so to speak."

"You're expecting trouble?"

"Only what I've laid in store for the others." Chapman's expression was still thoughtful. "There's too many nobs in this for my liking. That bit of muslin isn't only Felbridge's sister—she was betrothed to Ardenley."

"Do you reckon we'd do better to stick fast to the rules then?"

"Hardly, not if the Nonpareil's to get into Brighton first!" snapped Chapman irritably. "I need that £50,000 and intend to get my hands on it, so we'll do it like we planned, only I'll come with you now instead of staying back here in London." His glance moved beyond the Swan then to the landau which had drawn up behind it. "God above!" he exclaimed, seeing Aunt Derwent's face grinning out at him.

Sewell saw her too and recognized her as the widow who had been wined and dined. So, for once Chapman had been duped instead of doing the duping! The coachman had to grin, nudging the furious coachmaster. "Here, isn't that—?"

"No!" came the snappish reply. "It just happens to look like her!" Chapman scowled at the landau.

Henry had been so stunned to see Jane on the box that he didn't notice that Will had the ribbons instead of Arthur. Seeing his sister perched up there so conspicuously was a galling experience, and Henry's blue eyes had darkened with fury. So, she thought to make a fool of him, did she? What a gull he'd been, not realizing what a viper she was in his trusting bosom! Far from being really interested in his coaching, she'd been pumping him and telling Ardenley and Wheddle everything he said! He rounded on Lord Sefton, suspecting him of complicity. "Sir, I don't find this trick at all amusing!"

Lord Sefton didn't like the tone. "Steady on now, Felbridge, there's no need for that. I didn't know Lady Jane was involved. I only knew about Ardenley, and I told you about *that*. You've been asking for a poke on your handsome snout for some time now. That business of the Lyndon ball was evidently the final straw for your sister." He chuckled a little. "What spirit, eh?"

"That's not what I'd call it," grumbled Henry, giving Jane another dark look. He hadn't noticed the landau behind yet.

Lord Sefton was looking thoughtfully at Will Huggett and then at Chapman, who hadn't exactly seemed all that surprised to see the son on the Swan's box instead of the father. "Felbridge, there appears to be something you've overlooked in your apoplectic rage with your lovely sister, and that is the howling fact that Arthur Huggett is nowhere to be seen."

Henry stared at Will, forgetting Jane for a moment. "I wonder what's happened? He was hail and hearty enough when I saw him yesterday."

"Look at Chapman. He's been up to slightly more than that

fire last night, you mark my words. With Will on the box, the Swan doesn't stand an earthly. It's going to be between you and the Nonpareil after all.'' Lord Sefton glanced at the landau then and saw Blanche. He pursed his lips. ''Felbridge, I'm afraid that I've got some bad news for you.''

''Eh?''

''Miss Lyndon is evidently in on the Swan as well. She's in the carriage behind.''

Henry stared at Blanche, his eyes hurt and accusing. It was bad enough that Jane had stabbed him in the back, but that Blanche should do it as well. . . . Then he saw his aunt and he turned away. So Charles had only seen fit to warn him about Dursley and had kept the rest to himself. Sworn to secrecy, no doubt! He'd show them! He'd show them that they couldn't make a fool of him!

Lord Sefton pursed his lips. ''Well, my boy, I'll warrant you wish now you'd behaved yourself the night of the Lyndon ball, eh?'' He chuckled again. ''Your womenfolk are tweaking your nose, and doing it publicly.''

Henry didn't reply. He didn't find anything amusing in the situation, especially as he now understood the knowing smirk on Dursley's odious face. Even Dursley had been in on the plot, his archrival and the man he loathed most in all the world! He'd never forgive Jane for this, or Blanche, or his aunt! Never! He vaulted lightly up onto the box of the Iron Duke, making the roans toss their heads in anticipation as he picked up the reins. He sat stiffly, ignoring the Swan and keeping his back toward the occupants of the landau.

Blanche had watched his every reaction and now she lowered her eyes sadly. If he'd given her the chance, she'd have smiled at him and shown him she still loved him, but he hadn't, and now he seemed more angry than ever before.

Aunt Derwent sniffed. ''Tiresome boy,'' she muttered. ''When will he ever learn? Don't pay any attention to him, Blanche, he's being extremely disagreeable.''

''But I love him.''

''I know.'' Aunt Derwent patted her hand, and then smiled at Betsy. ''Come on now, ladies, we're off to Brighton and it's going to be very exciting. Smile at the world, we've a stagecoach to cheer for and it certainly isn't the Iron Duke! Or that horrid Mr. Chapman's Nonpareil. Did you see the look on his face when he spotted me? Oh, it was a sweet moment.''

Blanche managed a laugh then, and Betsy smiled shyly, a

little overawed to be with such elegant ladies in a carriage more luxurious than any she'd ever been in before.

Lord Sefton looked at his watch again and decided that it was more than time to start the race. He signaled up to the battlements of the Tower, where a cannon was waiting to be fired for the off. An answering wave signified that they were in readiness, and a hush fell over the gathering, even the queen's yahoos standing in quiet anticipation for a moment. As the marshal walked toward his curricle, every other vehicle prepared for the big moment, ready to set off in hot pursuit the moment the stagecoaches left.

Chapman nudged Sewell, hissing through clenched teeth. "I want that £50,000! Needle Felbridge, I want him rattled!"

The coachman was confused for a moment, but then with a taunting grin he leaned across, pointing his whip at the Iron Duke's splendid roans. "What a poor, lean lot you've got there, my lord. They must cost you more in whips than hay!"

A ripple of amusement passed through those in the crowd who heard.

Henry scowled at him, goaded more easily than might otherwise have been the case because of the Swan. "I can't imagine how you've got the gall to criticize my cattle considering you've got the most miserable set of bo-kickers I've ever seen stagger from a stable! They look as if they've had three sweats already! Claw them up the hill, did you? You'll have to find a better style, Sewell, you looked like a damned windmill when you arrived. Not that many will have noticed, they were all too busy laughing at that tea crate you call a coach!"

Sewell and Chapman glowered at him, while the crowd curled up with mirth at this display of unfriendly rivalry. On the Swan, Will remained still and quiet, the beads of perspiration still standing out on his pale forehead. Jane noticed how his hand trembled on the ribbons. Her own nerves were far from steady, and her heart hadn't stopped its wild thundering since the moment they'd left the Feathers.

On his curricle, Lord Sefton was looking at his watch for a final time. The queen stood up in her carriage to watch, and everything was suddenly so quiet that the animals in the royal menagerie could be heard very clearly indeed. The marshal raised his hand. The three stagecoaches were poised, their teams screwed up to a veritable pitch as they responded to the change in the atmosphere. Then Lord Sefton dropped his arm, the cannon boomed, and the three coaches sprang forward together toward the narrow confines of Eastcheap.

Jane clung to her seat as the Swan surged into action, the chestnuts pulling so effortlessly that the stagecoach could have been weightless. Will had anticipated the signal to absolute perfection, stealing a slight march on the others so that unbelievably the Swan entered Eastcheap in the lead.

Twisting in her seat, she saw the Iron Duke and the Nonpareil thundering neck-and-neck behind, with beyond them the medley of following carriages, led by Lord Sefton's yellow curricle. The noise was incredible as the whole concourse poured along Eastcheap, jostling for position and driving as fast as the stagecoaches.

The crowds passed in a blur, their cheers reverberating between the houses as Will prepared to negotiate the sharp turn to the south directly ahead, using the brakes for the first time. He'd avoided using them all the way from the Feathers, but his speed was too great now to postpone the moment any longer. Jane tensed, not knowing quite what to expect.

Then they were upon the corner, the brakes snatching fiercely so that the team's heads came up. Jane held on tightly, her eyes closed as the coach swung around the corner, losing precious inches on its rivals because Will had applied too much pressure and lost too much speed. She heard him curse under his breath as he tooled the chestnuts up to a swift pace once more.

Ahead rose the two-hundred-foot column called the Monument, built to commemorate the great fire of 1666, which had started close to this spot. There was a gallery at the very top, and people were crowded into it, waving and cheering as the three coaches swept closer, followed by the company of fashionable carriages and the light vehicles of the sporting gentlemen.

London Bridge was in sight now, and although Jane could hardly believe it, the Swan was holding on to its lead. This was about to change, however, and it was because of a misunderstanding between Will and herself. An open landau was drawn up at the foot of the Monument, and as she saw it she remembered that Charles had said, Alicia and her newly reconciled husband were to join the carriages following the race from this point. The landau was theirs and because its hoods were down she saw its occupants quite clearly. They sat side-by-side, their backs toward the oncoming race, and there was an ominous gap between them. Jane stared at them as the Swan thundered past. The duke's thin, elderly visage looked pinched, to say the least, while Alicia looked positively furious, her face flushed and angry. They'd quarreled already. "Oh, no." she breathed, still staring back at the landau, which was moving forward as it joined the following carriages.

Will heard her and thought something was wrong. Automatically he began to rein in. "What is it, Lady Jane?" he cried.

The Swan's speed fell away dramatically. "Nothing's wrong, Will," she cried looking back again to see to her dismay that the other two coaches were on the point of passing. "Drive on, Will! Quickly!" But it was too late, the Iron Duke and the Nonpareil galloped by, and she distinctly heard Chapman's triumphant laughter.

Will urged the chestnuts into action again, but as they crossed the bridge toward the southern bank of the Thames, the Swan was trailing in third place.

THIRTY-ONE

Chased by the throng of sporting vehicles and carriages, the race dashed noisily through Southwark, cheered on from every pavement and window. As the Elephant & Castle was passed, the two leading coaches were together. Sewell resorted to his whip to try and edge the Nonpareil into the lead before they reached open country, but on the flat the Nonpareil's revolutionary design had no advantage over the more conventional Iron Duke, and Henry's skill was anyway equal to his opponent's.

Bringing up the rear, the Swan was cheered on as well, especially by the women, but Jane could see that very slowly the other two coaches were pulling away. She looked anxiously at Will. "They're getting away! Can't we go faster?"

He hesitated, knowing that it was his timidity which was at fault; then with sudden resolve he cracked the whip. The team sprang forward as if stung and the wind buffeted Jane's bonnet, forcing her to hold it tightly on. The parasol had long since been placed safely by her feet, where it lay with its blue fringe trembling in the draft of air which swept against the coach from the speed with which it was traveling.

Looking behind again, she gazed at the following concourse. A cloud of dust was rising above the company of carriages, curricles, cabriolets, and horsemen pursuing the race out of the capital, and she could see Lord Sefton's yellow curricle in the lead, with the Duke of Dursley's purple cabriolet close behind. Beyond their accompanying band of sporting gentlemen, she could just make out Blanche's landau, one of the only ones to be sensibly hooded, and the Brantingham landau, its hoods down so that its occupants must already be liberally covered with the choking dust. She stared at the elegant vehicle, thinking that far from assisting the Brantinghams to mend their quarrel, the dust would make it ten times worse, since Alicia loathed being anything other than perfectly turned out.

Her attention was whisked back to the front again then as the race passed through the open turnpike at Kennington. The leading stagecoaches seemed to be a little closer now that Will had urged the team on, but even as she thought it a sharp bend in the road made Will check the Swan's flight just a little too much. Sewell and Henry suffered no such hesitation; they drove on without slowing at all, again drawing inexorably away from the Swan.

They were in open country now, the city sliding away fast behind them as the fresh teams pounded along the almost deserted road, few other vehicles risking being caught up in the helter-skelter of race day. There were still people lining the wayside, but they were becoming fewer and fewer in number, just little groups here and there as the workers from the fields came to the road to watch the race.

Cow parsley and blue flax swayed and bobbed as the leading coaches drove furiously by, still neck-and-neck, and Jane could see her brother's lithe figure bending forward just a little as he sought to coax just that little extra pace from his flying team of strawberry roans. The Iron Duke's bright green panels were already a little dulled from the dust kicked up, and she could taste that same dust on her lips.

With each bend in the road, Will's lack of confidence and inexperience cost the Swan precious inches. He couldn't bring himself to use the brakes, his training and instinct telling him that each application put a strain on the wheels, and so Jane had the torment of watching the others draw inexorably further and further away.

Will knew his failings and glanced apologetically at her. "I can't do it, Lady Jane," he shouted above the noise of the coach, "I'm just too afraid!"

"It's only for one day, Will."

"I know." His whip cracked again, but although the chestnuts flung themselves willingly forward, making the coach lurch tangibly faster, the next corner saw those inches lost once more.

Ahead, Henry was fighting to stay with the Nonpareil now, for the corners gave the low, wide Nonpareil the upper hand and Sewell wasn't slow to capitalize on this. At the bridge where he had almost overturned his unfortunate rival on the day that Jane and Lewis had traveled to Brighton, he at last gained the advantage, squeezing the Nonpareil into a definite lead, one which Henry would have to work very hard indeed to snatch back. Behind them both, the Swan thundered on, catching up a little on every straight, losing again at every bend, bridge, and descent.

There were crowds again at Mitcham, where the air was sweet with the scent of lavender and herbs from the surrounding market gardens, but Jane was hardly aware of anything, clinging to the edge of her seat as the Swan flew along the street. The taste of dust seemed to have spread now from her lips to her entire mouth, but she didn't really notice. Taking yet another glance behind, she saw Lord Sefton's curricle some hundred yards away, with the Duke of Dursley close behind, and beyond them the light racing vehicles of their gentlemen friends. Then there was a gap before the brilliant company of following carriages could be made out through the dust. She saw Blanche's landau, still managing gamely to stand the pace, but the Brantingham landau was nowhere to be seen.

Mitcham faded away behind as they raced on toward the end of the first stage at Sutton. Ahead now lay the dell where the ox-wagon had so nearly managed to cause such a dreadful accident to the Nonpareil. The memory was suddenly very vivid indeed, like a warning cry in her head, and she quickly put a hand on Will's arm. "Have a care, this is a dangerous place!"

She could see the lane now, and smell the perfume of lily-of-the-valley. The overhanging trees muffled the passage of the coach, making everything seem oddly quiet after the noise of the open road. The road curved, taking the other two coaches out of sight, and eliminating for the time being the view of the following spectators; the Swan was to all intents and purposes alone. Jane could hear her heart pounding with rising fear as she stared at the entrance of the lane, so hidden still by leaves that to the uninitiated it was quite invisible. Something was going to happen again!

Suddenly the road wasn't clear any more—a small flock of sheep spilled from the lane directly into the Swan's path, milling around frantically as two dogs snapped and barked at them.

Jane screamed as it seemed the coach must plough straight into them, and Will gave a startled oath as he struggled to rein the flying horses in. The team's heads came up and their haunch muscles bulged with the effort of trying to stop, but the coach's impulsion was too great, it hurtled on toward the terrified, helpless sheep.

Jane clung to the seat. "Will! The brakes!" she screamed. "Use the brakes!"

At the very last moment he grabbed at the handle, applying the brakes with all his might and fighting back a cry of pain as he wrenched the muscles in his hand. The coach shuddered and the brakes whined against the wheels, but the speed was almost immediately checked, the horses rearing and plunging as they managed to halt within inches of the panic-stricken sheep. The dogs didn't give up, but continued harrassing their prey.

With another curse, Will rose to his feet, snatching up his whip and cracking it like a pistol close to the ears of first one dog and then the other. The effect was electrifying. With frightened yelps, they took to their heels and vanished back along the lane. The sheep immediately broke away in the opposite direction, streaming into the undergrowth and making good their escape before the dogs returned.

Jane was too shocked to speak as Will sat down again. He winced as he took up the reins, for a pain lanced through a torn muscle in his right hand. Clicking his tongue to soothe the unnerved horses, he moved the Swan forward once more, just as Lord Sefton's curricle headed the spectators around the curve behind.

The team came swiftly up to a spanking pace once more, but precious time had been lost and there was now no sign at all of the other two stagecoaches. Moreover, it was soon obvious that the injury to Will's hand had made matters much worse as far as the unfortunate Swan was concerned.

Jane looked anxiously at him. "Can you manage?"

"Just about. God damn that villain Chapman!"

"Chapman?" Her eyes widened then. "You don't mean that the sheep were his doing?"

"Reckon so. There was a man in that lane, and I'd swear I'd

240

seen him at the Black Horse." His whip cracked and he whistled encouragement to the team to fling themselves into their collars as they drew the coach out of the dell on toward the first cottages of Sutton.

The other coaches were to change teams at the Cock Inn, but the Swan's fresh team waited beyond the town at a fork in the road. As the Swan passed the inn, Jane saw the skewbalds and roans of the Nonpareil and Iron Duke, but of the coaches themselves there was no sign. Will shouted out to an ostler as the Swan dashed by, and was told that they'd driven on one minute earlier, the Nonpareil still marginally in the lead.

Lewis's second team waited at the appointed place, and as the Swan drew to a weary standstill, the grooms from Maywood rushed forward to unharness the tired team. Jane's heart was pounding as she watched, for it seemed that they were taking an age. Lord Sefton, the Duke of Dursley, and their friends had all taken fresh horses at the Cock Inn and were now coming along the road again, slowing and finally halting altogether as the Swan remained obstinately stationary by the fork in the road. The fresh team were almost harnessed, but one of the traces was refusing to untwist. It couldn't be left, for if it untwisted on the road, the resulting snap might break it. The grooms rattled and shook it, but the metal links stayed where they were. Will glanced at his father's watch. Precious time was slipping away, and the leading coaches were moving further and further out of reach with each second.

"Can't you finish?" he cried out in desperation. "We want to reach Brighton today, not next week!"

"Keep your hair on, we're doing the best we can!" growled the man in charge, scowling as much in embarrassment as annoyance.

Jane turned in her seat to see the following concourse beginning to catch up as well, all coming to a gradual standstill behind the earl and his friends. It was so humiliating, as if fate was determined not to lift a finger to aid the poor Swan. She could have wept with frustration, especially when she saw the Brantingham landau again, its hoods wisely raised now.

Suddenly the trace capitulated, straightening so easily that it was hard to believe that it had put up such a struggle. Will didn't wait a second. His whip cracked and the fresh team plunged forward, almost snatching the coach out into the road again. Their hooves clattered on the tinder-dry surface, and the wheels rumbled, while Jane heard whip after whip cracking behind as the following carriages began to move again as well. But how much time had they lost? She looked anxiously at Will, raising her voice above the noise. "How late are we?"

"Five minutes on Dad's reckoning," he shouted back.

She stared ahead in dismay. Five minutes, five ignominious minutes, and they'd only covered the first stage! There were another four stages to cover yet, how much more time would they lose before trailing into Brighton a disgraced third? Oh, please, *please* let luck be on the Swan's side for a change!

THIRTY-TWO

*O*nly once during the next stage did they even catch a glimpse of their opponents, and that was when the road ahead rose over Banstead Downs. Jane could see the others quite clearly, and it seemed that somehow or other Henry had taken the lead, dashing over the summit with the Nonpareil at his heels.

Will's injured hand was giving him a great deal of pain, but he struggled valiantly to continue, and he was gradually coming to terms with the brakes, which had after all probably saved their lives in the dell. But five minutes was a lot to make up, and Jane knew that with each mile to Reigate, only seconds were being clawed back.

After the incident with the sheep, and Will's certainty that it hadn't been accidental, she was still very nervous, scanning the road ahead and the fields for a sign of further trouble. She was trembling inside, and clinging to the edge of her seat more tightly than necessary. Oh, how she wished Lewis was with her and that he'd never gone back to Maywood the night before.

The air on the downs was sweet and warm, and she could hear the high-pitched songs of larks far above. She saw Tumble Beacon again, and remembered wryly the defiant thoughts she'd had when last she'd seen it. She'd been so convinced that the Swan was going to take the others on as an equal, challenging them on their own level; the truth was proving very different.

They reached the top of Reigate Hill with no further sight of the other two stagecoaches. The spectators following were now stretched in a long, straggling line, with a considerable gap between Lord Sefton and his friends and the first of the carriages. As the Swan began the dangerous descent, Will applied the brakes with something approaching confidence. The countryside of the weald stretched ahead, hazy with sunshine, allowing only a vague impression of the distant South Downs, beyond which lay Brighton, their goal.

The Swan dashed through the town of Reigate, where people lined the pavements to cheer the tardy coach on its way, the women again calling encouragement as they saw Jane on the box. At the White Hart, where the Iron Duke and the Nonpareil had changed teams minutes before, the lapse of time was sufficient for the tired teams to have been led away out of sight. Will shouted an inquiry as he drove past, and an ostler called back that the others were still nearly five minutes ahead, with the Iron Duke still somehow in the lead. Jane's hands clenched and unclenched with frustration. In spite of their efforts, they weren't making any impression on that gap!

On the far side of the town, more grooms from Maywood were waiting with the fresh horses, and to Jane's great joy she saw that Lewis was with them. He was mounted on a nervous, capering black horse, his head uncovered so that his golden hair shone in the bright sunlight. He wore a dark green riding coat and beige breeches, and he looked concernedly at Jane as he maneuvered his horse close as Will drew the coach to a weary standstill. "Are you all right?"

"Yes. Just."

He reached over to put his hand on hers. "What's been going on? Why isn't Arthur driving? And why on earth are you so far behind?"

She explained a little breathlessly, glad of the reassurance his hand gave her.

His gray eyes darkened as her story unfolded. "Chapman should be strung up!" he breathed. "But you still haven't explained why you're so far behind. The business with the sheep would explain two minutes away, but not five."

"Will's hurt his hand rather badly. He's in a lot of pain, Lewis."

He looked quickly at the unhappy coachman. "Is this true, Will?"

"Yes, my lord. I only wish it wasn't. I wasn't doing that well before it happened, but now . . ." His voice trailed miserably away and he shook his head. "I'm just not up to it, my lord.

Even with both my hands good I haven't got what it takes for something like this.''

Jane looked equally as miserable. "Oh, Lewis, we're going to fail utterly, and it just isn't fair!" She felt foolishly close to tears.

His hand tightened over hers. "I think you should wait here for Blanche to arrive and go the rest of the way with her. In safety.''

"No! No, Lewis, I won't hear of it! I'm going to stay with the Swan!''

He studied her insistent, rather dusty face for a moment and then smiled. "Yes, I rather see that you are," he said softly, "which means that I must too." He dismounted then, glancing at the grooms, who had unharnessed the old team and were leading them away while the fresh horses were brought forward.

Lord Sefton's cabriolet was fast approaching along the road now, together with the Duke of Dursley and the rest of the little coterie of light vehicles, but of the carriages of the other followers there was as yet no sign. Lewis hurried over to the yellow curricle. "Good day to you, my lord."

The marshal tipped his top hat back and gave a wry smile. "After the Swan's abysmal performance so far, I'll refrain from wishing you a good day in return, Ardenley.''

"It isn't the Swan's fault, not by a long chalk. There's been more than a little interference from Chapman.''

"I take it you're referring to the fire?''

"And the nobbling of Arthur Huggett, to say nothing of sheep blocking the way before Sutton.''

Lord Sefton stared at him. "Sheep? So *that's* why I nearly caught the Swan up! I couldn't understand why it was suddenly so close. Chapman's a tricky customer, and no mistake. If I actually catch him at it, I'll have his conniving guts for garters.''

"I'm tricky enough myself when need be," replied Lewis. "Tell me, is there any reason why *I* shouldn't drive the Swan from now on?''

"You?" Lord Sefton grinned. "No reason at all, dear boy.''

"And is there anything in the rules which lays down the exact route which must be followed?''

"Not as far as I know. Why?''

"If foul means are Chapman's order of the day, then I can match him.''

The marshal cleared his throat uncomfortably, leaning closer to prevent the nearby gentlemen from hearing. "Ardenley, I must warn you that if I see anything untoward, I shall be forced to disqualify you.''

"Oh, there won't be anything like that. I intend to content myself with *legal* trickery, I promise you.''

"I'm relieved to hear it.'' Lord Sefton glanced at Jane, who was watching them anxiously from a distance. "Is your interest due to the lovely lady?''

"Why should it be?''

"Because I can't imagine that you really meant to settle for the fool's gold of Brantingham when you could have had the real thing in Felbridge's delightful sister.''

"I didn't settle for anything, sir; it was settled for me.'' Lewis turned to look back at the coach, where his grooms had almost completed the change of team.

The noise of the following stream of carriages was beginning to fill the air now and then the first one appeared around the bend in the road behind them. Lord Sefton nodded at Lewis. "Hadn't you better get on with it, then? Time, the Iron Duke, and the Nonpareil wait for no man.''

Lewis hurried back to the Swan, where Will had climbed down now and was pacing nervously up and down, trying to flex his aching hand. He turned sharply as he heard Lewis approaching. "My lord?''

"I'll take over, Will; you're in no condition to carry on.''

Will couldn't hide his relief. "I'm sorry to have failed you all, my lord.''

"You didn't fail, man, you did damned well! Driving a coach and four with an injured hand is no easy matter.''

Will smiled with pleasure at the praise. "Thank you for that, my lord.''

"Credit where credit's due,'' answered Lewis, climbing lightly up onto the box next to Jane. Then he leaned down to Will again, nodding toward Blanche's landau which had at that moment drawn up behind Lord Sefton and right alongside the Duke of Dursley's purple cabriolet. "Go to Miss Lyndon, Will; I'm sure she'll gladly convey you the rest of the way.''

"I'll do that, sir. Good luck.''

"We'll need it,'' replied Lewis, gathering the ribbons and watching the Duke of Dursley, who was doing his utmost to attract Blanche's attention and was being ignored for his pains. Then he looked at Jane for a moment. "Well, madam, it seems you must trust yourself to my care for the rest of the race.''

"I do so gladly.''

"Gladly? I'm overcome by such enthusiasm."

"I mean it, Lewis."

He met her gaze for a moment. "Yes, I can see that you do," he said softly. "I wonder what Charles would say? However, first things first, so let's see what we can do about this race, eh?" He nodded at the waiting grooms, who released the horses. At a barely perceptible command, the team sprang eagerly forward, moving the Swan swiftly on its way once more.

Will dashed across to the landau, where a curious Blanche had opened the door to see what was happening. Still ignoring the rather cross Duke of Dursley, she called out to Will, "What's wrong? Why has the Swan lost so much time?"

"I'll explain, Miss Lyndon, if you'll please be so kind as to take me with you."

She nodded, sitting quickly back for him to climb in.

Aunt Derwent looked a little sternly at him. "Sir, Betsy has already regaled us with dreadful tales of fires and my niece's miraculous escape from death. I do trust that you aren't going to give me further reason for recourse to the *sal volatile*."

Will looked uncertainly at her as the landau lurched forward once more. "I don't know what you mean, my lady, but what I've got to tell isn't good." He told them what had been happening and Aunt Derwent tapped her parasol crossly on the floor of the swaying coach. "That wretched, wretched Mr. Chapman! Just wait until I catch up with him in Brighton—he'll wish he'd never been born!"

On the Swan, Jane felt as if she was flying now, for somehow Lewis managed to coax that little bit extra from the horses. The flower-dotted meadows of the weald passed swiftly by, the hedgerows bending to the rush of air as the coach thundered along the dusty highway. She felt a surge of excitement now, a thrill which she hadn't experienced before, for she knew that Lewis was a different class of driver entirely from the unfortunate Will. She remembered that even Henry had grudgingly admitted that he considered Lewis to be the finest whip in the land, and now, as the Swan dashed through the countryside toward Crawley and the next change, she knew exactly what her brother had meant. She could almost feel the seconds being snatched back, and knew that no other man could have better negotiated the bends, ascents, and descents or covered the flat ground at such speed. Whereas Will had visibly driven the coach, Lewis seemed hardly to move. His commands were subtle, sometimes barely discernible, but he achieved far more, making the horses seem fresh when they must have begun to tire. Glancing behind, she saw that Lord Sefton and his friends were having difficulty keeping up, and there was no sign at all of the following throng of carriages. She wanted to laugh aloud with anticipation, and her eyes shone.

Lewis glanced at her and grinned. "I see you begin to appreciate the lure of coaching," he said, his voice raised above the rush of wind and the noise of the coach.

"Yes, I do! Oh, Lewis, can we possibly catch them up?"

"Going the way I intend to go, the answer has to be yes," he answered rather mysteriously.

"What do you mean?"

"Wait and see." He returned his attention to the road then, easing the team over the brow of a hill and then gently applying the brakes so that the Swan slid down the incline without putting any strain at all on the horses. There was no jarring or jolting as there would have been with Will, just a smooth flowing motion which didn't seem to check the coach's speed at all.

The crowds of Crawley passed in a blur, she hardly saw them, she was too intent upon the knowledge that gradually they must be catching up with the other two coaches. She didn't glance at the George Inn, and she could hardly bear it when Lewis halted the tired horses for his grooms to change them. Seeing him on the box, the men worked as fast as they could, informing him that the Iron Duke was still in the lead, and that both coaches had passed by only four minutes before. Jane's excitement grew. Only four minutes! Oh, hurry, please hurry!

The change was completed in less time than usual, and then the Swan was speeding on its way, driving swiftly up through the cool greenness of Peasepottage Forest on its way to the fourth change at Maywood.

As they emerged from the forest and saw the South Downs beginning to loom in the distance ahead, she searched the road for a sign of the other two coaches, for surely they would soon see them! But there was nothing and they passed through Handcross, where more crowds were waiting, without seeing their quarry.

It was just outside Handcross, before they reached the gates of Maywood where the next change of horses would be waiting, that they at last saw the Iron Duke, but it was in circumstances which made Jane gasp with horror and alarm, for the magnificent coach was overturned in a ditch, with a small crowd of farm laborers gathered around it from the field where they'd been working.

Lewis immediately began to rein the Swan in, and Jane stared anxiously for a sign of her brother. The coach lay there, its beautiful paintwork scratched and spoiled, its axle quite obviously broken, while the horses, shaken but not injured, were being tended to by several of the men in smocks.

As the Swan at last came to a standstill, she saw Henry, leaning against the side of the Iron Duke, his face ashen and stained with blood from a cut on his forehead. With a mixed cry of relief and anxiety, she scrambled down from the box and ran to him. "Henry! Are you all right?"

He was very shaken, but managed to catch her close, hugging her reassuringly. "Yes, sis. I took a nasty tumble but no bones are broken."

"Oh, thank God, thank God!" There were tears on her cheeks as she clung to him.

He smiled a little, stroking her hair. "Ah, so I'm back in your good books again, am I?"

"Of course you are," she whispered. "You were never really out of them, you just left a few pages dog-eared now and then."

Lewis joined them then. "You're all right, Henry?"

"Just about. The poor old Duke isn't though."

"What happened?"

Henry nodded toward the silent group of workers. "There were two others, strangers I gather. They flung a log of wood through the wheels as I was passing. I didn't stand a chance."

"And they hopped it, I suppose?"

"Like stags into that wood over there."

"Chapman?"

"Well, since I hardly imagine it was the Swan's connections, I have to think that he's the villain of the piece. Besides, I recognize their descriptions."

Lewis smiled a little. "He usually is." He looked at the wrecked coach, and the ugly piece of wood which had shattered the spokes of the wheels and brought the whole vehicle crashing so dangerously into the ditch. Chapman was ruthless beyond belief.

Henry looked curiously at Lewis then. "You've taken up the ribbons again then?"

"The time seemed, er, appropriate."

"You'll never catch that son of a jackal—he's long since gone on his way. He must be at Maywood by now."

"I'll catch him."

"You better had, dear boy; my £50,000 is depending on you. Besides, the Iron Duke must be avenged for the indignity that's been heaped upon it." He glanced at Jane. "Am I forgiven enough for you to avenge the poor old Duke?"

"Of course you are."

"Was I really that bad?"

"Worse."

"Oh, cruel heart."

She smiled.

At that moment, Lord Sefton's curricle appeared along the road, closely followed by the Duke of Dursley, who didn't hide his delight to see the Iron Duke turned over in so demeaning a way.

Lord Sefton reined his bays in swiftly and came over to them. "What on God's earth happened?"

Lewis quickly told him, and the marshal's face darkened with cold anger. "That's it! I won't brook any more from that blackguard Chapman! I'll see to it that he loses his license and never regains it! And to think that he's going to get into Brighton first!"

"Oh no he isn't," said Lewis quietly.

Lord Sefton look at him as if he was mad. "How can you say that given the lead he's got now? Dammit, man, he'd have to go backward not to get in first!"

"Maywood's not that far ahead," explained Lewis, "and where Chapman has to go around it, I am at liberty to cut straight across. You did say there was no hard-and-fast rule about the route, didn't you?"

Lord Sefton stared at him for a moment and then a slow grin spread across his good-natured face. "That's right, you can go any way you like so long as you get to Brighton, and if you cut out that loop you'll gain at least ten minutes. But is that enough?"

Lewis nodded. "Enough for me."

"Have a care at Bolney, for if he knows you've got him in your sights, the lord alone knows what he might resort to to stop you."

"I'll be on my guard, of that you may be sure."

The following carriages were beginning to catch up now, Blanche's landau still valiantly in the forefront. Leaning from her window and seeing what had happened to the Iron Duke, she gave an audible cry of dismay and gestured frantically for her coachman to stop as close as possible. Then she was running like the wind toward Henry, her ribbons fluttering and her eyes bright with tears. "Henry! Oh, Henry, my love! Are you all right?"

"Blanche?" He went to meet her, swinging her into his arms and kissing her on the lips in front of them all. "Don't cry, my sweet," he murmured, showering kisses all over her face. "I'm all right, it's all right. . . ."

Lord Sefton tipped his top hat back on his head. "Well, that's them sorted out, I suppose. But we've a race to get on with, Ardenley, and the longer you dilly-dally here, the further ahead that damned rat's going to get."

Lewis caught Jane's hand. "Come, my lady, we'd best be on our way."

They ran back to the Swan, just as the Duke of Dursley, furious to realize that Henry's overturn had had the opposite effect upon Blanche to the one expected, turned his purple cabriolet in the middle of the road and drove away again back toward Handcross, causing considerable difficulty and danger to the stream of carriages pouring in the opposite direction. Through the dust which still swirled above the company, Jane distinctly heard the furious curses of the other coachmen as they informed His Grace of Dursley what they thought of him.

Lewis lifted her lightly onto the box again and then vaulted up beside her. He grinned at her. "Hold on to your bonnet, madam, we're about to take to the air!" Then, with a sharp click of his tongue, he stirred the team into action again. They pushed into their collars, coming up to a swift pace and leaving the scene of the accident far behind.

Within a minute or so the north lodge of Maywood loomed ahead, and the fresh team attended by their grooms. The men's jaws dropped with astonishment when they saw Lewis himself with the ribbons and none other than Lady Jane Derwent beside him. They set about changing the horses, while Lewis learned that the Nonpareil had passed some nine minutes earlier. By his calculations that meant that Chapman was actually ten minutes ahead, for it would take another minute to complete the change of team. If his arithmetic was right, the Swan should emerge from the south lodge gates at precisely the same time the Nonpareil was due to pass. It would be close, and if the Nonpareil managed to pass the gate first, it would be very difficult to get in front again, Sewell not being one to behave according to the rules on the king's highway.

The grooms had almost finished, and the one in charge looked up a little uncertainly. "I don't like the look of that trace, my lord."

Jane stared where he was pointing. "It's the one we had trouble with at Sutton!"

Lewis nodded at the man. "Will it do?"

"I reckon so, but keep an eye on it."

"Jane, you'll have to watch it. Tell me if there's the slightest sign of anything wrong."

"All right."

He gathered the ribbons, pausing for a moment then before bending his head toward her and kissing her very briefly on the lips. "For luck," he murmured.

Then the grooms were standing back and he was urging the coach forward again, through the open wrought-iron gates where the cool shadow of the copper beech dappled the drive, and then on up the long, straight incline toward the great house.

Jane's heart was singing. Could she hope that fleeting kiss had meant anything? *Dared* she hope?

THIRTY-THREE

*T*he appearance of a public stagecoach in Maywood's elegant park caused a great deal of amazement. A line of men scything the grass paused to stare as the Swan swept past, and they hastily removed their hats as they saw that it was Lord Ardenley himself on the box.

Wheels crunching and gravel scattering, the coach dashed on toward the house. A small herd of red deer fled in alarm, making for the shelter of the trees by the lakes, while from the kennels to the west of the house came the sound of excited baying as the hounds picked up the change in the hitherto tranquil atmosphere pervading the estate.

The Swan was close to the house now, and Jane could see the servants gazing down in astonishment. They seemed to be pointing beyond the coach. She turned on the box to look back, and she couldn't help laughing, because everyone was following the

Swan! Lord Sefton's curricle was close behind, and then the lively company of sporting gentlemen, while beyond them were the private carriages, all of them driving for all they were worth in the wake of the stagecoach. The freshly-raked surface of the drive had already been ruined, and the head groundsman was standing watching with the utmost dismay as the work he and his men had completed only an hour before was undone in a moment.

Lewis eased the team past the front of the house, the noise it made echoing from the mellow stonework, and then they were approaching the kennels. The hounds were almost frantic with excitement now, setting up such a clamor that it was as if they were in full cry after a fox. Men emerged from the stables to watch as their master tooled the stagecoach swiftly by, the fresh team moving easily and with a firm rhythm which spoke volumes of their strength and fitness.

Jane's eyes were shining with excitement and the new feeling of anticipation began to quiver through her again. In Lewis's hands, the Swan was a different coach. She watched how he drove, his grip firm without seeming to be, his commands so light that she could hardly believe the team was conscious of them.

The kitchen gardens were to the left now, and the faces of the startled cooks and scullery maids peeped over the wicket gate to see what all the noise was about. Then the drive turned southward again, passing the great terrace and the magnificent parterre, where the gardeners straightened from their work to gape as the noisy cavalcade swept down toward the south lodge.

Jane could smell the roses in the formal beds, and see how the sunlight sparkled through the dancing waters of the fountains for which Maywood's parterre was renowned. It was all so peaceful, but the thunder of hooves and wheels, and the crack of whips made it all seem so unreal, as if she was asleep and in the middle of a wild dream.

The open park was in front of them now, the long ribbon of the drive stretching toward the great copper beech which marked the position of the south lodge. She glanced along the stone wall guarding the estate, wondering if at any moment she would catch a glimpse of the Nonpareil on the highway beyond, but there was nothing. Maybe it had already passed! Maybe the wall was too high and that was why she couldn't see.

Closer and closer to the lodge the Swan drove, moving at such a pace that she didn't think it would be possible to negotiate the turn onto the road in safety. Then, to her horror, she saw that the gates ahead were closed! "Lewis! The gates!"

Lewis grinned at the alarm on her face. "Have faith now, Jane."

"But . . ."

He urged the galloping team even faster, as if the gates weren't there! Jane stared at him and then at the gates. She heard him laugh then, before he shouted out at the top of his voice. "Hallo! The gates! Get a move on Tom Martin, or I'll have your damned hide!"

A startled face appeared at one of the lodge windows and then disappeared again. Jane felt as if her heart had stopped. The man could never open the gates in time! They were going to hurtle straight into them!

The lodgekeeper was struggling to push the heavy gates, and then she heard another sound—a whip cracking somewhere beyond the wall on the highway. The Nonpareil!

Lewis's control was complete. He didn't check the team's headlong speed at all, and the Swan swept through the opened gates onto the road just in front of the oncoming Nonpareil. Jane clung onto her seat as the coach lurched sharply, and she heard the furious shouts of Chapman and Sewell as they were pipped for the lead by a rival they thought they'd long since seen off.

As the Swan straightened and Lewis once again urged the team to full pace, she looked back, just in time to see Sewell have to swerve the Nonpareil in order to avoid Lord Sefton's curricle, which had hurtled out of the gates as unexpectedly as the Swan. Chapman had been standing on the box, waving his fist after the Swan, and the sudden swerve almost catapulted him over the wall into Maywood. He sat down again quickly, cursing Sewell for being a ham-fisted Johnny Raw who'd be better employed on a brewer's dray!

Lewis grinned at Jane again. "There now, that wasn't too bad, was it?"

"I think I left my stomach somewhere back there!"

"Have you lost your liking for ribbons, my lady?"

She smiled. "No."

"Stubborn to the bitter end, eh?"

"Derwent leopards don't change their spots, I'm afraid."

"*That's* something I've come to realize," he replied, laughing as he sprang the willing team toward the hill rising sharply ahead of them.

Her breath caught as the coach seemed to leap forward, and she found herself laughing aloud with the sheer exhilaration and excitement of the moment. She looked back again, to see the

Nonpareil close behind, George Sewell having recovered his aplomb and driving with gritted teeth as he sought to close the gap. Behind the Nonpareil the cloud of dust marked the progress of the race followers, some of who were traveling so sedately that they'd barely half-crossed Maywood. She wondered where Blanche's landau was, and Alicia's. She glanced at Lewis again. Was it really over between him and his mistress?

The team's sheer impulsion carried them up the hill, and at the top they stretched out almost joyfully, as if they exulted in the wild pace. Bolney was only a few miles in front of them now, and then would come the final change of horses. It was the one place where precious time might be lost and the Nonpareil be able to snatch the lead again. The other coach was very close, she could hear it above the noise of the Swan.

On they dashed, over a windy common where gorse and heather bloomed beneath the warm summer sun, and then the cherry orchards of Bolney were in front of them; in the distance she could see the hump-backed curves of the South Downs, beyond which lay their destination, Brighton.

The people of Bolney had gathered to watch the race, and they cheered as the Swan swept at full pelt along the village street, the team flecked with lather now they were almost at the end of the stage. Jane could smell the purple thyme in the cottage gardens, a sweet, heady perfume which she knew would in future always remind her of this day, just as lilies-of-the-valley would always make her think of danger.

They passed the inn where the grooms had the Nonpareil's final team ready and waiting, and she laughed to see their open-mouthed astonishment that the unfancied Swan had not only survived Chapman's tactics, but had snatched the lead!

The Maywood grooms were waiting beneath the overhanging boughs of an ancient oak tree, not visible until the last moment because of a sharp bend in the road as it went around a farm with a huge stone barn. As Lewis drew the coach to a standstill for the change, the grooms gave a loud cheer to see their master in the lead, then they went quickly about their work. Lewis sat back, tipping his hat further back on his head before looking almost lazily at Jane. ''Well, madam? What is your opinion now of the noble art of ribbon-tooling?''

''Well, I suppose I have to admit that I can understand its fascination.''

''Good God, you mean you actually relent that much?''

She smiled. ''Yes.''

"What about the leopard's spots?"

"I'm afraid they've become a little washy."

"They have indeed. So, you're enjoying this little caper?"

"Yes." She hesitated. "I find it exhilarating."

There was a strange light in his gray eyes as he reached out to put his hand to her hot, dusty cheek. "Oh, Jane," he said softly, "I can think of something much more exhilarating. . . ."

"Lewis, I—"

But she got no further, for at that moment the groom in charge called out to him. "My lord?"

"Yes?"

"This trace doesn't look too healthy."

The trace! She'd forgotten all about it!

Lewis sat forward to look at the heavy metal chain. "Will it stand the miles to Brighton?"

"I don't know, my lord. Under any other circumstances I'd say no, but when it's a race. . . ." The man shook his head helplessly. "It's the devil of a choice, my lord."

"Well, Beelzebub and I have an understanding, so I'm sure he'll waive his rights upon my eternal damnation just for this one day. Now then, for God's sake get those fresh horses harnessed so we can be on our way before the Nonpareil gets here!"

"Yes, sir!" The man touched his hat and beckoned to the man waiting with the last horse, but even as the animal was at last in position, the Nonpareil came seemingly out of nowhere, erupting from behind the stone barn which had muffled the sound of its approach. It was moving at such a reckless pace that Jane could only stare in horror. Surely it would overturn, it couldn't possibly hold the corner!

A low whistle escaped Lewis. "Great God above," he breathed, "has Sewell taken leave of his senses?"

Jane clutched his arm as the other coach swayed alarmingly. "Oh, Lewis. . . ."

His hand was over hers. "It's all right," he murmured.

The Nonpareil seemed on the very point of capsizing, but the low, wide design saved it, just as Sewell had gambled it would. The straining, frightened team heaved themselves into their collars as the whip cracked over their heads, and with another alarming lurch, the Nonpareil righted itself and was thundering past the stationary Swan. She saw Sewell's delighted grin and heard Chapman's derisive, triumphant shout.

It had only been a second or so since the Nonpareil had appeared from behind the barn, but to Jane it seemed like more than a minute. She grabbed at her seat as Lewis galvanized their own team into action, willing them up to a pace to match that of the other coach, but already she could taste the Nonpareil's dust on her lips, and as the Swan came swiftly up behind, Sewell kept his coach in the center of the road, weaving it from side to side to make absolutely certain there was no chance of passing.

Lewis's mouth was pressed in a thin, determined line, and there was a steely glint in his eyes as he tooled the Swan easily along. He glanced briefly at Jane and smiled. "I'll get him," he said, "on the Steyne itself if need be, but I'm damned if he's going to cross the line in front of me. Keep your eye on the trace," he added. "We don't want to do an Iron Duke into the next ditch."

She stared down at the trace, its heavy links taut now as the team drew swiftly along the road. She could see the suspect link, but it didn't seem to have changed.

"Sefton's keeping up!" said Lewis.

She turned and saw the yellow curricle moving through the dust kicked up by the battling stagecoaches. Of his companions and the other followers there wasn't a sign, and she could imagine them pausing to take refreshment at leisure in the inn at Bolney. Looking to the front again, she watched the dust being kicked up from the Nonpareil as it wove from side to side. "If he does that all the way, we'll never get past!" she cried.

"If he does that all the way, he'll have a spent team by the time he gets to Brighton. Let him get on with it, I'll bide my time." His voice was almost drowned by the noise of the coach.

"As you did at the south lodge gates?"

"We got through, didn't we?"

"Just."

"I like to live dangerously."

"I believe you, sir."

He laughed then, and she found herself laughing with him.

The laughter seemed to release the pent-up emotion inside her, making her sharply aware of the sheer stimulation of the race. Excitement began to spill through her in time to the motion of the coach and the thunder of the hooves. Sunlight gleamed on the harness and the team's coats, and on the ring Lewis wore. She watched his hands, so strong and confident and so completely in control of all the power generated by the galloping horses. It was that strength that had attracted her to him in the first place, for in those few moments when they'd been introduced, she'd sensed that as well as physical strength, he had strength of character as well. Everything about him had drawn her like a pin to a magnet, and it drew her still. She was conscious of the whiplike tension in his body as he concentrated on what he was doing, manipulating the horses with deceptive ease, making it seem that he was doing so little, when the very opposite was the case.

He felt her gaze upon him. "Apply your close scrutiny to that trace, madam, not admiration of my lily-white paws."

She looked hastily at the trace, a quick flush leaping to her cheeks at having been perceived studying him in such a way.

On and on they drove, over the South Downs where the gulls soared and the tang of salt was in the air, and then they breasted the final hill and the white elegance of Brighton stretched away before them. She willed Lewis on, unable to tear her eyes away from the coach in front as George Sewell flung his team down the incline. Lewis didn't fling the Swan, he held the team back gently, giving them their heads when they'd almost reached the bottom. But the Nonpareil was still in front. She stared after it in dismay.

Lewis grinned. "We'll give him the go-by, you wait and see! His cattle must be almost on their knees after all that needlework on the road. He wove enough to darn his grandfather's stockings!"

In spite of her dismay, she had to laugh.

There were carriages and gigs along the roadside now, waiting to see the race. Ladies and gentlemen stood up to cheer as the coaches thundered past, their cheers redoubling as they recognized Lewis and Jane. The closer to the town they came, the more people lined the wayside. Noise and excitement filled the air and Jane's pulse was rushing almost unbearably as the first villas loomed on either side. They must get past, they must!

Beside her, Lewis sat quietly, his whip untouched, whereas Sewell's could frequently be heard as he discarded style in favor of an absolute desperation to hurl his coach over the line first.

The Steyne lay ahead now and the road widened. Lewis picked up his whip and cracked it just once. The Swan sprang forward as the team threw themselves into their collars, instantly gaining on the other coach. Sewell couldn't weave now, not in such a very public place, and so he had no option but to watch the Swan creeping inexorably up on him.

Jane could hardly bear to watch. The finish seemed so very near. There wasn't time! They'd never do it! The team's ears were pricked, they had energy in hand, but the Nonpareil's skewbalds didn't have any more to give. As Lewis had predicted, all that weaving had used them up. Gradually the Swan was drawing alongside so that the leaders were neck-and-neck, but then something made her remember the trace. Her eyes fled toward it and her heart leapt with panic—the damaged link was slowly giving way! She stared at the exposed metal, too frozen with fear to do anything but whisper a warning. "Lewis, the trace is breaking!"

He didn't hear her above the crescendo of noise all around as the race neared its climax and the two stagecoaches flew headlong toward the streamers and bunting marking the finish.

She heard the sickening snap as the link finally parted company, the broken trace striking sparks from the cobbles as it dangled loose. The team checked perceptibly, swerving to one side, but Lewis caught them back, cracking his whip again so that they made a final effort to keep going, sheer impetus carrying them over the line half a length in front of the Nonpareil.

Jane hardly knew that they'd won, she was too rigid with fear as the coach careened on, the horses unnerved by the broken trace and consequent lack of tension on one side. Screams of alarm rose from the crowd as it parted hastily to let the coach through, and an orange girl dropped her tray of fruit so that it rolled in all directions. The off-side wheel struck a gingerbread stall, bringing it crashing to the ground, and all the time Lewis struggled to bring the team back to hand, applying the brakes and calling out soothingly. Jane stared at the royal pavilion which was coming up fast now right ahead. Surely they must drive straight across its grounds! But then Lewis regained full control, easing the sweating horses to a surprisingly gentle halt right at the entrance to the royal drive.

She remained where she was, still too taut with fright to move. He looked at her, smiling a little. "Are you at a loss for words, madam?"

"Yes."

"It's a dire length a man has to go to to achieve that satisfactory state of affairs," he said lightly.

The crowds were pressing around the coach now, cheering enthusiastically because the outsider had won, and because the finish had been so very exciting. Lewis paused only long enough to be sure Jane was all right; then he vaulted down to push his way through the press toward the Nonpareil.

Chapman had already alighted and had his back toward the

Swan, but he span around in an instant on hearing Lewis's cold voice. "Chapman! I want you!"

A hush fell on the gathering as everyone craned to see what was happening. From her vantage point on the Swan, Jane could see quite clearly.

Chapman's face was ashen as Lewis strode up to him and without warning flattened him with a deadly blow to the chin. The coachmaster sprawled motionless on the ground, knocked out completely by the force of the punch. The crowd gasped, and Sewell looked down in fear as he in turn received Lewis's lethal attention. The coachman was jerked down bodily from the safety of the box, and shaken like a rat, his head wobbling so much that his pristine white hat fell off and rolled under the hooves of the nearest wheeler.

"P-please, my l-lord!" stammered the unfortunate man.

"If you ever cross my path again, Sewell, I'll ram your nasty little head down the nearest gutter, is that clear? Tread the straight and narrow, my laddo, like a good boy." Lewis flung the terrified man away so that he stumbled over Chapman, who had just begun to sit up. The two sprawled back again, much to the mirth of the onlookers, and then Lewis turned on his heel to come back to the Swan. He smiled up at Jane. "That was a little unfinished business, but I'm sure you understand its urgency."

"I do, sir."

He held up his hand to assist her down, and the crowds began to cheer again. Her yellow skirts whispered as she slipped down from the box, and he smiled into her eyes as he drew her hand to his lips. "Well done, Lady Jane, you showed them all."

She was about to reply, when a man pushed through the crowd toward them, an immense basket of roses in his hands. "Lady Jane Derwent?" he inquired.

"Yes?" She turned in puzzlement.

"These are for you." He pushed the basket into her arms and then gave her a sealed letter before vanishing into the crowd again.

Slowly, she put the roses down and then, with Lewis still next to her, she broke the seal on the letter.

My darling Jane, I know that you will do well on race day, which is why I'm taking the liberty of having these flowers waiting for you. I love you. Charles.

She turned quickly back toward Lewis, but he had gone. She knew that he'd read the brief note and put entirely the wrong interpretation upon it.

very much to him, for the important thing was that Kristen Blanche-
field. Jane could smile wryly to herself about this, for at least
she'd succeeded in what she'd set out to do; she'd brought her
brother to his senses and made him realize what was
really important in his life.

THIRTY-FOUR

As the weary race followers began to arrive, everyone of
consequence adjourned to the Castle Inn to enjoy the iced champagne which had been promised. There was much celebrating of
the Swan's famous victory, and Lady Jane's ribbons were toasted
time and time again, but Jane found little to celebrate, for Lewis
hadn't spoken to her since she'd received Charles's roses.

The vanquished Nonpareil was the object of much interest
from the crowd which still milled around on the Steyne, having
been left there when Chapman and Sewell had taken to their
heels after being soundly whacked by Aunt Derwent and her
vengeful parasol. Furious at all they'd done, she claimed from
Henry the right to deal out their punishment, marching up to
them in full view of everyone to tell them exactly what she
thought of them.

Lord Sefton had already dealt with them, having lost no time
at all on arriving to inform Chapman that he'd soon be losing his
license, Sewell being told that he'd be wise not to try finding
work in London for a goodly time, since word of his participa-
tion in such villainy as today's on the high road would soon be
put about everywhere that mattered. Neither man denied anything anymore when they learned that the men used to break the
Iron Duke's wheels had been recognized from their descriptions
and could definitely be linked to the Nonpareil. By the time Aunt
Derwent and her parasol came on the scene, the two wished with
all their hearts that they'd never even heard of the race, let alone
tried to win it.

Henry would dearly have liked to punish them himself, but he
bowed to Blanche's pleas that he shouldn't risk any further
injury after all that had happened. He was philosophical about
the defeat he'd received at his sister's hands, admitting quite
openly that he'd deserved to be beaten, and even going so far as
to magnanimously propose a toast himself to Lady Jane and her
ribbons. It was quite evident, even to the astonished sporting
element in the gathering, that losing the race didn't really matter

very much to him—all that mattered was that he had Blanche back. Jane could smile wryly to herself about this, for at least she'd succeeded in what she'd set out to do; she'd brought her ninny of a brother to his senses and made him realize what was really important in his life.

Naturally enough, Will and Betsy wouldn't have felt at ease in such company, and so as Betsy hadn't been to the seaside before, they'd gone to the beach to celebrate the Swan's victory in their own way.

Jane sat in a windowseat gazing out at the crowded Steyne, an untouched glass of champagne growing steadily warm and flat on the ledge beside her. Street musicians were playing a fiddle, drum, and penny whistle just by the window and some of the crowd were dancing to the music. The jaunty notes clashed with the more restrained playing of the military band outside the pavilion.

The basket of roses stood on the floor beside her and now and then she caught their perfume, in spite of the cigar smoke drifting so heavily in the crowded room. She ran her fingertips over the cool petals. Oh, Charles, it was a sweet gesture, but it could not have happened at a more inopportune moment. And the accompanying letter could not have been more ambiguously worded, leaving Lewis with the firm impression that she and the writer had more than a slight understanding. She'd tried to speak to him, but he'd gone out of his way to avoid her, and when she had managed to say a few words to try and explain, he'd cut her short in a way as cold and distant as any he'd employed in recent weeks. He was a stranger again, and it was as if the companionship and shared experience of the race had never happened. There had been moments on the Swan when she'd felt sure he loved her still, but now there was no trace of warmth in him— he seemed to loathe the very sight of her.

Aunt Derwent came to sit beside her. "Alicia and the duke appear to have patched up their quarrel. She's all over him, like some horrid creeping vine."

Jane glanced toward the Duke and Duchess of Brantingham, who were lounging together on a large sofa as if they'd never been apart. Alicia had attended to her rather dusty clothes and was supremely elegant once more, her heavy hair pinned up but looking as if it might tumble deliciously down at any moment, which of course it never would. She looked radiantly happy and genuinely so, which Jane found surprising to say the least, considering the unlikely appearance and age of the gentleman who appeared to inspire such joy. The Duke of Brantingham was elderly, balding, and rather on the thin side, and even though he dressed elegantly enough he didn't have that style or charm that Jane would have thought a woman like Alicia would require.

Aunt Derwent sipped Jane's champagne and then wrinkled her nose. "Good lord, it's almost boiling." She glanced at her niece and saw how she was still looking at the Brantinghams. "Yes, it *is* rather surprising, isn't it? But then, perhaps it isn't. . . ."

"Oh?"

'Brantingham may look a dry old stick, but he's got hidden talents."

Jane looked at her in astonishment. "Don't say *he's* part of your past as well?"

"Part of Jenny Lindleigh's past, and she confided everything in me. I thought when Alicia snapped him up that she'd done remarkably well for herself, and I was more than a little startled when the marriage came to such a rocky parting of the ways so very quickly. Alicia's a fool, of course; she always has been and she always will be."

"Men find her fascinating."

"She knows how to be fascinating, but she hasn't a clue how to be sensible. She fell in love with Brantingham in spite of herself, and then she couldn't bring herself to face the fact that she'd given her heart to such a Methuselah. She played around like the immature creature she is, and as a consequence lost him. I gather that it was left to Lewis, who in my opinion has never loved her, to make her finally realize what she wanted. Which brings me to you, my girl. Why on earth are you moping over here by yourself? And why hasn't Lewis even glanced at you since we arrived? Well?"

Jane lowered her eyes. "It's the same old story."

"And I'm the same old aunt, prepared to listen in the old way as usual. Come now, Jane, tell me what's happened, because I confess to being quite astonished that after dashing away together on the Swan you should arrive victoriously in Brighton and not even be speaking. Did you quarrel all the way?"

"No, quite the opposite. Everything was wonderful until these were presented to me." Jane touched the roses.

"But they're lovely. Who are they from?"

"Charles."

"Oh."

"And this letter was with them."

Aunt Derwent took the letter and read it. "Oh, dear."

"Lewis saw it."

"And put two and two together to make five?"

"Yes."

"Why don't you tell him then?"

"I've tried, but he won't even speak civilly to me. At least, that's not quite true, he speaks civilly, but so coldly that I couldn't bear it." Jane looked across at Alicia again, for she'd deserted her husband and gone to speak to Lewis.

He smiled as she came up to him, slipping his arm lightly around her small waist and kissing her on the cheek. Alicia smiled up at him, whispering something in his ear which made him laugh.

It was too much for Jane. "Excuse me, Aunt Derwent, I can't stay here any more. I'll be out by the Swan if you need me." Gathering her skirts, she went quickly from the room, just as Lord Sefton proposed another toast to Lady Jane's ribbons.

Aunt Derwent looked sadly after her as she hurried out onto the Steyne, and then rose determinedly to her feet, crossing the crowded floor to tap Lewis on the shoulder. "A word with you, sir."

He turned from Alicia, his smile fading when he saw who was addressing him. "Lady Agatha?"

"I want a word with you, in private."

He inclined his head. "Very well."

"I will join you outside in the courtyard in a moment, but first I wish to speak to Alicia."

He bowed and withdrew, and Aunt Derwent faced Alicia. It was time to intervene as much as possible, and to fib more than a little into the bargain. "Now then, I think we have a few irritating details to sort out, don't you?"

"Irritating details?"

"Yes. You told my niece a despicable lie about your relationship with Lewis, and I think it only right that you should now tell the truth."

Alicia raised an eyebrow. "Really? And why should I do that?"

"Because I think you want to keep your husband now that you've managed to win him back."

Alicia's green eyes were guarded. "And what can you do to make me tell Jane anything?"

"I can go to Brantingham and tell him a few home truths about you, truths he doesn't even dream about. You've been behaving very badly in recent years, my dear, and I know rather more than you'd like to have him find out."

263

"He wouldn't listen to you."

Aunt Derwent crossed her fingers behind her back. "My dear Alicia, Brantingham was listening to me when you were still learning your alphabet. Perhaps you would be convinced if I told you he has a sickle-shaped scar on the lower righthand side of his back, a scar I'd hardly know anything about unless I'd shared some, er, intimate moments with him." Thank goodness Jenny Lindleigh had had such a wagging tongue after her brief escapade with the duke all those years before, an escapade which had been a companion prank to the pretend elopement with Percy Byrde, but which had gone that little bit further!

Alicia was staring at her. "You and Brantie?" she breathed.

"Brantie? So that's what you call him, is it? I won't bore you with my name for him. Now then, my dear, what's it to be? Will you do the right thing by my niece, or do I toddle across to, er, Brantie right now and tell him the painful truth about his beloved?"

"You wouldn't dare."

"Try me."

Alicia hesitated then. Lady Agatha Derwent was perhaps too much to take on at this particular time. "Very well, I'll do as you ask. Not that it's going to avail Jane of anything, since it's quite obvious to me that Lewis isn't in the least interested in her anymore."

"You do what you're required to do, missy, and leave Lewis Ardenley to me."

"Where will I find Jane?"

"I believe she's out by the Swan."

Alicia coolly inclined her head and went out.

Aunt Derwent drew a long breath. Dear me, how easy it was to tell fibs and be totally convincing; it was a rather disreputable talent she'd no idea she possessed to such a degree. There, that was the first part of it out of the way—now for the rest of it. If Alicia confessed the truth, Jane would be finally convinced that Lewis had never deceived her, but equally Lewis must be persuaded that there was nothing going on between Jane and Charles. And if that didn't work, she'd knock their silly heads together!

It was relatively quiet in the courtyard and Lewis was leaning on a rail smoking a thin cigar. His head was bare and his hair very bright in the afternoon sun. She observed him for a moment, thinking that poor Charles had never stood a chance—he couldn't hold a candle to this man.

He saw her and straightened, quickly putting out the cigar. "You wished to speak with me, Lady Agatha?"

"Yes, Lewis, and I rather think you already know what about."

"Jane?"

"How perceptive of you." She studied him critically. "I didn't take you for a fool, sir, but that is nevertheless what you appear to be."

"There are times when I can see where Jane's sharp tongue comes from."

She smiled a little. "That's as may be, but I cannot for the life of me think where your stupidity comes from. Jane isn't going to marry Charles—she isn't even encouraging him. She's turned him down once and for all, and he realizes it. Those roses were ordered several days ago, and if the wording of the note is rather unfortunate, it still doesn't mean that she returns the sentiments it expresses. She's fond of Charles, but that is all. It's you that she loves, Lewis Ardenley, and I think it's high time you went to her and apologized for your disgraceful behavior. You *do* love her, don't you?"

He gave a wry smile. "Oh, Lady Agatha, if you only knew how much."

"My dear sir, I believe that from my own experience I can hazard a very fair guess." She surveyed him. "Lewis, I'm very fond of you, and I know that you're the only man for my niece. Indeed, as far as she's concerned, no one else will do. Now then, I've done all I possibly can to smooth your paths. I've even, er, leaned a little on Alicia to confess her past fibs. The slate is absolutely clean at this moment, so it's up to you and Jane to put the past behind you and get on with things."

He came toward her, taking her hand and raising it gently to his lips, then holding it for a moment as he looked down into her eyes. "You're a very wise woman, Lady Agatha, as well as a very lovely one, and I think that the Duke of Wellington made a very sad mistake when he failed to make you his duchess."

"Just see that you don't make a similar mistake, Lewis, for you and Jane were put on this earth to be together. Now, go to her. You'll find her out by the Swan."

He kissed her hand again and then left her. She took a long breath. Henry and Blanche had sorted out their problems, and if all went well, soon Jane and Lewis would have done the same, which would bring a very memorable day to a more than satisfactory conclusion.

Jane was seated on a bench watching the small crowd gathered around the Swan. The team had long since been removed to the inn's stables to be baited and the coach stood alone on the Steyne, its blue panels still dusty from the race. She gazed at the box, remembering the moment when Lewis had first taken the ribbons, and the brief touch of his lips over hers. For luck.

The street musicians were still playing, as was the band by the pavilion, and there was an air of festivity which would carry on until well into the night, when a fireworks display was planned on the beach. She felt no such festive spirit, even though she now had Alicia's confession that she'd lied all those months before. Lewis hadn't been unfaithful; everything he'd said had been the truth. But she, like a fool, hadn't believed him. Oh, had there ever been a greater fool since the beginning of creation? She'd put her so-called pride first and given him his ring back, and thus plunged them both into heartbreak. At least, she'd plunged herself into heartbreak—she no longer knew what Lewis's feelings were. There had been times during the race when she thought she could detect something more than mere warmth in his eyes, but now he was so unbelievably cold and remote that she felt he really loathed her. Perhaps he did, perhaps he'd never really forgive her for her lack of faith. Today on the Swan she'd felt closer to him than at any time since the dreadful day she'd paid heed to Alicia's lies; Charles's roses had put an end to that. Now there was only coldness and she didn't know how to reach past it; she didn't even know if it was possible to reach past it. Maybe it was too late.

"Jane?"

With a gasp, she turned. He was standing only a few feet away, the Corinthian perfection of his appearance giving him a presence that made the crowd around the Swan automatically shrink back a little. The light breeze ruffled his golden hair, and his eyes were very steady and gray. Slowly, she rose to her feet. "Lewis?"

"I believe that I owe you yet another apology." His voice was soft, almost drowned by the raucous music from the street players. A faint smile touched his lips. "I seem to have owed you many an apology of late."

"I owe you one as well, Lewis; in fact, I've owed it for more than six months now."

"Alicia wasn't my mistress. Not then."

"I know."

"That she became so afterward was because I felt myself to be the dog that had been given a bad name, and I behaved as such. I wanted to hurt you, Jane, because you had hurt me by having so little faith in me."

Her heart was pounding so wildly that she felt a little weak. She put a trembling hand on the back of the bench, her fingers moving nervously over the smooth wood. "I—I believed her." She hesitated. "She's so very beautiful, I thought. . . ."

"That she'd succeeded in stealing my affections?"

Her violet eyes were huge. "Yes," she whispered, the single word inaudible above the noise all around them.

"Oh, Jane," he said softly, "can it really be that beneath that brave exterior you are so lacking in confidence? Don't you know how beautiful you are yourself? And don't you know that you are everything I've ever loved in this world?"

The tears which had been pricking her eyes for some time now shone on her lashes. "I love you too, Lewis," she said, her voice choked. "I love you so much that I can't bear to continue without you. . . ."

He came swiftly to her, catching her close. "Don't cry, my love," he murmured, his voice muffled against her dark hair. "I'm so sorry for behaving as I did when I saw those roses."

She raised her tear-filled eyes. "I'm not going to marry Charles, and there's never been an understanding between us."

"I know." He put his hand gently to her chin, lifting her lips to meet his. He could taste the salt of her tears, and feel the quivering of her body as he pressed her to him. His mouth moved slowly, savoring the moment as if they had never kissed before, and they were both heedless of the astonished stares from the watching crowd.

Her heart ceased its frantic pounding and seemed to melt within her. She felt weightless, as if all the cares of the past months had suddenly been lifted from her.

He smiled down at her then. "Will you marry me, Lady Jane?"

"Oh, yes," she whispered.

He took something from his pocket and held it out to her. It was the ring she'd returned. "Perhaps you should put this on again then."

"You had it with you?"

"I've carried it ever since the day you gave it back to me."

She stared at him. "Oh, Lewis. . . ."

He took her hand and slipped the ring on her finger. The diamonds winked and flashed in the bright afternoon sun. Slowly, he drew her hand to his lips, turning it palm uppermost to kiss it.

A delicious joy swept through her and her fingers closed over his. His lips were on hers then, but as he kissed her again a voice interrupted them.

"And about time too. I was beginning to think you were completely beyond redemption." It was Aunt Derwent.

They turned quickly to see not only her, but also Henry and Blanche. Aunt Derwent was holding some empty glasses, and Henry was in the act of opening an extremely large, extremely cold bottle of champagne.

The glasses were set carefully on the bench and the champagne frothed and foamed as it was poured into them. When they all had a glass, Aunt Derwent proposed a toast. "To Henry and Blanche, who were the first to put their untidy house in order."

Blanche blushed as Henry kissed her.

Aunt Derwent smiled at them, but wagged a finger at her nephew. "And mind how you go from now on, my laddo. Blanche must always come before your coaches."

"She will." He turned to Jane. "I've much to thank you for, sis."

Aunt Derwent nodded. "Yes, indeed you have."

"And we *all* have your health to toast, Aunt Derwent, since you've always had our happiness so much at heart."

She smiled, pleased. "Thank you. Henry, it's good to know the four of you appreciate my efforts."

"We do," they replied in unison.

She gestured to Henry. "Come now, fill up the glasses again, we have another toast to share." Henry hastened to comply, and then she held up her brimming glass to Jane and Lewis. "After the unconscionable length of time you've taken to get together again, I feel I should box your ears, but instead I'll content myself with wishing you every happiness for the future."

It was Lewis who proposed the final toast. "We've drunk to ourselves, but there's one thing of considerable importance that we've yet to properly salute. He smiled into Jane's eyes. "Your ribbons, Lady Jane," he murmured, raising his glass.

The other glasses were raised as well. "Lady Jane's ribbons," they all said, and Jane laughed with sheer happiness.

About the Author

Sandra Heath was born in 1944. As the daughter of an officer in the Royal Air Force, most of her life was spent traveling around to various European posts. She has lived and worked in both Holland and Germany.

The author now resides in Gloucester, England, together with her husband and young daughter, where all her spare time is spent writing. She is especially fond of exotic felines, and at one time or another, has owned each breed of cat.

FOLLIES OF THE HEART